ASHEN DAWN

ASHEN DAWN

Midnight War: Book 2

ADAM FERNANDEZ

Clover Hill Press

New Jersey

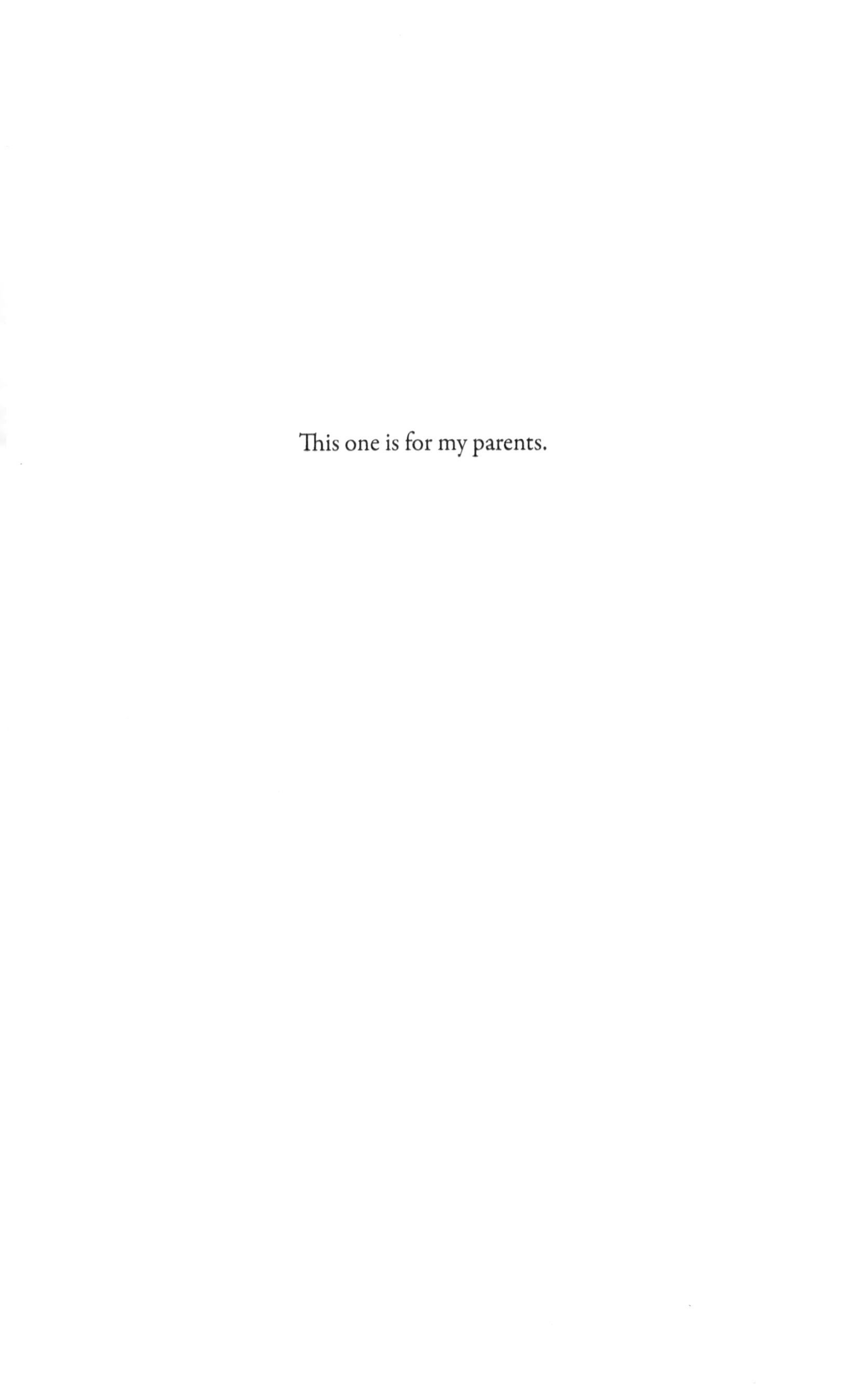

This one is for my parents.

"Ashen Dawn will descend from the heavens, masking their light from the darkness of this realm. They shall tread the path of mortals, measuring the depth of their conviction. If found wanting, the nine worlds will be cleaved by their smoldering hand and voice. For only through flame and pressure can new life be cast."

Excerpt from the Holy Scripture, Book of Judgment 2:10-15

TABLE OF
CONTENTS

PROLOGUE

Aelius

3592 U.E.T. – Unterwalden, Earth

Aelius looked up at the Sun, or at least where it should have been. He couldn't see it save for the faintest glow. In fact, the thickness of the ash in the air made it so he didn't even need to avert his eyes at all. His watch was broken but he looked at it out of habit. It hadn't been very long since the initial blasts, but he was becoming disoriented.

The Iron Cage continued its periodic bombardment of the surface with maximum efficiency. There was a mass exodus in the early moments of the disaster, but they didn't get far. The starships were quickly cut down by the cage's ion guns as they attempted to escape the atmosphere. Only a few brave or desperate people attempted to flee now.

There was hesitation in his steps. The feeling of uncertainty that settled in his chest was an unfamiliar one. Aelius had not felt anything like it since long before he left his home for this system.

His plan had been progressing well, and then in an instant he lost control of the situation. He tried to convince himself that this was only a setback, but he was forced to admit it was now one of many mistakes. The husk continued to achieve victories, even after so many centuries. While his personal victories became far more sporadic.

His exoarmor died hours earlier, so he had abandoned it on the roadside. Still, he wandered from burned-out town to burned-out town, seeing few survivors. Aelius was looking for any kind of escape or refuge, but he still hadn't found his salvation. It was the same story for the tired souls he encountered wandering the roads. *Was it the lucky or unlucky who survived the initial blasts?*

His armor had helped save him, but the desolate, burning landscape around him made it obvious that most weren't so fortunate. Bodies were everywhere. The few who survived wandered or huddled in their homes, praying for deliverance. He knew the odds of their survival were infinitesimally small.

He had done the calculations. The odds of his own survival however were over ninety percent, and yet here he still was, stranded. Wandering alone amongst the detritus of Empire, looking for salvation like the others. He needed to get to the closest research facility as soon as possible.

Thoughts of home and family came unbidden and unwelcome to his mind as he wandered. The probability of having a family had always been low for him, but he had achieved it here on Earth and now was haunted by their absence. His love, Eresh, had abandoned him years earlier, leaving with her servant, Namtar, to places unknown, so strong was her renouncement of his methods.

She even convinced others from their crew to abandon him. She was convinced he had chosen the wrong path. Convinced that his approach would end in their ruin. Their daughter Semiramis likewise had left his side to pursue her own path. They both warned him not to continue, but he declined to listen.

The Iron Cage had been the pinnacle of his plan, the surest defense against the onslaught of the Kra. He knew the people of his home system would arrive one day to address his betrayal. They would undo his unsanctioned tinkering with the feral humans and revert these worlds to their proper order. He always intended to prepare himself and the humans for this eventuality. His mission hadn't changed now.

His calculations had been promising, the chance of success was well above the most conservative thresholds, and yet...had he been too confident? Had he succumbed to that disease of hubris that was so common among the yantuk, the feral humans? *Had he become feral himself?*

He wanted an answer, but he struggled to quantify the facts in a way that could be measured and computed. It was a problem that came up frequently when dealing with yantuk.

He kept track of the relative time in his mind, each passing minute noted with almost perfect accuracy, but the conditions made the exercise increasingly difficult. His mind was becoming muddled by lack of food and constant exertion.

Meanwhile, the acrid smoke of burning plastic was strong enough to make even his eyes water. He knew his body was struggling with repairing the damage at the pace it was being caused by the flood of radiation. He couldn't keep this up for long.

A quiet town came into view once he crested the nearest rise. As he suspected, there had been no direct blasts aimed at this remote facility, but that didn't mean there was no danger. He could see a team of security droids patrolling in the distance but didn't pay them serious attention. He assumed his credentials should still grant him safe passage. If not, he could fight several of them even in his current condition.

When he approached them confidently, as predicted, they did not attack. The droids saluted once he was in range and offered their support, but he waved them away to continue their previously assigned mission.

The town was empty, its inhabitants having already left and quite quickly by the look of things. His destination was past the other side of the village, so he pressed on. Beyond the village limits, he found the gravel road he was searching for and began walking up the slightly inclining hill.

He had never been to this research station but knew the road would eventually lead into the wilderness beyond. Nestled deep in those high mountain valleys were the prized groves of Jiddi trees. One of very few such groves on Earth and perhaps one of the last remaining at all, at least for now. He knew it wouldn't be long before radiation, storms, and neglect ruined whatever trees survived the initial blasts.

He made it several kilometers up the road before he heard rustling in the trees. Stopping in his tracks, he searched the tree line but found nothing. After a moment, he decided to keep walking. He calculated the noise was likely a falling branch with a probability over eighty-five percent, but as soon as he had the thought, he received a heavy blow to the back of the head.

Stumbling forward, he saw a distorted form move past him, followed by another. The falling ash made spotting their cloaked silhouettes easier than it would have been in clear conditions. It was something he should have noticed, but this was another sign he was getting worn out.

Three figures came to stand before him, deactivating their cloaking devices. They wore shining black exo-armor devoid of markings. The plasma blade hilts hung at their hips, and large rifles were strapped to their backs.

They looked prepared to siege a star cruiser. Aelius didn't try to draw his own plasma blade. He knew he could kill them, but he needed information and a way off this planet more than he needed to be alone.

"That was unnecessary," Aelius said, checking for blood on the back of his head and finding none.

The one who was in charge stepped forward and retracted his helmet. He was a young man with a handsome face and black hair braided tightly to his scalp. His bright-blue eyes contrasted sharply against his umber skin. His striking appearance was accented even more by the falling ash.

"Did you think we wouldn't look for you and your inventor, Widukind?" His voice was cold and hard.

"Archduke Leopold," Aelius said, offering a perfunctory nod to the prince. "I wasn't hiding. I expect I'm looking for the same thing you are. A way off this planet and Widukind, of course. Is he with you?"

Leopold ignored his question and grunted. "It seems unlike you not to plan an escape route, or do you have a ship hidden in these mountains?"

"I assume you already looked," he said, and Leopold smiled.

"We did. The workshop has already been raided and the orchard burned. Now, you are coming with us."

So Widukind wasn't hiding away in his workshop. The math was beginning to look worse for what happened here.

The pair of soldiers who accompanied Leopold searched Aelius roughly. His plasma blade was confiscated along with a smaller plasma dagger. Then they shoved him along in front of them as they marched slowly up the hill.

"Is he with you? Tell me," Aelius asked again.

"No. We hoped to find him with you," Leopold said, but the bitterness in his voice was obvious.

"I'm glad you survived. I assume your mother is also well if you've not already killed me," he said, and Leopold laughed.

"Don't patronize me, Aelius. Was this your plan for the Iron Cage from the beginning, or was it Widukind's maybe? Was it the theists who put you up to it?" He waved his hand. "You know, it doesn't matter now. By purpose or ignorance, you've both doomed us all. My grandfather was right to distrust you and sail away from this ruined Solar System. The war was so nearly won, and now..."

"This was not by design. We have all been betrayed," Aelius said, his typical flat intonation returning to him. "When we reunite off the planet, we can set to work repairing the damage to the planet. All is not lost."

Leopold laughed again, harsher and more bitter this time. "You misunderstand, artificer. There are no more ships to take us off this planet, and the ones that have tried to leave have been blasted to pieces by your little machines."

"Widukind can devise a way. We only need to find him," Aelius said, as they arrived at a transport craft. It would be small enough to fly low and undetected by the satellites.

"It's too late for that, artificer. Billions lie dead, and millions more will die every day if we can't get them off this planet. With Earth in ruins, the war will be lost. How many billions more will die then?"

Aelius began the calculations before considering the question was rhetorical. "There is still hope. The Empire will continue to fight, and with Widukind the Earth can be repaired," Aelius said as a foreign feeling began to creep into his chest. Was he...nervous?

Leopold shook his head, his eyes heavy. "Aelius Najm, you are under arrest for treason. You have betrayed not only the Empire but all of humanity. You will answer for your crimes for the rest of eternity."

Aelius worked through the permutations of his situation. The well of support he had garnered over centuries was gone. He was even more alone than when he first arrived in this system. Semiramis, Eresh, Widukind, and so many others were gone, and the feeling in his chest rose again. He had to find a way off this planet, a way to try again. To figure out who had betrayed them and reconnect with the pieces of his life.

That math was simple.

He struck out with his hand, catching the left guard in her armored throat, the armor doing little to stop the force of his blow. The guard stumbled back, and Aelius kicked out at Leopold, knocking him away before retrieving the hilt of his blade, kindling it in a single motion.

"Take him alive!" Leopold shouted and ran toward Aelius without kindling his weapon. Leopold was brave and noble, but it didn't matter.

Aelius swiped down at the right guard, catching him in the shoulder blade and driving the plasma deep into his center mass. The soldier collapsed in a heap as Leopold leapt onto Aelius, pushing him toward the open transport.

Aelius stumbled back as Leopold's armored hands cinched around his throat. He was forced to swipe out at the other guard as they tried to lock down his sword arm. The guard lost a leg for his effort, and Aelius punched at Leopold's face with his free hand. To his surprise, Leopold didn't let go.

"You will answer for your crimes," Leopold growled as he tried to cut off his air supply.

Aelius wanted to reply but could only hold on so much longer. He had to finish this now. Bringing his plasma blade back up, he pushed it into Leopold's left arm.

"No!" he yelled as his armor melted away, revealing his mechanical arm beneath. The metal resisted at first, but Leopold was unable to let go of Aelius's throat. It became a battle of attrition, and the plasma was winning.

Leopold tried to readjust as his arm lost its function, but one hand wasn't enough to hold on, and Aelius shoved him away. The mechanical arm crashing to the ground as Aelius gasped for breath.

"I told you we were betrayed. I will find the answers, and we will win this war," Aelius croaked out as he caught his breath and stepped into the transport. Leopold looked up at him from where he panted on the ash-covered ground, blood streaming from cuts on his face. Electricity sparked from the frayed wires of his ruined arm.

"You won't make it off this planet!" Leopold said, spitting blood. He sprang to his feet and charged toward the open hatch, but it was too late.

Aelius slammed the door shut and rushed to the pilot's chair. He had the transport started and in the air as sparks showered the hatch where Leopold's blade dug into the metal of the hull. It was too little too late, and the ship was airborne before he could breach the door.

Aelius considered taking the transport into orbit but knew that would be a death sentence. Instead, he flew as far from this location as he could. He needed a place he could regroup with his thoughts before finding a way off the planet. He also needed to settle the odd feeling in his chest that refused to go away.

ACT
1

CHAPTER

1

July, 4103 U.E.T. – *Rubah*, Interplanetary Space

Silas hadn't slept since they left Mars. Instead, he stayed by his daughter's side, unable to release her charred hand. The touch, the smell, it had all been nauseating, but he couldn't leave her alone. Even the pain from the wounds he sustained fighting Ajax hadn't been enough to keep him away.

He was glad he stayed because ultimately his prayers were answered. Surely there was no other explanation for Catherine's survival except that it was a miracle. He thanked God, but he might have thanked the devil himself for saving his daughter.

It had taken Marcus and several others to restrain him so the physicians could move Catherine to a room with the proper medical equipment. He remembered Marcus telling him that his prayers had done their part but now the physicians needed to do theirs. With the pain of losing her so fresh, he was reluctant to let her go but eventually relented.

Now his solitude was filled with grief for his lost wife. Diana was the best among them, but it seemed he was only allowed one miracle.

Silas moved to sit with Marcus beside the table where Diana's lifeless body remained. There they quietly worked through their grief. Silas at losing his wife and Marcus his sister. Diana had been the only family Marcus had left, besides him and Catherine.

"I always thought I would be the one to go first," Marcus said, looking out the window. "All she wanted to do was help people. That's why she joined the Hospitallers, to save lives."

Silas remained silent. It seemed so unfair. Marcus was right—it should have been one of them. The kind always seemed to bear the brunt of misery.

"Who did it?" Marcus finally asked.

"It doesn't matter now," Silas said. He didn't want to tell Marcus it had been his nephew, Henry. He had replayed the scene in his head so many times, looking for answers to what had happened.

Ultimately, he was confident it had been unintentional, despite his desire for someone to blame. He wouldn't blindly blame Henry for the sins of his father.

Marcus grunted but didn't push. "Well, we'll just have to make them all pay, won't we?"

"Yes, we will get our retribution," he said, and one of the *Rubah's* crew came to inform him that an escort arrived from the *Specter*. He acknowledged the sailor, who promptly saluted and left.

Silas pulled back the white sheet and placed a hand on his wife's forehead. "She made me a better person in more ways than I can express. I wouldn't be here at all if not for her."

"You have that right. I told her she deserved better, but she stayed with you anyway," Marcus said, standing up to put an arm on his shoulder.

Silas laughed. Marcus really had said that, and to his face. As much as they were friends, Silas also saw Marcus as the little brother he wished he had got instead of Simon. "Now imagine how lonely you would be if she had left me."

"Don't get so excited. You're hardly that entertaining," Marcus said.

The warmth of the interaction was comforting in the sudden sea of change. Silas didn't think he could have made it this far alone.

A pair of soldiers in Pandora Fleet uniforms appeared in the doorway, keeping a polite distance.

"We should start making our way," Marcus finally said.

"I'll be right there," he said, and Marcus nodded, giving his sister's hand a squeeze before walking off to talk to the soldiers.

Silas stood with a grunt, the wound on his side from the duel with Ajax radiating pain through his body. Composing himself, he looked down at his wife and leaned in to kiss her forehead.

"I will find a path to the Celestial City, however dark and painful the road. And when I do, I will see you again. I love you," he whispered into her ear.

Stifling a tear, he went to join Marcus. There he ordered the soldiers to collect Diana's body and take it to the shuttle for transport to the *Specter*.

Silas and Marcus made their way toward the bridge of the *Rubah* after asking several sailors for directions. Silas was limping slightly but waved away any attempts from others to inspect his injuries. He would be fine because he had to be fine. There was far too much for him to do now, and others were depending on him.

The *Rubah* was only a tiny fraction of the size of the *Specter*, but it was still big enough to get lost in. However, despite its age and size, it had performed admirably in extricating them from Mars under heavy fire. He would have to commend the captain for their exceptional skill.

In the aftermath of the battle, he hadn't had the time or energy to regroup with his own crew or even the crew of the *Rubah*. He wasn't even entirely sure how many days had passed since they left. The whole experience had been such a blur.

"I feel like I just stopped spinning and can't fathom which direction to go," he muttered to Marcus.

"Probably why you didn't make it as a pilot," Marcus quipped as they arrived at their destination.

The Mercurian guards at the door saluted and waved them in. On the bridge, sailors went about their duties with military precision. It was a level of discipline Silas wouldn't have expected on a civilian vessel before their escape from Mars. The bridge was spacious for a ship of the *Rubah*'s size but packed with displays and consoles, not unlike similar warships of his fleet. The ship hid its true origins well.

At the rear of the room was a large digitable flanked by several transparent digiscreens arrayed around the table like a stadium. The screens displayed various navigational charts and systems data.

Around the table stood several familiar figures. Theodore, Kaya, and Reina flanked another woman who Silas assumed was the captain based on her uniform. She looked familiar, but he didn't think they had ever formally met.

For the briefest moment, he made a mental note to ask Diana, because she was always better at recalling these sorts of things. His heart sank when he remembered.

"High Commander," Theodore said with a nod to Silas, and the captain saluted. The other two women looked at him warily.

Silas returned the salute and nodded. "Captain, thank you for your fine display getting us off planet. However, I apologize. I don't know your name."

"Captain Masoumi, Milord. Thank you, it was challenging but luckily never a close thing," she said, confident but not smug. Silas appreciated people who were good at what they did and were unapologetic about it.

"I have you all to thank for still being here, especially you, Lady Vardan. Your bravery was beyond anything I have seen in decades," he said, looking from one face to the next.

Kaya smiled. "I only did what needed to be done. I heard there's good news about your daughter."

"Yes, a miracle unlike any I have ever heard or seen, but I'm cautiously optimistic. From what I'm told, we aren't clear of the danger yet."

"I'm sure things will continue to improve, High Commander. She's a strong woman," Kaya said.

That didn't assuage his fears.

"We are glad to have someone of your caliber with us now," Theodore said. "Your shuttles have begun transporting survivors from your fleet to your ships."

"Thank you, I'll be joining them shortly, but I wanted to speak with you all first and give you my heartfelt thanks."

"Yeah, nice work out there, kid, and I guess you too, Reina," Marcus said with his characteristic smirk, looking from Kaya to Reina. Reina glared at him and rolled her eyes, though it seemed more playful than angry. Perhaps there was still hope for the two of them to work out their differences, Silas thought.

"I'm sorry to say that I feel quite out of the loop. Perhaps you can apprise me of the current situation?" Silas said, growing more serious.

Theodore took a deep breath and swiped his finger across the digitable, producing various charts with marked groups of ships, telemetry data, and orbital paths.

"We are only several days out from Martian orbit, but we seem to be free of enemy forces. Tiberius and the Mercurian fleet are covering our retreat, but we expect them to join our formation within the next few hours," Theodore surmised.

Silas studied the map, his brow furrowing. "We seem to have lost a lot of ships."

"Yes, unfortunately there have been some losses, but your Captain Lancaster refused to provide more details until you returned," Theodore added.

Silas rubbed his jaw, wincing as pain radiated from the wound on his side and leg.

"Are you alright, High Commander?" Theodore asked.

"Fine." He waved. "I will provide you with a status report once I return to my ship and assess the situation. Do you plan to rejoin the Mercurian fleet?"

Theodore nodded. "I assume so, but there are still a lot of variables in play. It is my understanding that Tiberius wishes for us all to meet once he returns. Perhaps he has a better picture of the overall situation."

Silas studied Theodore as he spoke, looking for some sign of deception and finding none. Although there did seem to be some hesitation at the mention of Tiberius. Silas wasn't surprised that it might rankle Theodore to be taking orders from the duke's young son, however talented he might be.

"How has your ship here fared? Is there any aid we can provide?" Silas asked, looking to Captain Masoumi.

The captain grinned. "I think the *Rubah* may have fared better than your own ship, High Commander. I think we will manage. The ship itself only sustained minor damage, although we took some crew losses during the evacuation."

"Will you be able to maintain the ship's operation?" he asked.

"Yes, we're still at full strength regarding operational crew. What we have lost in marines has been made up for by Coalition refugees, most of which should be fit for some form of duty," she said, and Silas nodded.

Silas didn't like the idea of having so many Coalition members aboard, but it wasn't his ship. He only hoped they took proper precautions to avoid any unfortunate incidents.

His discomfort must have been obvious, because Reina said, "Don't worry, High Commander. We've been the good guys all along." It was Marcus's turn to roll his eyes.

"When we all meet again, we can begin to develop a sustainable long-term plan," Theodore said, trying to redirect the discussion.

"Very well, we'll regroup soon. Hopefully by then we will all have more clarity." Silas paused and looked Theodore in the eyes.

"Tell me truthfully though. The day you came to me in the palace, why didn't you tell me the might of Mercury was sailing for Mars. Did you know?" Silas didn't expect the man to answer honestly but he wanted to gauge his reaction anyway.

"No, I didn't know," Theodore said bitterly. It was the truth Silas wanted, but it didn't make him feel any better. Duke Vardan acting independently of his own nobles seemed uncharacteristic of such a measured man. "Although the Pandora Fleet seemed ready to fight as well."

Silas nodded his acknowledgement. "The Pandora Fleet is always prepared to fight." His face turned rigid. He owed his life to these people but still didn't know their goals or intentions. He had to be cautious now more than ever.

"I hope we can enter this new age with the transparency these endeavors require," Theodore said diplomatically.

The admonishment was clear in Theodore's voice, although Silas never intended to set the world ablaze. Even if he had given the orders to prepare for war, he didn't expect it to come to this, but perhaps he should have. How many lives would have been saved if he had been more decisive?

"I see no other way we can proceed," Silas said, and the others agreed. It was a strange union he found himself in, but it was also one he would have to learn to manage if they were to come out of this unscathed on the other side.

The group talked for a short while longer about what they knew before Silas received word that they were the only ones left aboard. After saying their farewells, Silas, Marcus, and the last remaining Pandora Fleet members departed back to the *Specter*.

CHAPTER

2

Silas

July, 4103 U.E.T. – *Specter*, Interplanetary Space

Silas studied the hull of the *Specter* from the small window of the transport. As they got closer, the billowing smoke and damaged panels became more and more apparent. Straining his eyes, he could see teams of workers floating through space to conduct repairs as sparks from dozens of welders filled the darkness.

What really drew his eye was a large smoking hole in the rear of the ship near one of its main engines. Things looked worse than he had imagined, and he felt guilty for only now arriving to address the problems. He had placed aside his duty to his fleet in service to his grief.

Marcus echoed his sentiment. "It's worse than I thought."

"I've never seen the *Specter* damaged this badly. We need to see Lancaster and figure out what's going on," Silas said.

They landed in one of several bustling docking bays, the air locks closing behind them as the shuttle entered. The bay was as chaotic as the outside of the ship, with crews moving everything from food and water to heavy metal plates and missiles.

After exiting the craft, they walked quickly through the corridor. Sailors stopped to salute and cheer him. Silas returned their greetings and waved them back to their work. He knew the operations of the *Specter* inside and out, so it was impossible for him not to notice the reduction in manpower. Then there were the banners.

"What is that?" Silas asked as he stopped to pause at the several large banners hanging on the wall of the hanger bay. The Pandora Fleet banner with its silver cube on a black background sat next to one for the falcon squadron, which operated from the hangar bay they arrived in. However, what really caught his eye was the third banner.

"The Republic flag sure looks different," Marcus quipped, and Silas pursed his lips. Where the Republic banner would have been now hung a hand-painted one that included the twin falcons of house Beckett soaring above a red circle representing Mars. Except it wasn't simply his normal coat of arms. This version included a crown above it all.

His staring had the unfortunate effect of drawing the attention of the nearby soldiers, who stopped what they were doing and turned to watch. They looked nervous, as if wondering how he would react to their art project.

"Can one of you explain this to me?" Silas asked no one in particular. He kept his voice firm but neutral. As he scanned the assembled faces, he saw they had torn the Republic badges from their uniforms. Silas suddenly felt self-conscious about his own uniform.

A young lieutenant approached hesitantly when no one else would. His expression was cautious but full of obvious pride. "My Lord, we've torn down the enemies' banner and hung one we've chosen to follow," he said as his eyes darted between Silas and Marcus.

"And explain this crown to me, Lieutenant. Last I checked that wasn't part of my heraldry." Silas knew it had been once, long ago when the Becketts branched out from the old Solar Emperor's family tree. None of that was common knowledge, but there might be some among the crew who appreciated the old and secret histories of their world.

"Some of us fight for our home moons or planets, but all of us fight for you, for the King of Mars," he said and dropped to his knee, head bowed. The others in the hangar bay did the same.

"For the king!" they all shouted.

Silas stood rigid and shocked. Surely this was some kind of jest, but they seemed serious in their acclamation.

Marcus sported a wide grin. He was enjoying Silas's discomfort.

"All of you, stand," Silas shouted. The soldiers reluctantly got to their feet, looking at him expectantly. They were waiting for his approval, and he wanted no part of it.

Silas chaffed at the thought of a crown. Even the ducal crown felt far too heavy on his head, and now they were asking him to be a king. No, they didn't even ask. They presumed to make him one against his will.

He was ready to disavow them of this terrible thought, but something stopped him. He saw the faces of the soldiers, their tired but longing expressions. Many had given their lives for this fight, and he owed it to them to see it through, to deliver them victory.

If they wanted to fight under his personal banner, was it his place to deny them? For now, he could do nothing worse than deny his most loyal supporters. He would need every one of them soon. He let their energy wash over him and embraced its significance.

"I pray I can do justice to this honor you bestow on me. I'm no king, and I don't need a crown to accomplish our mission. I will not rest until our homes are liberated and the enemy is destroyed. We will all have our vengeance. God wills it, Pandora eternal!"

The hairs of his arms stood on end as the soldiers returned their own cries, "Pandora eternal!"

Others shouted, "For the king!"

Cries of "God wills it" were far fewer, and Silas wondered if the phrase was too closely associated with the Republic now. He prayed they weren't losing their faith.

The cheers didn't subside until Silas and Marcus were well away from the hangar bay. Even as they navigated the labyrinth of corridors, dozens stopped to offer oaths of their own. It was as if a fever had overcome everyone on board. The feeling was overwhelming, but he also felt shame for the small part of himself that welcomed their adulation.

When they finally found an empty corridor, he pulled Marcus aside, speaking quietly, "What was all that back there?"

"Something that should have happened a long time ago, I think. Your head is maybe a little big for a crown, but I'm sure we can find one that will fit."

"I never wanted to be duke, let alone king," Silas said, ignoring the joke.

"Well, looks like it's not up to you, and maybe it never has been. I think it's obvious the people have been looking for a symbol to guide them. At least here and now, they've picked you," Marcus said earnestly.

"There hasn't been a king of Mars for millennia. Why revive one now? As if I don't have enough targets on my back."

"What you're saying is you'd rather be emperor then? Would that make the risk more worth it?" Marcus said, and Silas looked at him exasperated. "Listen, what did I tell you before the trial? This isn't only about you. These people all have their own hopes and dreams. They know the Republic isn't going to be where they accomplish them. It's been rotten to the core all our lives. They were given an opportunity here, and they grabbed it."

Silas shook his head. "They picked the wrong person. I can lead on the battlefield, but I don't know how to lead a nation."

"Tell me, Silas, who else has the authority and strength to unite so many disparate people than the Duke of Mars and hero of the Pandora Fleet? The catalyst of change."

"I'm no hero. Catherine could better claim that title," Silas said adamantly. "I've already failed my own family. I barely knew how to be a husband and a father. How can I be a king?" he said, his heart aching for Catherine and Diana most of all.

"How many have you saved? How many more could you save if you only stopped getting in your own way? If you don't give up when the road gets difficult. This is a war. Maybe a fleet commander is what we need the most. There will be a separate time for martyrs and politicians," Marcus said, grabbing his forearm. The admonishment stung. He was never a quitter, but it was what he was proposing now.

He let Marcus continue. "I told you I'm with you, and those men and women in that hangar bay are with you. There will be many more who share the same vision as us. We need to find them."

"And once we find them, then what?" he asked.

"Then you deliver what you promised, to reduce the Republic to ash and build a new world."

Silas held his gaze for a long moment, the silence between them serving to solidify their bond to this bloody course of action. He wanted to back away; to shirk from the responsibility his soldiers were placing on him. He had emerged from the capital with his life and daughter. All he wanted to do was hide to protect them both.

Before this moment, he wouldn't have thought he was capable of that level of cowardice. Marcus and the others had suffered the same or worse by his side, and yet they stood ready to fight. Catherine met the flames of the pyre with unmatched commitment and grace.

His own cowardice stank like a foul bog. He was becoming driftwood on the relentless tide. It was why accepting their praise made him feel like the grifters he so despised.

"We can't let this king business spread out of control. It will send the wrong message about why we are doing this," he said.

Marcus nodded. "I'll do what I can to stop it, but I'm not sure if we can put the genie back into the bottle."

"Do what you can, please," he said, and Marcus grasped his arm.

"Pandora Eternal."

"Pandora Eternal," Silas echoed. He would not shame Diana's memory by quitting now, and he would continue the fight his daughter believed in until the day came when she could join him.

The ship's meeting room had a very different atmosphere. When Silas and Marcus finally arrived, they found Captain Lancaster already present, along with the fleet's other senior officers.

They stood to salute, and he waved them back into their seats as he moved to take his own. He winced as he finally sat down. He felt like he had been standing for an eternity but avoided grabbing his side. He didn't want the others to know he was injured.

There was an uncomfortable silence.

"Well, someone tell it to me straight," Silas ordered, scanning the assembled faces.

Unsurprisingly, it was Captain Lancaster who answered, "We're thoroughly screwed, Your Grace." A bandage wrapped around his neck added to his hard appearance.

"That good then," he said with a deep sigh. The table was much emptier than it should have been. "Perhaps someone could walk me through the events of the last day and where we stand now."

A younger woman, Captain Dvorak, cleared her throat to speak. Her short blonde hair was neatly cropped and styled. Noticeably, her face lacked the tired expression the others all seemed to carry.

"We were preparing to execute the Tenebris Protocol, but before we had the chance to fully deploy our forces, the Mercurians' opened fire on the capital from their orbital formation. A capital ship and two destroyers formed the bulk of their forces, but they had more of their battlegroup hidden in interplanetary space. Their initial attack was as devastating as it was unexpected," said Captain Dvorak.

Captain Dvorak was an effective and confidant woman who served as the captain of a destroyer-class ship, named *Mist*. She was the youngest in the room by more than a decade, but she was also amongst the most gifted. Silas indicated she should continue.

"When the fighting began, Captain Lancaster issued the order to execute the protocol, and we initiated combat maneuvers. Luckily, the Mercurians seemed content to target the Republic's ground-based weapons and left us enough time to regroup. After that, things went to sarding hell. I think Captain Lancaster could better explain," she said, motioning to the older man who looked like he was on the verge of smashing a hole through the table.

"Sarding traitors is what it was, Zhou and the rats he infested our fleet with all these years," the man snarled.

"We've known about them just as long. That's why we've been tracking them," Marcus said.

"Aye, we have, but there were more than we thought. They were a crafty lot, and when the shooting started, they were happy enough to try and take our ships by force. Shooting their own officers in the back. The cowardly sards." Lancaster slammed his fist down on the table, causing water glasses to shake. "They underestimated my resolve and ability. This ship has been my home longer than anywhere else. I'll be damned if I let some traitorous worms take it from me."

Lancaster pulled down the bandage from his neck, revealing a large bloody cut that ran the length of his throat. "They tried to hang me, the bastards."

The others watched with varying degrees of sympathy and anger. Silas maintained his stoic silence, but his anger was rising with each passing moment.

"Our own men tried to hang you?" Marcus asked with a raised eyebrow. He said to Silas, "Didn't we handpick the bridge crew of the *Specter*?"

"Seems like mistakes were made in their choosing," Lancaster said dryly.

Marcus looked angry at the insinuation, but Silas didn't think it was useful to try and point blame. "You've done well Captain. I thank you for keeping control of my flagship. We will need it now more than ever. What of the rest of the fleet?"

Dvorak, perhaps feeling the tension from Lancaster, spoke again, "We've lost roughly half, Your Grace. Only one omega class battleship, the *Elysium*, remains. There are also several destroyers, such as mine and many of the smaller frigates and corvettes.

"There have also been significant losses among the marines. We're still getting accurate numbers, but nearly half are dead or deserted. Many more are severely injured," Dvorak said, her voice mechanical and businesslike, but the pain was obvious in her eyes.

Silas looked around the room, searching for the captain of the *Elysium*. "Where is Captain Horner?" He hoped the news would be good. It was already bad enough they had lost so many of their ships, including several of their largest. The loss of so many men made matters worse.

"Dead, sir, along with most of the *Elysium's* senior officers. From what we can tell, they fought aggressively on the bridge before the crew could regain control of the vessel." Dvorak left the rest unsaid.

Silas rubbed his chin. The stubble that took root there had begun to itch. He never liked having a beard, although Diana always thought he looked better with one. The thought of his wife threatened to derail his composure.

"Captain Dvorak, I want you to take command of the *Elysium*. I trust you're up to the task?"

Normally, someone so young wouldn't be selected for such a challenging position. But he didn't have anyone else here he would trust with the vessel besides Lancaster, and his skill was required aboard the *Specter*.

Dvorak stood as if surprised and saluted with a hand to her chest. "Your Grace, Highness," she said, clearing her throat, "I will see it done. For the king!"

God's bones, not them too. Marcus hid a smile, and the others began banging their fists on the table in approval.

"For the king! Pandora eternal!" echoed those in the room.

Their energy temporarily washed away the pain he felt radiating from his wounds and the anger that occupied his mind. Still, he raised his hands to try and quiet them. When their fervor died down and the room regained its senses, he spoke.

"Thank you for your enthusiasm, but we can't let any of that spread further than it already has. Be sure to let your men know. I am Lord Beckett, Duke of Mars and High Commander of the Pandora Fleet, nothing more," he said adamantly. The others seemed disappointed.

He then turned to Colonel Taylor, the Republic Army liaison who had been among the first to support their rebellious actions. "What do you make of the losses to the marine units Captain Dvorak described? Can we still fight?"

"The captain's assessment is generous. We've lost a large number, mostly to defections. We still have enough to defend the remaining ships, but it's a slim margin. I was going to suggest that recruiting more troops needs to be a priority."

"How will we feed and supply them even if we can find them?" Lancaster interjected. "Our supplies will be strained repairing the fleet and sustaining our current numbers. Solidifying our control of the ships took time. During which, the Martian anti-orbital guns did a great deal of damage to our vessels, the *Specter* in particular."

"We saw extensive damage as we came aboard," Silas said.

Lancaster nodded. "It's even worse than it looks. The engineers think the auxiliary engine may not even be repairable with what we have onboard."

"What does that mean in plain terms? Are we operational or not?" Silas asked.

"Right now, we are sitting ducks," Dvorak chimed in. "With the *Specter's* reduced power and maneuverability, the rest of the battlegroup would be forced to stay nearly stationary to defend it."

Silas cursed silently before voicing what he knew would be an unpopular option, "And if we leave the *Specter* behind, scuttle it into a large asteroid?"

"Then we lose this war before we even start. The *Specter* is one of the few advantages we have. Its fire power is superior to all but a handful of ships," Lancaster said gruffly.

"What if we could take control of the fleet base on Phobos, or even the one on Enceladus?" Marcus asked.

Silas didn't expect their bases to be viable options. There were only two, and neither were well placed for what was sure to be a challenging war ahead.

Lancaster shook his head. "We tried to secure the base on Phobos, but it was a lost cause once the Republic navy began to regroup. We managed to collect several shuttles' worth of supplies and troops before we retreated, but it wasn't much. The Far Coast base is anyone's guess. We could spend months getting there only to find it burned to the ground."

Silas rubbed his eyes. The picture they were painting was quite grim and left them with few options.

"Do we know anything about what the Mercurians want out of all this? Can we trust them to support us with men and supplies?" Taylor asked.

"We should know soon. For now, we seem to be on the same side," Silas offered, but he wasn't entirely convinced.

"The young Lord Vardan fought well. He commanded the field as if he were an admiral twice his age. It was impressive," Lancaster said, and the others echoed his sentiments.

"If the ship requires serious repairs, Mercury isn't very useful. They don't possess docks or facilities suitable for repairing a ship this size. That leaves us with Venus or Luna as viable targets," Dvorak said.

"It's too soon to make that big of a decision. We need the dust to settle, while we complete whatever repairs we can with available materials. Until then, everyone is to remain on high alert," Silas said, and everyone nodded. "Anything else immediately pressing before we return to what I'm sure is a long list of tasks for all of us?"

Dvorak said, "One last thing, Your Grace, what do we do with the bodies of the dead? There are more than we have the space for and repatriating them to Mars or anywhere else seems impractical for now."

"Prepare the honored dead for a space burial at the earliest opportunity," he said easily. The practice was common enough for people in their profession.

"For the traitors," he began to say as the others watched him tentatively, "we will launch them to Earth orbit. There they can start down the road to salvation or burn with the rest of Eden."

The others offered no objections. It was a practice typically reserved for pirates and criminals, but it felt appropriate in their current situation.

"If there are no other questions, let's regroup once the Mercurians arrive," Silas said.

When he was greeted with silence, he dismissed the room and walked tiredly toward the bridge. The wound in his side began to throb, along with his head. He wanted nothing more than to shower and rest, but that would have to wait.

CHAPTER

3

"Lord Beckett looks like he's already given up," Kaya said to Theodore and Reina. Captain Masoumi returned to her regular duties on the bridge. "Considering he nearly lost his family and everything else, I thought he'd be more committed to fighting."

Theodore fixed Kaya with a steady gaze. "His world is a shattered wreck of what it was. It's a miracle he's standing at all. How long did it take you to even leave your room when you heard about your mother's death? You especially should be capable of more grace than you're giving him."

Kaya knew he was right but didn't want to admit it. From the moment they arrived on the *Rubah* she was anxious to continue the fight, and that fact was making her impatient with everyone.

It was one thing to pay lip service to her mother's dream and another to make it a reality. Then there were those who let Catherine stand in her mother's place to die. At the very least, Kaya felt she should have been asked before the role was given to Catherine.

She thought she had made peace with Theodore, but she couldn't shake how he had lied about her mother from the beginning. Back in New Olympia she didn't have the time to put it all together, but now she had more questions than answers.

"Do you know for a fact that Lord Beckett killed my mother?" she boldly asked, and even Reina seemed taken aback by the question. She wanted to ask how long he had known she was Hex and when she had died

19

if it wasn't in the shuttle explosion, but she didn't want to say too much in front of everyone.

"I don't know what this is all about, but I don't think we need to have this conversation now," Reina said. She was eyeing the sailors on the bridge who lingered, trying to overhear what was happening.

"It's alright, better we get this out of the way once and for all," Theodore said, the tension on his brow expressing his exasperation. "No, I don't know that Lord Beckett was the cause. I have presumed as much, but there was never any proof one way or another because her body was never recovered."

"Then why did you tell me that it was him?" Kaya's eyes narrowed, with her rising temper.

Theodore wouldn't look at her. "I didn't want you mixed up in any of this. I thought if you hated him, it would convince you to leave things be and abandon this cause. I wanted to keep you safe, like I promised I would."

Kaya hated being manipulated, and it was becoming too common of an occurrence. "Like I told you before, this is my life and my choice. I'm entitled to the truth as much as any of you," she said, pointing a finger to each of them in turn.

Reina looked annoyed. "Careful where you point your finger, princess. Did Aron always have a choice when you dragged him around the capital?"

"That was different," Kaya said, locking eyes with Reina.

Theodore broke the angry stalemate before it could escalate. "We all do what we think is best in the moment for ourselves and those we love. Everything I have done has been to keep you safe, nothing more."

Kaya broke her stare and looked back to Theodore. She thought he sounded sincere, but his stack of lies was becoming unstable.

Kaya tried to calm her breathing. She had to be cautious now, especially with her choices becoming more and more limited. She needed Theodore, Captain Masoumi, and the *Rubah*, and it wasn't only her. Reina and the rest of the Coalition members on board needed them too if they were ever going to get home again. She had to remember that.

"Okay," she finally said, and everyone relaxed. "So, what now then?" The others seemed happy to change the subject.

Theodore said, "Like I told Silas, once your brother arrives with his fleet, we will discuss the next steps. I wager he will want us to return to Mercury,"

Kaya frowned. "Mercury isn't where the war is."

Theodore shrugged halfheartedly. "If it isn't yet, it will be soon. We know that the Republic is actively jamming long-range communications, and we have had no news from back home in days. In either case, we cannot allow our base of support to disappear."

"So, Mercury may be as unsafe as here." Reina crossed her arms.

"I doubt that, but it's likely not fully secure either," Theodore said.

"What makes you so sure?" Kaya asked.

"There were plans in place for this eventuality."

"More secrets then." Kaya leveled him with a biting gaze. "I have no intention of abandoning the real fight alongside the Coalition."

"I'm with the princess on that," Reina added. "Besides, I never liked the heat."

"Reina and the coalition members," he said with a hint of distaste, "can do whatever they like. We appreciate their support in getting you and everyone else out of the capital, and we will deposit them when and where we can. However, you are a Vardan, and your place is at your family's side."

Kaya scoffed. "No, it sarding isn't. My place is wherever I choose to be."

Reina was smiling or at least what passed for a smile on her grumpy face.

Theodore looked exasperated. "This will be out of my hands soon. You can take it up with your brother or your father if we are able to reach him. I have already shown I won't force you to do anything," he said. Kaya knew he was talking about how he let her leave the family estate in New Olympia before the execution. "But I doubt your family will be as accommodating."

She thought he was likely right and didn't push any further. She could appreciate that at least Theodore seemed to be mostly on her side. It was a small victory, but one she would take.

"Reina and I collected the information you asked for on the Coalition members," Kaya said, and Reina reluctantly handed Theodore a paper with some rough numbers and affiliations.

Reina didn't want to provide such detailed information, but accountability was important on a spaceship, and Kaya couldn't see any harm given the current situation.

He looked over the paper Reina handed him. "A little less than eighty," he said to himself. "We can accommodate that many comfortably for now. I will have someone see to getting them assigned barracks. I assume they won't be causing any trouble?"

Reina laughed, "I should be the one asking you that about your own men."

Theodore scowled. "Our marines are well-trained soldiers, not terrorists."

"I think that's a matter of perspective, isn't it?" Reina put her palms on the table and leaned over to put her face closer to Theodore's.

"Hey, we're on the same side now, remember?" Kaya said, stepping between the two. She was the reason any of them were together, so she felt responsibility to deescalate the conflict. "And not that it should matter, but most of the Coalition members here used to be professional soldiers. Without them, we would have died in Trinity Square."

Kaya moved her gaze to Reina. "You took part in the Midnight Raids, didn't you? Are you and the rest of Prometheus the only ones capable of changing sides?"

Reina glared daggers at her, but Kaya didn't back down.

"That is your one free pass, princess. Next time, don't talk about things you know nothing about," Reina said and turned to leave.

Kaya was surprised by her sudden change. Reina had never talked about what she did during the Midnight Raids, but Kaya didn't realize it was such a sour subject. Like Theodore, there were things Reina kept from her.

"That woman is dangerous, Kaya," Theodore said when Reina was out of sight.

"I trust her with my life, like I trust you, but neither of you seem to trust me."

"It isn't that simple."

"I've been hearing that a lot lately, but what's simpler than the truth?" she said, trying to keep her anger and frustration in check.

Theodore looked like he was about to speak when Captain Masoumi came back over to inform them the Mercurian fleet was approaching. The conversation would have to wait.

CHAPTER

4

Kaya

July, 4103 U.E.T. – *Paragon*, Interplanetary Space

THE MERCURIAN FLEET ARRIVED with limited fanfare but a buzz of activity. The captains of the various ships on both sides coordinated transfers of food, equipment, ordnance, and troops while senior leadership from the Pandora Fleet was requested to meet aboard the Mercurian flagship, the *Paragon*.

Kaya wasn't personally included in the meeting invitation, but as a member of the Vardan family she insisted on attending. She also insisted on taking Reina with her.

The *Paragon* was more massive than the *Specter* and had played a decisive role in the fight over Mars. Kaya had only ever been aboard it once, years ago when her father went to meet the ship's new admiral, a woman who was installed by the leadership of New Olympia. A position only the most loyal would receive.

Kaya wasn't a soldier, but she had spent a lot of time around them. Respect for the chain of command was critical, which made her wonder now how Tiberius ended up in control of the vessel at all. She even asked some of the senior sailors aboard the *Rubah* how it might have been possible, and they seemed to think it wasn't. It was a curious thing.

The shuttle ride from the *Rubah* to the *Paragon* was quiet. Reina refused to speak to her after their last interaction, and Theodore seemed lost in his own thoughts. So, she sat in silence.

With so many eyes watching these first moments of their revolution, it was decided that the meeting should be formal in appearance. Theodore explained it was important to ensure the right optics to instill confidence in the troops and potential civilian allies.

Theodore had said, "The people need to know this war is no longer a battle of the slums but the entire Republic."

Kaya thought it was a waste of time, but she didn't argue. The ship's crew found black marine uniforms suitable for Reina and herself. They lacked any adornments but would suffice for the moment.

Theodore meanwhile wore an ornate military uniform she didn't think she had ever seen him wear before. The decorated hilt of his plasma blade hung at his hip. The odd part was that Theodore was not serving in a military role as her father's lord steward. So it was strange he had the uniform now. He would have had to pack it before leaving Mercury. Another clue to what he knew and when he knew it.

She knew he was in the military once, but that had all been before she was old enough to really remember. Growing up, he had always been a gentle and thoughtful person, making it hard for her to reconcile the man she knew as Uncle Teddy with this new man of war. Reina's distant expression suggested she found it all much less interesting.

Their small delegation was among the last to arrive, and they were ushered swiftly from the hangar bay to the main meeting room of the ship. Unlike the *Rubah*, the ship contained expansive hallways that resembled something closer to a posh high-district condominium than a war ship. The meeting room was similarly ornate. On the walls were lifelike paintings of landscapes and scenes from history alongside ancient war banners, trophies taken from the Great Solar War. In the center of the room was a massive wooden table surrounded by comfortable-looking leather chairs.

Most of the seats were occupied, and she made note of Silas and several others she recognized on one side of the table. Her brother Tiberius sat at the head of the table, with his own cadre of officers interspersed with the Pandora Fleet members.

The soldiers eyed each other warily. Days earlier, they were allies under the Republic banner, and now they stared at each other as potential enemies. Nods and salutes were the only language being spoken at the table.

Kaya found it interesting that the Mercurian forces were largely united in their origin and culture. The Pandora fleet meanwhile was an amalgamation of people from nearly every planet and moon in the system.

Her party took the nearest available seats as the last few guests filed in behind them. Tiberius broke the silence.

"Lord Parker, thank you for returning my dear sister to me safely. I'm glad to see you well, little cactus," Tiberius said with a wide grin. Some of the others chuckled. Kaya forced a smile.

She was glad to see him, but she didn't appreciate being belittled in front of so many leaders. It was obvious he was putting on a show like he always did. Maybe anticipating her next action, Theodore put a firm hand on her arm.

Tiberius continued, "We will speak more after the meeting, but now let us get to the matters at hand."

Kaya saw the serious expressions in the room and relented to Theodore's silent suggestion. She had to remember there was a time and place. Reina watched with an even more sullen expression than she normally had. Reina was the only Coalition representative in attendance besides herself, but Kaya wasn't sure she was even officially a member.

"Lords, ladies, and knights of the realm, I welcome you to the beginning of our journey to a new frontier," Tiberius began, his voice strong, confident, and oozing natural charisma. "I wish my father, the Lord Eminent were here with us, but unfortunately he is leading the pacification of Mercury as we speak, and our long-range communications are currently jammed."

Before now, Kaya had considered this conflict was being driven by de facto Coalition groups, but it was becoming increasingly clear that was not the case. Reina had likely realized that already, which was the cause of her angst.

"We are at war, and to win this war we must all come together in a unified front the likes of which haven't been seen since the fall of the Solar Empire," Tiberius said. A divide was materializing between the Vermillion Coalition, Republic, and this third group of separatist nobility and warlords who lacked a unified organization.

Kaya wondered what this undefined faction wanted out of this conflict. More specifically, what drove her father to join? Maybe he wished to be emperor, she thought, but something felt off about that. He was well known for very reluctantly ascending to the role of lord eminent.

"Your support in this conflict is already much appreciated, Lord Vardan, but before we can think of winning a war, we must secure our base of operations," Silas said. His voice was firm and carried obvious authority. There was an edge to him now that was different from what Kaya saw earlier in the day.

Silas continued, "What was the status of the war over Mars when you disengaged?" The Pandora Fleet officers turned to see what Tiberius would say.

"You are in luck, Lord Beckett. We have an entire planet that will serve as our base of operations," Tiberius said, and he sounded even more smug than usual. It seemed like his recent victory was already going to his head.

"Mercury is small and a long way from here, and last I visited, it didn't have any dockyards of notable size. That is assuming it is fully within your father's control," Silas said.

Kaya looked at her brother, wondering what he would say. Silas didn't seem convinced. She had been worried about her father and hoped things were going better back home. Although, she knew the Alhazen castle had stood as a rock for their family since even before the Time of Chaos. Something that gave her a lot of comfort.

"Mercury will be fully in our grasp in short order, but you have a point when it comes to the docks. This is the main reason why we are all here. The might of Mercury sails for Venus, and I hope the Pandora Fleet will sail with us." Tiberius surveyed the reactions from the room.

The answer surprised Kaya. "Shouldn't we be returning to continue the fight on Mars?" she said, and everyone turned to see where the sound had come from. It became obvious no one was looking to her for guidance.

"We will continue to fight for Mars, but Lord Beckett is correct that we must secure dock yards if we are going to sustain the war effort," Tiberius said, speaking as if he were one of her professors correcting a naive mistake. She hated it when he spoke this way, like some wise old teacher.

"There are dockyards on Mercury, Luna, and a dozen other moons we could use. Why would we ignore them all to wage war on another planet?

The fighting has already started on Mars, and the people are dying while we sit here and talk." She felt like she was having this same conversation repeatedly and no one was listening.

While Tiberius had seemed accepting of her first question, he seemed less pleased with the second, casting her a disapproving glare. He may have expected her to remain silent, but she had no intention of doing that.

Aron stayed behind so they could escape, and then there was Jimmy and the rest of Prometheus and countless others. There was even a small part of her that longed to shake Hal to his senses despite his recent actions. Surely, he never meant to hurt his own aunt.

For a moment, Tiberius's demeanor changed. "If we stay to fight over Mars, we are doomed to lose before we even begin. The might of the Republic will surge forth and overwhelm us before we can even secure our own lines. Venus has the largest docks within the inner ring and access to a larger pool of manpower than Mercury and Luna combined. No, there is no way to win this war but through Venus."

Kaya wasn't sure she had ever seen Tiberius this passionate about anything beyond his own appearance. Something about the way he talked about Venus also felt somehow personal.

Silas interrupted, "Before we can contemplate the larger campaign, we have more immediate concerns." He motioned to one of his subordinates, who typed into her digipad and produced several schematics and graphs that displayed above the large table for everyone to see. Kaya thought Silas looked to be in some pain but hid it well.

"As you can see here, during the fighting, the *Specter* was severely damaged, along with several other ships in our fleet. Until we get them repaired, I cannot commit them to the larger campaign."

Tiberius clenched his jaw. "Surely the repairs can be conducted en route to Venus."

"No, we have exhausted all our options for repairs. We need permanent facilities, and an active war zone would not be ideal. Since Ganymede and Europa are on the other side of the asteroid belt, that leaves Luna as the next best choice," Silas said, eliciting several laughs from the Mercurian leaders.

"You aren't joking, are you?" Tiberius said with a smile. "I suppose there is some merit to it, but the Lunese can't be trusted. I shouldn't need to tell you that."

Silas wasn't laughing. "That is true, but they are also the most likely to be sympathetic to our cause. We haven't had any contact due to the jammed communications, but I would guess the Duchess Engstrom has already taken this opportunity to begin her own rebellion on Luna."

"That would be fitting of her family name, I suppose," Tiberius said, his smile disappearing as he wrapped his fingers on the table. It was something he usually did when he was thinking.

Kaya knew the Lunese had always been a—for lack of a better word—difficult population to control. Their history of rebellions was nearly as infamous as their pirates but far less successful. Beyond that she knew very little about the place because no one traveled there unless they needed to. It was a moon full of factories and hard people. Not the kind of place anyone with means would choose to vacation.

"Very well then, go to Luna and secure their support for our cause. I will need to rejoin with the rest of our fleet on Mercury and ensure the Republic didn't have any creative ideas to attack my home, before sailing for Venus to properly begin," Tiberius said, and it was the leaders from the Pandora Fleet who laughed this time. Kaya could see her brother's body tense and she assumed an outburst wasn't far behind.

"I have come here as a curtesy, Lord Vardan," Silas said, keeping his tone respectful but firm. "Nothing more. I thank you for your aid, but neither your father, nor you, have earned my blind loyalty in this endeavor. You can tell your father if we are to fight this war together that it will be as equals."

Kaya wondered why Tiberius thought he could so easily command their obedience. He seemed on the verge of saying something untoward, but then his posture returned to his typical well-practiced manners.

"Of course, Lord Beckett, I simply mean to suggest a course of action, in case repairing the communication beacons takes longer than expected. It is important we coordinate our efforts."

Silas nodded, his body language softening. "Let us discuss the rest of the particulars then so we can get underway with the utmost haste."

The meeting went how Kaya would have guessed, with politicking amongst the senior leaders. It was disheartening that the Coalition was being left out of the discussion completely despite how many years they committed to fighting the Republic.

Tiberius had always seemed carefree and unbothered by stressful situations, and she envied him for it. Except now something about his behavior seemed more...desperate. She had never seen him break like he almost did confronting Silas. The others might assume it was because he was facing a career commander with decades more experience, but she didn't think so. Tiberius never backed down, not even with their parents, and who was Silas in comparison to them? Now he seemed to care enough about the outcomes to consider being prudent. It was uncharacteristic.

The two groups continued their discussions of supply transfers and troop movements. Followed by an exchange of information regarding what they knew and didn't know about the state of the Solar System. There were too many topics and not nearly enough time to cover them all.

Kaya was left to watch quietly. Not because she didn't try to speak but because she had been thoroughly ignored every time she tried suggesting they refocus their efforts on Mars. Reina still wasn't speaking, but they shared a silent look that suggested she felt the same way as Kaya.

When the meeting had finally ended, the two groups bid each other fair travel and headed to their vessels. It all felt cold and transactional, and she wondered if necessity was enough to keep these groups working together. Jimmy had said the Coalition needed Silas Beckett, and it seemed like Tiberius felt he did too.

She stood to leave with the group from the *Rubah* but waited for the rest of the room to empty before approaching Tiberius. Her brother greeted her with a hug that she awkwardly returned. "It is good to see you again, Tiberius."

"You look a bit taller than I remember," he said, appraising her. They now stood nearly at eye level with each other, which was impressive considering he was quite tall at a little over six feet. He had always been tall as long as she could remember, even as a teenager.

"It wouldn't be such a surprise if you had come to visit me," she said, crossing her arms.

"Yes, well, it's been a busy couple of years," he offered with a shrug.

"I can see that."

"But that doesn't matter now that we are all reunited. I had rooms prepared for you aboard the *Paragon* for the trip back to Mercury," he said with genuine warmth.

"That is kind of you, Lord Vardan," Theodore said with a respectful bow of his head.

"I'm not going back to Mercury," Kaya said less respectfully, and Reina gave her a quizzical look.

"Well, that isn't up for debate. Father wishes you home, and so home you will go," Tiberius said, as if that would be the end of the discussion. "You have had your fun, Kaya, now be sensible."

Sensible. She seethed at the word. What was sensible about any part of their situation? He would march off to war while she did what, sat in her room reading? "I would have sooner died back on Mars than run away. The people we left behind don't get to hide inside castle walls, so neither will I."

"Those people are not important like you are," he said, ignoring Reina's icy stare. "Your place is with your family, not insurgents pretending to be soldiers."

She had no reason to expect better of him. He had always been a proud and elitist person, and now he was leaning into those beliefs harder than ever. She loved him as a brother but hated him for who he was choosing to be.

"Lord Vardan, if I may," Theodore said, clearing his throat, "perhaps Lady Vardan and I can continue with Lord Beckett to Luna. There we could ensure that he follows through with his promises."

"No. Absolutely not, it is far too dangerous," Tiberius said instantly.

"No more dangerous than sailing back to Mercury. If we are acting in the capacity of emissaries for Duke Vardan, even the Lunese will respect that tradition," Theodore said. Kaya was confused as to why Theodore was helping her now. Was it guilt or something else? Either way, she hoped it worked.

Tiberius stayed silent for a long moment as if considering the proposal.

"Very well, you will travel as emissaries, but let me be abundantly clear,

Lord Parker. Should *anything* happen to Lady Kaya, I will hold you personally responsible," Tiberius said, and the threat was unmistakable. Normally, she would have laughed at him making such a declaration, but he seemed deathly serious, and even Theodore hesitated before replying.

"Yes, of course, My Lord, I will protect her as I always have, as my own kin," he finally said, bowing his head deeply. "You have my oath."

"Very well. Let us at least dine before we part. Your *friend* here can see to transporting supplies to the *Rubah* for your journey. I won't see my sister off without proper care and equipment," Tiberius said, looking to Reina, who harumphed loudly.

He didn't wait to get a response before grabbing Kaya by the shoulder and walking her off down the hallway. "Theodore, come along as well," he shouted back, laughing as his jovial manner returned.

CHAPTER

5

Sailors quietly marched into the large hangar bay. They lined up in formation before the cluster of missile-shaped caskets. Silas was saddened to know this scene was being repeated in several other hangar bays. So many dead and so little accomplished. Normally, he would learn each name and commit it to memory, but there were far too many for that now.

The caskets were draped with plain white cloths in place of the traditional star and cross of the Republic, all save for one at the front covered with his own house Beckett banner. His eyes lingered on that casket. Diana's body would be laid to rest soon, but it didn't bring him much comfort.

His eyes moved on to the large guns that would launch the assembled caskets into deep space. The bodies of the traitors meanwhile had already been jettisoned toward Earth during the dead of night with no one in sight to mourn them.

He wiped his brow and adjusted his stance. The pain from his wounds was continuing to intensify, and he had to suppress the occasional grimace.

He held it together during the meeting with the Mercurians, but his strength was fading. Luckily, none of them were in attendance now save for Lady Kaya and Lord Parker. He wasn't sure why they remained, but courtesy dictated welcoming them.

"Do you think they are here to keep an eye on you?" Marcus whispered beside him. "Also, have you been to see one of the physicians yet? You look awful."

"I told you I'm fine, and I don't know."

"Yeah, I figured Emperor Tiberius back there would have wanted his sister to stay with him," Marcus said.

Silas chuckled, which transformed into a groan.

"Yeah, totally fine."

"I'm glad you found your sense of humor again," Silas said.

"Our situation is a sarding mess—we all know that—but it doesn't mean I can't find joy in the little things, like your misery."

The fleet's senior cleric, Bishop Vesivi entered last, eliciting quiet murmurs from some. Others bowed their heads respectively or looked to Silas for guidance on how they should behave. Silas opted to remain at attention with a neutral expression.

"Is it really the best idea to still have the bishop aboard?" Marcus asked quietly.

"I'm not sure. Lancaster seems to want him gone, but other reports said he fought to protect the ship, even taking up a rifle at one point."

"I'd hate to agree with Lancaster, but he's a bishop. How can we trust him?" Marcus said before Vesivi neared them.

The man was roughly their age and had been stationed as the bishop for the Pandora Fleet for the last eight years. He wore a plain white robe in place of his normal ornate vestments.

"Lord Beckett, Commander Higgins," the bishop said, bowing his head deferentially. The man was still fit and youthful in a way most clerics weren't. He stood at roughly the same height as Marcus, although they were both several inches shorter than Silas.

"Bishop," Silas said respectfully, "are all the preparations in order?"

"Yes, My Lord, we're ready to proceed when you give the order."

Silas nodded, and the bishop walked to a temporary alter that was assembled beside Diana's casket. All the Republic's symbols had been removed from their normal places beside the altar and replaced with a plain and unadorned white cloth. Eventually new symbols would be chosen, but that required the luxury of time.

"Children of God, we gather now not to say goodbye but to wish our comrades and loved ones safe travel as they continue their journey through the cosmos. We pray that God's light guides them to the Celestial City, where one day the faithful will be reunited," Vesivi intoned.

The bishop moved to stand in front of the first casket and bowed his head. He made the sign of the star and cross and placed his hand on the casket, delivering the final rites to its occupant. He continued this process until he had visited each casket, stopping before Diana's last.

"Oh, mighty God, observe this child we send to you and judge her worth. May your victorious hand and guiding voice deliver her obedient soul to your eternal kingdom," he intoned one last time.

Silas stood motionless, watching the ritual he had seen hundreds of times with new eyes. His heart ached, and he yearned to reach out and hold Diana one more time. He swallowed his regret for all those long months he spent away from home and the time he could have spent with the love of his life, lost for nothing.

Then his mind went to thoughts of Diana floating cold and alone through space, and his heart broke anew. He reminded himself that God would surely lead her swiftly from her cold wandering. He would welcome her into the warm embrace of the Celestial City, and there she could have everlasting peace by the fire.

Whether Silas would ever see her there again, he didn't know. Maybe if he could rectify his wrongs and earn his absolution. Maybe then he would find a place by her side again. He vowed that even if he had to wander the icy cold of space for millennia, he would gladly do it to see her smile one more time. Then he realized he was crying, as wet tears dripped down his cheeks, his mask broken.

"My Lord, with your blessing, we will send the children home to their creator," Vesivi said.

Silas tried to speak, but no words came out, and Marcus motioned for the bishop to continue.

Then one by one the caskets were loaded reverently into the large guns and launched on their journey into the deepest reaches of space, their trajectories carrying them further than any human had ever gone. There in the darkness, they would search for God's guiding light and the Celestial City.

When only Diana's casket was left, Silas and Marcus moved forward to join the other pole bearers in placing it within the launcher. Silas stepped aside so Marcus could say his own private goodbye. When he was done Silas returned.

No simple words would encompass how he felt, and he struggled to know what to say, so he leaned in and kissed the casket, placing his hand softly on the cold metal. "I will love you forever, and no matter how long it takes, I will see you again. I promise you."

The gun fired and reverberated through his body. His physical pain forgotten as he watched the casket travel into the void from the small viewing windows. Then, just like that, it was done.

The bishop said a few more words to close out the ritual, and everyone was dismissed. Several people looked like they wanted to speak with Silas, but he turned to Marcus before they got close. "I'm going to see Catherine. I can't stomach any more condolences."

"I will join you," Marcus said and turned to accompany him. For now, the others would have to manage without them.

The physicians had nothing new to report, and Catherine remained in critical condition. Her body was covered with wires and tubes connected to machines that did most of the work of keeping her alive.

Silas worried this would be her future forever, but he tried to keep his faith that God brought her back to him for a reason. He wanted to stay there with her even though he knew he couldn't do anything that the physicians couldn't do better.

At Marcus's insistence Silas allowed the physicians to look him over before they returned to their duties. They were unhappy with his condition but sent him off with medication and a strong recommendation to rest. Silas knew as soon as they said it that he would be doing no such thing.

When they returned to the bridge, he received a message that Kaya and her party wished to speak with him. Mr. Beach had taken the liberty of setting them up in his private suite.

The Vardans were distant relations to the Becketts. Both families could trace their lineage back to the last Solar Emperor, so Silas knew Mr. Beach would welcome Kaya to his table for that reason alone. His sense of propriety wouldn't allow for anything else.

"What do you think they want?" Marcus asked as they made their way back to his quarters.

"Maybe to convince us to stay, or perhaps to keep an eye on us," he said, shaking his head. "It could be anything with that bunch. I've seen more surprises out of them in the past few weeks than I would have ever imagined possible."

Marcus snorted, "That's putting it mildly."

"They still know things we don't, which could be important. Kaya did try to come to us before all this happened. She tried to warn us."

Marcus begrudgingly agreed. "I think the only ones we can trust are each other."

"I'm not saying I trust them fully, but don't let your history with Reina get in the way of making an honest assessment," he said.

"My integrity is not so easily cast aside," Marcus quipped, and Silas rolled his eyes. "It's been years since we were together. I barely think of her at all anymore.

"Whatever you say."

"I hope Mr. Beach put out some snacks at least. I'm starving."

Silas swallowed hard at the thought of eating. Between the pain of his wounds, stress, and the medication the physicians had given him, he had no appetite.

The guards stationed out front of his quarters saluted and opened the door. Mr. Beach stood ready to greet them.

"They are waiting for you in the dining room, Your Grace. Should I have a meal brought out?"

"Yes, thank you, Mr. Beach," Marcus replied. Mr. Beach waited for Silas to respond.

"Yes, thank you," he said and entered the dining room where Kaya waited alongside Theodore and Reina. They rose as he entered and bowed in greeting. He and Marcus took their seats, and the others followed his lead.

"I admit I wasn't expecting guests, particularly Mercurians." Reina snorted. "And one Lunese," Silas added, smiling. "Are you not rejoining the fleet to return to Mercury?"

"We won't take up too much of your time, High Commander. The reason we came, beyond paying our respects, was to inform you that we would be accompanying you to Luna," Theodore said. He was apparently the spokesperson for their group.

Silas assumed some kind of Mercurian detachment would remain with him, but he was surprised it was this group. "In what capacity? As you know, my fleet in its current state can offer only minimal support."

"As emissaries on behalf of the Lord Eminent, we will travel with your fleet but will operate independently."

Silas considered for a moment. It was a liability having them along, and they would likely try to influence his actions, but they had also proven to be resourceful allies.

"You are of course welcome to sail with us. We will offer what protection we can, but I would advise you to remain in a position to easily escape into interplanetary space. We can't predict how we will be received by the Lunese. There might be another battle to fight."

"We will remain out of the way, but our frigate is capable, and I will of course offer whatever aid we can. I only request I be included during any negotiations," Theodore said, and Kaya interrupted him. "*We*," she added emphatically.

Silas raised an eyebrow to Kaya. Her fire reminded him quite a bit of Catherine's own personality. The desire she showed on the *Paragon* to defend his Martian home was also commendable. Although her tact could use work, she was young, and that would come in time.

"Reina and I are representing the Coalition forces that are onboard the *Rubah*."

Theodore let out an exasperated sigh. *It seems like they don't have a united front after all.*

"You speak for the Prometheus Group or the entire Coalition?" Silas understood what she meant, but it felt appropriate to clarify. The Coalition as it existed was hardly one unified force.

Kaya looked unsure of what to say, but Reina bailed her out. "I speak for Prometheus, along with Kaya. In lieu of any other members of the Apex Group present, we are assuming control of available Coalition resources."

Silas assumed this really meant they controlled a small ragtag group of refugees and little else. They were on a Mercurian ship after all, full of Mercurian soldiers. Unless the Mercurians were in bed with the Coalition, which he doubted, their resources would be very limited now. In any event, he owed them a debt and would honor that. In time, they could be properly returned to the fold.

"You are both welcome. I owe you at least that much for getting me safely here. Although," he said, turning his head to address Reina specifically, "you know you always have a place here with the Pandora Fleet."

Marcus let out a disgruntled groan.

"Thank you, High Commander, but I have my place here," Reina said, and Kaya looked relieved.

Mr. Beach returned with stewards carrying trays of roast chicken, vegetables, and pitchers of water and wine out to the table. The interruption gave Silas a chance to collect his thoughts.

"How long has it been since you were home on Mercury, Lord Parker?" he asked as he ignored the food on the table, choosing instead to sip from a glass of cold water.

Theodore didn't seem to hear, as Mr. Beach lowered a tray of steamed vegetables on the table. "Mr. Beach, was it? Have we met before?"

"I believe so, My Lord, in passing," the old man replied, not stopping from performing his duties.

"He's been here since time in memoriam," Marcus said through a mouthful of chicken.

Theodore chuckled politely, but Silas watched how Theodore eyed Mr. Beach. Was he looking for some weakness he could exploit to get near him?

Seemingly satisfied, Theodore answered Silas's question. "Nearly two years now, I think. It has been a long time, but please call me Theodore. I care for formality as much as you do."

"Please call me Silas then."

Theodore raised his glass, and Silas did the same. "Thank you for that privilege. I will admit I don't have much to return to on Mercury, so being here seems like a better use of my time."

"I can relate, although there is a lot of unfinished business for me on Mars."

"You will return to Mars then, after Luna of course?" Kaya said, leaning against the table.

He scratched the stubble on his face. "I have pledged to support your father and brother over Venus." He tried to keep his answer as diplomatic as possible.

"It will be a long road to New Olympia," Theodore offered, and the others lowered their heads, likely coming to the same conclusion.

"That it will be, but together and with God's guidance we will make it through. Where that will take us in the next day, weeks, or months, who can say with any certainty?" In truth, Silas hadn't decided at all what he would do next, but he didn't need to tell them that here and now.

He wasn't sure who he could trust, and there was still the issue of repairing his fleet and replacing lost manpower. There was no firm timeline for when they could potentially launch any kind of substantial campaign.

The meal continued with bursts of conversation followed by long periods of silence before the guests departed. Marcus followed closely behind them. Finally leaving Silas to get into bed for the first time in days.

CHAPTER

6

Kaya

July, 4103 U.E.T. – *Rubah*, Interplanetary Space

Kaya had been replaying her role during the trial and their escape from Mars. Her mind kept getting stuck on how she struggled to subdue the guardsman. Even Mistress Blaiset had nearly overpowered and killed her. She would have died if it wasn't for Professor Moreau's intervention.

She got out of bed and put on her gym clothes. She would need to be stronger and faster if she wasn't going to let that happen again. That day highlighted her lack of experience fighting real opponents. Lifting weights wouldn't make her a soldier, but it was a start.

Outside her room, the lights were set to a soft glow, signaling it was still the middle of the night. Walking through the quiet corridors, she turned to musing about all the things she would gladly give up for a chance to run through the sands of Mercury again.

This elicited a momentary pang of regret. Had she made the right decision to stay? Also, why had Theodore agreed so easily to stay as well? Maybe he also believed in her mother's dream.

She made her way to the large gym reserved for officers and the ship's guests. When she opened the door, she found it wasn't empty. The crew worked strange hours, so it wasn't completely unusual to see people in there during whatever breaks they had, but it wasn't one of the ships officers she found.

In the center of the room was a large mat covering the floor. There she saw a shirtless man kneeling before a bowl that was emitting a sweet-smelling smoke that filled the room.

She closed the door softly behind herself so as not to interrupt whatever ritual was transpiring. On closer inspection, she realized it was Namtar, the Mercurian who had retrieved Catherine's body and helped them escape New Olympia.

His back was turned to her, and she could see that his tan skin was covered with geometric black tattoos. The markings appeared old, faded, and far rougher than any tattoo she had seen before, but the markings were oddly beautiful in their complexity and symmetry.

She stood staring at them, trying to decipher their meaning but came up empty. Although, she felt convinced they looked purposeful.

The man prostrated himself before the bowl of smoke and raised his hands as if in supplication before repeating the ritual several times, all while chanting a series of sounds or words she didn't understand. Eventually, the smoke dissipated, and he placed the bowl reverently into a small bag. He turned to look at her.

"I am finished, Lady Kaya, my apology," he said in his heavily accented voice.

She was told he was Mercurian, but his accent was totally foreign to her. He stood gracefully, his powerful muscles tensing slightly, and she found herself staring again.

"Oh, sorry I interrupted," she said as he came to stand near her. He was nearly half a foot shorter but carried himself with an effortless grace she had only ever seen in dancers or famous duelists. As far as she knew, he was neither.

"There is no interruption." He bowed his head.

"What were you doing? I've never seen that before." She was embarrassed by her nosiness.

"I offer prayers to my gods."

"You have more than one?"

"Do you not?" he asked, and she tilted her head in surprise. What a strange question.

"There is only..." she began to say before realizing the Republic and its church no longer ruled her. Maybe it was his honesty that surprised her. She wasn't used to people openly expressing their beliefs, but it was her turn to embrace the new way.

"I believe in no God or gods," she said.

He considered her answer. "Some people are created and shaped by the gods. Others are born in the heavens."

Great, another person with riddles, as if one prophet wasn't enough, she thought.

Kaya replied, "Or there are no gods or God at all, and we all get one chance to do things right." She knew there was no afterlife for her, no second chance in the Celestial City or elsewhere. She had a finite life here and now to make a difference.

"Even if you don't know them, the gods shape us and the world. They gave us life, and in return we work with them to maintain harmony and stability in the world. For that, we honor them, like I have now."

Kaya studied him again. There was something entirely foreign about his demeanor. His tattoos reminded her of the ones worn by the Armanic people, but they came from the ice moons of the Far Coast. His dark skin and accent didn't align with that hypothesis.

"God has never done anything for me to give thanks for," she said, and he seemed to understand.

"There are many days I feel cursed, but many more when I feel blessed to be where I am. I have led so many lives, but the gods always return me to this same path. I think you will find yourself in a similar position one day. Fate is inescapable."

"I'm in control of my own life," she said defensively.

He smiled sympathetically. "We can control our bodies, but the gods control the seas and the wind. They also control the minds of lesser men and lead the herds as they will. It is that weakness demons will exploit to their own gain. But I've taken enough of your time and will leave you to your training." He began to move off the mat.

"Wait," she said, and he paused. "Are you some kind of prophet?"

He seemed amused. "I have tried to live several times as a priest, but it never lasts. The gods always lead me back to the warrior's path. I think that we have in common."

"I'm no warrior," she said, thinking of how she had so nearly died at the hands of an old woman. Namtar had fought through the streets of New

Olympia with a body on his shoulder. He was like some mythical hero made flesh. She was nothing like him.

"You are untrained, but you have the spirit of a warrior. I'm not often mistaken about these things, but if you prefer to hide behind the strength of others, that is your choice. Like I said, the gods will lead you back to your proper path."

His eyes pierced into her in some unspoken challenge. It felt like she was facing a lion empty handed.

"You don't know anything about me."

"I know many follow you now, and many more will follow you soon. How can you lead them if you refuse to fight?"

She looked blankly at him and felt the familiar anger rising in her chest. She didn't like being accused of hiding, of cowering in fear while others fought for her. She wasn't a coward, so she took a step closer, looking down at him.

"Good," he said and moved to take a practice sword from the rack and threw it to her before returning to the middle of the mat.

"Where's your blade?" she asked, confused.

"I don't need it."

She stared a moment then said, "Suit yourself." She charged toward him, sweeping the wooden training sword out to catch him in his side. She wasn't in a mood to play games.

She swung, and he dodged, moving in a blur, so her strike hit nothing. He twisted to grab her free arm. With another twist of his hips, he sent her launching over his body and into the air before she came crashing back down to the mat. The air wheezed from her lungs, and the wooden sword flew from her hand.

"That..." she gasped, "...was not fair." She hadn't been expecting a wrestling match.

"Fair? What is fair in combat?" he said, circling back to the center of the mat to watch her.

She got to her knees, still breathing heavily, "This is only a gym, not a battlefield."

"You must be ready to adapt to your enemies. You must be ready to do what it takes to achieve victory. They will not wait for you to be prepared or follow imaginary rules. Come, strike at me again," he said, motioning.

She sighed. Why was everyone like this? She just wanted to lift some weights and relax, not do whatever *this* was. "Why are you even here? Aren't you with the Pandora Fleet?"

He considered the question for a long moment before answering, "No, I have always served the gods, no one else. First, I protected the Lady Beckett, and now the gods have put me in your path, so here I will stay."

"What if I don't want you to stay?" she said to be argumentative. She had nothing against him, but his presumptive attitude was off putting. She wondered why this man with no obvious ties to her or their cause cared so much about staying.

"I serve the gods and will do as they guide me."

She thought he might be as deluded as Silas was, but there was no doubt that he was a spectacular fighter. She had never seen anyone move the way he did during their escape from New Olympia.

She stood up and regained her form., holding the wooden sword out in front of her body like her mother had taught her. She began to circle, looking for an opening, but he easily matched her movements.

She swung out, gripping the sword in both hands. She feinted an attack to his head before shifting to swipe at his legs. She thought she had him, but then he rolled forward, sweeping her legs out from under her. She landed roughly, her head slamming back into the mat.

She let out a cough and rolled onto her knees. "Where are you really from? Are you Armanic?" she asked, motioning to his elaborate tattoos.

He stepped gracefully back to the center of the mat and went to his knees in a resting position. "No, my tribe is older and long forgotten. A small place in the desert beside a mighty river. I'm all that is left of my people."

He spoke of his home with a passion that broke the stoney features of his face. It was obvious he missed the place. His mention of the desert made her think of her own home, and she assumed his origins on Mercury were a given.

"Did you learn to fight in the army?"

He shook his head. "I learned to fight when I stared down death with only a spear and my wards," he said, fingering the lines of the tattoos.

"They're like your armor?" she asked, studying the designs. She could see the pattern hidden in the geometry, but its meaning was still lost on her. It was like finding a map without a key.

"Yes, they protect me from demons and ward off evil," he said seriously.

His superstitions were curious, but they didn't change her immediate thought. This was someone who could teach her.

"I don't know how long you intend to stay with us, but maybe you could help me train? At least while we're all stuck on this ship."

"Of course." He bowed his head deferentially.

"You can certainly use the help," a voice called from behind. Kaya turned to see Reina entering the room. "I guess no one can sleep around here."

"Yeah, seems that way," Kaya said and stood up from the mat.

"I will meet you here again tomorrow," Namtar said, collecting his shirt from the ground along with the bag that contained his ritual bowl. She agreed, and he left the room.

Reina gazed for a long moment at his body as he left. "Well, he's easy on the eyes."

Kaya laughed as a lot of the pent-up tension left her. She never thought she would be so happy to hear Reina joke with her again, but she still felt reluctant to address the source of the tension.

Kaya realized now she should have never brought up the Midnight Raids and Reina's role in them. It also wasn't right of her to lash out at the one person who had stood by her side. Even so, she struggled with forming an apology.

"Is he with Prometheus?" Kaya asked.

"No, he isn't one of ours. I assumed he was with the Hermes Conglomerate, but I can't say for sure. There are dozens of people from different coalition groups onboard but given how well he fought... Hermes is my guess."

The awkward silence returned, and Kaya tried to build up the nerve to admit she was wrong. She had already lost Aron and Henry, but she was still behaving the same way she always had. She was taking Reina's presence for granted.

"Listen Reina, I..." she began.

"Save it, princess."

Reina's words took her aback, and she stared at the older woman wondering if she was playing some mind game. "I shouldn't have said what I did," Kaya blurted.

"That's true, but you did, and I probably would have done the same thing if I were you," Reina said, looking into her eyes. "I understand what it's like to be angry, but you also need to recognize who your enemies really are. You also need to stop thinking you know everything."

"I never claimed to know everything," Kaya said, her face reddening.

"Then why do you keep speaking so flippantly about things that happened when you were barely out of diapers or assuming everyone is a coward for wanting to stay alive or protect their homes and loved ones. Just because you don't worry about those things doesn't make them meaningless. This war isn't only about you, and the sooner you realize that, the better it will be for everyone."

The accusations stung but Kaya understood her point, or at least thought she did. "I understand if you don't want to stay. I don't think it's too late to change your mind."

Reina snorted and shook her head, "Tell me, princess, why are *you* still here?"

The answer for her was simple, and she didn't hesitate. "To make my mother's dream a reality. To get back to Aron and the others who stayed behind in New Olympia and help make a better life for every citizen struggling in the slums. To make the sacrifice of every member of the coalition who fought and died to get us this far worth it."

Reina smiled. "That's why I'm not going anywhere, even if you act like a spoiled brat sometimes. Have you seen how those coalition soldiers look to you for guidance? No, you probably haven't even noticed," she said, waving dismissively. "Hardly any of them had ever left New Olympia, let alone flown in space. They're terrified and drifting in a world they know nothing about."

Kaya had to admit she hadn't noticed. She was so consumed with her own plans that she hadn't really considered the coalition members at all beyond the fact they were there and safe. She wanted to help them, but she didn't really know them.

Kaya rubbed her forehead. "They listen to you, not me. I'm not even officially a member of Prometheus. You're one of Jimmy's great captains."

"Yeah, that's true, but I know who and what I am," Reina said, and Kaya tried to cut her off, but she continued. "No, I do. It's important to understand who you are, and I'm a tool more than a leader. I don't have the vision that you do for the future, and even if I did, I don't have the means or temperament to make it a reality."

It was Kaya's turn to laugh, "Like I do? My father and brother want me back on Mercury, while Silas and Theodore look at me like a child showing them an art project."

"But they do look your way. When you spoke in that meeting, no one tried to stop you. They listened, even if they didn't act on it. I may as well have been invisible," Reina said.

"You aren't invisible. I wouldn't even be here without you." Kaya tried to be reassuring.

"I don't want compliments, princess. I want you to realize there are things you can do that all those soldiers and even I can't. None of those commanders believe in us or what the Coalition can accomplish, not even Silas, who has known Jimmy and I for years, but *you* do."

Kaya was normally confident, often irrationally so, but now self-doubt creeped in. She felt like she didn't deserve any praise, not after how badly things had gone. Aron was likely dead, along with so many others. She felt terribly guilty. "I've barely accomplished anything since joining Prometheus. The others will be able to help us better than I ever could."

Reina rolled her eyes. "You're so caught up in what little you think you've done in the past few months that you're ignoring what you could accomplish in the next two, five, or even more years. This is a long game, princess, and you need to be in it for the whole time. There are no quick fixes here."

"Theodore-"

"Theodore is a hypocrite," Reina interjected, raising her voice. "He acts like the Coalition offers no value, meanwhile Hex and her Hermes Conglomerate were funded by your family this entire time. Your mother wasn't the only one with a dream fighting for something better. She wasn't the only one making progress. Jimmy changed lives in the slums every day and that matters." Her face was flush, and she looked on the verge of crying, something Kaya had never seen the woman do.

Kaya was never good in these situations. Reina was opening up for the first time, and Kaya didn't know what to do. She had to say something, but no words of comfort came easily to her lips. Her mother had been Hex before Catherine and her mother's fight was Reina's fight as well. Surely Theodore and her father understood that, especially if they were also a part of her Hermes Conglomerate somehow.

"I don't know that I can do what you're asking, but I do think Theodore understands the Coalition and what it can accomplish. My mother wore the armor of Hex before Catherine, she died for the Coalition, even if no one knows it," she said, waiting to judge Reina's reaction.

Reina stopped pacing on the mat and looked back to Kaya, her brow furrowed. "Your mother, Duchess Vardan, Grand Marshall of the Void Knights, and hero of the Republic...was Hex?" The disbelief was obvious on her face.

"You didn't know then," Kaya said more as a statement than a question. "Seems like Theodore and Aelius were the only ones who did."

"Of course, the prophet would be involved," Reina said with a sniff. "I had only met Hex a few times when she came to meet with Jimmy or at meetings of the Apex Group...but she was always masked, and I never knew who she was. I'm not sure if Jimmy even knew, but it does make sense now that you say it.

"Their access, knowledge, everything about the Hermes Conglomerate always felt too good, too polished," Reina said, almost talking to herself. "So when she died in that shuttle explosion...it was a cover-up?"

Kaya shook her head with a shrug. "I don't really know. I think she must have died fighting the Pandora Fleet, but Theodore says he doesn't know either, and Aelius only talks in riddles. I wish my father were here so I could find out what he knew."

"Have you spoken to Tiberius about it?"

"No, we were never very close given the age gap between us. Even when she died, we never really talked about it. Now with everything going on, it doesn't feel like the right time," she said, adjusting her hair to distract herself from the shame of admitting that fact out loud.

Reina said, "I would think now is the perfect time."

Kaya took a deep breath through her nose. "I…" she lowered her voice. "This is going to sound horrible, but I never got the sense he even cared."

"We all mourn in our own ways. Maybe his masculine pride wouldn't let him show any emotion. That seems like something he would think," Reina suggested.

Kaya's mouth scrunched. "You aren't wrong, but I don't think it was that. It was like he was relieved when she was gone. After that, he was hardly ever back home in Alhazen. He said it was because of his military service, but I never thought that was it. I'm not sure I can explain it."

"Maybe all the more reason to speak with him."

Tiberius had been away for much of her youth either in school or training and what little time he was around he tended to be even more aloof than she was. His constant lecturing made her even less interested in spending time with him when she was little. He always spoke to her like a child, even when he was basically one himself. It was always quite grating.

"If I thought it would be productive, I might try. We've never been close, and even the way he speaks to our father you would think he was the Vox himself."

"Sounds like a typical noble brat. I'm sure he earned his fair share of punishments."

Kaya shook her head. "You would think so, but he always seemed to get away with everything. Whatever discipline I ever saw him get seemed more like a show than anything of substance. I always assumed he was their favorite. Anyway, you don't want to hear all my family drama." She turned her back on Reina. She was a bit embarrassed to be sharing so much.

"So if the truth is what you want, why didn't you agree to go back to Mercury. You could have gotten your answers," Reina asked, and it felt like she was still suspicious of Kaya's motives even with her recent declaration of support for her goals.

"There's nothing I want more than to know the truth, but that information is a luxury right now. I will keep looking for it, but others have already suffered enough for my selfishness…" she said, lowering her head. "Victoria, Henry, Aron, all of them. Even the guard I killed when I was where I wasn't supposed to be during the trial. How many more are there that I don't even realize?"

Reina stared at her thoughtfully. Kaya thought Reina could see through her bravado.

"All of them made their own choices, even if they don't see it that way. Eventually they might realize that, but even if they don't you can't undo the past, no matter how hard you try. All we can do is strive to make the future better," Reina said, and Kaya felt like the woman's mind had wandered beyond Kaya's own problems and into the realm of her own. She wondered what choices Reina regretted making so much but knew now wasn't the time to ask.

Reina moved in closer. "As for the guard, I'm sure they would have killed you given the chance. It's sad, but this is war, and war is sad. It's grim, dark, and dirty, but that's the point. It should never be easy. When it's easy, you know you've gone too far and given up your soul. So keep your head up, princess, and appreciate the fact you're still human."

Kaya looked to Reina, searching her face for any sense of malice, lies, or political maneuvering but couldn't find anything but support. Support she didn't feel she deserved. Before this moment, she wasn't even sure Reina liked her. Kaya didn't feel absolved of her guilt, but for the first time in recent memory she felt like someone acknowledged the pain she felt.

"You're sarding awful at being comforting," Kaya said to break the tension and laughed.

"I'm even worse at hugs," Reina said with a snort and turned to walk toward the area where various weights and benches were arrayed. "So are we going to stand around here for the rest of the night, or can we get a workout in?"

Kaya was thankful for the change of subject and wiped her eyes with the back of her hand.

"Yeah, do you think you can finally match my weight? I'm feeling a bit lazy to keep changing them," Kaya said, and Reina glared before adding another heavy plate to the bar.

Then, in a moment of déjà vu, Kaya heard the ship's comms click on.

"General quarters, all hands man your stations, entering Earth orbit," the captain said, and Kaya looked to Reina, who nodded without a word. They both made their way from the gym to gather their things and join the others on the bridge.

CHAPTER
7

ARON

JULY, 4103 U.E.T. – ECHUS CANYON, MARS

"CONVOY APPROACHING, TWO CLICKS out," the scout relayed from a treetop perch farther down the valley.

Aron had joined the small strike team led by First Sergeant Gwen Lin, formerly of the Pandora Fleet, for this mission. They had been hiding in the wooded valley watching the main roadway between New Olympia and the port cities of the Acidalian Sea to the east for nearly a week.

Aron looked through his binoculars and scanned farther down the valley road, but the heavy tree cover and steep cliffs made it difficult to make out much detail.

"Nothing visible yet," he relayed to Gwen and the rest of her squad through the comms device.

They all sat ready to spring their trap and ambush any unsuspecting Republic convoys. A strategy the Coalition forces had been employing on various roads around the capital to great effect, but this was the first outing Aron had joined personally.

"Copy that. Tell me when you see what you are looking for, and we'll do the rest," Gwen replied.

Aron wiped his brow and returned to peering through the binoculars. He wasn't a soldier and never imagined he would become one, but he was trying his best to learn quickly.

The evacuation from New Olympia had been a chaotic thing once the fighting erupted. Even with a well-laid plan, it proved an arduous endeavor. Luckily, Jimmy had the foresight to evacuate as many people from the city as possible prior to the day of the execution, or as people were calling it now, the Ashen Sunset. That day turned out to be the hardest of his life but in some ways the most fulfilling.

It was also why he now found himself scouting the roads for Republic convoys looking for tools they could use in their fight. Gwen knew her business, but he had a trained eye for hardware and equipment. The coalition had plenty of soldiers, but they had very few engineers, particularly now.

Aron wasn't hopeful this next patrol would carry anything useful, but he was diligent in performing his duty, because he knew others were counting on him. Like his sister Clara, who was safely back at the facility with Jimmy and the others. He wanted to make sure it stayed that way.

Some of the Coalition members advocated for hitting every caravan that passed, and at first Aron agreed with them. They needed all the supplies they could get. Then Gwen explained it would only cause the caravans to be more heavily guarded or even lead to a more substantial military presence in the region. That would only hurt their cause in the long run and make it harder to gather the rarest supplies they needed most.

"Still nothing," Aron called out again.

The terrain had been a challenge since they first arrived. They were in a part of the planet he had never seen before outside of pictures. There were fast-flowing rivers that came down from the heights of Mount Ascreus, carving an immense network of valleys and narrow canyons. From the floodwaters grew lush forests that cloaked the red Martian soil.

It was in these wooded mountain canyons that the Prometheus Group hid the bulk of their forces and continued their fight.

"Wait, I see them, three trucks... Sarding hell," he said.

"Want to elaborate on that?" Gwen said, annoyed.

"I uh, what...oh," he said, stumbling over his words. He hadn't gotten used to the official comm protocol. "Good news, I see some communication gear, just what we were looking for, also a couple of large, covered trailers. I can't tell what's on them."

"Want to hurry up with getting to the bad news before they pass our position?"

"Yeah, well, there's a tank with them and at least one... No, make that two large truck-mounted rail guns," he said, sitting back on his haunches. It was finally a good find, but the risk would be too great to go for it. Which is why he was surprised when Gwen spoke.

"Copy that. Strike Alpha moving into position. Overwatch, prepare to provide suppression," she said, relaying her orders and sounding, to Aron at least, like a general sieging a castle.

"Copy that, Sergeant. Overwatch is weapons hot. Standby for contact, one click out," replied a grizzled-sounding man named Jacob who Aron had met a couple days earlier.

"No, no, no, what are you guys doing? Not this one! It's too guarded," Aron shouted back on the comms.

"Without this equipment, we can't communicate reliably with our other forces, right?" Gwen asked.

He scrunched his brow and looked back through the binoculars. The convoy was close now. "Yeah, we need it," he said reluctantly. Without a direct connection to the Republic's military satellites, long-range communication was impossible.

"Then settle down and let us do our job."

They were less than a dozen people about to take on a fortified convoy of at least twice as many. It was crazy, even if they were all veteran soldiers, but all Aron could do was watch.

Before they left, he had asked Gwen for a rifle, but she laughed in his face. She said from the distance he would be scouting from, he was more likely to hit her own squad or nothing at all. If things went sideways, his instructions were to make it back to the Prometheus facility as soon as possible and warn the others. A job that she stressed was more important than a few stray bullets.

Everything seemed to slow down as he watched through the narrow lenses. The tall trees stopped their gentle swaying, and leaves stopped rustling as the convoy turned the final blind corner, directly into the ambush. It was then he could see clearly the occupants of the trucks and the burnished blue armor they wore.

"Gwen! These aren't regular transport troops; it's armored Republican Guardsmen!" he shouted into the comms.

He briefly considered going down to help, but what would he even do? He could barely stop Kaya from bludgeoning him with a book, but he was going to fight armored guardsmen? It was a ridiculous idea.

"Acknowledged," Gwen replied curtly, as he continued to look through his optics. He wished he hadn't, as a blinding light flashed, causing him to drop them. A thunderous boom echoed through the valley, violently shaking leaves and dead branches from the trees.

Sarding hell. He ducked behind the rocky outcrop even though he was well outside the blast radius. The experience in New Olympia had left him jumpy about explosives.

Gathering his wits, he fumbled through the dirt and leaves before finding the binoculars. Gunfire was ringing out in regular bursts as he tried to scan the mayhem looking for Gwen and her team through the chaos.

The smoldering cab of the lead truck was the first thing he saw, the mounted gun destroyed in the initial blast. No movement was coming from the truck, so he kept scanning looking for the source of the gunfire. By the time he found it, blue armored bodies were falling quickly to the ground. It was frightening how easily it all seemed to happen.

Then he saw Gwen rushing toward the tank, its big gun useless against a lone person on foot. She leapt onto the heavily armored vehicle and deposited a grenade into some open slot. She seemed to know where to place it and jumped from the vehicle before the grenade exploded, the force of the blast popping the heavy canon off its turret and likely killing the occupants.

The guardsmen managed to group up and form a meager defense, but they seemed to be no match for the phantoms that assaulted them from the trees on either side of the road. Gwen's sharpshooters were armed with high-powered rifles and special ammunition that could even pierce the shields of the officers' exoarmor.

Aron genuinely felt bad for the guardsmen, dying before they even got a chance to fight. Weren't they only trying to do a job like they were?

Aron couldn't look away until only one soldier was left standing, a young woman with a terrified expression. Unlike the officers, she had no exoarmor protecting her. She fired her rifle into the trees haphazardly until she ran out of ammunition and dove behind one of the truck wheels.

"Take her alive!" Aron shouted through the comms. He prayed there was a way this could end without more blood.

Either his words came too late, or they didn't listen, and a single shot rang out loudly from somewhere to his left. His eyes were glued to his optics as the woman's hand fell limply to the ground from behind the truck tire.

He put down the binoculars and didn't look again after that. Several more shots rang out sporadically, and he knew what they were for. He didn't need to see it.

"All clear, overwatch confirm," Gwen said over the comms.

"Confirmed, all targets quiet, but I'd expect a response soon," Jacob replied.

"Copy that. Aron, get down here," Gwen said.

Aron hesitated, taking a deep breath to calm himself. He'd seen his share of violence before the Ashen Sunset and since, but it still bothered him more than most it felt like. He had rarely been this close to it before, and now it felt more personal.

"Quickly would be nice," Gwen said.

"On my way," he said, lowering his shoulders while he half slid, and half jogged down the hillside to the roadway. He tried his best to avoid the bodies of the soldiers and the bent metal of the vehicles.

"Take a look at all this," Gwen said to him when he arrived, motioning to the one covered truck. The rest of the team stayed in their positions, guns at the ready.

Aron stepped into the back of the truck and whistled. What he saw was far better than he expected. Each side of the truck was lined with an array of communication devices and associated consoles. They were the kind of high-end comm devices they needed to fix their facility systems, in particular their security and encryption capabilities.

"This is the best thing we've found yet." He smiled back at her. "What's on the trailers?" he said, motioning behind Gwen. "It looks big."

Gwen walked over and drew a knife from her vest. She cut a hole in the canvas covering the trailer's load.

"By God's bones..." she said, peeling back a flap of canvas.

Aron walked over to get a better look, but all he saw were random-seeming pieces of metal stacked on top of each other. "What is it?"

"Look behind the first couple pieces. There in the middle, what do you see?" she said, pulling out a flashlight to make it easier for him.

He moved closer and saw the glint of glass and electronics. His heartbeat faster. "Is that a cockpit?"

"Yes," she said, grabbing him by the shoulders, "for a falcon. I'm going to guess the other trailer has one too. Do you think you could assemble them?"

"I...I have no idea," he said honestly. "I never took any courses on military or aerospace maintenance. I did rebuild a few tractors once though."

She looked undeterred. "We can figure out that part later." She turned to the rest of the team. "Get ready to move, people. Strip the bodies and load the functional vehicles."

Aron paused at the door of the vehicle when he saw one of the soldiers dragging the body of the young woman out of the way. He stood fixated until Gwen physically pulled his head away.

"Why didn't you stop?" he said, trying to keep the emotion from his voice. "Didn't you hear me?"

"Would they have?" Gwen said, her expression cold and serious. She had spent her life fighting as part of the Pandora Fleet, so he didn't expect her to understand how he felt.

"We can be better than them."

"First, we need to win. Right now, we can't afford to take care of prisoners while our own people can barely eat." She leaned in and whispered in his ear, "This is what war is. There's always a cost, but don't forget what you're fighting for and who the enemy is, what they're capable of."

He nodded because he didn't have anything else to say. When all of this started, when he first got involved with the Children of Men and the coalition, he had only wanted to keep his sister safe. He had failed at that, but Kaya and Jimmy had bailed him out. Now he was involved in a war he never asked for.

At least Clara was still safe, but he knew that safety wouldn't come for free. Next time, someone might not be there to bail him out. They had to win this war if there was ever going to be lasting peace for people like them.

"Now let's hope we can get these rigs down the canyon roads," Gwen said, and Aron's eyes went wide.

"I don't know how to drive," he said, suddenly very self-conscious.

Gwen raised an eyebrow. "Seriously?"

Aron shuffled his feet. "We never had a car. Why would I learn?"

"Fair enough," she said. "Going to need someone else up here. The rookie doesn't know how to drive."

The others shared a laugh at his expense as they loaded into the trucks and began the difficult journey back to their new base.

CHAPTER

8

Aron

July, 4103 U.E.T. – Echus Canyon, Mars

THE THREE STOLEN TRUCKS rumbled into the subterranean garage hours later. As they expected, it was a complicated journey bringing the large vehicles down the winding mountain roads. The entire affair left Aron wishing the Republic invested more heavily in air transport vehicles.

Aron hopped out of the passenger seat and stretched his back with a groan.

Jimmy strode into the garage to meet them. He was taller than average like many from the Far Coast, and his muscular build gave him a commanding presence. He wore a plain black uniform that contrasted sharply with his pale-white skin. "By God's bones, what is all this? When did communication equipment get so big?"

Gwen saluted. "Commander, you're going to want to see this."

Jimmy followed her to the back of one of the two larger trucks with the covered trailers. She cut the straps that held the canopy and waved over a pair of soldiers to help her pull it off.

Jimmy whistled as he scratched his beard. "Well, sarding hell. The guns from these alone are a great find. What about the comms equipment though? That's what we really need."

Aron said, "The other truck is loaded down with it. I think we should be able to get systems up and running in no time."

"The escort on all this must have been substantial," Jimmy said.

Gwen adjusted her rifle strap. "It was, but the kid said it had what we needed, so it seemed worth it."

"How were you so sure?" Jimmy said, looking back at the truck with the equipment. "Looks like any other transport truck to me."

Aron shrugged. "The wiring on the antennas gave it away. Among other things. It's not something most people would've noticed."

"I guess it was a smart bet not killing you the first time we met," he said, a grin growing across his face, and slapped Aron on the shoulder.

Jimmy was much larger than Aron, so the blow put him off balance, and the soldiers shared yet another laugh at his expense. The abuse rankled him, but it was nice to feel a part of things for a change. Especially since his experience with the Children had been far less jovial.

A bark echoed through the garage, and a ball of fur came running at full speed toward Jimmy. Except once the dog got close it changed course to leap on Aron. No one had ever been so excited to see him before.

Jimmy grunted, and Aron reached down to settle the dog by running his hands through its blue merle coat. The dog had striking heterochromatic eyes and panted in pleasure when Aron began rubbing its sides.

"I missed you too, Argos. Who's a good boy?" he said as he ruffled the dog's mane and relished Jimmy's forlorn expression. It couldn't feel good when your own pet abandons you for the love of another. Maybe this was how Aron would get the last laugh.

"No loyalty anymore. I save the mangy mut on the road, and this is how he thanks me," Jimmy said, his muscular arms crossed on his chest.

Aron discreetly held out a piece of the uneaten ration bar in his pocket to Argos.

Jimmy turned to Gwen. "Let's get these things unloaded and get Demitri in here to see if he knows anything about putting these Falcons back together. Did you find anything else useful?"

Gwen motioned, and two soldiers dragged a crate over from behind one of the trucks. She reached in and pulled out a blue and gold breastplate. "We got a few sets of these. Wash off the blood and they should be pretty good," she said, tossing it to Jimmy, who caught it deftly.

"Republican Guardsmen, yes, that could be very useful. Looks like they will need some repairs though. Anything else you need from me to get the comms equipment up and running?" Jimmy said, turning to Aron.

"No, I don't think so. I need some time to look over everything. I will run it by Demitri too, if that's okay," Aron said.

Theoretically, the equipment would help them use the Republic's own comms channels against them. He had taken a course on maintaining these types of systems, but Demitri had real-world experience with secure military equipment that he didn't have.

"Okay, but make this a priority before any of you get lost playing with these new toys. We need to get communications up and running. Anyway, I don't think we even have anyone who can fly these things," Jimmy said.

Aron gave a clumsy salute and immediately felt silly, but it felt like the right thing to do, so he did it. Luckily, Jimmy didn't seem to notice or care, and Gwen only seemed bemused.

Jacob, who had run overwatch for the mission, helped Aron unload several crates of comms equipment. They moved them into a small office off the garage bay.

"Good job out there. We might make a soldier out of you," Jacob said when they finished and held his arm out. Aron grabbed his forearm to shake it, but when he did, Jacob yanked him in closer. "But there's no room for bleeding hearts out here. If you hesitate, people die, simple as that. They don't sarding care about you, so you shouldn't care about them."

The older man's breath smelled of tobacco and six-day old rations. Aron turned his face away slightly to try and get a breath of fresh air. Jacob pulled him in even closer, their eyes locking together. "Do you understand me?" His yellowed eyes dug deeper into Aron.

"Ye-yeah of course. I know that," he said, trying to pull away from the man.

"Good," Jacob said, releasing his arm. He was suddenly much more cheerful than he had been. "See you around." Jacob lit a cigarette and walked away.

Aron reached up to wipe his face, following Jacob's back as he left. His demeanor reminded him more of soldiers he met with the Children than those of Prometheus.

The odd interaction left Aron uneasy. He wanted to be a part of Prometheus, but then interactions like the one with Jacob made him feel like he wasn't as welcome here as he thought. Except this felt like something more than that.

When he couldn't shake the uneasy feeling, he decided to come back to the boxes later. He could go find Jimmy and let him know what happened first before talking to Demitri. Maybe he was overreacting, but it was better to be careful. He wanted to find more ways to show Jimmy he was a valuable member of the team.

The hallways of the old mining company facility were busy at this time of day. Who he saw were mainly Prometheus members who operated closer to the surface in the old maintenance and administrative areas of the mine. The refugees meanwhile set up camps in the abandoned mining towns deep underground.

Aron and his sister Clara were given quarters with the rest of Prometheus. Aron insisted Clara should get a room near his instead of moving to the "deep vils," as the people were calling them. The mining tunnels would be safer if they were suddenly attacked, but Aron preferred she was closer. Somewhere he could keep an eye on her.

Luckily, Jimmy agreed to his request. Rooms were limited near the surface, so it wasn't a light decision. Still, he gave them a room to share near his own. Since then, Clara had been working as Jimmy's personal assistant. Everyone seemed pleased with the arrangement.

He passed dozens of doors and corridors that led to different offices or makeshift barracks. He followed the old, faded signs on the wall that led him to the central atrium, which served as the new headquarters for the Prometheus Group. The facility was a bit confusing to navigate, but he knew he would learn his way around. It would be easier now that they had the comms equipment, and he wouldn't need to leave again anytime soon.

The central atrium was a large open space with a tall, vaulted ceiling meant to simulate an open-air courtyard. However, the glass ceiling that would have once held screens to simulate the sky was long broken and covered in cobwebs. Wires crisscrossed the courtyard in every direction, powering stands of lights and other equipment.

In time, the plan was to repair the facilities' original utilities and improve everyone's quality of life. Aron was surprised to see that in a week they had made so much progress in cleaning up the dust and debris. They also moved in tables, chairs, and other serviceable furniture for people to work and relax.

He saw Jimmy speaking to several of his lieutenants in front of a digitable displaying various maps of the region. He paused, wondering if this was really a good idea. He didn't want to seem too sensitive. Maybe he needed to grow some thicker skin. Was complaining to Jimmy about a mean joke really going to make him seem more valuable?

Before he could muster his nerve, Clara shouted from across the room, "Aron!"

He saw her waving from an old sofa pushed into a dimly lit corner.

He was happy to see her and thought it might be the universe telling him he should rethink his original plan. When he got closer to Clara, he could see she was knitting something with red-colored yarn. "What are you doing?"

"Well, I was making you something, but I thought I'd have more time." She held up the half-finished garment, her lips pursed. "It's a sweater."

"When did you learn to knit? I've barely been gone more than a week," he said, looking over the garment. It was far from done, but to his surprise it looked pretty nice.

She shrugged. "I found the supplies when I was cleaning up one of the rooms. I was bored, so I started trying. One of the hospitallers taught me a couple of tricks."

She always found ways to surprise him, and this was no exception. She had learned a new skill in a few days and didn't even think anything of it.

"I made Jimmy a scarf first, but he won't wear it," she said, glaring at the man from a distance in a way only a teenager could.

"Well, it's pretty hot outside for a scarf."

"Yeah duh, I know that. The scarf is for in here. It gets drafty," she said, pulling on the collar of her own sweater. "I feel like I'm turning into a mole person. Look how pasty I'm getting," she said, pulling back a sleeve and revealing her white skin, which had been equally pale before they got here.

"You've always looked like a ghost. What else is new?" he said, and she threw the ball of yarn at him.

"How long are we going to be here?" she asked, her eyes searching for good news. He retrieved the yarn and tossed it back to her while he thought of an answer.

"I don't know. It might be a long time," he said honestly and sat down next to her, a cloud of dust rising around him. He batted it away with a cough. "Has everyone been treating you alright?"

"Yeah, everyone's been okay," she said, wringing her hands. "Jimmy's been keeping an eye out, but I think he's running out of things for me to do that aren't fetching coffee or delivering messages. I want to do more."

He wanted to argue with her, but he had a job by the time he was thirteen. Clara was nearly fourteen already. "I'll talk to Jimmy and see what he says. How's that?"

She smiled, and her whole face seemed to light up. Despite everything that had happened, she had a level of enthusiasm unmatched by anyone he knew. "That'd be great, thanks, Aron. You know..." She stopped.

"What is it?"

"Well, the hospitaller who taught me the knitting stuff, she said I could help her in the infirmary..."

"No! Absolutely not that. Are you crazy?" he responded.

"Why not?" she said, raising her own voice. "She's a *knight*, a *real knight*. How cool is that? I'll be right here perfectly safe like I am now."

"I...no, you don't need to see all of that, Clara," he said softening. He didn't want to see that beautiful light of hers snuffed out by the pain she would see there.

"I'm not a little kid anymore."

"I know, but...this is different." He felt his resolve slipping.

They were both distracted from their conversation when a small group of people came bursting into the room in a flurry of activity.

Aron turned back to Clara. "Why can't you keep helping Jimmy, or how about you help me in the comm room? We'll have a lot of work to do, and I could use the help."

"I want to do my own thing, not follow you around. I don't want to stare at a digiscreen all day."

He sighed. "You can do all sorts of things as an engineer. I spend as much time repairing circuits as I do writing code," he continued to say until the commotion became louder, drawing his attention again.

Others began to crowd around Jimmy, and he felt like he was missing something important. Maybe an opportunity for him to contribute.

"We can talk about this later," he said and stood.

Clara followed him over to where Jimmy was assembled with his lieutenants. He was facing down a woman who stood calmly with her hands bound behind her back. She wore the robes of a professor at the Sanctum, but they were dirty and torn. Her hair looked equally unkept.

"Who is she?" Clara whispered at his side.

"I have no idea," he whispered back, but he thought she looked familiar.

She was a tall woman with long brown hair and a serious expression. Exactly what he would expect from a scholarly type.

A guard brought in another prisoner with a cloth bag over her head and bindings on her hands and feet. Unlike the first, the guard carried her on his shoulder. Her robes were equally filthy, but Aron could clearly see they were cleric's robes. The guard deposited her on the floor where she struggled against her bindings.

Jimmy's eyes narrowed as the second woman was brought in. He moved closer to the unmasked woman, pulling a knife from his belt.

Clara gasped.

Aron's heart skipped a beat, and he struggled with whether to protect the strange woman or cover Clara's eyes.

Before he could do either, Jimmy had closed the gap between them and with a swipe of his knife cut the ties binding her hands. Aron and others in the room seemed to let out a collective breath.

"Professor Moreau, I'm surprised to see you here," Jimmy said, and the woman rubbed her wrists. Moreau... Was this the Professor Moreau who Kaya worked with? She was dirty but appeared healthy and unharmed.

"James, good to see you too. Please call me Elyna," she said and attempted to straighten her hair.

"Alright, then call me Jimmy," he said, running a hand through his beard.

"With the pleasantries done, can you tell me what you're doing here? You were supposed to stay in the Sanctum last I heard from Hermes."

So she was in the Hermes Conglomerate then.

"Well, things got...complicated," she said, spreading her hands apart. "I didn't make it to the transports in time, so I came here."

Jimmy continued to stroke his chin. "Is the complication this mystery prize here?" he asked, motioning to the writhing form wearing the hood. Whoever was under there seemed quite agitated. "Maybe you can tell me why you brought a cleric into my hideout."

Elyna walked over to the other woman and pulled off the hood, revealing a mass of golden curls. Aron could see now the woman was gagged, and she struggled to move her hair from her eyes so she could see. Elyna brushed the hair from her face, and Aron's eyes widened when he saw who it was.

"What is it? Who is she?" Clara whispered, prodding him in the ribs.

Jimmy whistled and relaxed his shoulders. "Well, that's a complication alright," he said and moved closer. "Lady Pendlebrook, welcome to my home."

Aron could hear Victoria scream through the bundle of cloth in her mouth and knew things had gotten much more interesting.

Aron
July, 4103 U.E.T. – Echus Canyon, Mars

Jimmy directed a pair of guards to take Victoria into his private quarters, along with Elyna who followed closely behind.

Clara pulled at his arm and whispered into his ear, "Do you know who she is?"

"What? Yes, but not now, okay?" he said, pulling away from her grasp.

"You said we would finish talking about…"

"Are you ever going to drop this if I say no?" He was anxious to go and tell Jimmy what he knew about Victoria.

"No, this is what I really want. When was the last time I ever asked for anything?" she said, and he knew she was right. She had dealt with a lot and never asked for much.

"Yes, okay, I agree," he said reluctantly. She shrieked, hugging him tightly.

"Thank you, thank you."

"As long as you stay in the base and listen to the hospitaller, okay? Now I need to go. We can-"

It was Clara's turn to dismiss him as she ran toward what he assumed was the infirmary, forgetting all about the new visitors. Aron made a mental note to check in with her later.

Aron went to where Jimmy was talking with Gwen and his other lieutenants. There was a part of him that worried if he didn't continue to make himself useful Jimmy might get tired of keeping him and Clara around. He was intent on telling him what he knew about Victoria, even if it wasn't much.

"Jimmy, I think I can help," Aron said, interrupting him.

Jimmy glared, and Gwen looked ready to forcefully remove him. "What I need you to do is work on those comms. Find Demitri and talk to Sebastian too. He can maybe help."

"I mean, I know about Victoria and…"

"Yeah, yeah, I've spoken to Kaya too. For now, do what I'm telling you to," Jimmy said and turned his back, entering his quarters. Gwen moved to block the doorway so Aron couldn't follow. He sighed in frustration.

"Stop trying to be everywhere, and stick to doing what you're good at," Gwen said. "You have your job, and we have ours. That's how this all works."

"Well, who the sarding hell is Sebastian?" Aron said, throwing his hands up. He didn't feel less anxious, but he was tired of being reprimanded.

Gwen smirked and motioned with her rifle to a chair at the other side of the room.

The man in the chair sported long, luxurious brown hair tied back with a red ribbon. He wore stylish clothes that were clean and properly pressed. Even his boots seemed allergic to the dust that clung to every inch of the underground hideout. He looked like a high-district fop who had strolled into a night club for an evening of debaucherous merriment. Except now he sat there polishing a gleaming silver pistol.

"What club did they pull him out of?" Aron asked.

"Jimmy said he showed up a couple days ago in a truck laden with supplies. His dad is some magnate in a city in Northern Aonia. I don't remember the name," she said.

"Northern Aonia is a long way south of here. How did he even know where he was going, and better yet, what is he even doing here?"

"I guess his father did some work with Prometheus, and Jimmy gave him a heads up, but who knows? Seems like the kid is here to fight though, from what he's said. He's more sarding annoying then you, but he's enthusiastic."

Aron felt wounded. "That was uncalled for."

"See, you keep talkin' to me instead of doing what yer told. Now, get out of here," she said and gave him a light shove of encouragement.

Aron reluctantly obliged and walked over to where Sebastian was sitting. He was humming some kind of tune. Aron hadn't spoken to him and already found everything about him irritating.

"Hey, Sebastian, come with me," he said, sparing the niceties. Up close, he thought it looked like they were probably similar in age, so he didn't feel it was necessary. He was also struck by the vibrant hazel hew of his eyes. They were clear and free of the common yellowing.

"Ahh, Aron, right? Good to meet you, chap. I'm Seb," he said, holstering the gun under his jacket and extending his arm. Aron reluctantly grabbed it in greeting. He hated these high-district posh types.

"Come on. Jimmy wants you to help me," Aron said.

Seb smiled broadly. "My first task then, hurrah. Lead the way," Seb said in his awful accent.

"Nothing to be that excited about. You realize we're at war, right?"

"Yes, of course. I'm here for all of it," he said, raising his hand in a fist. "The fight for liberty, heroism, sacrifice, pain, and the drama of it all. How thrilling, am I right?"

"Sarding hell!" Aron said and turned to shove Seb into the wall, but the man dodged him easily.

"Ha, easy there, chap. We're on the same side, aren't we?"

Aron felt foolish, but he wasn't going to let this clown cast a shadow on the pain and sacrifice of so many people. He took a deep breath before pointing a finger at the pompous fool.

"I don't know who you are or what you think this is, but it isn't a game. I suggest you keep your head down, shut your mouth, and make yourself useful."

Seb stopped laughing, and his smile softened to something that seemed slightly more serious. "Alright, I get it. I was just lightening the mood. It's felt like a funeral parlor around here."

People fought and died for the Coalition every day here, so in many ways it was like a funeral parlor. In a few short weeks, many of them had lost more friends than Aron had ever had in his life.

It was a sobering experience, even for people who grew up with the specter of death hanging over them in the low or mid districts. He supposed it was something someone like Seb had probably never experienced, and his anger faded.

"If you want to lighten the mood, come help me. What we need is to get our comms array up and running, not a stage performance. Jimmy said you might be able to help, why?" Aron asked, looking him up and down as if it would answer the question. As far as he could tell, he was good-looking and little else.

"Our company manufactured various digidevices, like screens, tables, handhelds, and many others. I don't know much about comms arrays, but I understand a lot about the components," he said brushing an invisible piece of dust from his jacket.

Aron was a little surprised. He had expected him to be altogether more useless. "Did you attend the Engineering University of New Olympia or maybe another one?"

He shook his head. "Sorry, chap, my father sent me to the military academy in Aonia."

"Not one of the business schools?" It was odd that the son of a magnate would choose a military path. That was typically reserved for the nobility or less wealthy individuals hoping to make a name for themselves.

Seb shrugged. "I have other siblings, more...suitable, to business. My father thought it better I try to create my own fortunes elsewhere," he said, and his expression soured.

"So how did you avoid your military service?" Aron asked, starting to sympathize with Seb.

"I was put in charge of a checkpoint that got bombed, and I took that opportunity to fake my own death," he said, a wide grin returning to his face. He put his arms out as if waiting for Aron to congratulate him.

Aron didn't want to laugh, but he did. "Sarding hell, and it actually worked? That is creative. I'll give you that." He secretly hated how charismatic Seb was turning out to be. "Come on, I'll show you what we're working with. We also need to find Demitri."

"Who's that?" Seb asked as they walked toward the comms office.

"Lieutenant Orlov, he used to be with the Pandora Fleet, was a tech officer," Aron said, leading them on a wide berth around the large blast door at the entrance of the logov, or "Berserker Cave" as some people called it. Seb must have already heard the stories, because he also eyed the door warily.

Aron wanted to avoid any run-in with the berserkers he knew slept behind that door like monsters from ancient legends. He had never seen a berserker before arriving in this place and was surprised to find out the stories weren't all made up.

The berserkers were a frightening amalgamation of man and machine. Their limbs and bodies were more metal than flesh. At first, he thought they simply wore heavy armor, but up close he learned it was welded to flesh and bone. He didn't know how berserkers were created, but like everyone else he knew it was unnatural. Jimmy insisted they weren't the monsters people assumed, but he wasn't so sure.

They found Demitri in the main garage, near the makeshift comms office Aron had started assembling. Demitri was practically slobbering over the partially assembled Falcons, which were now offloaded from the trucks and uncovered on the ground.

"Are those...Falcons?" Seb asked as he rushed over to join Demitri and several others who were poking around at the various components.

"Demitri!" Aron shouted to get the man's attention.

Demitri shot up from where he was crouching, admiring one of the engines. He hit his head on one of the crafts fairings, his glasses falling from his face.

"God's bones!" Demitri shouted as he fumbled to pick up his dropped spectacles. "Did you have to yell?"

"Sorry, you looked distracted," he said to Demitri. "Seb! You too."

Seb reluctantly joined them. Aron felt like he was trying to herd cats.

Demitri was a reserved kind of guy who spoke softly and often avoided making eye contact when he spoke to others. Despite Demitri's military background, Aron felt like they had far more in common than he did with soldiers like Jacob or Gwen.

Demitri had gotten separated from his unit during the events of the Ashen Sunset. Luckily, he got picked up by a coalition team in the chaotic aftermath and brought here. From what little news they had gotten, they knew the entire Pandora Fleet had been marked as traitors for their role in those events. Some had turned themselves in hoping for amnesty, but most either died in the fighting or went into hiding.

Despite being abandoned, Demitri was usually in a good mood. Now the two of them represented the most knowledgeable members of the Prometheus Tech Corps remaining in this location.

"Demitri, my name's Seb. Pleasure to meet you," Seb said, holding out his arm like he had for Aron. He sounded like a merchant ready to sell, all smooth and confident.

Demitri reluctantly took the offered arm. "Oh, hey. Demitri," he said while simultaneously admiring the floor.

"Heard you were the one who found the Falcons," Demitri said, looking at Aron. He had a thick Jovian accent and spoke in a slower, more measured tone than the people Aron was used to working with.

"I spotted the trucks, didn't really do anything else," he said honestly. He wasn't looking for any special praise.

"Good work," Seb said, his gaze traveling back to the Falcons and the piles of parts that encircled each one like religious offerings. "But do you think you can actually make them fly?"

He shrugged. "Maybe, I don't know. I was hoping Demitri had worked on them before."

Demitri ran his hand through his hair and shook his head. "Nah, not me. Been around them plenty, but never worked on one. My specialty was security systems."

Aron frowned. "I haven't either. I wasn't on a military track at the university. Anyway, I don't think we have anyone who can fly them."

"Oh, I can fly one," Seb said and looked at Aron as if it was something most people knew how to do.

"You never thought to mention to anyone you're a pilot?" he said.

"I assumed there were plenty of others, and I never made it to a Falcon squadron. I got injured and never made it through the selection process, I was going to try again, but then I died, and all this happened," he said as a matter of fact.

Aron pinched the bridge of his nose. "Alright, we can sort this out later. For now, Jimmy wants us to get the comms array up and running.

It's important we finish as soon as we can. Without it, we may as well be stranded on an asteroid."

Seb and Demitri shared a bewildered look. Neither of them looked ready to offer any solutions on how to accomplish their new task, and Aron knew it would be on him to figure it out. It always seemed to fall to him to just figure things out.

"Alright, Seb, there should be a large spool of wire in one of the supply rooms. Go ask around and bring it here when you find it. It should be orange and about 10mm thick," he said, motioning with his hand.

"I can do that," Seb said and walked off without any complaints. Aron was surprised he was so willing to listen to instructions and supposed his military training may have been good for something.

"Demitri, you remember those batteries we found in one of the old mining rigs?"

"The micro reactors?" he asked, scratching his head.

"Yeah, those are the ones. I think we're going to need them if we want to get our signal out further than the local area."

"Hmm, I think they were using them to power some of the barracks," he said.

"Tell them to light a candle or something. This is more important," Aron said, trying to keep his tone level.

"Alright, I'll try that," Demetri said and slinked off.

Aron wondered if he assigned each of them the wrong task. Hopefully they would manage and get everything working relatively easily. In the meantime, he would work on what he could.

Aron retrieved a dented box that held a nest of equipment wires he collected for this type of project, along with several tools he had hidden in a corner of the garage. Moving them into the comms room, he set them down with a thud.

The comms room was a mess of boxes, components, and wires that lacked any rhyme or reason in their layout to Aron's tired mind.

The original comm equipment from the ancient mining operation had a thick layer of dust over lifeless screens, and many of the switches were either broken or missing. Frayed wires protruded from empty compartments where thieves long ago stole the valuable items, and based on the smell, rodents now built their homes in them.

He flipped one of the switches and jumped back when it sparked violently and began to smoke. That was when the panic began to set in as he watched his dreams of success disappear with the billowing smoke.

The job turned out to be much more difficult than he originally thought it would be. It took them more than two days to clean out the existing equipment and remove anything that was either too damaged or antiquated to be of any use.

Meanwhile Jimmy continued to come around to stand over their shoulders unannounced. He was anxious to contact the other elements of Prometheus, and Aron didn't blame him. The longer they were out of touch, the more likely people would die. The added urgency had pushed them all to work harder.

Seb had proven to be particularly resourceful despite his silver-spoon appearance. He had even played a critical role in retrieving the microreactor when Demitri had failed. When Aron pressed him on how he did it, he said simply, "Everyone has a price, chap."

Now, after four days, they were finally making positive progress and were on the cusp of testing the system.

"Okay, pull again," Seb said. His feet were the only visible part of his body from under the console, his once-pristine clothing stained beyond repair.

Demitri pulled up on the wire and snaked it through the last-remaining opening. He then set to work attaching the last control unit, while Aron made the final connections to the micro reactor.

"Now what?" Seb asked, getting up with a grunt. He brushed hopelessly at his clothing. "I hope this was worth it. These were my favorite pants."

"Did someone check all the components on top of the tower?" Aron asked.

"I sent one of the mechanics up there yesterday," Demitri said as he soldered the last wire into place. "And I think we're done, finally," Demitri said before collapsing into one of the rickety chairs they found to furnish the claustrophobic room.

Argos barked from the corner where he had set up watch near the door, perhaps feeling that the long wait was almost over. Seb sat down beside him and rubbed behind his ears, which looked to be what he actually wanted.

"Now we have to connect everything to the tower array, and hopefully we should be able to reach out through the jammers and to the satellites," Aron said as he moved to one of the consoles to work through the system bios.

"Why did we need all this new hardware for that?" Seb asked, motioning to all their pilfered military equipment.

Demitri answered, his head hanging off the back of the chair, "Republic protocol."

"Thanks, so that means what exactly?"

"He forgets not everyone spent years in the military," Aron said, stopping what he was doing to turn to Seb. "Jimmy explained it to me. Standard Republic security protocol for mass unrest initiates a full lockdown of all long-range communication satellites. I'm sure you noticed how your comms device stopped working."

A light seemed to turn on in Seb's mind. "That explains a lot. So once this is up and running, we'll have the comms network back?"

"No, not really." He motioned to the new equipment. "This will let us connect to the Republic's military satellites, and from there we can send messages to other outposts. Hopefully there are some Coalition members listening as well."

"That is a good thing, isn't it? You don't seem very excited."

"We can expect them to be tracking any data transmissions once we connect to their network. We can try to mask our movements, but..."

Demitri finished the thought, in his Jovian drawl, "If they track us or the others, God himself won't be able to put the pieces back together."

Seb's expression went from ecstatic to deflated in a matter of seconds.

"Go get Jimmy. We're ready to turn it on," Aron said and began saying a silent prayer.

Jimmy arrived with Gwen and several of his lieutenants, but the room was hardly big enough for all of them. Jimmy had everyone wait outside except for Aron, Gwen, and Argos, who stubbornly refused to surrender his chosen corner.

"How sure are you?" Jimmy said.

"Maybe seventy-five percent. This isn't my specialty, but I think I have it figured out." He pulled out his notebook where he had worked out every step in painstaking detail.

Jimmy waved it away. "I won't understand any of that. This is a big gamble, kid. Will the others be able to respond to us?"

"Once I relay the proper security protocols, yes. The Republic will figure out they aren't authentic eventually, but it should buy us time to take control of an actual satellite."

"Without being able to coordinate with the others," Gwen said, "we're just rats in a cave. We need an army if we're going to stay here or a ship to get us off this rock."

Jimmy ran his hand through his beard, but it looked like he had been considering this point for days if not weeks. "I need to *know* you're sure. Otherwise, we're potentially signing death warrants for millions."

Jimmy's expression was somber, and he searched Aron's face. Aron imagined Jimmy was trying to look past any false confidence, but Aron didn't have a habit of boasting. His life had always been about numbers, logic, and probability.

"I would have destroyed all of this and never told you anything if I didn't think I could do it, but I've also weighed the odds and know we need to try." His cold practicality made way for his real feelings.

"I don't want my sister to grow up in a cave. I don't think you want that for anyone else either. This isn't life. It's waiting."

"Okay," the big man said, and then he stepped back and pulled up one of the rickety chairs to sit beside Argos. "Well, what are you waiting for?"

Aron snapped back to the present and called for Demitri to come back into the room.

"Get ready to load this when the console kicks on," Aron said, and handed him a data chip loaded with software he had been working on.

"Roger," Demitri said, adjusting his glasses and pulling up a chair. He seemed content to have Aron calling the shots. "Ready on your count."

Aron went through the checklist again and ensured everything was in its place and then said, "Anyone want to say a prayer?" looking over his shoulder one final time.

Gwen said, "Press the sarding button." That seemed appropriate enough, so he did.

The machines fans whirled to life with an accompanying series of beeps and clicks. Displays lit up with scrolling lines of text and numbers as the main systems booted up.

"Now!" he shouted and started typing furiously as Demitri did the same.

"Raising the curtains," Aron said, biting his lip.

"They haven't found us yet," Demitri said.

"Upload in progress," Aron said as a loading bar crept slowly across his screen. He could feel the sweat building on his brow. "One last..." And suddenly it was done. The glow of a solid green light filled the small dusty room.

"That's it?" Gwen asked.

Aron let out a long breath.

Jimmy pulled a slip of paper from his pocket and handed it to Aron. "Here, can you connect us to this address?"

"Let me try." Aron punched in the series of codes.

The sound of the electronics intensified as fans accelerated and the array pumped its signal into the ether. A few moments later, there was a single word on the display, "Connected."

Jimmy grinned and stood up to stand beside Aron and Demitri.

"What's their callsign, sir?" Demitri asked.

"Forge Alpha."

Demitri nodded, and Aron left him to it, since he could tell he was in his comfort zone now.

"Forge Alpha, this is Torch One Actual, radio check, over."

There was nothing but silence.

"Forge Alpha, this is Torch One Actual, radio check, over," Demitri said again.

Aron had to remind himself to breathe.

Demitri was about to send the message again when the comms clicked and there was faint static.

"Torch One Actual, this is Forge Alpha Actual, read you loud and clear. By God's Bones what took you so long? Over," said the deep voice of an old man.

Jimmy leaned in further and pushed them both aside so he could take over the device. "Temujin, you sarding old bastard, I never thought I'd be happy to hear your voice."

"The dream isn't dead yet, but I might be soon. You called just in time. Now we have a lot to talk about and not long to say it, so listen. The Forge Knights and Coalition still hold Deimos, but that's the only good news," the man said, and Aron grabbed his notebook and settled in for what he knew would be a chaotic and stressful conversation.

CHAPTER

10

Silas

July, 4103 U.E.T. – *Specter*, Great Cislunar Plane

"Your Grace."

Silas sluggishly opened his eyes. His vision was cloudy and unfocused.

"Diana, is that you?"

"No, but you must rise. There isn't much time."

He turned over in the bed. The sheets were damp with sweat and clung to his body, reminding him that he was cold and alone. The fog became thicker until a sharp pain from his wounded side cleared it.

"What..." he said with a start and tried to sit up, realizing Charles was there by his side. "Mr. Beach?"

"Your Grace, be careful," Charles said, inspecting his wound. "It is badly infected. You are in a worse way then you've told anyone."

Silas knew there was no point in lying.

"I have no time to be unwell."

"You will have plenty of time when you're dead if you continue like this." Silas blinked. Was he making jokes now? "Here, take this. It should help." Charles said, handing him several capsules and a glass of water. He swallowed the pills without hesitation and waved away the glass. He was no stranger to aches and pains.

"Thank you," he croaked and tried to get out of bed, but he found it so hard to move. Everything hurt, and the world moved around him in slow motion.

"You can and will be able to do this," Charles said answering a question

Silas hadn't even put to words. He was just so tired. If only Diana were with him, she would know what to do.

"I've lost the path, Mr. Beach." He didn't know if it was the infection speaking or his fears.

"The path might be obscured, but it hasn't disappeared. It is only hiding underneath the newly fallen leaves."

"I didn't take you for a poet," he said and let out a laugh as hollow as his soul. Even the haunting image in his mind of Catherine's charred body did nothing to rouse him from his stupor.

Charles struck him with the back of his hand. The blow twisted Silas's head and left his ear ringing. The unexpectedness of it jolted him into action. He violently threw the damp blanket aside and stood eye to eye with the old man. Charles didn't flinch or back away, he only stared.

"Good, that is the fire you need. The fire of your house and ancestors." He bowed his head. "Your Grace."

Silas wanted to strike him, but he couldn't bring himself to violence against a man who nearly raised him since he was a little boy. It wasn't the first time in his life Charles had reprimanded him, but it was the first display of violence.

Silas relaxed his shoulders and grabbed the sheet to wrap it around his waist to cover his nudity. He limped toward the bathroom, clutching at the visibly bloodied bandage on his side.

Stopping at the door, he looked back. "How do I find the right path?"

Charles shrugged. "The same way as everyone else. You look for it, instead of assuming you already know everything you need to."

"If only my eyes weren't so old. I might find it sooner and save everyone a lot of pain."

"Maybe it's time to get spectacles then, but first we need to dress you for the show," Charles said and proceeded to set out a fresh uniform, alongside a new bandage for his side.

Silas grimaced, knowing the man had rough hands for a physician, but he was the only one who could help him keep up his charade a while longer.

They reached the Great Cislunar Plane soon after he emerged from his quarters. It didn't take long before their ships were hailed by the Lunese fleet, and a tense standoff began to take shape.

A cold shower had helped Silas feel more human for the time being, and Charles had done well to make him look the part of a strong and healthy commander. Underneath the façade, he used every ounce of his strength to remain standing and keep his eyelids open.

"After this, you're going back to the med bay, even if I have to drag you there myself," Marcus said in a low whisper. He knew his friend would be able to see the truth. Like Diana, he had a knack for reading him.

Silas watched from the monitors on the bridge as their formation moved into position. The engineers had done a good job putting out fires and stemming the flow of smoke from the hulls of their ships. At least on the surface, the fleet appeared strong and intact. He hoped the illusion would hold up long enough for them to establish an advantageous position.

"Update," Silas asked the comm officer.

"We're establishing a connection now, sixty seconds, standby."

Marcus said, "I think they have nearly their entire planetary fleet mobilized."

Silas scanned the digiscreen to his left before turning to the screens that showed images from outside the ship. They weren't always very useful since up and down was relative in space, but there was something he found grounding about them anyway.

While deep inside his own ship, he found it grounding to see an outside world made of real and tangible objects. It was a reminder that what he decided would have real consequences for real people. Hiding behind screens and sterile telemetry data made it far too easy to forget his enemies were human.

"Confirm their fleet numbers against the naval records," Silas said to a young officer. It looked like several larger ships might be missing from the Lunese fleet, but he wasn't positive. If the entire fleet wasn't present, it would help their chances if it came to violence.

"All personnel to battle stations," Lancaster called from the captain's chair.

"We should armor up," Marcus said.

Silas shook his head.

"Is that a good idea?" his friend asked again.

"We can't arrive like conquerors, especially not here. It will only have the opposite effect with the Lunese."

"Dirty pirates," Marcus sneered.

The young officer returned with a slip of paper she handed to Silas. "High Commander, it looks like they're at roughly fifty-percent strength with only one carrier on our radars. No dreadnoughts."

Silas took the paper and dismissed her.

"Hiding the rest of the ships maybe?" Marcus theorized.

"Maybe in reserve on the other side of the moon," Silas concurred.

"They won't do them any good that far away," Lancaster said.

"High Commander, the Lunese are hailing us," the comms officer interjected.

Silas cleared his throat and stepped forward, wiping the sweat from his brow. Marcus helped to steady him when he swayed slightly. "Put them through."

The largest digiscreen illuminated and revealed the bridge of another vessel that appeared much like his own. A cadre of commanders glared back at him with stoic expressions, his camera meanwhile only focused on him.

"Lord Beckett, this is Admiral Moore, commander of the 3rd Lunese fleet. Your presence in our orbit is surprising given recent events. We have only received limited information, and none of it is comforting." He was an older man with a bald head and a serious expression. Silas didn't know him personally.

"Admiral, I am here to parley with the duchess. I must ask you to break your formation and allow us to proceed to the capital unmolested with all due haste," he said, his voice level and measured.

"Forgive me, High Commander, but I cannot do that until I ascertain your intentions. Come and meet me aboard my ship, and we can discuss the current situation," the admiral said. He spoke in the same, contemptuous tone Republic naval commanders like Zhou had directed toward him for most of his career.

Off camera, Lancaster made a rude gesture with his hand. Silas didn't need anyone to tell him that what the admiral suggested was a horrible idea. On his own ship he held the advantage, and given the state of their fleet he would need it. If he left and Moore decided to take him prisoner, this all ended here and now for them.

"Admiral, you're welcome to come aboard and discuss the situation with me here. This is within the bounds of courtesy afforded me as Duke of Mars."

"That may be true, Lord Beckett, but you are still High Commander of the Pandora Fleet, are you not? As senior-ranking officer, I must insist you come aboard my vessel."

"No," he responded without hesitation.

Silas could see Lancaster motioning to various crew members behind the digiscreen, no doubt issuing orders and directing vessels for a potentially hostile response.

Then all they could do was wait for the admiral to make the next move. They were out-positioned and outgunned without the Mercurian Fleet for support. Fighting would be a last resort.

The comms remained connected, but the silence that followed was as immense as the void of space between their ships' hulls. Silas and the admiral were locked in a battle of wills, waiting to see who would avert their gaze first. Silas had no intention of backing down, even as his eyes strained to maintain focus.

"Very well. I will see you soon, High Commander," Admiral Moore said, and the transmission ended abruptly. His face had been a placid mask, and the ease with which he agreed left Silas feeling uneasy.

"Prepare a delegation to meet them in the hangar bay. I'm going personally," he said to Marcus.

"Wouldn't it be more secure in one of the meeting rooms?" Marcus asked.

"Yes, but I want them to see as little of this ship and its condition as possible." The Lunese couldn't know how vulnerable they actually were.

Marcus nodded. "I'll get Colonel Taylor and have him gather an entourage."

Silas turned to Lancaster. "Keep everyone on high alert and be ready to fight, but don't make any obvious movements. We don't want to scare them into making bad decisions."

"Your Grace," the gruff man said, lowering his voice, "we should strike first and end this now. Take what we need from the Lunese and return to Mars."

"The Lunese are citizens like us. We need to give them a chance to be on the right side or we're no better than our enemy."

"Your Grace," Lancaster saluted, but it was obvious he disagreed. "Let's hope there is honor among pirates."

Silas found Marcus and Colonel Taylor in the Alpha Hangar, a bay normally reserved for special guests and non-combat related travel. It was spacious and had massive air locks capable of accommodating large shuttle vessels.

What made it unique was that unlike the other hangar bays, which were utilitarian in their design, the Alpha Hangar was clad in ornate finishes, giving it an air of opulence.

Marcus approached, a string of red licorice hanging from his mouth. "I still think we should be armored, and don't look at me like that. If you want some, ask."

"No thanks," Silas said, returning a salute from Colonel Taylor.

"Your Grace, I agree that we shouldn't take such a big risk, but I've taken the liberty of keeping marines on standby."

"The risk is acceptable," Silas said. "If we lead with the promise of violence, it will be all we get from them. You both know the Lunese are a hard people."

"But you think they will capitulate? We haven't even heard from the duchess," Marcus said, loading his mouth with more licorice. Taylor was more sensitive to proper military decorum and gave Marcus a disapproving look.

"The Lunese have never been the most loyal citizens, but that doesn't mean they aren't honorable. This might be a test to find out what side we're on. The problem is we don't even know how much they know or what they've been told," Silas said.

"Now you're trying to confuse me on purpose," Marcus said.

"That isn't usually very hard to do," Taylor said dryly, and Silas would have laughed if his side didn't hurt so much. Taylor appraised him silently.

Silas knew he was doing a bad job of hiding his discomfort. "Either way, we don't have a better choice, unless we want to limp back to Mercury with our new benefactors." From their expressions, Silas knew neither of them thought that was a better idea.

Two transport shuttles landed not long after, accompanied by the sound of fans and motors as the airlocks opened and closed. After safely landing, the shuttles powered down, and hatches opened to allow the occupants out. Each transport was large enough to hold a couple-dozen occupants.

Silas tensed slightly as armored figures emerged. Luckily their weapons were holstered, helmets retracted. Silas didn't second guess his own decision not to wear armor. His honor dictated that he adhere to tradition.

The admiral approached flanked by his aids. Silas, Marcus, and Colonel Taylor stood to greet them, flanked by their own honor guard. The admiral waved for his guardsmen to step back, and Silas did likewise. The man wore the standard gray armor of the Republic navy, a ceramic blade at his waist and a rifle on his back. He stood several inches shorter than Silas, and his bald head shone brightly.

So he came ready to fight. Someone should have told him to bring more men.

"Lord Beckett," the admiral said without offering a bow or any sign of deference.

"Admiral Moore," Silas replied without a salute. He would play the game however the man chose to. "Why have you come armed and armored to a parley?"

"Parley?" he said with a tone of surprise. "You're the most wanted man in the Solar System. A criminal by all counts. Since when do we parley with criminals?"

"I advise you to choose your words carefully," Taylor sneered.

Moore looked Taylor up and down, making a sound of disgust, "It is you, Colonel, who should remember your place. These are naval matters."

"That is Lord Taylor to you. I have no need of the Republic's poultry recognitions."

"All the better, as you will likely be stripped of them soon enough."

Silas seethed as he had flashbacks to Zhou and his scheming.

"You misunderstand our purpose, Admiral Moore. The star of the Republic has burned out, and soon it will be a cold and dead remnant. Stand down and let us pass to the capital so we can treat with Duchess Engstrom and discuss the future of our system."

The admiral stood quietly as if he were considering something and then his tone changed. "As you say, Lord Beckett. I needed to be sure of your position. We have only heard limited news, but citizens from Mars have begun to appear with many different tales."

Moments before, the air in the room was becoming thin, and the promise of violence hung in every word. Now the winds blew in the opposite direction, and he wasn't sure what to make of it.

"There was fierce fighting above Mars, but the 1st Fleet was quickly silenced by the might of Mercury and the Pandora Fleet," Silas said, his shoulders back and rigid.

"Yes, that is what we've heard. Was it really the young Vardan boy? I have my doubts. Imagine being beaten so easily by a child, shameful," Moore said.

"We must treat with the Duchess immediately," Silas repeated, trying to move things along. He had no patience for gossip.

"I'm afraid she is indisposed securing our realm. I can take you to the archbishop at once. He will be able to aid you further," Moore said.

Silas fought back a grimace. The pain was getting worse, and the lengthy period on his feet was taking its toll.

"The archbishop has forsaken his oaths to New Olympia and God?" he asked, not trying to mask his suspicion.

Silas knew Duchess Engstrom well, even if they had barely spoken for decades. Her quiet contempt for religion and God had been the primary cause for their incompatibility.

Although, once she inherited the duchy, she was happy to support cooperative clergy. Unfortunately, he knew very little about the archbishop of Luna and the circumstances of his ascension and couldn't say if he was one of her trusted few.

Moore spread his arms. "Why would you be so surprised? The Lunese propensity for putting profit first extends to every tier of society. Why should the clergy be immune?"

"The clergy put God above all else, as should the rest of us," he offered. Clergy who only paid lip service to their vows were worse than atheists in his eyes.

"Then why is it a God-fearing man like you is standing here after spilling so much holy blood in New Olympia?"

The question wasn't surprising, and it should have been simple to answer, but it struck a nerve. A lifetime of guilt was difficult to leave behind. "My problem is not with God. It's with false prophets and tainted messengers."

Moore's smile grew. "Then what more is there for me to explain. Piety comes in many forms, and the truth isn't reserved only for you. Unless you claim to be a prophet yourself. Do you receive divine messages, Lord Beckett?"

Silas said with a scowl, "I claim no special link to the divine. Our Republic is rotten and needs treatment if it is to survive and serve the people it promised to protect."

Moore laughed, "I guess the tales of your delusions were greatly exaggerated. Come, let's put this ugly business behind us and start anew." Moore motioned back toward their shuttles.

Silas let his muscles relax. The prospect of finally being able to rest filled him with joy, but then Silas noticed something. One of the figures standing next to the admiral, a young man, perhaps a little older than Henry, ever so slightly shook his head.

That was curious. He searched the boy's eyes and noticed Marcus shifted his feet. He must have seen it too.

"Yes, time is of the essence," he said, stepping closer to the admiral. "Tell me though, the duchess, has she kept her faith?"

"Of course, there are few on Luna as devout as she. Come, let us have a drink," Moore said, trying to usher Silas toward the shuttle.

"You know her well then?" he asked, holding his ground. He had no intention of leaving his ship.

"Yes, better than most," Moore said, and Silas knew he was lying. There would be no rest for him tonight or any night for a very long time.

"This is your final chance to throw down your weapons," Silas said, letting his pain and anger stain his words. The air in the room shifted again, and he could hear the rustle of armor behind him as soldiers prepared to unholster their weapons.

Moore scoffed, "They were right. Watching your daughter burn has finally broken you. Now you're destined to earn the same fate as her."

"And your words will earn you only death," he said, drawing his plasma blade and kindling it. He swung the blade toward Moore, but his movements were uncharacteristically sluggish, and the man dodged his strike easily.

Marcus drew his own blade and stepped in front of Silas. In that moment, the boy who signaled them drew his ceramic blade and buried it deep into Moore's side. The thin blade sliced easily through his armor and into his body. He lived only long enough to watch his plan fall into ruins.

"Issue the orders, full attack. Their commander is dead!" Silas shouted to Lord Taylor as Marcus pulled him back behind their line of defense. Enemy troops poured out of the vessels like demons. They fired on their position, forcing them to retreat deeper into the ship.

The boy must have acted on his own, as they fired indiscriminately at him as well. Marcus pulled the boy back with them as they fell back. Only in the narrow corridors were his men able to secure a defensive position and begin fighting in earnest.

"Shut the doors and vent them," Silas commanded, trying to regain his senses. The blood vessels in his head pulsed nearly to bursting, and he struggled to hold it together.

"It's too risky. We will rip a hole in the hull if we do that now. Reinforcements are coming. We need to fight them off. Lie low," Marcus shouted over the gunfire, and Silas began to act on instinct.

He shoved Marcus away and holstered his blade. He took the rifle out of the hands of one of the nearest marines. He knew he couldn't fight in the hallways with his blade without armor.

Raising the rifle, he took a position in the front of the line and opened fire on the fiends attempting to storm his vessel. Meanwhile, larger explosions began to ring out, and the hull quivered as the ships began to exchange fire over Luna.

CHAPTER

11

Kaya

July, 4103 U.E.T. – *Rubah*, Great Cislunar Plane

Kaya fingered her sapling pendant as she watched the ships on the screen nervously. She and Reina had rushed to the bridge when the announcement came that they'd entered Earth's orbit. They had taken up seats at the meeting table, which had become their go-to spot when they weren't in the observatory or the gym.

Reina was trimming her nails with a knife, and Kaya tried her best to ignore her. Releasing the pendant, she leaned over the table and swiped through the video feeds displayed on the digiscreen.

"How do we know if they're going to fight?" Kaya asked.

On the screen, she saw the distant shapes of ships arrayed before them and the glow of Lunese cities beyond. Then she switched to the feed that showed Earth and its swirling array of satellites, forming the Iron Cage. The dark and brooding clouds underneath echoed her own feelings.

"You don't," Reina said, putting the knife away.

The ships appeared still and unmoving from their distance, making it impossible for her to discern their intentions.

Kaya shook her head. "I'm not sure why we are so far back. We're closer to Earth than Luna. We could gather the Coalition forces we have here and mount an attack of our own."

"We don't have the equipment for that. Look at the size of those ships. They are crewed by thousands. Besides, this ship won't add much to Beckett's formation and having you on it makes it a bigger liability. He would have to focus too many resources to protect it. Back here, we can contribute with the other ships of the rear guard while avoiding the heaviest fighting."

Kaya rolled her eyes. "How chivalrous of him."

"The rear guard is important. You should try to learn something about naval combat," Reina scolded.

"I will add it to the list," she said and went back to studying the enemy formation.

"I wish you spent some time in the military, then you could have gotten used to what it means to hurry up and wait. Enjoy these quiet times. They won't always be here."

"If I wanted a quiet life, I would have never left my room in Alhazen," she said, and Reina laughed. "What?"

"Teenagers are always so sure of themselves. Unless you claim to see the future, you never predicted any of this would happen. You didn't *choose* any grand life of adventure. You made some bad choices and fell into the shit like the rest of us. Now you can enjoy the agony of flailing about trying not to drown."

"I'm nearly twenty." That was the best retort she could come up with, and she immediately felt silly. What better way to seem childish than declaring her age.

Reina turned to look at Aelius as he entered the bridge.

"What's he doing?" Kaya asked, following Reina's eyes.

Aelius paid them no attention and went to speak quietly with the captain and Theodore. Neither looked happy to speak to him.

"Who knows? He always shows up like a raven to signal dark tidings," Reina said, pursing her lips.

Kaya let out a short laugh. "Now who's the dramatic one?"

"I can't say he's the cause, but nothing good ever happens when he comes around."

Kaya knew there was truth in that statement. "I'm going to go see what is going on-"

Sirens blared as red flashing lights filled the bridge with their threatening glow.

"Enemies inbound," a steady voice said over the comms. "Tighten formation for combat maneuvers."

"What's happening?" Kaya shouted to Reina over the noise.

"Dark tidings, I think," Reina shouted back.

"Sarding hell," she said and rushed toward Theodore. She had found herself in this position one too many times now. Maybe Reina was right that she should learn something about naval combat. Then maybe she could be useful for a change. "What's going on?"

"It looks like the Lunese aren't open to a parlay. We will need to reposition," Theodore said, looking over the readouts on the various digiscreens.

"Enemy ships closing range from Vector 9-0 Omega. Captain, they're coming right for us, twenty-four ships. Looks like a full Falcon squadron," one of the bridge crew relayed.

"Initiate evasive maneuvers. Deploy flak screens. Full power to shields and engines. We need to get back to the main formation and in range of the fleet's Falcons," the captain relayed.

Kaya ran back to the digitable and flipped through the available cameras. There she saw the chaos erupting as missiles sped from ship to ship, leaving trails of fire like comets before unleashing their nuclear payload into the shields of enemy vessels. Some made their way through those shields to dramatic effect, as debris began to vent into space. The pieces of shrapnel coalescing around shattered hulls in thick clouds. The few ships of the rear guard began returning fire on their attackers.

Then the *Rubah* began to change direction rapidly, causing the objects in the camera's view to shift violently, making Kaya nauseous.

Reina took her by the arm and helped guide her to a pair of nearby flight seats. "This is going to get worse before it gets better, princess."

Kaya strapped herself in, grateful for the help. Reina looked only slightly less bothered by the maneuvers.

Kaya thought of the Coalition members in the open barracks and reached for her comm device. "I need to let Rudra and the other Prometheus members know what's coming." Reina agreed and handed Kaya the digipad.

Kaya knew the Coalition members onboard weren't likely to get any detailed updates from the *Rubah's* crew. She was able to establish a connection with the other part of the ship and relayed the information that they were actively under attack. They would have to do what they could to brace themselves.

Then the ship began to shake, and she knew from experience they were under fire.

Sailors relayed information in a constant stream of consciousness, and Kaya tried to follow as best she could.

"Two Falcons eliminated."

"Shields at seventy-three percent."

"Radar shows seventeen craft remaining."

Seventeen, she thought, panic rising in her chest. That seemed like far too many.

The first mate relayed the most ominous message. "Captain, our current vector is becoming untenable. Debris and enemy vessels are going to cut us off before we make it."

"Specter Actual, this is Rubah Actual. Requesting new vector. We are under heavy fire. The rear guard is being overwhelmed. We need support. Over," Captain Masoumi said, and Kaya really began to worry.

"Can we outrun them? How can a few Falcons take out a frigate?" she asked Reina.

"No, they're too fast. This is exactly what Falcons are best at. Normally we could fight them off with our own, but the *Rubah* doesn't carry many, and most of them are damaged anyway. I...I don't know what we can do," Reina said, and the worry was plain as day on her face. Kaya had never seen Reina scared.

While everyone rushed to take their seats, Aelius and Theodore stood beside Masoumi like a pair of sea captains from some ancient painting. Stoic and unmoving in the face of ship swallowing waves.

"Rubah Actual, Specter Actual, maintain original vector, we will cover as best we can. Over."

"So much for chivalry," Kaya said and fought back her nausea as the ship continued to lurch violently.

"This isn't going to work," Theodore said, stating the obvious.

Aelius reached over the captain's shoulder and tapped several things into one of her displays. Theodore looked at what he entered and turned to him with a shocked expression.

"It is the only way," the prophet said, and the captain cursed loudly.

Kaya missed what was said next as all her attention went to not vomiting. She rejoined the conversation as Theodore finished some kind of impassioned plea. "What...is...going on?" she struggled to ask Reina.

"They want to land on... Ahh!" Reina shouted as the ship lurched again even more violently then the last time.

"All personnel, prepare for emergency reentry. I repeat, prepare for reentry," the captain relayed to the entire vessel.

"Emergency reentry to where? We're thousands of miles away from Luna."

"Earth," Reina said in a panic.

Kaya tried to get Theodore's attention, but he had moved to take his own seat, and the captain ignored her. Only Aelius saw her flailing arms and walked over as if taking an afternoon stroll.

"Don't be afraid. This has the best probability of success," he said with a smile that was more creepy than comforting given the situation.

Probability. They were about to die, and this crazy old man was talking about probability!

"What about the Iron Cage?" she shouted over the growing noise of alarms and combat.

"I know a way," he said as cryptic as usual. "It should be alright. Hold on now," he said and walked back to take a seat beside Theodore.

Should be alright? Did he say should instead of will? Aelius never said anything by accident.

Kaya tried to take it all in but struggled to focus on any one thing. She saw untethered objects smashing into consoles, and even the experienced crew looked panicked as they tried to execute their jobs. Gone was the brave stoicism she saw during the exit from Mars.

Her head was pushed back into the seat. She wanted to look at Reina but couldn't turn her head. Her arms were likewise pinned to the chair. The booming sound of explosions began to ring out. Kaya thought the shields may have been failing. Even some of the hardened crew began to cry out.

It was so much worse than the escape from Mars. The ship felt and sounded like it was being torn apart.

Kaya tried to scream, but no sound came out. She imagined the *Rubah* falling through the gray clouds of Earth before crashing into some fiery, molten pit. She imagined the fiery hell conjured by zealous clergymen. There was nothing but pain and misery in the garden now. There was no way out. There was no clever trick to get out of this. She was going to die.

Kaya clutched at the arms of her seat because it was all she could do. Her nails dug into the thin padding, and the veins of her hands strained under the effort of holding on. She didn't want to give up, but she couldn't move. There was nothing she could fight, and there was no chance to run away. She was utterly and completely trapped.

Her mind caught up with that realization, and she saw an image of her mother in her mind. She wanted to reach for her, but then she saw Aelius and remembered his words. If the ageless were real, then her mother could still be out there waiting for her. If her mother really was ageless and still alive, there wouldn't be a reunion in the afterlife for them. She had to live because she had to know the truth.

Kaya pushed aside the thoughts of safety and comfort her mother's memory gave her. Kaya wouldn't die, couldn't die, until she knew for sure that she was gone, and her mother's dream had become reality. She had a mission to complete, and she had only just started.

She clenched her jaw and fought against the g-forces. A sense of determination washing over her despite the pain. Then blood rushed to her head and her grip on consciousness began to slip.

"I will see you some other time," she mouthed, and then there was nothing.

SILAS
JULY, 4103 U.E.T. – *SPECTER*, GREAT CISLUNAR PLANE

SILAS WAS PANTING, HIS uniform soaked with blood and sweat. He struggled to get to his feet after falling again. Without the benefit of his armor's magnetic boots, he was slipping in the blood that coated the *Specter's* corridors.

The Lunese had been able to establish a beachhead, however brief, to launch their assault. The fighting had been fierce and bloody but luckily brief.

He felt an arm under his shoulder and saw it was Marcus helping him to his feet.

"Marcus... What's the status?" he said through labored breaths. Marcus's face was bloody from a gash over his eye, and he scowled.

"Think that was the last of them," he said and pulled Silas down a corridor their reinforcements came streaming out of.

"Lancaster, report," Silas said, activating his comms device.

"The sarding bastards came from our rear, but we're regaining control. It isn't over yet," Lancaster's gruff voice relayed.

"God's bones, the Mercurians were in the rear guard. How didn't we spot them sooner?"

Marcus wiped his face with a sleeve and assessed the blood. "Maybe they used the Earth to mask their movements, or our sensors were too damaged. I don't know. I'm no engineer. I told you we should have worn armor."

Silas ignored him and waved down Lord Taylor, who he saw in the distance. Taylor was covered in blood but seemed less battered than he and

Marcus. "Lord Taylor, lock down this section. Then I want the ship swept. Find anyone who might have gotten through."

"Your Grace," the man said with a salute and ran back toward the Alpha Hangar.

Silas stopped to grab the wall, willing the world to stop spinning.

"Taylor and Lancaster can handle this. We need to get you to the medical bay," Marcus shouted. Alarms were still blaring in the corridor. His head was throbbing even worse than it had been earlier in the day.

"To the bridge," he said. Marcus sighed and half dragged him in that direction.

He battled to keep his eyes open, and if Marcus had decided to take him somewhere else, he likely wouldn't have had the strength to stop him. However, his friend did as he asked and took him to the bridge, where he garnered no shortage of concerned looks.

"I'm fine," he said, waving away any assistance. "Lancaster, give me better news."

Lancaster expertly scrolled through various displays showing complex vectors and trajectories for a hundred different objects.

"Your Grace, some of their ships are turning to flee, and the formation in our rear has been eliminated, but we've sustained some heavy damage." Lancaster issued commands to his subordinates to begin compiling damage reports. "The *Pelican* looks to have taken critical damage and… God's bones."

"What is it?"

Lancaster switched to a video feed and pulled it up on one of the bigger screens for Silas and Marcus to see.

"Tell me that isn't…"

"Aye, it is," Lancaster said. "I didn't see this until now."

"How old is that video?" Silas said as his stomach sank.

"Approximately twenty minutes ago."

"Pull up the *Rubah's* position."

"Your Grace, there's no active telemetry data for the *Rubah*," replied one of the young officers on the bridge.

The ship's hull quivered as it was rocked by more missile strikes. Silas struggled to maintain his feet through the pain and exhaustion.

"I want that sarding carrier, captain," he said, slamming his bloody fist on the table. "And scramble Falcons. I want to know where that Mercurian frigate went."

"Aye, Your Grace, but I think she's lost to the cage," Lancaster said coldly.

"You better hope it isn't, for all our sake's." Their alliance with the Mercurians was already tentative enough. They couldn't afford to strain the relationship so soon.

"Why did they sail that direction at all?" Marcus asked, and Silas wondered the same thing.

The same young officer turned as if he were going to speak but then seemed to change their mind.

"What is it, sailor? Do you know anything that might be helpful?"

"Your Grace..." The young man looked from Lancaster to Silas.

"Out with it!" Silas demanded.

"Our rearguard was busy engaging the enemy incursion when the *Rubah* was set upon by a Falcon squadron. They requested additional aid because there was no clear path for them to reach our formation," the officer said, staring at the ground.

"Lancaster, what did you do with this information?" Silas snapped.

"This the sarding first I'm hearing of it," Lancaster said, and Marcus narrowed his eyes.

The young officer looked nervously at Lancaster, who stared at him. Turning back to Silas, he swallowed and said, "Your Grace, I didn't relay the information. I advised the *Rubah* we had no resources to spare and that they should continue their original course."

Silas closed the gap between himself and the young man. He reached a bloody fist down to grab his shirt and lifted him from his seat before depositing him on the floor.

"You sarding fool," Silas said. Then the dizziness struck again, and he fell to the floor beside the man.

If he had been in his right mind, he would have demanded the crew of the *Rubah* stay aboard the *Specter* or at the very least within their immediate formation. He was worse than a fool, and now Lord Vardan would certainly seek his head for the death of his only daughter.

"We might still find them. Maybe it's more scanner trouble," Marcus offered while helping him up. Silas knew that wasn't true. This was one more failure for the pile.

"Your Grace, our marines have established a foothold on the enemy carrier," Lancaster said, distracting Silas from the young officer.

Small victories. "Spare the crew who surrender. Kill any who resist," he said.

"Aye, Your Grace."

Silas looked at the young soldier and noticed him looking to Lancaster, perhaps for salvation. Unfortunately for him, he had overstepped his authority in making his decision to keep quiet. "Lieutenant, you're relieved of your duty. Marcus, see that he makes it to the brig."

Marcus took the man by the arm and escorted him to a pair of waiting security officers. Silas turned back to the array of displays to monitor the battle.

The Falcons reported no sightings of the *Rubah* as the battle continued to rage, albeit with a lower intensity. The Lunese formation was beginning to break, and several of their ships were either left drifting helplessly or had already fled the field, searching for safety somewhere in interplanetary space.

Silas watched all of this transpire with vague recognition. He issued orders and collected information, but it didn't feel like something he was doing. Instead, he felt like a low-district puppeteer pulling strings on some ruined and ragged puppet.

If Lancaster had been a less competent naval commander, they surely would have already lost. Except victory only offered so much comfort now that Kaya, Theodore, and the rest of the *Rubah's* crew were likely dead. He repaid their trust in him with incompetence, and he knew it would come back to haunt him. His choices always did.

Taylor arrived at the bridge sometime later. Silas wasn't sure if it had been minutes or hours. If someone had told him it had been days, he might not have questioned them, but the new arrival pulled him from his self-loathing.

"Your Grace, I thought you should hear this right away," Lord Taylor said, pushing a bloody form in front of him. It was the young man from the Alpha Hangar, except his armor had been removed and his hands were bound behind his back.

On closer inspection, he looked to be older than Henry. Perhaps closer to Catherine's age. He was fit and carried himself with quiet confidence. Even bloodied and in chains, he held his head high. He reminded Silas of himself at that age.

"You killed your commander. Why?" he asked, skipping the formalities.

"They murdered my father."

Silas appraised him. "What's your name?"

"Viscount Hayashi, Your Grace," he said with a bow of his head.

"Lord Hayashi is an old man," Silas said, looking him over.

"He was. I'm Ichiro Hayashi, his only child."

Silas only had a passing knowledge of the old Lord Hayashi and even less about his family, but they could verify his claim against their records later.

"Where is the duchess, Lord Hayashi?"

"No one knows."

"Explain," Silas said impatiently.

"When the news came of what happened in New Olympia, an emergency session of the Lunese council was called. During the meeting, the duchess attempted a coup against the archbishop, but her plan failed. The cowards among her contingent were happy to throw her to the wolves for a pittance.

"When it became clear the tide had changed, the duchess and her retainers fought against the Frumentarii and security forces. Except, it was too little, too late, and many lords and ladies were killed."

"How do you know all this?" Silas asked.

"My father was among those lost in the fighting."

"And the duchess?"

"When the bodies were cleared from the meeting chamber, the duchess was not among them."

Silas considered his features as he spoke. The story seemed plausible, but he had to be careful.

"How did you end up by the side of the admiral?" Silas asked probingly.

"I was in his service before these events transpired. When I found out about my father's crimes, I denounced him, and for that I was allowed to stay. I don't think the admiral or even the archbishop fully understood the scale of what happened in New Olympia."

Silas didn't fault the boy for that decision. At least if what he said was true.

"Did you think to garner favor with me as the winds shifted again?" he asked.

Lord Hayashi returned his gaze, steady and unblinking. "With all due respect, My Lord, you were going to lose this fight."

"The battlefield says otherwise," he offered.

"The rest of the Lunese Fleet, at least the portion of it that isn't loyal to the duchess, remains in reserve in the moon's shadow. I suspect they would have already been here if Admiral Moore had been able to issue the order."

Silas considered that. It was strange the rest of the fleet never engaged if it was indeed close by and within the admiral's control.

Silas studied his face a moment longer and then said, "Provide Lord Hayashi with quarters and see he gets what he needs. He is to remain there until summoned."

Lord Taylor saluted and escorted Hayashi from the bridge.

When he was gone, Silas felt his knees buckle but steadied himself against one of the displays.

"Captain Lancaster, I expect news of our new carrier ship and the Mercurians soon. Marcus, see to the security sweep, and then get yourself cleaned up and rested." He turned to leave before adding, "You look like death."

"No worse than you. Where are you going? The med bay, I hope," Marcus said, skeptically.

"I need to inspect the damage and consider what I will say to Lord Vardan."

Marcus grabbed him by the arm before he could leave. "You need medical attention," he said in a low whisper.

"See to the men and the completion of the battle. We will reconvene in an hours' time," he said loudly for Lancaster and anyone else nearby to hear. He couldn't afford to be seen as weak.

Marcus reluctantly released his arm. "Stubborn bastard."

Silas walked purposefully through the corridors, ignoring the pain. He could find his way through his ship in pitch blackness if he needed to. The unblemished hallways near the bridge gave way to large corridors used to muster entire battalions and ferry them off on missions to distant planets or enemy starships.

He vaguely remembered offering passing salutes to armed marines that streamed past him in the corridors. Several stopped to ask if he required aid, but he put on a confident demeanor and dismissed them to their duties. They were more use defending the ship than caring for him. He continued his deathlike walk through the vessel.

Eventually he came to the place of the battle and saw welders and engineers already hard at work repairing panels, pipes, and wires. The bodies had already been removed, and deckhands took mops to the blood-soaked floors.

Clerks meanwhile dutifully collected weapons under the watchful eye of one of the ships' junior supply officers. So much death, and yet all that remained was cold efficiency. There was no room for anything else. It had been centuries since someone died in combat aboard the *Specter*. Yet everyone continued as if it were just another day.

He considered it a testament to their training and the quality of his commanders. Training kept men alive and gave them the confidence to act under immense pressure. Quality leadership empowered them to take initiative toward common goals, from the lowest man at arms to the highest officer. He hoped he could continue to maintain the high standards the Pandora Fleet had come to represent.

The lights flickered, and he shielded his eyes against the sudden flash. He opened his eyes slowly as the light dissipated and found the corridor was suddenly empty. No deckhands or clerks, only him and the bloody floor. No, it wasn't only him, he thought as he saw the bodies of the fallen men and women were there now.

Except they no longer maintained their cold silence. They writhed at the places of their deaths, reaching out for him as he tried to pass. There were so many of them. He tried to run, to rush past the ghosts that haunted him now, but his feet struggled to move.

The bloody floor took hold of his feet, and he reached for anything on the walls that he could grab to propel himself forward. Anything that would give him leverage to break free of this new torment, but it was no use.

The corpses moved closer, and he saw their faces. The faces of the countless lives he had seen ruined by war. The faces of the men and women he couldn't protect and the innocent citizens he had let down in their time of need.

"No, I tried," he said to them, but they didn't relent. "I tried!" They shambled closer, pressing their weight onto him.

He fought back against the pressure of the mob, but they pushed him to his knees. The blood rising like the tide around his legs. He realized they were going to drown him in it, and a shiver went up his spine.

Silas thought he would be afraid in this moment, but instead he only felt numb. He was prepared to release himself into their cold embrace. He had longed for the moment when he could finally atone for his many sins. He always knew this day of reckoning would come.

They pressed harder, and he relaxed his body, slumping down into the bloody pool. It was warm, and he only felt peace within the sinister tide. He imagined his mother tucking him into bed as a child, and there was no fear. He imagined the fields of stars he had always dreamed of. The wild and alien worlds of the universe that were waiting to be discovered.

He felt a pang of regret that he never had the chance to explore, to build. He was tired of destruction. He opened his eyes hoping to view the world one last time, but all he saw were the ruined and leering faces of the dead.

It was then he realized his weakness. They hadn't come here to save him. They had come here to test him, to test his resolve, and he had failed. He thought of Catherine's charred hand and realized he was about to abandon her again. He was becoming everything he taught his troops not to be. He had become a cautionary tale of failure. The man who let the Republic crumble. The man who cast aside his family.

"Catherine!" he shouted, taking the undead soldier by the collar. "Are you here for her? Well, I won't let you take her."

He shoved the corpses away and reached through the viscous liquid for his plasma blade. He found it still at his hip and kindled it, swiping madly at the corpses that tried to drown him. He saw the blade cut through bone and gristle with ease.

Hands, arms, and heads fell from the bodies around him. He pushed through the gore and broke free, rising out of the bloody pool. He ran and stumbled away, sliding in his haste to escape. The dead only offered light resistance, but he still breathed heavily from the exertion.

He stopped at a closed doorway at the end of a large t-intersection, turning back to see if he had gotten away. Sweat dripped from his brow, and he could see the bloody trail he had left behind but there were no pursuers. He looked anxiously down the adjoining corridors but couldn't find a sign of anyone else. He was utterly alone.

Turning slowly, he saw that his subconscious mind or perhaps divine guidance had brought him to the ship's chapel. He fumbled with the door controls, yearning for the safety he knew would be inside. A loud whoosh of air nearly knocked him over as the door opened, and he was sucked into the room. He was hit by a surge of heat from a fire that blazed in front of him.

Seeing the flames, he tried to stumble back, but the door was already closed. He tried to use the controls, but nothing happened. He instinctively tried to use his comms to call for help, but there was nothing but silence.

"Dear God, I beg your forgiveness," he shouted into the maelstrom. The altar was fully alight, and the metal around it was beginning to twist and glow under the heat. Smoke for the moment was still being pulled through the ship's ventilation ducts, but the fire suppression system seemed to be inoperable. He averted his eyes from the light and heat.

Then he thought of the relics hidden within the altar. Bones of the early martyrs and broken fragments of their weapons. He turned again, shielding his eyes to get another look. He was surprised to see the altar seemed undamaged despite the flames and heat.

"Is this meant to test me again? Am I supposed to reach into the flames this time to save the holy objects?"

There was no response save for the crackling of the fire. The flames grew in intensity but didn't spread closer. He took that as a sign to approach. He wondered which angel it was that finally showed itself to him.

He had abandoned Catherine, his only daughter, in the flames. He had listened to her cries and did nothing but watch. It was a shame he had avoided facing until now. He thought this must be the angel of life and death that was visiting him. He approached somberly, collapsing to his knees before the unburnt and glowing altar.

His body ached, and the pain in his side intensified. He dropped his head to the floor, but a wave of heat rushed over the ground, forcing his face upward. God appeared to be displeased with his display.

The heat instead forced him to gaze into the flames as they blazed ever hotter in hues of orange, yellow, and blue. Perhaps he had been destined to burn all along. Did that mean Carlo Ajax, the Praefectus Frumentario, had been on the correct side?

"What is it you want of me, God? I have so little left to give."

Light erupted from the center of the flames, bursting out like a super nova. The wave of energy hit him in the chest, and he fell back, the wind knocked from his lungs. As he struggled to breathe, he saw it. The message he had been waiting for. There in the fire stood a figure, tall and vibrant, wielding a molten blade.

The figure was an angel with flame-cloaked wings that were only barely contained by the vaulted ceiling of the chapel. The fiery angel looked down and flicked its blade in his direction. He raised his arm defensively, but he couldn't look away. It was one with the flames and as it approached, so did the heat. He continued to crawl backward. He could feel and smell his burning hair.

He was pressed against the wall, unable to move back any further. The heat forced him to look upward to God's messenger. Pitch-black wells took the place of eyes, but they weren't dead eyes. Their shape and position rippled with the flames.

The scripture told many stories of God's angels and how they took their forms from the natural world. There were many angels, but it was the council of archangels, led by the Ashen Dawn, that had preeminence.

Among the council, there were many angels that depicted God's fiery radiance, but it was the angel of life and death that was fully embodied by flame. The angel was neither male nor female but something entirely celestial. And now its fiery wings shone brightly and spread like a protective energy dome over the room.

He stared into the fire and considered what God's message meant. Was the angel here to extract retribution? No, not that. If it had been, he would have already been consumed by the flames.

"Tell me what you want from me. What more do I have to give?"

The flames swirled up as if answering his words, blazing around his head in a fiery tempest. He thought of the scripture.

Only flame can cleanse the sins of man.

Perhaps God had finally sent a messenger to come and lead him from the darkness. Except the angel raised its blade, and this time he didn't look away. He did not raise his own weapon because what could he do against divine will? Instead, he braced himself and began to mutter a series of prayers, except an attack never came.

Instead of cleaving him in two, the angel pressed the blade into his left shoulder. The molten metal burned through his uniform and bit deep into his skin. He cried out from the pain, but he couldn't hear his voice over the sound of the crackling fire. His pain was excruciating, and his eyes were forced open by the shock. In his agony, he looked upward to the heavens but only saw the angelic face outlined in the flickering light.

He struggled to maintain control, his mind a muddled mess. The angel of life and death, the divine messenger, had marked him, but he didn't know why he was the one chosen. Although he knew in his heart the why didn't matter. He had been called to serve, and he would answer. He swore an oath to face the darkness without fear, and what better way to do that than with the light of heaven at his back.

It had been years since the last time he spoke with God. He had begun to consider he might have been alone all along. He had nearly abandoned his faith, but God still believed in him. Now he would be the one who through God's fire would cleanse this corrupt world of its evil. Not Ajax, the Manus, or even the Vox could claim such a right. His failures made him question if he was the best person for this mission.

"Divine spirit, I am your servant. Deliver me from this storm, and I will achieve victory in your name," he shouted into the flames, and the fire intensified.

The light shone brighter and brighter, until finally in one large blast of energy the angel and flames disappeared. The explosion of light and pressure was so violent that it snapped his head into the wall.

He only had a vague sensation of what happened next. In the maelstrom, the angel departed, but as it turned to leave, he thought for the briefest moment he saw God's face beside it.

It wasn't the face of a man or woman. It wasn't the face of a human at all. It was as if all the matter of the cosmos coalesced into a mass of swirling energy. The colors were vibrant and overwhelming. The beauty felt at odds with the angelic visage that had loomed over him with its violent request.

The divine forms began to dissipate as he felt hands grabbing to pull him across the floor. He wanted to remain in that moment, to understand it, but he had no choice. He had no strength left to fight, and he was once again pulled away from God.

CHAPTER

13

Silas

July, 4103 U.E.T. – *Specter*, Great Cislunar Plane

"He's awake," Marcus said, catching Silas's ears.

He squinted against the light. Marcus stood beside Colonel Taylor, both staring at him. He had tubes in his arm delivering intravenous drugs, and the physician came to check on the equipment when he stirred.

"Where am I?" he croaked. His throat was dry and his voice raspy. He covered his mouth to cough and smelled the familiar odor of smoke that clung to him.

"Med bay," Marcus said, leaning in to look him over. He waited for one of the physicians to back away before leaning in closely. "Don't you remember what happened?" There was a look of concern on his face.

"The raid, Hex, did we get her?" He couldn't remember the last time he felt so rundown. How long had he been here? "Why is no one answering me?"

The physician came to his side. He was a serious man who wore the insignia of his profession and rank within the Knights Hospitaller. "High Commander, you were terribly afflicted with an infection to your side. You're lucky to be alive from that alone. That you survived the explosion is a testament to your strength."

"I'm not so easily undone by coalition tricks," he said, rubbing at his temples. The physician looked to Marcus and Taylor for some kind of guidance. There was obvious concern in their eyes, but none of them spoke.

Taylor tried to sound reassuring, "Your Grace, it's been..." Before he could finish, memories began to return to Silas.

Like a nightmare, he relived the agony of the execution and his wife's death. The visit from God and the divine messenger. It was all like a bandage torn from his soul.

"No...no, I'm alright," he said, silencing Taylor and waving away the physician. "I remember now." Although, part of him wished the memories never came back.

He checked over his body and was surprised to find himself relatively injury free. Minor burns covered his arms and neck, but the pain in his side had subsided significantly. He moved to pull the collar of his shirt from his left shoulder, revealing a white bandage. The angel's fiery brand was real.

Marcus replied to an unasked question, "It's a deep burn. They think it may have been some arcing wires. Looks like your shoulder took the worst of it."

"You said there was an explosion?" The details were muddy, but he remembered a blast. When the divine messenger had left with a display worthy of its name, its fiery writ marked him as a tool or perhaps a weapon. He still wasn't sure he was the right choice for either.

"Yeah, a gas line exploded near the chapel wing. Engineers think it must have been nicked by a stray shot during the fighting, and something set it off, and..." Marcus paused. "Why are you smiling? It's creeping me out."

Silas didn't dare tell Marcus about what he saw because he knew the man would never believe him. "Nothing, I'm glad to still be here, that's all. How is Catherine? How long has it been?" He didn't ask about the explosion because he didn't think it mattered. He received a message from God, and the others saw what they needed to.

"She's the same," he said sadly, "but it's only been a couple of days."

"A couple of days!" Silas threw the blanket off his legs and attempted to climb out of the bed. Colonel Taylor grabbed his arm to steady him.

"Relax, things are under control. The battle is won, and we've been regrouping. Our fleet has gotten a little bigger, and now it even includes a proper carrier-class vessel," Marcus said like a proud new father.

His men and the mission needed him to lead them. He was finally able to get on his feet with the help of Taylor. His sweaty feet clinging to the cold metal floor of the med bay. "Good, good..." he said, gathering his thoughts, "we will make for the docks at once. I need to visit my quarters, but then we'll set things right on Luna."

"That might be more complicated than we thought, Your Grace," Taylor said, stepping back once Silas was firmly on his feet.

Silas wrapped himself loosely in a robe a passing medical assistant handed him. Then he remembered the young Lord Hayashi and his story. "Has the Lunese boy said anything new or useful?"

"Why don't we regroup in the meeting chamber?" Marcus said, looking at their surroundings. He was right that this wouldn't be the best place to have this discussion. The only thing that spread faster on a ship than fire were rumors. Silas agreed, and the group separated.

Silas took a few moments to stop and see Catherine before he left the med bay. She continued to sleep peacefully, but he could already see signs of life returning to her. Blotches of fresh pink skin were beginning to crop up amongst the field of ash that was her ruined body. For the first time since the trial, he had real hope. She was a fighter, which meant he would need to be also.

He leaned in close to her bandaged head. "With you, I received my miracle, and now through the divine messenger I have received my mission. Stay strong, and soon we will be delivered from this nightmare and through the fire, reborn in God's image."

With his oath given, he left and made his way back to his quarters.

Walking through the familiar halls, he felt a little lighter than he had in months. With the infection subsiding, he was able to think more clearly. He could formulate a more logical plan on how to proceed, but he still had a lot of doubt about his ability to lead them from this mess. From a young age, he had always been eager and ready to command others and in his youth proved to be an adept military leader. Now, in the twilight of his career, he had made so many mistakes that he wondered how he had ever made it this far at all.

The divine messenger had returned some of his confidence and the fire that had propelled him into his current position. Except the fire also reminded him of his greatest mistakes, the firebombing of districts during the Midnight Raids and Catherine's execution. The idea that violence begets violence had never felt so true to him. Except, what choice did he really have? Only through fire could sin be absolved.

He received odd looks from sailors as they passed, likely a result of his robed appearance, but he assumed they had already heard stories of the explosion and his injuries.

He had expected to find Charles in the medical bay, a fresh uniform in hand, but the man was curiously missing. It was unlike his valet to be indisposed when duty called, so he assumed whatever it was must have been important. If it wasn't important, it was at least unplanned. He could picture the horror on the old man's face at the thought of Silas navigating the halls in a bathrobe.

When he reached his quarters, he was even more surprised to find Charles wasn't there either. Their quarters were connected, and so he went to knock on the man's door. Propriety and respect stopped him from simply opening it, but no answer came. He struggled to think of a single time in the last twenty years his old servant had ever absconded. He wouldn't even take a day off without being nearly threatened with violence to do so.

Whatever it was, he resolved to leave the man to his business. Perhaps the recent skirmishes had shaken him. In truth, they had shaken Silas, even if he was loathe to admit it. This had been the first time in his lifetime that the *Specter* had ever truly been threatened by armed opposition. He knew intellectually this was what the future held, but living it was something else entirely.

He dressed quickly in the same Pandora Fleet uniform he had worn most of his career. His uniforms still all bore the marks of the Republic, and it felt strange to wear them now after everything that had happened.

He had never set out to lead a revolution. He only ever wanted to protect his family, but here he was. Still, looking at himself in the mirror, something felt wrong about it all. He went to the nightstand and removed a small pocketknife. It was red and bore a white cross. The man who sold it to him had said it was a genuine relic from Earth. Silas wasn't sure it was, but he appreciated the salesman's energy, so he paid three times more than he should have for it.

He flipped open the blade and used the sharp edge to cut away the Republic's star and cross from his uniform. If the men had burned the banners, he wouldn't be doing himself any favors keeping the symbols on his uniform. Even if his intention wasn't to destroy the Republic, it would need new symbols. Then they could rebuild it into what it was always meant to be, a beacon of hope and salvation. He placed the knife back in his nightstand along with the patches.

Charles still had not returned by the time he left, and the guards posted at his door couldn't offer any information about his whereabouts.

Silas would have to find him later. For now, he had to get to the command room. There they would devise a plan for their next steps on Luna. The docks would need to be secure, and the surface pacified. Preferably both could be done quickly. It was their best chance of creating a position they could fight from moving forward.

The Pandora Fleet often spent long periods of time away from their headquarters on Deimos. However, this was heavily reliant on resupplies from friendly ports and the larger Republic Navy. In the absence of resupplies there was only a finite amount of time they could continue to operate.

Before he reached the conference room, he saw the familiar form of Charles walking, no, running toward him. The man's demeanor was becoming increasingly unhinged, and Silas truly began to worry.

"Your Grace," Charles said, bowing his head. He somehow wasn't out of breath. "I must speak to you right away."

"Of course, Mr. Beach," he said, stopping in the corridor. Sailors continued to pass by, offering sharp salutes.

"No, not here, we should return to your quarters."

"I'm afraid I must attend a meeting, but we can discuss whatever it is when I return," Silas said genuinely. He had no intention to brush the man off, but there were pressing matters.

"Yes, Your Grace, that is why I came to you right away once I heard you were awake. Unfortunately, you had already left by the time I arrived. I must insist we go and speak now. It won't take long, but there are things you must know."

Silas had never seen Charles so animated. He paused, trying to consider what problem could be serious enough to delay this meeting further.

Charles leaned in close. He stood roughly the same height as Silas, and so was able to speak discreetly into his ear. "I know the *Rubah*, and the Mercurians have gone missing. Finding them *must* be your highest priority. Above all else."

Silas didn't try to hide his surprise. He was ashamed to admit that with the skirmish and his injuries he had forgotten completely about the Mercurians. He was even more confused by why Charles suddenly cared.

"Don't worry Mr. Beach, we will find them," he said.

"No, Your Grace, you don't understand," Charles looked suspiciously at the passing crew members. Silas had never seen him so rattled.

"Okay, well, can we discuss it when I return?" he said, placing a firm hand on Charle's shoulder.

Charle's eyes took on a sharp and focused appearance. He leaned in even closer, grabbing Silas by the shoulders. "Things are not as they seem with Lord Vardan. He is far more dangerous than the Vox or your brother could ever be. Especially if he feels he has been wronged."

The comment caught Silas off guard. "I don't really understand."

Charles exhaled sharply. "This isn't the best place to discuss these things."

Silas looked at his comm device and didn't think he should delay his meeting much longer. "Is this something we need to address right at this moment?"

Charles paused. "No, Your Grace, but finding the Vardan girl should be your priority. Above anything else."

Silas still didn't understand why Charles cared so much. His point seemed reasonable, but he wasn't sure the perceived slight of the Lord Eminent, thousands of miles away was their top priority.

"Don't worry Mr. Beach, their safety remains a top priority. We can discuss this more when time allows."

Charles sighed, lowering his head. "Yes, Your Grace," he said and took a step back. "I will be waiting for your return but remember what I said."

Silas assured him he would and continued on his way. He had already spent too much time in the med bay. His fleet was in imminent danger from the Lunese, and that had to take priority. Whatever anger he might incur from the Vardan's if he was unable to find the *Rubah* would have to wait. If they lost the coming battle for Luna, it wouldn't matter anyway.

The meeting room was full of activity when he arrived. Junior officers came and went with files and reports while his more senior commanders brooded at the table. Captain Lancaster and Lord Taylor seemed particularly displeased. The assembled officers rose from their seats and offered their salutes as he entered.

Marcus remained seated beside a table with small sandwiches. He was more interested in eating than planning, it seemed, or maybe he had given up on arguing with the older men at the table.

"At ease," he said, waving them back to what they were doing. He groaned softly as he sat back in the leather-bound chair. Marcus placed a sandwich in front of him after he sat down. "You have to eat," Marcus said, sounding like Diana.

Silas pulled up a view of the outside on one of the tables digiscreens and frowned. "Why aren't we docked, Captain Lancaster?"

Lancaster looked annoyed. "Lord Taylor here thinks he knows more than me about sailing now. Thinks we shouldn't risk docking yet." Lancaster began raising his voice. "What he forgets is that we weren't supplied for an extended siege before we left Mars. We need food, ammunition, fuel, and most importantly to repair our broken ship so we can get sarding out of here." Lord Taylor leaned back in his chair, crossing his arms. He looked like he was trying very hard to contain his temper in front of Silas. "There are other factors we must consider. Like the fact an enemy fleet remains in play nearby. You're a talented captain, but you're no admiral. This conflict is already bigger than anything fought in all our lifetimes. We need to consider the big picture."

Silas listened quietly. Nothing either man said was incorrect. There was no shortage of variables now.

"We must first agree on what our goals are. With Mars compromised, we need a base of operations, and Luna offers us dockyards, supplies, and the manpower we need to retake New Olympia." Silas waited to see if anyone would offer disagreement, but no one did.

Lord Taylor leaned forward in his chair. "We have won one small skirmish. Perhaps we can take the docks as well but holding them indefinitely would not be so simple. We don't know what the situation is on the surface or how much support we can anticipate. We are only thousands against millions, or more." The air seemed to leave the room.

"We don't need to hold anything. We need to dock, pillage, repair, and sard off," Lancaster said.

"Now you're suggesting piracy?" Taylor accused.

"It's not piracy when you're stealing from pirates. These people are criminals and not worthy of our time and blood," Lancaster said, and Silas put up a hand to silence any further rebuttals.

Their task seemed nearly impossible. They were too few, and the Lunese were many and unpredictable at best. Although, what choice did they have? God had put this path before him, and the angel of life and death had anointed him with its fiery authority. He would find a way to succeed.

Silas said, "Not all the Lunese are our enemy. We need to secure the support of local leaders if we're going to accomplish anything here. The Lunese are a proud people, and it is unlikely they will appreciate foreign conquerors marching through their cities. First, we need to find the duchess. She is the key to our success here. We also need local leaders like the young Lord Hayashi to help us legitimize our mission."

"Are neither of you going to tell him about the letter?" Marcus chimed in through a mouthful of sandwich. Silas looked at Lancaster and Taylor questioningly.

"It's nonsense, Your Grace," Lancaster said confidently, and Marcus stood up with a scoff.

"You lot really need to start opening your eyes. The world is changing, and it's apt to leave you both behind with that kind of attitude," Marcus said, shuffling through papers on the table before producing a letter he handed to Silas.

"What's this?" Silas asked, briefly scanning the paper. It was handwritten in a formal script and bore the seal of the Duchy of Luna. That it arrived on printed paper spoke to its significance.

"Seems like the Lord of the Silent Sea wants to be our friend," Marcus said.

"God's bones!" Lancaster interjected. "We don't need the help of pirates."

Marcus swallowed the mouthful of food and said, "We need all the help we can get."

Taylor seemed to be quietly considering the situation.

Silas scrunched his brow as he read the letter. It was in fact from the Lord of the Silent Sea. Some also called him the pirate king, while others called him the master of the belt. By whatever name, he had a fearsome reputation.

"Do we know who sent this? Is there any way to verify it?" Silas asked.

"It arrived via courier. They came from the docks via a transport ship. We nearly blew them to pieces, but it was only one small transport, and they came under a white flag," Taylor said.

There was a time when Silas chased the pirate king through the inner Solar System and the asteroid belt, but that was before Hex became the priority target of his career. It felt like so long ago.

"They claim to have command of the docks and the remaining Lunese fleet," Silas said, reading the letter. "It could be the ships Hayashi alluded to."

"An obvious ploy," Lancaster said.

"Can we confirm the existence of this remaining fleet?" he asked.

"Based on information we have so far, it was the 3rd Lunese Fleet that we engaged. The 1st and 2nd fleet are known to be currently on rotation through interplanetary space on various missions. We can't say who they're loyal to, but since they aren't here, they're not an immediate concern," Lancaster said.

"That leaves the 4th Lunese Fleet unaccounted for," Silas said.

"A fact they are using to their advantage to trick us, Your Grace. If they had so many ships at their disposal, they could have driven us away."

Taylor aggressively set down his mug, spilling coffee onto the table. "This is one of the many reasons why I do not want to rush to the docks. If it turns out not to be a lie, we would be nearly helpless to stop another counterattack with our forces so heavily committed elsewhere. Not to mention, the docks are not without their own defenses."

"Have the scouts reported anything yet?" Silas asked, looking over the available maps and diagrams.

Lancaster responded, "I haven't risked any deep patrols. Most of our fleet is damaged and in desperate need of major repairs. We can't risk losing any more ships, not even scouting vessels. Which is also why we can't afford to lose the dockyards. We need to get this next move right." Lord Taylor continued to stare at Lancaster, and it was clear the two men were never going to come to an easy agreement.

Silas considered Lancaster. The man was a good, perhaps even great captain, but he also tended to have narrow vision when it came to tactical matters. It was the main reason he was never promoted to commander. Narrow-minded thinking was not going to help them win a larger war. Lancaster dismissed the quality of their enemies, but fire, steel, and radiation killed as easily, no matter who wielded them.

Marcus started pacing as he spoke. "I know you all remember our days combing the belt for the pirate king, or whatever he wants to call himself now. It was the first assignment of my career, and I'd love to see that bastard hang for the things he's done. I'm sure you all have your own reasons too." They all listened quietly.

"But we can't pretend they're some ragtag group of asteroid raiders. We spent our careers worrying about optics and pretending no one could threaten the Republic's military supremacy. But we all know their captains and pilots are some of the best we've ever seen. We can argue about their ethics, but their quality isn't debatable." Even Lancaster grudgingly agreed.

"My feeling on traitors is well known, but if this is real," Marcus grabbed the letter, shaking it in his hand. "These are people we need on our side. This conflict is bigger than only us, and we all need to come to terms with that. Besides, piracy is a matter of perspective. They could make a good case for us to start sailing under their colors."

Silas grimaced along with Lancaster and Taylor, even if the suggestion had been rhetorical. None of them wanted to openly admit that Marcus was right. Marcus only echoed Silas's own thoughts, but his pride bristled at being lumped together with brigands.

They all looked to Silas for the final answer.

"Summon Lord Hayashi. I want to get as much information as we can before we commit to anything," he said and one of the junior officers left to fulfill the order. "In the meanwhile, what is the status of the Mercurians?"

Lancaster seemed unconcerned and continued looking at his charts. Taylor filled the silence. "Nothing yet, but it doesn't look good. Our scouts haven't found any sign of them. The only good news is long-range communications are still down, so Lord Vardan has no way to hail them. Which means we still have time to consider a plan before he knows anything."

"What plan can there be to explain to the Lord Eminent that his only daughter is dead?" Silas said to no one in particular. The warning Charles gave him came to his mind. Charles was right. This could create a major problem. Even if Lord Vardan only retracted his support, it would be enough to doom their Lunese campaign in the long run. It would be even worse for everyone if he decided to prioritize revenge over the greater war effort with the Republic.

"How about we don't get killed by pirates first, then we can worry about the Mercurians," Marcus said.

There was collective agreement, and they set to work figuring out how they would take the Lunese docks and avoid being trapped in the process. Lord Hayashi was brought in during that time to answer logistical questions about Luna or provide insight into what he knew of the pirates. Unfortunately, most of his knowledge about the pirates was anecdotal, and its usefulness would be difficult to verify.

The conversations were long and often tense. None of them were willing to admit they felt a little bit out of their depths. They had all spent their lives fighting the Republic's enemies, but those conflicts were isolated and often mismatched affairs. The Pandora Fleet or some other unit would swoop in like they had on 132 Aethera or Deimos to easily overwhelm and capture an enemy facility.

The scale of this new endeavor was something else entirely. Their training was thorough and included expansive war games and the study of battles from the Great Solar War and before. They understood military theory but never had to apply it at scale. Their lack of practical experience was glaring in those early moments of planning. It had been generations since any unit larger than a brigade had been deployed on an active campaign.

"We don't have enough men for what we intend to do," Lord Taylor said, tossing his pencil onto the table. "Accounting for the marine units we have left, we have about seventy-five thousand personnel spread throughout the fleet. Most will have to remain aboard their ships to defend against attacks. Several thousand more are already assigned to securing the captured Lunese vessels. That leaves us with maybe twenty to forty thousand men to subdue all of Luna."

No one spoke. They all knew Luna was home to billions. Even if most were noncombatants, there were still large contingents of the Republic military spread throughout the moon. In terms of sheer manpower, the Republic had them beat by a wide margin.

"We need to rush the docks and bombard them from orbit. If we can do that, they will be outgunned, and we can safely take what we need and leave," Lancaster offered.

Silas was becoming annoyed by Lancaster's lack of desire to acknowledge their larger vision. The plan he proposed might give them a short-term advantage, but it would doom any future efforts to achieve peace and security. But Taylor was right that they didn't have enough soldiers.

Lord Hayashi, despite his earlier silence, took the hanging silence as an opportunity to speak unbidden. "Bombarding the cities of Luna from orbit will not endear you to the people."

"Do you have another suggestion?" Silas asked. He was going to need the Lunese one day if he was going to retake Mars and reestablish proper order. However, given his divine edict he would take the path of fire and ash if that was where God led him.

"There are many within the military who would be loyal to my house. They would have openly joined the duchess in her coup if things had gone differently. Also, as I already said, the pirate king was an ally of the duchess, albeit privately."

Silas considered his words. "We can only solve these problems one at a time. I think we can all agree the docks are our primary objective." He took a deep breath to solidify his course of action. "Let's arrange the details of the meeting with the pirate king and see where it leads us before committing further."

Lancaster offered several more colorful complaints but relented when the others pressed. Silas dismissed the room and stood to stretch. He had to prepare himself for the visit while the others continued their assigned tasks.

Lord Hayashi spoke before he was led from the room. "One last thing, Lord Beckett. A warning." Silas narrowed his eyes. "Despite the reputation of the Lunese as separatists, there is still a sizable faction of Republic loyalists. The fighting will be hard and bloody no matter what we do."

"Then this is our chance to make our ancestors proud. Show them that we will protect this world they built for us and leave it better than how we found it," Silas said. He would supplement his lack of experience in interplanetary war with faith and conviction.

It would be the edge that would bring them victory. He knew the Republic's commanders were in the same position as him. Silas only hoped they would learn faster than their enemy and that God continued to be on his side.

ACT
2

Aron

July, 4103 U.E.T. – Echus Canyon, Mars

It had been a long call with so many people in such a tiny room. Aron learned that the old man who answered their transmission, Temujin, was in fact the Grand Marshal of the Forge Knights. Aron was glad to know that such high-ranking officials were a part of the Coalition's forces, but he wondered what use an order of seneschals and magistrates would be in fighting a war. Jimmy seemed to think highly of the man, but he was cautious in his own optimism.

Although without news from the other planets, they didn't know if the defection by the Forge Knights was unique. It was possible the knightly orders that administered justice to the other planets and moons had also defected. It was even possible the Void Knights, that oversaw interplanetary justice may have already defected. Without reliable communication, it was impossible to know how far and wide the war had already spread.

"What now?" Aron asked when the call had ended and the room went quiet.

"We continue our mission here and in the meanwhile figure out a way to help those on Deimos," Jimmy said, putting a hand on Aron's shoulder. "You did well, kid. One of the best engineers I've ever seen if I'm honest, and I've met quite a few."

Aron beamed at the compliment. "Thanks, but it was a team effort."

Jimmy reached into his pocket and produced several folded pieces of paper. He flipped through them until he found the one he wanted and handed it to Aron.

"Here are some other addresses. See if any of them produce results. Your goal is to collect data and say as little as possible. If you reach any units related to the Children of Men, cut the connection. We don't want those lunatics knowing where we set up shop."

"Aren't they on our side?" Aron had no interest in working with the Children again, but it seemed like an extreme measure. Especially in their current situation.

Jimmy shook his head. "They only care about their own agenda. Nothing else. You know that better than anyone. The less they know about what we're doing, the better."

Aron nodded.

"When you're done with that, see what you can do with the Falcons out there. If we can't get them flight ready, I at least want to cannibalize the guns."

"I'll try to assemble one at least," Aron offered.

It was already a fully functional aircraft, only disassembled. In theory, it shouldn't be that hard. Since it wouldn't require any specialized manufacturing.

Jimmy congratulated them again on a job well done and left with Gwen following close behind.

"Do you actually think you can rebuild one of the Falcons?" Seb asked when the room had emptied.

"Now you have something to say," Aron chided.

"You had it all well in hand, but can you really rebuild it?" Seb asked again.

Aron sighed. "Maybe. I don't know. It should be straightforward. Between the three of us, I think we can do it."

Seb grinned broadly. "I can't wait for the chance to fly it."

"Who said you would even get the chance? Jimmy might have other pilots in mind. Actually, I would guarantee you he does."

"Well, we still need a test pilot, right? Look no further. No use risking the life of an experienced pilot when you can use me instead," Seb said enthusiastically.

"Have you always been such a madman? You do realize none of us actually knows how to build these things. It could as easily explode as fly," Aron said, shaking his head in disbelief.

Seb waved away his concerns. "You seem smart. I trust you will figure it out, and if not, don't worry about it. You can't kill a dead man twice."

"Let's get it up and running first, then we can talk about your martyrdom in its first test flight," he said with a smile. Demitri seemed distant as he stared at the comms equipment.

"You okay, Demitri?" Aron asked.

"Oh yeah, I just zoned out for a minute," Demitri said, returning his focus to their conversation.

"Alright, before any of that, let's run through this list Jimmy gave us and see who we can find," Aron said, and they set to work.

They spent nearly the rest of the day attempting to reach other outposts but only had limited success. More than once they also had to quickly terminate the connection, hoping to avoid Republic counterintelligence efforts. It made for a stressful but fun game of cat and mouse. Aron was glad to prove he was the equal of and often better than the Republic's military engineers. This was a task he was particularly well equipped for.

Eventually, Argos's persistent barking told them it was well past dinner time, and Aron made the decision to call it quits for the night. They could continue again in the morning.

As they finished up, Demitiri said, "I think I'm going to stay here for a while, see what I might be able to overhear."

Aron shrugged. "If you really want to, I guess, but don't try to send any messages. I don't want to poke around anywhere Jimmy hasn't asked us to."

"Roger that," Demitri said and leaned into one of the displays.

Aron assumed Demitri wanted to stay in an environment he felt comfortable in. So he left with Seb. Argos plodded along happily beside them as they went back to the canteen in the main living area. The stress of the day was washing away, and Aron's shoulders felt light.

At least until they ran into Jimmy, who pulled Aron aside to speak privately. "Oh, Jimmy, nothing new to report yet."

"This is about something else." Jimmys expression was serious.

Aron frowned. "Is everything alright?"

Jimmy's face softened slightly. "Yeah, a lot on my mind. We didn't have time before, but I wanted to ask you about Lady Pendlebrook."

Aron perked up at the new opportunity to be useful. "Sure, though I don't know much beyond what Kaya has told me."

"So you've never spoken to her?"

"I've never actually met her," he said honestly. "What are you going to do with her?"

"I'm not sure," Jimmy said. "I don't get the impression she wants to help us."

"I'm sure she will come around, like me and Kaya."

Jimmy rubbed his beard as he thought. "I hope so, kid, but one more question. Did Kaya ever mention that her and Lady Pendlebrook were related?"

"No, not that she ever told me." Aron felt confident he would have remembered a detail like that. "What's going on?" He couldn't help his curiosity.

"There seems to be a lot of interest in our new guest, and I'm trying to figure out why, so if you think of anything that seems important, come let me know," Jimmy said and turned to walk away.

Aron rejoined Seb, and they continued to the canteen.

Aron spent much of the next week bouncing back and forth between the communication room and their makeshift hangar bay. Seb became an enthusiastic supporter of the Falcon project. It even turned out he knew quite a bit more about the machines than Aron would have thought. They were steadily making progress, but the Falcon was a long way from taking flight.

Meanwhile, Demitri spent most of his time in the comms room. The problem was with each passing day the positive reports from allied positions were dwindling.

Only the Forge Knights on Deimos seemed to be able to put up any real resistance. They had control over docks, supplies, and several large neighborhoods, but the Republic's blockade left them stranded.

It was clear the Republic was only looking for a solution to remove them that would minimize the destruction of resources. The terrestrial outposts like the one he was in now were not so lucky. Those, they were vaporizing as quickly as they were found. No matter the collateral costs.

Aron was busy calibrating one of the Falcon's many sensors when Demitri shouted, "Aron, come quick."

He rushed to the room and saw Demitiri quickly scribbling a note. Argos stood up from his guard post in the corner and wagged his tail excitedly. He might not understand the standard tongue, but he obviously wanted to be involved.

"What is it?" Aron asked, coming up beside Demitri. He absently scratched Argos behind the ear.

"We got a report from an outpost near Chryse requesting aid. Sounds like they had to fall back from their position."

Aron took the note. "Chryse is on the coast, isn't it? That must be hundreds of miles away."

"Yeah, it's not close, but they sounded desperate. They planned to fall back into the canyons, but that's all I found out before the feed died. Do you think it makes sense for us to stay here?"

Aron played back the messages. He wanted to know for sure what was said before he updated Jimmy.

"Almost everyone we've found sounds desperate. I don't think there is anywhere safer than here right now," Aron said. "Let me go get this to Jimmy. He will want to know."

Demitri nodded, and Aron left with Argos faithfully by his side. The dog had become quite attached to Aron and often chose to stay with him over Jimmy. A development Jimmy didn't particularly like, but the dog had a mind of his own, so there wasn't much to be done about it.

The facility had also become increasingly crowded over the last week, with more and more refugees arriving every day. Jimmy didn't turn anyone away, but their resources were becoming strained. Most of those who came couldn't offer much, but they tried to be useful. Then there was the small but vocal minority who criticized them daily for not doing enough.

All this left Jimmy and his lieutenants extremely busy putting out metaphorical and occasionally literal fires on a near-daily basis. It also meant people like Aron, who Jimmy had grown to trust, were generally left to their own devices.

He spotted his sister Clara in the corridor and waved her down.

"I feel like I haven't seen you in days," he said when she came up beside him. She offered Argos a warmer hello than she gave him.

"Dame Heather keeps me pretty busy, but I don't mind," she said, referring to the only Hospitaller knight they had left in the base. Dame Heather had been a physician at a local hospital before joining Prometheus. Now his sister was becoming increasingly involved in the day-to-day operations of the infirmary alongside her.

Aron was worried about what she might see spending so much time among the sick and wounded, but Clara had taken to it easily. It turned out she had a much stronger stomach than he did.

"I'm sure she's happy to have your help. Did you drop off a meal to someone?" he asked, motioning to the empty tray in her hand.

"Yeah," she said, not offering any additional information.

"All the way up here? Why would you be delivering anything outside the infirmary?"

"It doesn't matter. Did you speak with that lady they brought in yet? I would love to talk to her. She has such pretty hair," Clara said, twirling her own shaggy brown hair through her fingers. "Do you think Jimmy will let me talk to her? I've never talked to a noble before."

"She... No, I haven't, but really, where were you?" he asked. She didn't answer, and he became even more suspicious. "Come on, why are you being so odd?"

"I was in the Logov," she said with a nervous expression.

He stopped in his tracks, lowering his voice as others walked past. "That's where the berserkers live."

"Yeah, obviously, but they don't like to be called that. They have names."

"Clara, you can't be going in there. They're dangerous and all hyped up on nectar," he said, grabbing her arm.

She pulled away from him. "I knew you would be like this. They are people too. They're just in pain, but maybe one day I can help them."

His chest tightened. He only wanted to protect her, but she was more worried about protecting others. Even those brutes who only understood violence.

He shook his head. "They're still dangerous. They stay in the Logov for a reason. They aren't capable of existing with the rest of us."

"You only think that because you've never talked to them."

She was right that he had never spoken with a berserker, but then again no one really did. Their drug-altered minds had a hard time with speech and their general demeanor made them poor conversationalists.

"Someone else can go in there, Clara. I want you to be safe. You can't protect yourself against them. I sarding hell can't either. God's bones, I don't think most people here could."

Clara scowled. "I go in there because no one else will. It's not my fault everyone else is afraid. They're just people like you and me."

Aron didn't want to fight with her. Not here and not like this. He was worried, but he also thought maybe she should be allowed to make these decisions for herself. It was hard for him to let go of his sense of responsibility.

"Alright," he said, fighting back the urge to continue arguing.

"I promise I'll be careful," she said unprompted.

 "I know you will. Keep up the good work," he said and stopped at his intended corridor. "I need to go see Jimmy, but let's try and catch up later."

"Okay," she said, giving him an awkward wave. "I'll see you later."

He had hardly said goodbye before she was halfway down the corridor.

Argos barked and growled at his side.

Aron shook his head and looked down at the dog. "I wouldn't take it personally, boy. That's just how she is sometimes. I'm sure she'll make up for the missed belly rubs later."

When he turned to continue down the hallway, he bumped into Jacob, who had appeared out of nowhere. The former Frumentarii already unsettled him, but his sudden appearance now was not helping his opinion of the man. Then he slowly realized that was why Argos was growling.

"Uh, Jacob, what are you doing here?" he asked, trying to seem casual.

"Was going for a walk and saw you. Thought I'd say hi." The friendly demeanor felt out of place, and Aron wanted to be on his way.

"Off to see your lady friend? What's the hurry?"

"Who, Lady Pendlebrook? No, I'm going to see Jimmy." *Sarding hell, he had said too much.* Victoria's presence wasn't common knowledge, and even fewer people knew her name.

"So that's who he's been hiding? Not very nice of Jimmy to keep the rest of us in the dark," Jacob said, scowling. The scars on his face added to his intimidating presence.

Aron felt like an idiot. It didn't even take a Frumentarii torturing him to give up information. "I don't know anything about that. You'd have to talk to Jimmy."

Jacob suddenly grabbed the collar of Aron's jumpsuit and gave it a stiff yank. Argos began to bark and growl aggressively, baring his teeth. Drawing the attention of passersby.

Jacob exhaled loudly into his face before releasing him. The pungent smell of cheap tobacco and liquor overpowered Aron's nose. Jacob pretended to smooth out the wrinkles of Aron's jumpsuit. "She's nothing to you, kid. Let me know where she is."

Argos continued to growl.

"I...I don't know," Aron lied.

Jacob looked him up and down, studying him with his yellowed eyes.

"Well," Jacob said slowly, "make sure you tell me when you do. Maybe your sister might know. I could always ask her."

"You don't need to talk to her. I would tell you if I knew," he said tentatively. Now he was glad Clara was surrounded by berserkers. "Why do you care so much anyway?"

"I want to make sure I know where anyone important is so I can make sure to keep 'em safe."

"Alright," Aron said, but something didn't feel right.

Then as quickly as he appeared, Jacob turned to leave. Argos remained on high alert until he was out of sight.

"That's a good boy," Aron said, rubbing behind the dog's ear when he was confident he was alone again.

Then he hurried to his destination as if he had seen a ghost in the dark. He felt unsafe lingering in that corridor any longer, knowing he was probably being watched.

He made it to the central hall that now served as the base's command center. It was also where Jimmy's private rooms were located. He found Gwen standing nearby and moved to speak with her first.

"Is he in? We got another message. It's urgent."

"Yeah, he's in there. How bad is it?" she asked, looking up from the table of maps she had been staring at.

"Bad. They're making progress," he whispered. Controlling information and more importantly people's fear were their biggest tasks in such close quarters.

"Sarding hell. Jimmy can fill me in later. I need to finish these scout assignments," she said and waved at the soldiers guarding the door to let him pass.

Jimmy occupied an apartment historically used by the mine superintendent in the days when the facility operated. Inside was a series of interconnected rooms that included its own small kitchen and multiple bathrooms. It was large enough to house several people comfortably.

Aron walked through the entrance hallway and into a small living space that was attached to the kitchen area, Argos following close behind. Two large sofas dominated the center of the room. The fabric of the sofas was torn and broken, but they had done a decent job repairing them with clean scraps of cloth. If they stayed here much longer, he assumed they would find some paint for the walls and polish the rust from the metal fixtures.

Jimmy sat on one of the sofas conversing with his guest, Professor Elyna Moreau of the Sanctum. Aron didn't know her personally, but he had learned some details from Kaya. Based on what she told him, he was surprised to see her here. Although, every time Aron thought he had the world figured out, he realized what he knew was only the tip of a very large iceberg. That was proving to be especially true when Kaya was involved.

On the other sofa was Lady Pendlebrook, another one of Kaya's... acquaintances, maybe. He wasn't sure, but she had arrived bound like a prisoner, so he assumed that was what she was. She was unharmed and seemed quite well.

Aron wasn't worried about her being a prisoner because he had been one too. He knew Jimmy wouldn't be unnecessarily cruel; it wasn't in his nature. Argos ran into the room and jumped on the empty half of the sofa to curl up beside Victoria. She gasped, attempting to pull away, but Argos only moved closer, thinking it was a game. Victoria eventually gave up, and Argos plopped his head in her lap.

"That dog will spend time with anyone but me," Jimmy lamented. "What news is there?"

Aron looked at the two women in the room before saying anything. He had already shared enough sensitive information today.

"It's fine. This one can't leave the room, and I'm pretty sure Elyna knows more than both of us combined."

Aron had not spoken to either woman directly, but if Jimmy was satisfied, that was enough for him. "Another outpost near Chryse is being forced to retreat into the canyons."

"That is still a few hundred miles from here," Elyna said.

Jimmy stroked his beard. "Yes, but it means the Republic forces are fully mobilized now."

"They requested aid, but we didn't give them our location," Aron said.

"Good. They will find this place eventually without us lighting a beacon. I will have Gwen send scouts farther out. There might be a way to collect our people discreetly. Has there been any other news from Deimos?"

Aron shook his head. "We're still trying though."

He noticed Victoria out of the corner of his eye pulling what looked like dog hairs off her already dirty robes with a frown. "They're coming for me, you know. All of you will wish you had let me go already," she said. "It is not too late to cooperate with me. God is merciful."

Jimmy chuckled, "You saw what God's mercy looked like during the Ashen Sunset. Would you call it mercy if I decided to give you the same treatment?"

Victoria paled but managed to keep her head held high, even if her lips trembled. Her golden curls framed the sharp aristocratic features of her face. Even in dirty robes, Aron found her beautiful. She managed to remain proud now, even though she arrived like a frightened sack of potatoes. He found her experience oddly relatable.

"I didn't think you would, but you can relax. I have no plan to mistreat you so long as you cooperate. I have a decent track record with training obstinate thoroughbreds," he said, and Victoria looked confused. "Was there anything else, Aron?"

He considered his next words carefully. He knew something needed to be said, but he couldn't think of how to say them.

"What is it?" Jimmy asked again.

"It's Jacob, he was asking about your new guest," Aron said, motioning with his head toward Victoria.

"Well, what was he asking?"

"He wanted to know where she was, but I didn't tell him. I don't think he's going to drop it though. I don't know what he wants, but I don't trust him."

"Because he was Frumentarii?" Jimmy asked.

"No, because he's a sarding ass."

Elyna chuckled.

"We will make sure to keep an eye on him. In the meantime, we need to continue consolidating our forces. The defenses of the facility are also far from completed," Jimmy said.

Aron wasn't sure if his worries about Jacob were being dismissed. He supposed the man hadn't actually done anything yet, but Jimmy kept speaking. "That is going to mean coordinating more closely with the Children. I'm going to need you to get a message to the Father."

Aron instinctively recoiled at the mention of his old employer, or perhaps captor was a better term. He had hoped to never see or speak to the Children again, but he rarely got what he wanted. Why should this be any different?

"You didn't even want to tell them where we are."

"I still don't want them to know. I know you don't want to do this. I don't either, but I've decided we need the manpower. At least until we can get some breathing room."

"Don't worry, child. Those zealots won't be able to harm you here. We will make sure of that," Elyna said, but the reassurance of a stranger meant very little to him. "Even if none of us like it, they have an important part to play in all of this still."

"What do you know about the Children?" he said to the professor. "I can tell you that I lived with them, and they didn't accomplish anything important beyond chaos, murder, and their own delusional games. That's not to mention the Father's generals, who are almost madder than he is." Aron couldn't believe he had to be the one to point this out.

Professor Moreau stared him down in a way only an angry professor could. "I've known the Children longer than you have been alive. I know their wants and desires better than anyone in this room. What they portray on the surface is only the murky film on top of the water that hides a very deep pond. Don't confuse their strange proclivities with incompetence. They have a plan, like Prometheus and Hermes do. So long as their plan aligns with ours, they have resources worth exploiting."

Aron didn't like it, but he understood the practicality of having the Children as allies. "I will see what I can do," he said simply. "If that's it, I will get back to my duties." He didn't feel much like lingering anymore.

Jimmy nodded, and Aron spared a quick glance at Victoria, who seemed as scared as he was. He didn't know much about her, but she seemed as much a victim of circumstance as he was. He offered her a weak smile and left the room.

Kaya

July, 4103 U.E.T. – North America, Earth

KAYA HAD ONLY LOST consciousness briefly before the world snapped back into full speed. The straps of her flight seat dug deeply into her shoulders, and she struggled against the force of gravity. She could see Captain Masoumi, pinned to her own seat but still able to shout commands to her crew. The ship's engines roared louder than she had ever heard. She expected shards of turbines to come crashing through the bridge at any moment.

The displays flickered on and off as the ship's power surged. Red emergency lights kicked on a second later, illuminating the bridge in an eerie red glow.

Suddenly, they hit something hard, and her neck snapped forward and back violently. Then all she could hear were the cries of the ship's occupants.

Kaya groaned as she tried to test her arms and legs. The pain in her chest and neck was intense, but she was able to move. Captain Masoumi, along with Aelius and Theodore were stirring in the dim light. When she looked to her left, she saw Reina was slumped forward, her arms hanging limp.

Thankfully, it looked like she was still breathing. If it wasn't for the straps of her seat, she would have been tossed like a rag doll. Kaya spared a brief thought for the poor crew members who lacked proper flight seats for such an intense maneuver and hoped they survived.

"Activate triage protocol. I want auxiliary power up and running!" Captain Masoumi shouted as she ran from the room.

Theodore approached to assess Kaya's condition. "Stay here. It's the safest place to be," he said and made to follow Captain Masoumi. Before he left the bridge, Theodore instructed a pair of sailors to keep an eye on her and Reina.

Kaya's adrenaline was pumping, and she knew it was time to do something. She had been given a second chance and wasn't going to waste it sitting around here, waiting yet again for someone to tell her what to do. She unbuckled the straps and slid out of the chair as quietly as she could. The sailors were still very much distracted by trying to keep the ship operational and failed to notice.

She came up beside Reina and looked her over. When she saw there were no obvious injuries, she slapped Reina's face. Gently at first, and then harder when she didn't wake up.

"What the sarding..." Kaya slammed her hand over the woman's mouth.

"We aren't dead. Come on," she whispered and helped Reina undo her seats restraints.

As Kaya turned to lead her from the room, she saw Aelius in the distance looking at them, but he only nodded.

Reina pulled on her arm. "Are we going or not? Actually, where are we going?"

"Shh," Kaya reiterated and led Reina quickly from the room.

They had to leave before Aelius decided to change his mind. The hallway was still eerily quiet and lit only by emergency lights. She could hear the shouts of crew members in various parts of the ship, but only a handful of people could be seen darting down the hallways in front of them.

When they had gotten a fair distance from the bridge, she felt like she could relax slightly. They hadn't seen the captain or Theodore close by. "Did you forget all your own talks about operational security?"

"I didn't realize we were in enemy territory. How are we not dead?" Reina said, rubbing at her temples. Then she stopped walking and stared at Kaya. "Are we on..."

"Earth, yes. We must be. Unless we somehow maneuvered into the right orbit to slingshot back into Luna."

Reina jumped. "No, I grew up on Luna. This isn't Luna. Especially since the gravity generators are down." Kaya hadn't been serious about her suggestion.

She continued her path through the corridors with Reina following close behind. She stopped in front of the armory door.

"Are you planning a mutiny?" Reina asked.

"No, I'm planning to get off this ship, but we need exosuits. Good ones."

"Do you—" Reina began to say, but Kaya cut her off.

"Don't try and talk me out of this. I'm sick and tired of people trying to tell me what to do. We crashed onto the *Earth* and *lived*. How many people can say that. I'm going to see what's out there," she snarled.

"I was only going to ask if you knew how to use combat armor," Reina said dryly. "It's more complicated than your average radiation suit. Wait, there was one more thing." She raised a finger dramatically. "Are you absolutely out of your mind?"

Kaya exhaled sharply and turned to scan her security card. The light turned green on the lock, and the door slid open with a sharp hiss. "It's going to be fine. Don't go soft on me now."

The ship's armory was large and had enough space to house equipment for hundreds of soldiers. The armory, which had previously been sparse when she left Mercury years earlier, was now brimming with equipment Tiberius had given them before departing for Venus.

"Maybe we should find some others to join us on this little expedition," Reina said, picking up a rail rifle and inspecting it.

"Are you afraid, Reina? That is very unlike you. What is there to be afraid of? It's a dead planet, remember."

"Yes, but you never know, right?"

"You've read too many stories." Kaya opened several lockers until she found armor that should fit each of them. "Perfect, here we go. I still can't believe we survived."

"I'm Lunese. Tales of Earth are one of our favorites. Almost none of them are good. Growing up staring at a dead planet has a certain effect on you," Reina said, nervously.

Kaya paused, looking at Reina, who seemed on the verge of breaking. "I didn't think the stories of people visiting Earth were real, but here we are, living proof. It's incredible. You should be happier that we survived. It makes me think there's some reason why we're here, why we lived."

Reina shook her head. "You're right. It defies all logic, but that's what I'm afraid of. Think of all the other stories that could be true."

Kaya began stripping out of her clothes and putting on the suit's base layer. "We won't go too far from the ship in case the mutants attack." The possibility of what else they might find was exactly why she wanted to explore the surface.

"You aren't funny, princess," Reina said, unamused.

Kaya didn't know what to expect, but she was on Earth. That was amazing all on its own. The only thing she could think of was to set foot on Eden. She clutched at the Jiddi pendant around her neck one last time before getting into the armor and powering it on.

House Vardan perseveres. House Vardan remains steady. House Vardan remains as the keepers of the garden, until one day it can be restored. Perhaps this was the first step in doing exactly that. She thought this could be something close to her mother's dream.

"You okay, princess?" Reina asked.

"I'm ready," she said, snapping out of her thoughts. She attached the hilt of her mother's plasma blade to her hip and hefted a rifle from one of the racks. She kept her helmet retracted.

"I thought there was nothing to be worried about?" Reina asked with a raised eyebrow.

"It doesn't hurt to be careful," she said, trying to sound confident. Reina laughed, and Kaya joined her. Maybe from the stress or the ridiculousness of it all, but either way it felt nice to have Reina there with her for this. "There's a back way through here to one of the hangar bays. We'll pass through the barrack rooms so we can check on the Coalition people."

"I wonder how violent reentry was. I don't remember any of it, and I usually don't have that problem," Reina said, following close behind her, a rifle strapped to her back and her preferred pistols at her hips.

"Consider yourself lucky," Kaya said.

"You mean, you didn't black out?"

"I did, but not for very long. It was terrifying. I hope the others are okay," she said as they got to the rear entrance of the main barrack room. Reina was appraising her, but Kaya ignored it and opened the door.

Inside the room, people were running back and forth, trying to offer aid to the injured. Kaya turned on the lights of her armor and was able to clearly see a variety of injuries from minor cuts to severely broken bones and people who seemed not to be moving at all.

"Lady Kaya, is that you?" a young man said, approaching them. He had a large scar over his left eye that made him seem more menacing than he was. He had been one of Jimmy's lieutenants in Prometheus.

"Rudra," she said putting a hand on his shoulder. He was limping slightly but appeared mostly in one piece.

"What's going on? Why are you armored? Are we still under attack?" he said in a rush.

"No, we crash-landed. Reina and I are going out to see what's going on. Can you organize everyone here and try to keep them calm?" Kaya knew it would be a while before Theodore or Captain Masoumi thought to care for these people.

"On Luna?" he asked in a whisper as others tried to listen in.

She shook her head ever so slightly.

"God's bones," he said, making the sign of the star and cross. "I...I'll do what I can."

"Thank you, we should be back soon with news." He saluted, and Kaya left before others could press her with more questions.

She didn't want to lie to them, but she knew their situation was dire. No one made it back from Earth's surface. Everyone knew that. However, until she said it out loud, this could all be a bad dream.

When they had reached the hangar bay, Reina paused to look at her, a proud expression on her face.

"That is the leadership I was talking about, princess. You can't teach that. Good leaders either have it or they don't. I've seen enough leaders to know that you do."

"It isn't going to matter much longer, I think, but maybe there's some miracle that will get us off this planet."

"The Iron Cage didn't destroy us when we entered. Maybe it's not operational."

"Maybe," Kaya said and deployed her helmet. It clicked into place with a hiss of air, and a quick feeling of pressure inside the armor. Reina did the same, and they stepped into the air lock. Kaya activated the internal comms and linked up with Reina. "Testing."

"We don't have to do this," Reina said, perhaps more for herself than Kaya.

"Aren't you at least a little curious what's outside this door?"

"Not as much as you, but I promised Jimmy I would stay with you. I don't break my promises."

"I hope that's not the only reason you stay," Kaya said, putting a hand over her wounded heart.

Reina opened the airlock. "I hope a mutant eats you."

Kaya had only stepped foot on a handful of planets in her life. Mercury of course, then Mars and Venus. Each one had its own idiosyncrasies. Mercury with its long days and dominating heat or chilling darkness. Venus with its expansive oceans, and Mars with its sprawling cities and dizzying mountain peaks. None of them compared to how foreign Earth felt to her now.

When the door opened, she had been prepared for molten pits and fiery brimstone raining down from the heavens. What she got was a dull and gray landscape, coated in charcoal-like dust. The sun wasn't visible through the clouds and haze, but she assumed it must be daytime given the dim light. She stepped onto the ground and then stood there.

Reina came up beside her. "I thought it would be...different."

"I thought I would feel different," Kaya said, kicking at the layer of ash with her boot. "Let's look around."

The sensors of her armor scanned the immediate area, but no heat symbols were detected beyond the ship behind her. She took a few steps forward and turned around. The ship looked to be largely intact, but it was burned and singed all over and sported several missing panels. It was also dented and bent where it hit the ground and dug into the native soil. Its landing gear was likely smashed to pieces.

"I'm no engineer, but that doesn't look space worthy," Reina said.

Kaya ignored her and walked off into the distance. She kept the rifle strapped over her shoulder. It was obvious she wouldn't be needing it.

"Where are you going?" Reina asked, coming up beside her again.

"This can't be all that's here." They made it past the Iron Cage and survived. That couldn't have been an accident.

"Why can't it? Earth has been dead for hundreds of years. You didn't think the ageless were real, did you? Did you think they've been hiding here all this time?" Reina started to laugh and then stopped. "You did think that, didn't you?"

"It doesn't matter what I thought. If I'm going to die here, I at least want to see more of it than this dusty hill," she said with a heavy sigh. "This is the Garden, Reina, Eden! There must be something here we can learn."

"Look around, princess. This dusty broken world *is* the lesson. There's nothing left to find or fix," Reina said, eyeing their surroundings.

Looking out over the horizon, Kaya could see mountains to the west and gently rolling hills to the east. There were scraggly trees and bushes that looked more dead than alive dotting the landscape. She couldn't shake the feeling that there should be something, anything, more.

"Then we're the first people to step foot on this world in over five hundred years. They don't need us on the ship right now, and maybe there's something out here that can help us. Old tech the Empire left behind. Some ancient relics with mystical properties or who knows what. If it really is empty, at least we can stretch our legs for a little while," Kaya didn't mention there could be sprawling cities or hidden civilizations. Some of the stories said there were.

Reina sighed. "Fair enough. Where to then? It all kind of looks the same to me. Nearly makes Luna look tropical and diverse. We should have some time before they think to look for us and track the missing armor."

"Can't we disable the tracker?" Kaya asked.

"Not in standard-issue suits like these. Disabling the trackers will disable everything," Reina said, staring off into the distance. "Anyway, we want the crew to be able to find us if anything goes wrong."

Kaya thought that made sense. They wouldn't want to make it easy to abscond with expensive military hardware. Her helmet flashed with thermal alerts. There was movement behind them. Crew members were likely coming outside to inspect the damage. They needed to get going.

"This way," she said and took off at a jog down the gently sloping hill and toward a long and straight depression in the landscape. She tried to run but had to stop because of the pain in her chest from the crash. The armor only did so much to reduce the strain on her body. She knew there would be some serious bruises later.

"Why this way?" Reina asked.

"See the depression in the land?" Kaya said, gesturing as they slid and hopped down the hill. Dust and gravel spilled out in clouds from their footfalls. "It's long and relatively straight but also mostly flat."

Reina looked at her expectantly.

"So it must be a road, or at least it was. A river would meander more, and the sides would be sharp and steep like the canyons on Mars," It reminded her of following similar features in the deserts on Mercury.

Reina looked again. "I think you're right. Let's see where it goes."

They walked for nearly an hour. Kaya had been right. It was a road. In places where the sediment had been eroded from the surface, there were traces of smooth asphalt. Which of course wasn't surprising. Earth had been home to billions of people once, but there was very little sign of them left in this place.

It was like the Great Desert of Mercury. War had destroyed this place too and left little more than gravel, dust, and scraps of twisted metal. Except they also found the remnants of a long fence that ran parallel to their path. It was rusted, broken, or missing entirely in many places, but it was easy to identify.

"Does that look like a path along the fence there?" Reina asked. They had spent most of the last hour speculating about what the fence once guarded. They crossed over the fence line several times to look for an answer but hadn't yet seen any other structures.

"Maybe animal trails?" Kaya said.

"We haven't seen any animals."

"We haven't seen them but that doesn't mean they aren't here," Kaya said, but it did seem suspicious. "I think we should stick to the road. It's the most likely to lead us somewhere." She looked back the way they had come, thinking maybe she had seen someone following them. It was only her paranoia.

Reina nodded, and they continued walking. The feint path became more defined as they traveled further north, and they both became uneasy enough to raise their guns.

"You know how to use that thing, I hope," Reina said, motioning to the rifle. She kept her eyes scanning the landscape.

"Maybe not as good as you, but good enough. I used to shoot targets growing up with the master-at-arms of the castle."

"People don't usually stand still and let you shoot them."

"I'll have to shoot them before they move then, I guess," Kaya said dryly, thinking back to the first day she met Reina.

Reina had saved her life and taken another. It was justified, but it still stuck with her anyway. Kaya had no desire to shoot anyone, but she understood now that sometimes violence was part of survival.

"Don't get glib with me," Reina said.

"You only have yourself to blame," Kaya said with a chuckle. Then she stopped in her tracks. She thought she saw movement in the scraggly bushes to the west, near the fence line. Her armor didn't register anything. "Did you see that?"

Reina raised her rifle in a well-practiced motion and scanned the horizon. She had spent the better part of her life in the military and then the Pandora Fleet, and it showed in moments like this. Kaya was glad to have her there.

"I don't see anything, but look over there. Looks like a fork in the road," Reina said, pointing.

Kaya followed her raised arm and saw what she meant. There was what looked like the remnants of a gate and perhaps a sign. "Let's check it out," she said, and they approached delicately, their rifles raised. She felt silly for the precaution, but they were both obviously a bit jumpy.

When Kaya got closer, she could see that she was right. It was a gate. She walked up to the sign hanging from the remaining section of fence. It was heavily corroded with countless dents peppering its surface. She brushed ash and dust from the surface of the sign to see if there was any writing underneath. It was heavily faded, but she was able to make out some of the words, "Fort Carson — Earth Strategic Defense Command."

She took a step back studying the sign.

"What does it say?" Reina asked, from beside her.

"I don't know. Earth is the only word I recognize," she said, pointing to it.

"Imperial English, I guess?"

"It could be. Maybe we should have dragged Aelius out here with us. I bet he knows how to read it," Kaya said before another movement in the bushes caught her eye. She brought her rifle up. This time her armor had registered the movement.

"I saw that too. Look over here, the path. It continues up this way into the woods," Reina said and began walking, her rifle held at the ready.

Kaya followed behind her. "There, ten meters northeast," she said as the display in her helmet lit up with the heat signature.

Reina used a series of hand signals to indicate they were going to separate and flank the target. The hand signals were part of what Reina had taught Kaya prior to the execution.

They moved swiftly through the trees, getting into position. She saw the heat signature more clearly, and much to her surprise, it was humanoid. Turning around a large boulder, she raised her rifle and was stopped in her tracks by a man standing in front of her.

He was dirty, disheveled, and wore what looked like animal hides for clothing. She was so struck by disbelief that she stared at him unmoving. The man seemed similarly stunned.

"Don't shoot!" Kaya shouted into her comms.

She thought she might have been too late, but then Reina came charging up to her left through a stand of trees, and the man took off running up the hill. He was quick on the uneven ground despite the fact he wore no shoes.

"God's Bones, was that a mutant?" Reina asked, coming up beside Kaya.

"No, it was a man. We need to follow him," she said and took off sprinting.

CHAPTER

16

Kaya

July, 4103 U.E.T. – North America, Earth

Even with the aid of their exoarmor, they couldn't overtake the man. He ran gracefully like a wild animal as he bounded over stumps and boulders. He obviously knew the terrain, and it worked to his advantage.

Kaya tried to pretend it was the sands of Mercury, but it did her no good. She wasn't used to traversing thick forests in armor, even if this forest was short and stunted. The higher gravity of Earth only made things harder. Reina's Lunese roots and recent time on the Martian plains didn't help her either.

"Make sure you keep an eye on him. We need to see where he goes!" Kaya shouted as she tripped over another log, nearly falling over in the unfamiliar armor.

Reina sprinted forward and almost closed the gap with the man, but then he dove under a rock and disappeared.

Kaya skidded to a stop in front of the small opening. It was large enough for an adult to squeeze through but too small for someone armored.

"Sarding hell he was fast," Reina said, scanning the area around them. It looked the same as the rest of the forest had, with the ground sloping upward toward some kind of summit.

Kaya got on her stomach and shined a light from her wrist into the opening. Reina hovered over her, ready to pull her back if needed.

"I don't see him. It looks like some kind of tunnel. I can't really see how far it goes," Kaya said, getting up to her knees. "Reina, it was a *living* person! We need to go after him."

"That's why we need to gather the others and discuss our next move. We need a plan. There shouldn't be anyone or anything here," Reina said, looking concerned. "What if there are more of those mutants out here? He could be getting his friends right now."

"Like I said, it was a man. I saw his face. He looked scared, not dangerous."

"Fine, my point stands. What if there are a hundred of them down there?" Reina said, waving her arm toward the tunnel.

"I doubt it. He's the first person we've seen in hours of wandering around." Kaya stood.

"All the more reason to head back to the *Rubah*. The others will be looking for us by now, and this is information they should know," Reina said, trying to pull her back the way they came.

Kaya resisted. She was worried about the people on the *Rubah*, but they hadn't seen anyone on their path here, so she didn't think they were in any immediate danger. "If we let him go now, we might never find him again. This might be our only chance to find anyone at all."

"It's a big planet, princess, nearly twice the size of Mars. I grew up with stories of entire cities still on Earth. I always thought it was nonsense, but seeing this now with my own eyes..."

Kaya watched Reina's face as those stories faced off against naked reality. "Did you see how he was dressed? He looked wild, almost primitive. He's no threat to us, but imagine what he could know of this place. A key to the secrets still hidden on the planet. This is an opportunity no one has had in our lifetime."

Reina grudgingly relented. "I'm more surprised by his speed. Especially with how bad the air quality is. His lungs must be mostly ash by now. We probably scared him half to death. One more hour, and then we head back to the *Rubah*," Reina added firmly.

Kaya agreed to her terms, and Reina began walking slowly up the hill in the direction the tunnel ran. Kaya followed behind, looking for some sign of where it might lead.

Kaya looked at the display on her wrist. "Radiation seems minimal. No worse than the Great Desert on Mercury actually."

Reina looked up at the overcast sky, thick ash cover, and the silent landscape and said, "Maybe it was the fire and ash that swallowed the Earth."

"And the Iron Cage sealed the lid of the jar," Kaya said, noticing the remnants of a concrete structure in the distance. "Look over there, by that short cliff face."

When they got closer, it looked to be the end point of the road they had been following. The depression of the road disappeared into the rock face underneath a tangle of gnarled vines and fallen rock.

"Step back," Reina said, directing Kaya behind a large boulder before throwing a bandolier of grenades into the mess of brush and broken concrete. It exploded with a resounding bang.

Kaya instinctively ducked her head, despite her armor. "Sarding hell! You could have collapsed the tunnel. Not to mention now whoever is down there will know we're here." She felt any chance of finding the man and whatever answers he held melting away because of Reina's carelessness.

"We better be fast then. It's not like we were going to dig with our hands. Come on," Reina said, approaching the smoking hole that the grenades created.

Kaya rushed to climb up on the debris pile as the dust was still settling. Behind it she could see an open cavern with dim lights in the distance. Not the flickering flame of fires, but electric lights. She didn't wait for Reina before jumping down onto the other side of the opening.

She activated the lights of her armor. The cave was really a steel-lined tunnel that led to a large opening where a massive blast door once stood. It looked nothing like the dirt-carved tunnel the man had slid into. The door was half melted and leaned limply beside the door frame. The broken metal was heavily rusted, and it was clear the damage had occurred a very long time ago.

"Reminds me of the old mining colonies on Mars," Reina said, stepping up beside her.

Their boots crunching on the rocks underfoot was all Kaya could hear over her own breathing. "I haven't seen them, but there were places like this on Mercury too. Where the early settlers lived, before the atmosphere could be established and the surface terraformed."

Reina said, "Those facilities are notoriously big and complex. It's why Jimmy chose them for hiding Prometheus. We could search for days and never find him."

"Earth was always habitable; this must be something different. We need to at least try and follow. Imagine what he could know from surviving here for so long. Maybe it's something that could help us," Kaya said.

"Maybe, but like I said, we have an hour, not a minute more," Reina said, leading the way into the lit corridor, her rifle at the ready. "Stay close and keep your finger off the trigger."

Kaya didn't argue. This was Reina's business, and she was happy to follow her lead. The deeper they walked, the corridors became larger and more numerous in a web of rooms and hallways. Kaya used her plasma blade to mark their path on the concrete walls so they could find their way back out.

Not every light was functional, but there were enough to spread a dim glow through most of the corridors. There was no machinery, broken displays, or other signs of industry. Only bare concrete with holes marking locations where every useful item was likely salvaged long ago. There was no other sign of human habitation, although the lights being on struck her as odd given the primitive appearance of the man they saw.

"This feels like a waste of time. There's nothing here," Reina said.

Kaya didn't want to quit yet, when the greatest discovery of their lifetime was so close. Finding a living human on Earth was worth more than a little wasted time.

She had almost given up once in the Boundless Library, and if she had... who could say how different her life might be now? "It hasn't been an hour yet. Let's go a little deeper. Maybe that's where people stay to avoid the ash."

Reina acquiesced.

They descended several staircases and eventually started to see little signs of humanity. Not much at first, scraps of firewood and markings on the walls. They even found plastic containers in one empty room. None of it looked recent, but it seemed like her assumption might be correct.

They also found an opening in the concrete that led to another hand carved tunnel. Unfortunately, this one was also too small for them to fit through. They were both already naturally bigger than the man they were looking for. With the added height and width of their armor, they were never going to fit. Finally, they found a stairwell, but there was too much broken concrete and debris blocking the path down. Reina was also out of grenades.

When they finished searching the last room they could find, Kaya sighed, "I guess we'll have to come back with more tools if we want to go any deeper. These tunnels must lead somewhere. At least if Theodore doesn't lock us up after this."

"It's your father's ship, isn't it? Why don't you have more freedom? Why aren't you in charge of it?"

"I don't hold any titles or military rank in my own right, so I have no legitimate claim to it beyond my lineage. I don't think that would be enough for Captain Masoumi and the others to follow. Why would they choose me over an experienced leader and nobleman?" Kaya said, feeling especially deflated. She kicked an uneven piece of rebar protruding from the concrete out of frustration.

Reina raised her hand to quiet her. "Wait! Don't do that."

Kaya ignored her. "I don't want another one of your speeches about how the troops support me. I'm tired of..." As she ranted, Kaya gave the rebar another aggressive kick. The metal shifted, and in seconds the floor began to splinter like cracked glass.

Reina screamed as the floor collapsed and sent them freefalling.

The sensation didn't last long, and they crashed in a pile of debris and dust five meters below. Kaya groaned. The fall had been sudden and painful, but thankfully the armor took most of the impact.

"Sarding hell, I told you to stop. You're lucky we didn't get trapped in a cave-in." Reina threw a hunk of concrete to the side, waving her arm to see through the dust.

Kaya stood up, ready to argue, but when the dust cleared, there was a collection of faces staring at them in the low light. She scrambled to get her rifle up, and Reina did the same.

"Stay back," Kaya shouted, but the crowd didn't listen. Instead, they pushed forward tentatively, forcing her to back up over the uneven ground.

Brandishing the rifle did little to force them back. She glanced quickly to her right and saw Reina being likewise surrounded. *God's Bones.*

"Do we shoot them?" Reina asked, hitting one man who got too close in the face with the butt of her rifle.

Kaya tried to think fast. They looked more curious than threatening. She returned the rifle to her back and drew her plasma blade, kindling it. She swung it threateningly several times, stopping the approaching crowd. Even those who had been focused on Reina turned to admire the device.

She forced them back as she regained ground and stepped off the small debris pile. They seemed to respect the heat of her blade and moved back several arm lengths.

The tension was palpable, and in the stillness, she could see the dirty and thin faces around her. They reminded her of the people she had met in the slums of Mars but perhaps even worse. She noticed the man they had been chasing pushing his way to the front of the crowd. She could see now he was barely any older than she was. His face was gaunt and leathery, and his body bore several large and gruesome scars. His body told the story of a life she couldn't comprehend.

Kaya approached him now, assuming he must hold some authority with the others. She retracted her helmet and golden visor, revealing her bare face and emerald green eyes.

The man's eyes went wide. He shouted something in a language she didn't understand and dropped to his knees, prostrating himself on the ground before her. The others only hesitated a moment before doing the same.

Kaya stood staring at them dumbfounded. The air was musty and damp. The soft hum of machinery could easily be heard without her helmet, and it reminded her of being on the *Rubah*. Feeling the immediate threat had passed, she snuffed her blade. Reina moved tentatively beside her. The crowd, who numbered around twenty, didn't move.

"What the sarding hell is this?" Reina said, retracting her own helmet.

Kaya didn't answer. She instead went to the man and kneeled, placing a hand on his shoulder. It took some coaxing to get him to rise and look at her. "There's no need for that. We aren't here to hurt you."

The man seemed to be in shock and mumbled something else.

"I'm sorry. I don't understand," she said, spreading her arms in frustration.

The man stood tentatively, motioning to her. His head bowing in a continuous rhythm.

"Maybe he wants you to follow him," Reina suggested.

Kaya motioned for him to lead the way. It seemed to work, and she was glad basic communication seemed universal. As they left the room, she could hear the others stand up, but they didn't follow.

Kaya was overwhelmed by the sights and sounds of the place and kept stopping to look. Each room they passed was like a strange time capsule or window into an exotic world. The man waited patiently each time, before continuing to guide them.

There were tent-like homes, crammed into any available space. They had small fire rings burning, and a cool wind blew through the complex like a spring breeze. The crackling campfires meanwhile created a smokey haze that permeated the structure.

Then there were large rooms with rows of lights and racks with crops and water running from rusty machinery. The flow and drips of water reminded her of deep cave systems she had visited as a child.

The rough appearance of the people was at odds with the concrete structure and the old machinery. It was obvious these people lacked the ability to make the tools they still used. Like the people of the slums, they survived on the infrastructure of previous generations. Based on the state of the machines, Kaya wondered how sustainable their situation was.

They finally came to a large open room that was lined with crude candles and hand-drawn mosaics on the walls. She glanced quickly at the artwork and assumed it depicted whatever folk stories were important to these people. Kaya had spent enough time in churches to know a temple of worship when she saw one.

At the front of the room was an altar that looked like many she had seen before. Behind the altar, a glass-encased portrait hung in a place of honor. The glass was clean and looked to be immaculately cared for.

Kaya stared at the portrait for a long, long time, not wanting to acknowledge what she saw. Her lips moved, but she was unable to speak. It was all far too insane.

"Well, I may have had things wrong with calling you 'princess.' It seems like you were actually a cave goddess all this time. I guess I shouldn't be surprised. You've always been a bit broody," Reina said, looking up at the portrait.

Kaya blinked. The portrait was her, or at least it could have been. The facial structure, the emerald-green eyes, and olive skin. All of it. It was *her*, but it also wasn't. Which left only one explanation.

She stepped onto the altar and toward the large photograph. Reina stayed behind, guarding the man who had returned to his prostrated position. He started some kind of chant, which under normal circumstances Kaya might have found beautiful.

The person in the photograph…it was her mother, but it couldn't be. It was the kind of portrait used by military officers for their official functions. Kaya kept one like it of her mother when she became grand marshal of the Void Knights. It was one of the few photos Kaya took with her from Mercury. She had stared at that photo enough times to commit it to memory.

Now she felt like she was looking at a copy. The uniform was different, but the pose and facial expression were nearly identical.

"One of your ancestors, princess?" Reina asked, and Kaya thought that was the most logical answer. Then she saw the Ageless Legion insignia on the woman's chest above a collection of medals and ribbons. It was clearly and proudly displayed above the others, the same insignia she found in the Great Desert years ago. The same insignia Aelius identified for her on Mars from her mother's note. She was struggling to hold on to her own doubt.

"Any idea what he's saying? I don't like the idea of staying here much longer. This is getting kind of weird," Reina said, looking back at her nervously. The man hadn't stopped chanting since she stepped onto the alter. Kaya had ignored him, but Reina continued to keep a watchful eye.

"I have no idea," she said flippantly, ignoring the rest of what Reina said.

The discovery of this portrait had become the most important thing in Kaya's world. She brushed a loose strand of hair from her face. The dirt from her gloves smearing on her cheek. It was Gaian dirt. Dirt from the garden itself. Her heart sank and tears welled up in her eyes.

She knew it didn't mean her mother was alive, but all of this gave her new hope, except she was reluctant to reach for it. She didn't think she could take the loss all over again if it turned out to be wrong.

She looked back up at the portrait and spoke softly to her mother's memory. "Is this why you wanted to rebuild the garden so badly? Because you failed to protect it the first time?" If her mother was one of the ageless, maybe she felt some responsibility for Earth's destruction. Maybe the eternal dream was her way of making things right.

Kaya pulled the Jiddi tree pendant out from inside her armor and held it tightly. "What good is one tiny sapling, against all of this?" After seeing Earth now, the idea of rebuilding the garden seemed absurd.

Then she looked back at the praying man and allowed herself to hear his chant. The fervor of it reverberated through her skin and she felt ashamed for her lack of compassion. "I don't know what he's saying, but I think we owe it to these people to find out."

A new voice filled the temple from near the entrance. "He is saying, 'praise to the mother goddess. Bring us rain and bring us wheat. I am your vessel. Guide me with your hand.' That is a rough translation."

Kaya turned toward the doorway. There stood an armored figure, taller than herself with broad shoulders. His accent was strange, but she was able to mostly understand him. He wore jet-black armor, free of any markings.

Kaya drew her blade and stepped forward kindling it. "Don't come any closer. Who are you?"

Reina raised her rifle, and the half-dozen soldiers with the man fanned out into the room, blocking the exit.

"I should ask you the same, Martian. Where did you come from, and why are you here?"

Martian? What is he talking about? she thought. "Let us pass, and we'll be gone."

"No," he said and stepped toward her. "Come quietly. I don't know where you have been hiding all this time, but I will find out," he took another step forward and then stopped. A strange look on his face.

She thought it may have been recognition. He spoke again in a language

Kaya couldn't understand. He was trying to tell her something, but when she didn't answer, he continued his approach.

Reina brought the visor of her helmet down, and Kaya did the same. "I'll go left, you go right, and we'll meet in the center. I don't trust them," she said on their private line.

Kaya didn't want to fight these people, but their stance made her think they weren't going to let them leave. "Maybe we can comm the ship," she offered.

"They'll never make it in time. We need to make our move. Now!" Reina said and launched forward, firing a blast of bullets into the leftmost guard. The guard easily deflected the shots with an energy shield emanating from his forearm. He charged forward, knocking Reina to the ground with violent force.

Kaya tried to swing out with her blade at the man in front of her, but he easily dodged aside. Cursing, she turned back and swung again, but he dodged her blow easily a second time. He was quick, very quick. The fight, if she could even call it that, was going worse than her sparring session with Namtar.

The man who had been praying scrambled out of the way to crouch in the corner.

"No, you're not her," the armored man said, his voice tinged with sadness.

Was he referring to her mother? she thought. She dodged away from the other soldier who had come to her side, trying to subdue her. With a quick glance to Reina, she could see the older woman was already pinned to the ground, her wrists being bound.

Kaya shoved the new soldier with her shoulder, knocking him off balance. Then she charged again at their leader, attempting to score any kind of hit. In one breath, he had his own plasma blade drawn and deflected her comparatively clumsy blow. Another series of swipes and jabs with his free hand left her arm limp and the hilt of her blade rolling on the floor, where it snuffed out like her dream.

He swept her legs out from under her and held his blade to her throat. "Come peacefully or die here in this hole."

"I yield," she said reluctantly, retracting her helmet. "Who are you?"

The man retracted his own helmet. She was surprised to see a youthful face with short, cropped hair and brilliant blue eyes that popped against his umber skin. The harsh ridges of his face made him beautiful and terrifying all at once. He waited for a long moment without saying a word. "Do you not know who I am?"

Kaya continued to stare dumbly at him. He was certainly handsome, but she had not the slightest idea who he might be. With the number of surprises, she had endured in the last few years, she didn't even hazard a guess.

"Should I?" she said and heard Reina laugh in the background. The man seemed deflated or maybe confused.

He spoke in the strange language again, and the soldier she had hit came over. He lifted her roughly to her feet and bound her hands. He then used some kind of rod to unleash a jolt of electricity through her armor, rendering it lifeless. She supposed that it would have also fried the trackers Theodore, and the others could use to find them. It was difficult to move in the unpowered suit, but she didn't want them to see her struggle.

"How did you know we were here?" she asked.

"There was a large anomaly in the area. I thought maybe you were a stowaway we somehow missed. Now I think we will find a ship nearby."

"You better not go near it."

"You're in no position to make demands," he said, walking closer to study her face. "Descendent of Najm."

She didn't know how he knew her mother's maiden name, but it left her unsettled. "Hurt any of my people, and you won't get anything from me." Her knees buckled, and the soldiers were forced to yank her up again. Her reaction wasn't lost on the stranger.

"You do know something at least," he said and turned to lead the group away.

When she surveyed the room one last time, she saw the primitive man watching her intently from the corner. He made no move to help her, but it was clear he didn't appreciate what was happening. She hoped he wouldn't do anything stupid. Him or his people were no match for these knights, whoever they were.

She and Reina were led swiftly out of the underground facility to a wait-ing transport craft. Kaya was surprised the transport was not unlike the ones she was used to. It felt oddly normal after such an abnormal few hours on Earth. What she wanted to know now was how he knew her mother's name and why her portrait was hanging up behind that altar.

She was dropped into a seat by the window, across from their leader, Reina in the seat behind her. No one spoke as the transport took off and sped farther away from the *Rubah's* crash site and their only lifeline.

CHAPTER

17

Kaya

July, 4103 U.E.T. – Tilicho Lake, Earth

THE TRANSPORT FLEW LOW to the ground, which afforded her a clear, albeit brief view of the Gaian landscape. They were moving fast, faster than she had ever traveled planeside before. Her curiosity and the overwhelming numbness she felt were all that kept her from having an emotional breakdown.

The transport craft had looked much like the ones she was used to, but this one traveled at a far faster speed. From the higher position, she got a better look at the ruined landscape, large patches of scraggly vegetation and open plains. What she originally thought were mountains turned out to be, on closer inspection, ruins of city skylines. Behind those she saw a series of what looked like large volcanos billowing large plumes of ash into the sky. It seemed like Earth was full of fire and brimstone after all.

"Why are we flying so low?" she asked, curious. She looked for some possible destination but couldn't figure it out.

The leader stared at her. "To avoid the Iron Cage," he said, searching for something in her face. Maybe some hint of deception. "You really don't know, do you?"

"I..."

He raised a finger to silence her. "Don't speak."

"You kidnap us, presumably for information, and now you don't want me to say anything?" Kaya didn't attempt to hide her frustration. "Is it because you aren't the one in charge?"

He spun the hilt of her mother's plasma blade in his hand, glancing at it occasionally. "It's because once you begin speaking, I know my life will be irrevocably changed."

That hadn't been the answer she was expecting.

"The dark and brooding ones are always so handsome," Reina said behind her. He didn't acknowledge Reina at all.

Kaya wondered how Reina could make jokes in a situation like this. Her own mind was having trouble keeping up with the madness. She was worried she would break completely if she wasn't able to start getting some answers.

Eventually the landscape gave way to a large ocean that rivaled the ones she had seen on Venus. White-capped waves roiled on the surface as they sped along, gaining speed with each passing mile. The fact they still hadn't reached their destination, despite their travel speed, only reminded her how much larger Earth was than her home planet.

The further they went from the *Rubah*, the more worried she became. She wasn't sure if the trackers were still active in their armor, and finding them now could be nearly impossible. They could be taking them to a ship or some subterranean dungeon for all she knew. She had to fight back her rising panic at the unknown.

The hours continued to pass quickly as she sank into calming her mind and making sense of what was happening. While Kaya maintained her silence, Reina continued to speak to the knights who refused to acknowledge anything she said. Maybe it was some Pandora Fleet protocol for when you were captured, or Reina simply found it amusing. Either way, the woman's approach was only making Kaya more anxious.

Before long, they reached land once again and sped past a vast empty desert before eventually crossing into a rugged and mountainous region. There, painfully beautiful peaks rose sharp and jagged into the air, threatening to swallow them whole. In the complex web of valleys, ruined cities were replaced by windswept scrubland and massive glaciers. In the deepest valleys, she thought she saw rushing rivers and hints of green vegetation.

Then in the distance she saw what had to be their destination, a large transparent energy dome shimmering in the low light. From their approach, she could see it held a massive lake, flanked by tiered farms and a series of interconnected buildings. It looked almost like a miniature version of the Amaranthine Palace.

Inside the dome, the gray haze that had hovered over everything was gone. Color returned to the world, and everything looked lush and alive, like the jungles of Venus or the temperate forests of Mercury. She heard Reina whistle at the view. The unexpectedness of it only intensified the beauty.

They landed on a large, paved landing pad, flanked by relatively small pavilions that housed other similarly sized transports. She didn't notice any larger ships in the compound and assumed they must not have access to any. She and Reina offered no resistance when they were led from the craft. Kaya's pulse quickened in anticipation of what came next. There must be something they wanted. They wouldn't have brought them this far for nothing.

Kaya took a deep breath. The air was cool and crisp. Looking up, she felt the warmth of the artificial sunlight hitting her face. She had spent time in similar domes on Mercury during the periods of long night. Now, she welcomed the familiar and comforting warmth. It was a beautiful arrangement they had, but it wasn't lost on Kaya how different it was to the sorry lot she had seen in the underground compound.

They were stripped of their weapons and exoarmor. Reina sarcastically thanked them for not taking her thin bodysuit layer, although she also said their leader was welcome to it if he wanted.

They were led to a meeting room with large windows looking out over the lake and tiered farms that climbed the flank of the mountains. By Kaya's estimation, the dome covered at least twenty square kilometers.

Kaya shivered and wrapped her arms around herself. It was cold in the room, and she hadn't had time to adjust. The snow on the surrounding mountains suggested they were at a significantly higher elevation than wherever they had crashed.

"Could have at least given us sarding coats," Reina said to one of the guards who watched them silently.

"I'm fine," Kaya said, crossing her legs. "Colder than I'm used to lately."

"I was getting used to all the gray. It reminded me of my youth on Luna," Reina said.

"How are you so unbothered?" Kaya snapped.

"When people want you dead, they kill you. When they want information, they will ask you questions. When they do neither, that's when you know they want something more from you. They just haven't figured out how to ask for it yet," Reina said, adjusting her hair.

"So you think there's a way out of this," she whispered. "Alive, that is."

"Of course there is but we need to find it."

What Reina said made sense and put her a little more at ease. However, the woman also had a reputation for being overly confident.

"I think they want to know how we survived our journey to the surface. I got the sense he didn't even consider that's how we got here at first," Kaya said.

Reina spoke softly in her ear, "I think you're on to something, but we can't play your hand all at once. We need to secure our own way out of here first."

Kaya ran a finger absently on the table while she thought. It was a beautiful piece of furniture with an intricate inlay of gold and silver in red-tinted wood. It shined brightly and was easily one of the nicest things she had ever seen.

Everything in the room was exquisite really. From the light fixtures to the windows and the wall hangings. Everything screamed opulence. Unlike her childhood home, the Alhazen Castle, there was no chipped paint or faded tapestries.

Her thoughts were cut short when the man who had captured them strode into the room. He had removed his armor and wore finely tailored black trousers and a loose white shirt. She noticed a silvery glint from his right hand as he sat, and she wondered if it was her mother's blade. His outfit resembled something she would have seen in an old book. He wore it well, but it was horribly old fashioned. He kept his hand under the table, so she couldn't see what he was holding.

A woman whose features resembled his followed closely behind. She was roughly the same age or perhaps a little bit older. She wore a long yellow dress with matching yellow flowers in her hair. She was beautiful and regal but lacked the dangerous edge Kaya had recognized in the leader.

Her expression was neutral and offered no clues to who they were and what was happening here.

The pair took their seats across the table from them. Servants came in matching liveries to deposit tea and a collection of baked goods, cheese, and fruits on the table in front of them. Some looked familiar, while others were new to her.

"Are you ready to tell us what's going on here?" Reina asked without preamble. The Lunese were always quite direct, and Reina was truly a compliment to her people. Kaya remained quiet, studying the faces of their would-be kidnappers.

The regal woman said something in their unknown tongue.

"We don't speak your language," Kaya said.

The woman scrunched her brow and said something else.

"We aren't lying. We don't know what you're saying," she said.

The woman seemed increasingly frustrated.

"She wants to know how it's possible you're here on Earth with modern armor and weapons but cannot speak the Imperial tongue," the man said.

"How do you speak our language?" Kaya asked.

"I spent a good deal of time on Mars, unlike my mother. She never thought to learn their language."

Mother, Kaya thought, shocked. They looked like they could be siblings at most.

"This is the language everyone speaks. It's the Standard tongue. We aren't from Mars. I'm Mercurian, and she's Lunese," she said. "How does your mother look the same age as you?"

He looked curiously at her, and Kaya had another clue to what was going on. Her mind went to the only possibility, despite how unlikely. They were ageless.

"Tell me who you are and how you came to possess this," he said, placing her mother's blade on the table.

Kaya took a deep breath. She considered lying but... He knew something. Probably more than she could imagine. In any event, these people were obviously important, whoever they were. She looked at the regal woman and knew she couldn't come to them as some peasant.

"My name is Lady Kaya al Vardan, daughter to the Duke of Mercury." She motioned to her right. "And this is Captain Reina Kwon, my retainer."

Reina had never formally joined her service as a retainer, but she thought it afforded her some protection given the situation. Reina seemed irritated but content to let her handle the conversation.

He stared at Kaya appraisingly, placing his right arm onto the table. He then began tapping his fingers rhythmically on the wooden surface. She assumed it was one of his ticks.

Something about the sound seemed odd, and then she noticed his hand again. The glint she had seen hadn't been from her mother's blade. His hand and at least the rest of his arm she could see, was clad in some silvery metal. No... *made* of metal. The craftsmanship was amazing and inlaid with intricate geometric patterns in gold and black.

The arm moved with fluid motions, and if it wasn't for the designs and construction, she would have thought it was completely natural. It was as if all the stories of the Era of Empire were coming to life before her eyes.

When he didn't speak, Kaya said, "So are you going to tell us who you are and where we are?"

"This is the Dowager Empress Helena, my mother." The woman straightened at recognizing her name, and Kaya blinked. *Did he call her an empress?* The name seemed familiar, but she couldn't place it and racked her memory to think of why it was important.

There was another long pause.

"I am Archduke Leopold Corvidae, heir apparent to the Solar Empire," he said, leaning back in his chair. He said it in a matter-of-fact way, but he seemed to be waiting for her reaction.

Reina filled the silence that followed with laughter. It was a soft chuckle that quickly became a raucous laugh that left her gasping for air. Kaya had never seen Reina in such a state, and it scared her.

"I don't see what's so funny," Kaya said through gritted teeth.

Reina continued to laugh, until she eventually regained some control. "It's all so absurd. I must certainly be dead or dreaming. I crash-land on a dead planet with you and end up having tea with the sarding raven prince."

Reina wiped a tear from her eye. "I think I caught whatever madness you've been spreading around, princess." She paused for a moment before the laughter came again. "Wait, I guess you really are a princess then, aren't you?"

Kaya opened her mouth to say something untoward but then closed it again. The raven prince she'd said. No, it couldn't be possible, but here she was staring at the man with her own two eyes. The only figure in Republic history that struck more fear than the demons of the Holy Scripture. The man who had leveled cities, decimated fleets, and tried to shape the Solar System in his image. The man who would put himself above God.

He was also the man who personally led the defense of Alhazen Castle during the Great Solar War. Her father had always whispered that he single-handedly saved Mercury and ensured the survival of the Vardan bloodline. The raven prince eventually returned to Earth, where he died with the rest of Eden for his sins against God. At least that was how the stories went.

Kaya felt lightheaded.

The dowager empress left the room in a huff as the laughter continued. She was either annoyed by Reina's uncouth behavior or frustrated with her lack of understanding. Leopold looked at Reina with a confused expression but didn't share in any of her mirth. He seemed too busy making his own calculations. However, he made no attempt to stop his mother's departure.

"If you really are a Vardan, we would be cousins. Many generations removed, I assume, although I have never been very good at keeping track of that sort of thing. You said your father is the Duke of Mercury?"

"Yes, and his father before him. There have been many generations of Vardan dukes and duchesses."

"Who serves as archduke on Mercury?" he asked, continuing to tap his metallic fingers on the wooden table.

Kaya was surprised by the question and wondered if it was some kind of trick. "Well, no one is." She had heard the title used in a historic context regarding the prince and princesses of the Solar Empire, but no one had held the title since.

Reina, having taken control of her laughter, added. "After the Great Purge, the various dukedoms were destroyed, and their holdings spread to many minor nobles. Those houses were then consolidated under the rule of a single planetary duke with far less power. Then they eliminated the title of archduke."

Leopold seemed to take all of this in stride, and Kaya was a little surprised by Reina's knowledge on the subject. Then again, she probably had access to a lot of interesting information from her time in the Pandora Fleet and Prometheus.

"You didn't explain how it is you came to possess this," Leopold said, stopping his tapping and motioning to the hilt of Kaya's plasma blade.

"It was my mother's, and she left it to me."

"Who is your mother?"

"Duchess Semiramis al Vardan," she said, unable to hide her sadness.

"Semiramis is dead?" he asked bluntly, and Kaya's heart sank. He seemed to know her mother's name. She didn't want to believe she was who he was talking about. Maybe who he was thinking of was someone else. One of her ancestors maybe. She knew plenty of them had the name Semiramis.

"She..." Kaya wasn't sure what to say anymore. Was she dead? Part of her knew she was, but another part hoped it was all a lie. A terrible misunderstanding because she lacked the knowledge she was gaining in this very moment. The ageless were obviously real, but what about her father? His sadness at her absence seemed very real. "I'm not sure any longer. Did you know her well?"

He smiled as if remembering something and then frowned. "Yes, we served together in the war, but that was a long time ago now, before all of this," he said, motioning as if to the planet. "I still have many, many questions."

The quickening pace of her heart had taken away the chill she felt when first sitting down at the table. *He'd served with her in the war? Before all this? Did he mean the Great Solar War?* The prospect of finally having answers was exciting and terrifying all at once. Kaya didn't even know where to begin. "So do I," she said.

"What of your father, your grandparents?" he asked.

"I never knew my grandparents. They were dead before I was born. I haven't seen my father in years, but I've spoken to him recently. He remains well and on Mercury, but a war has broken out."

Leopold's head perked up. "The war is not lost?"

Reina laughed again, "Might want to get something stronger than tea for this conversation, Your Highness."

Kaya went on to explain as much of the last five hundred or so years of history as she could remember in only a few hours. When she had caught up to current events, she explained how they came to be in orbit over Earth and how they eventually crash-landed on the planet. She painted broad strokes but didn't leave much out. She couldn't see any reason to lie or obfuscate the truth of the world they lived in.

"The theists won," he said to himself. Kaya nodded.

Kaya knew either this man would help them, or they would die on this planet. Even with his help, they might die here anyway. If he was who he said he was, then he had been stuck here a long time, and she had to assume he would have left if he had the means. When she was done, Leopold, who had looked completely unflappable in the beginning, began to look as anxious as she felt.

"When you captured us, you called me descendent of Najm. Why?" she asked, taking her turn to become the interrogator.

"You called your mother Semiramis al Vardan. The Semiramis I knew went by the name Semiramis Najm. That you were staring at her photo and looked like her, I made a guess as to your origin. When you reacted to the name, I knew I was correct."

"That was my mother's maiden name, but a lot of women in her family had that name," Kaya said, lowering her head. "I can't say it's the same person you remember."

He studied her face more deeply and scrunched his brow, "When were you born?"

"4083," she said.

"You're not ageless then?"

"No one is. Or I mean, was..." She wasn't quite sure how to answer his question. "Up until a little while ago, I didn't know the ageless were even real. I'm still not sure I believe it."

"Is my presence here not proof enough for you?"

Reina leaned in. "Why don't you cut off your real hand over there so we can watch it grow back."

Kaya paled, but then again... There were hundreds of legends about the ageless and their physical capabilities. They were known for having tremendous strength and the ability to heal from any wound or disease. Some said a drop of their blood could cure anyone of any disease. They could even breath underwater or in the vacuum of space. The tales were as varied as the people who told them.

Leopold snorted. "I am ageless, not a lizard. It doesn't work like that."

Reina looked disappointed.

"Do you think I would still have this..." He waved his mechanical arm. "...if I could easily grow a replacement?"

Kaya didn't care if the wild stories were true. Knowing that the ageless were real gave her newfound hope that her mother could still be alive. That she could have survived her ship's explosion. Even if she wasn't the Semiramis he knew, she could still be ageless. Kaya had found the Ageless Legion emblem on her mother's note, and she was convinced that wasn't a coincidence.

Reina shrugged. "A stylistic choice maybe. How many more ageless are here?"

"How many men are aboard your ship?" he rebutted.

"Enough to keep it," Kaya said, "but I think you already knew that. If you had enough men to take it, you would have already." For all Kaya knew, he already had, but she bluffed, hoping to get information. She hoped everyone aboard the *Rubah* was still safe.

Leopold grunted, "Or did we need time to gather our forces in one place?"

Kaya stared into his face. In the silence that hung between them, the servants returned. They removed the plates of fruit and cheese, replacing them with heartier foods. Heaping plates of roast meat, cooked vegetables, and loaves of fresh bread were set between them. Kaya's stomach growled, and she realized it had been a long time since she last ate.

Looking at the food, she remembered the people in the cave. Their gaunt faces and dirty clothing. Then she remembered the boy Brandon from Tiyas who suffered from hunger in the slums on Mars while she ate in fancy restaurants with Hal.

"How can you eat like this in your palace while those poor people starve in that hell we landed in?" she said, and Reina stopped reaching for a loaf of bread. "Is that what you've done all this time, lord over these people like some divine figure? Is that why they worshipped that image?"

Leopold looked offended and perhaps even sad. "There are no gods here." He laughed bitterly. "There aren't even any emperors."

"Wouldn't you be emperor?" Reina asked.

"No. I never made it to my coronation, but that is hardly important now. As to your question, it's more complicated than you imply."

Kaya was unamused. She had grown so very tired of people telling her how complicated things were and why this or that couldn't be accomplished. For once, she wished someone would own their shortcomings and strive for a better solution.

"I can see you don't believe me, but there is much you also do not understand, child."

"I'm not a child."

He looked amused by her response. "When you measure your life in centuries, your perspective tends to shift. To me, you are both children, but I'm sure you don't see yourselves that way. Children never do."

Reina smiled. She seemed okay with being insulted.

"Spare me your condescension," Kaya said, feeling her face begin to flush.

His serious expression returned. "To answer your question, we eat like this because if we don't, we will die a slow and painful death. While agelessness is a gift, it doesn't come without a cost. We require a tremendous amount of fuel to keep our bodies operating so efficiently. When we're injured, we require even more to heal quickly."

"So you hoard it for yourselves?"

"We do what we must to survive. Once you have survived as a prisoner in a dead world for over five hundred years, you can judge me. We provide good lives for those we can here and on other estates. Who do you think maintains all their machinery? The lights that grow their crops and the wells that provide them with clean water from deep below the surface. I wish for nothing more than to rebuild my planet, but I lack the tools and resources to do so."

Kaya studied him, looking for any sign of deception. She studied his face like she did the clerics back on Mars who all too often had their own agendas when dealing with her. Her search didn't produce anything.

So she reached into her shirt and slowly pulled out the Jiddi tree necklace. Leopold's eyes lit up at the sight. He looked like he was ready to leap across the table for it. "I assume you know what this is then, a Jiddi tree sapling."

"How did you get that?" he asked.

"My father gave it to me before I left Mercury. He said I would need it to rebuild the garden. Rebuilding the garden was my mother's goal, and then it became mine. By some cosmic accident or divine intervention, I find myself here now."

Leopold stared at the pendant. "The Jiddi trees were the heart of the Empire. Now the ancient groves lie in ruins."

Kaya couldn't imagine an entire grove of these beautiful trees. "Can the Earth be fixed?"

"Don't you think they would have done that if they could?" Reina said sarcastically.

"With the right tools, yes. We have terraformed worlds far more hostile than this. But first we would need a way to disable the Iron Cage and get off this planet. Only then can we acquire the materials and the tools we need to accomplish any meaningful restoration."

"Why do you need us?" Kaya asked. She still wasn't sure what they could accomplish that Leopold couldn't. He obviously knew much more than she did about the problem and steps to fix it.

He paused as if considering how much he should say. "That you made it through the Iron Cage with such a large ship means you know a way back out of the net. If we captured it and went the wrong way, we wouldn't get a second chance. This is an opportunity we've never had before and I don't want to squander it," he said with a shrug.

"You want us to take you off the planet?" Kaya said. She was doubtful it was a real possibility, and worried Leopold might be desperate enough to rely on a long shot. But he had a point. They were able to make it through the Iron Cage the first time. Then Kaya remembered Aelius whispering into the captain's ear. Did he know how to get past it just right?

"Also my men. You said you wanted to rebuild the garden. In this, we are aligned."

"Do you have the tools we will need to begin repairing the planet?" she asked, trying to find the trap.

Leopold shook his head. "We lost what we had in previous attempts. The Iron Cage destroyed the drones, even in low orbit. First, we would need to disable the cage, then we can acquire new tools. Even if they no longer exist, we have the specifications and designs for new ones. We would only need someone capable of reproducing them."

Reina said, "There have been attempts for generations to destroy the Iron Cage. What makes you think you can do it?"

"We have studied it for a long time. We know the satellites as well as anyone, but their creators possibly could. Our remaining artificers have developed various ideas to disable the satellites, but the solutions can only be deployed from space," Leopold said, parting his hands. Kaya thought he seemed genuine.

Kaya felt energized by the thought of what could be. Then she began to wonder if Aron would know how to build the tools they would need. She knew he had a brilliant mind for machines. Then she wondered if he was even still alive, and her sadness turned to suspicion.

"Why should I trust you?" Kaya said, locking eyes with Leopold.

"I'm tired of my prison here. I've come to yearn for nothing and forgotten pain and pleasure equally. Anything that could be described as an emotion is absorbed by the event horizon of my soul." Leopold tapped his metal fingers rhythmically on the table again. "Perhaps this was the nirvana the ancient monks sought. I hope for their sake it wasn't. I realize now what a horrible feeling it is, the perfect equilibrium of your soul and body."

Reina looked unsympathetic. "Why not off yourself?" Kayas eyes widened at the suggestion.

Leopold didn't look put off. "Many have chosen that direction, even before being trapped here. Not every mind can tolerate an eternity of pain. If I remain stuck here, eventually I will drive my blade gleefully into my skull."

What he described was beyond Kaya's ability to empathize with.

"So, you see, there's no greater darkness than my own. When I look out, even the faintest light becomes a blazing beacon. Right now, Lady Kaya, you are my beacon, and I will gladly follow you to safer shores. No one else in five hundred years has given me the same hope."

Kaya didn't know what the right answer was. They could easily betray her, but without their help they would likely remain stuck on this planet.

"I can't guarantee you anything until I speak to the others in our party." Kaya didn't mention that she had no idea if they could even make it back through the Iron Cage. She only hoped Aelius would continue to have the answers no one else did.

Leopold frowned. "Whose ship is it?"

"It's my father's ship. His lord steward is the senior noble onboard," she said.

"If it is your father's, than it is also yours," he said as if there was no question.

"I hold no titles of my own."

"You don't need a title when you have the support of a prince and his retinue backing your claim. You're my royal cousin, probably," he said with a slight smirk. "I won't see you denied your birthright."

Based on his immature expression Kaya assumed it wasn't lost on him how ridiculous he sounded, although it was the first time she had seen him show any kind of joy.

Reina seemed equally amused. "I like how you think."

"Then we are in agreement," he said, slapping the table.

"I..." She was about to protest but then remembered how she had become a passenger over the last week. This was her chance to take charge of her life and what was happening in it. "Yes, I agree."

"Good, we can begin making the arrangements tomorrow. I apologize that we only have one guest room available, so you will have to share. We don't get many visitors," he said, rising from the table.

"Tomorrow? Why can't we go right now?" she said, concerned about the people on the *Rubah*.

"We've waited five hundred years. You can wait a couple of days. The servants will show you the way." He picked up the hilt of her plasma blade and began to walk from the room.

Kaya stood abruptly and shouted, "Hey, wait, that's my blade!"

"No. This is your mother's blade. Rest well, and in the coming days we will see if it's really yours." He left the room before she could say anything else.

Her heart sank to be separated from the blade, especially now.

"What are you doing?" Kaya said to Reina, who was busy collecting a plate of the untouched food. "He took our weapons and won't let us leave!"

"This is the nicest prison I've ever seen," Reina said and then lowered her voice. "They are probably watching. Keep your eyes open, but let's not get hasty until he breaks his word. We have limited options right now."

Kaya exhaled, dropping back into her seat. "What did he mean about seeing if the blade was really mine?"

"I don't know, but I've known enough people like him. I think he wants to make sure you earned it. Like my torches from Prometheus or the Pandora Fleet Cube," she said, motioning to the tattoos on her forearms. Some things you can't get by showing up. You need to prove you belong. Maybe he's not sure you should have it."

"Who is he to decide that? The Empire has been gone for hundreds of years. That blade was given to me. My mother would want me to have it. And I didn't ask to stay here."

"He certainly still thinks he's in charge, and he's measuring both of us. Maybe he's trying to decide if we're actually worth working with. We need to be careful because we don't know the rules to his game yet," Reina said, continuing to speak softly.

"What choice does he have? We have the only ship that can get off this planet. It's work with us or stay here, I guess literally forever," Kaya said.

Reina placed her plate back on the table and looked at Kaya seriously. "Princess, do you actually think they couldn't take the *Rubah* if they wanted it?" Reina looked genuinely confused, as if she thought Kaya had been in on some joke this entire time. "Did you see how easily they disarmed us? I felt like a child again, being leveled by my drill sergeant. That was only three of them. How many more could be here, dozens, hundreds, maybe even thousands?"

Kaya didn't really consider that possibility. She assumed because they hadn't already it was because they lacked the means. "Then why not do it? Why make this big show of speaking with us?"

"Speaking with you."

"What?" she asked annoyed.

"He wanted to speak to you, princess. Not me, or us, or anyone back on the *Rubah*," Reina said, stepping closer to her. "You saw that shrine to your ancestor or mother, or I don't know who, but he certainly knew who it was. Then he saw you, and everything changed. That blade was one more piece of evidence for him."

Kaya was struggling. "Okay, even then, so what?"

Reina shrugged. "I don't know, but I guess we will find out. Maybe he owes some blood debt to your family. Maybe he wants to decide if you're worth keeping alive, or maybe he's bored and looking for some entertainment. Like I said, we need to be cautious until we learn the rules."

Kaya's heart began beating faster as she considered the new possibilities Reina had put into her head. She took a deep breath and then another. She had to regain control of herself if she couldn't gain control of the situation.

"Whatever it is, I will succeed."

Reina smiled hopefully. "I know, princess. In the meantime, I'm going to enjoy what I can here. I suggest you do the same. We don't know when or if we might get another chance."

Kaya shook her head at the women's grim musings. *Reina really needs to work on her pep talks,* she thought.

Kaya made her own plate of meat and vegetables before the servants came to usher them to their quarters for the evening. Kaya didn't notice much as they passed through the halls because she was too busy wondering what challenge she would face next.

She had finally gotten one step closer to her mother's dream, and she wouldn't fail now. Surprisingly to her, she wasn't afraid. Nervous, yes, but not afraid. Maybe it was the stress stunting her emotional responses, or maybe she was finally beginning to cope with the demands following her mother's path had put on her.

She hadn't been able to save the people of Mars, but now she had a real chance to save the people of Earth. People who had been trapped in hell for generations. What better mission could there be for her than rebuilding the garden. Not metaphorically, but literally rebuilding it. The prospect of it excited her, while the reality of how monumental the task would be was crippling.

CHAPTER

18

Silas

August, 4103 U.E.T. - Artemis Dock Yards, Luna

"I DON'T WANT TO HEAR IT," Silas said as Marcus approached him in the hangar bay. "The days of leading from the rear are over."

"Leading from the rear is more important now than ever, but if you want to be stubborn about it, suit yourself. I won't miss all the paperwork."

"What makes you think there will be any less? Paperwork can only be delayed, never eliminated," he said, strapping the rifle to his back. He made the mistake of going unarmored once already and wouldn't be making the same mistake again so soon.

"We have the chance to create a new government, and you're already doubling down on bureaucracy." Seeing that no one was near, Marcus leaned in closer, speaking softly, "You doing okay? Feel like we've hardly talked since we left Mars."

"I'm fine," he said quickly.

"You don't look fine. Sarding hell, I might be more worried if you really were fine."

"Right now, my focus is on Catherine's health, securing these docks, and repairing our fleet. We need a base of operations and a safe place for our men, but don't be so concerned. God is with me again."

Marcus did look concerned, and he craned his neck again to see if anyone was close enough to listen. "Last time you told me that, I almost died on a sarding trash heap of a moon near Saturn. That aside, it's not only you I'm worried about but Lancaster and some of his old timers."

Silas turned to study Marcus's face. It was jarring because it felt like the first time he had looked at him in days. Silas thought his brother-in-law looked more tired than usual. His eyes were sunken, and oddly he wasn't eating anything.

Then he considered what Marcus had said. Lancaster was maybe more argumentative than usual, but he had always been steadfast in his loyalty to the fleet. "Where is this coming from?"

"While you were in the med bay, I heard some whispers that he was questioning your fitness to lead. From the people I talked to, it sounded like he was suggesting it might be time for new and more energetic leadership."

"Maybe he was being prudent in case my injuries were worse than they turned out to be," Silas said. He didn't want to believe he was already under threat from inside his own force. Although maybe he had been overconfident thinking his hold on the Pandora Fleet was unquestioned.

Marcus exhaled loudly. "I hope for both our sakes you're right." They both turned as more troops began assembling in the hangar bay for the trip down to the docks. "We can continue this conversation later. I don't think anything will change for now." Marcus's face was a mix of concern and annoyance.

Silas asked, "Not hungry?"

A sullen "nah" and a long expression was the only reply.

Lord Hayashi approached, flanked by a pair of Pandora Fleet knights that had been assigned to keep an eye on him. They allowed him some freedom, but Silas wasn't naïve enough to let the man roam the ship freely.

Hayashi had his armor and ceramic blade returned to him. The blood splatters on his armor were only partially cleaned, and they gave him a severe appearance. He offered a salute. "Your Grace, Commander. Thank you for this opportunity to accompany you."

Marcus eyed him warily. He hadn't been a proponent of including Hayashi in their plan, but Silas had decided it was important to have a Lunese representative.

Hayashi claimed that no one knew with any certainty who the pirate king was, so he would be of no use identifying them. Silas was more worried about avoiding other social pitfalls.

Having a Lunese lord supporting their cause would lend some level of legitimacy to their operation. They were not here as foreign conquerors, despite the aspirations of some of his other commanders. There were plenty in his crew who wanted revenge for recent events, but the Lunese were hardly the proper target for their ire.

Silas had instructed Lord Taylor and Captain Lancaster to remain behind. Lord Taylor would continue to organize the marines in addition to processing the thousands of prisoners who had been captured during the recent battle. Soon a decision would need to be made about what to do with them.

The captured Lunese carrier ship had been heavily damaged during the battle, but it was deemed a suitable place to temporarily hold the prisoners. It had enough space to house them and limited capacity to continue the fight should the Lunese become... unruly. If that happened, the fleet had standing orders to destroy the carrier permanently with everyone on board.

Lancaster meanwhile would ensure they maintain their orbital supremacy and guard against an assault from anti orbit weapons on the surface.

They didn't expect any other enemy fleets to appear in this theater, but with long-range communications unavailable, they couldn't let their guard down completely. Lancaster would also remain ready for his signal in case the docks proved to be hostile.

In private, Silas had also arranged for Captain Dvorak to take her new destroyer, the *Elysium*, and a small detachment of ships to flank the portion of the Lunese fleet that remained in orbit over the dark side of the moon.

Despite what he told Marcus, Silas didn't want to put all his faith in the hands of Lancaster. The man was capable, but he was also emotional, stubborn, and often shortsighted.

He needed people in key positions where they could have an impact on events as they transpired. Which was why he picked Captain Dvorak. He trusted her in a way he didn't trust Lancaster or his other captains. It wasn't common knowledge, but she had been a friend of Catherines in their university days.

She was also Venusian and came with a perspective different from the others. Most of all, she was creative and flexible, traits that all good commanders showed at some point in their career, before often losing them to age and overconfidence.

Silas boarded the corvette that would take them to the docks, Lord Hayashi and Marcus following closely behind. A small platoon of men-at-arms was on hand to provide security.

The Artemis Dockyards were one of the premier ship-building facilities in the Solar System. What started as a small Lunar probe during ancient times had grown to encompass a complex web of space stations, scaffolding, and manufacturing structures. Raw materials streamed from Mars and the asteroid belt to be processed into civilian and military vessels alike.

In the days of the empire, these docks had churned out some of the largest and most advanced vessels humanity had ever created. A fact the Lunese shipwrights took great pride in.

They didn't just build ships for economic reasons, although they certainly profited greatly from the enterprise. They built ships because it had become a core part of their identity. Where Martians had become cold and measured, the Lunese remained bold and determined.

Even now in the twilight of combat smoke spewed from orbital factories and sparks flew from the torches of welders who toiled on the hulls of a dozen different ships. Silas always thought of the Lunese as an industrious people, and that was only reinforced by what he saw.

He wondered if the Lunese today could build something to rival the *Sanctuary*, the legendary ark ship. Without the Republic's regulations restricting their creations, he thought maybe they could. That idea excited him more than anything else they were here to do.

Their corvette docked without incident. Silas stood from his seat and ensured his armor and weapons were ready. Marcus, out of habit, drew the ancient pistol from his chest. He chambered and checked the weapon before returning it to its holster.

"We are not here to conquer," he reiterated for the benefit of all on board. The others nodded their understanding.

"I have no desire to destroy my home, only reclaim what was taken from me and my people," Hayashi said.

"Aiding us now will only expedite your desires," Silas replied, thinking of his own home on Mars. He expected his brother, Simon, to have already moved into his estate before they even reached Lunese orbit. The thought helped him empathize with Hayashi.

The door of the transport opened slowly. Unlike the *Specter* and other governmental crafts or space stations, the Lunese docks didn't maintain gravity at the Earth standard. Instead, the artificial gravity of the hangar bays and other interior structures were designed to mimic the gravity of the Lunese surface.

Therefore, it was much lower than what most of them were used to. They were trained for fighting in low gravity, but like any other skill, it required practice to maintain proficiency. Practice none of them had gotten in quite some time.

Exiting the craft, they nearly glided across the floor as they got used to the new surroundings. They agreed to meet in one of the manufacturing sectors of the dock. The warehouses in these sectors provided more open lines of sight to help guard against any surprises. The hangar bay they docked in was plain and unadorned. He had expected to be greeted by some ragtag crew of militants, but instead there was a squad of well-armored soldiers.

Their exoarmor was of high quality, and it was obvious they were well trained from how they carried themselves. On the shoulders of their armor was an insignia with the image of a sea serpent. The soldiers on both sides held their weapons tentatively but left their helmets retracted, honoring the standard protocols of a parlay. This would have been more comforting if not for recent events.

The soldier in charge approached. "High Commander, you can follow me."

A small contingent was left behind to guard the transport, and the rest of them followed the escort. They kept a reasonable distance between themselves and their guides. Silas was considering their options as they walked. They had enough manpower to overpower these guards, but they also had no idea what was hiding behind every closed door they passed. He had raided enough insurgent facilities in his career to not underestimate his enemy.

Lord Hayashi was likewise scanning the corridor. "The soldiers are Protean Company contractors. They are officially neutral but typically handle sensitive matters outside of official channels."

Silas tried to rack his brain for what he knew of the Protean Company. There were many private security firms throughout the Republic, so keeping track of them all was no easy task. He couldn't recall a time the Protean Company was mentioned in his reports. Either they were mostly irrelevant or very good at their business.

"For the highest bidder," Marcus said softly.

Hayashi agreed. "They're particular about their contracts. Whatever they agree to, they finish. No more, no less. That much I can confirm."

Without knowledge of what that agreement was and with whom, Silas thought it meant very little.

They arrived at a pair of doors that slid open on their arrival. Inside was a small group of people waiting casually on the opposite end of the room. Silas waited at the door and sent several of his men-at-arms to investigate the space for any signs of foul play.

The soldiers returned an all-clear signal and moved to positions outside the door, along with the Protean Company escort. Meanwhile, Marcus, Hayashi, and himself entered.

Silas resisted the urge to place his hand on the hilt of his blade while Marcus kept his hand firmly on the grip of his pistol. Hayashi looked cautious but kept his hand off his ceramic blade.

The room was filled with rows of shelves that held a variety of boxes, the contents of which he couldn't identify. There were no tables, chairs, or anything else to indicate any meeting of importance was about to transpire.

In the center of the room was another pair of guards wearing high-quality exoarmor with their helmets equipped. They had rifles strapped to their backs and held lightning pikes at the ready. They stood protectively beside a slim man in a business suit.

The man adjusted his spectacles higher on his face as they approached.

Marcus made a show of taking in their surroundings. "Is this it?"

"Were you expecting a peg leg and a parrot?" the businessman said in a posh Martian accent.

Marcus looked amused. "You're the pirate king?"

"I prefer master of the belt, but others have styled me as the lord of the Silent Sea."

"Interesting choice for a Martian," Marcus said incredulously.

Silas studied the man. He was slim but not frail. His dark-brown hair was cropped short and gelled neatly. His horn-rimmed glasses gave him an air of intelligence. Everything about the man's appearance and mannerisms spoke of refinement and wealth. There was also something oddly familiar about him.

The pirate king spoke, "I have lived most of my life here on Luna, but we aren't here to discuss my origins. We came for business, and time is money. Both are in short supply, and we shouldn't squander either."

Something about the phrase or maybe the delivery of the words sparked Silas's memory. What at first looked vaguely familiar now felt almost like a window into another time.

"You are Orzone's son, aren't you? You're Qilin Orzone. I remember you now. You were there in your father's office, but somehow you got away," Silas said, his mind racing back to the time he watched Mars burn during the Midnight Raids.

"Yes, I'm glad you remember, High Commander, but we aren't here to discuss that either."

Marcus looked surprised, and Hayashi didn't understand the importance of what was said.

"Was it you we were chasing all those years in the belt, or did you inherit your crown?" Silas said quizzically. He felt a strange mix of anger and awe. He thought they had defeated the pirate king all those years ago, but it seems like all they did was relocate their operations.

Orzone sighed, "We are wasting time, High Commander. Your curiosity will have to wait. The duchess is being held by the archbishop, but there is no guarantee on how long he will keep her alive."

"How do we know she's still alive at all?" Hayashi said, latching on to a topic he understood.

"We have our sources, and they are reliable," Orzone said.

Silas moved his questioning back to the present. "Why do you even care? There is profit in disorder, isn't there?"

Qilin shrugged. "Yes, certainly, but only to a point. The duchess has been my oldest partner, and I value reliability above most anything else, even profit. The archbishop is not a man I care to do business with, now or ever."

"Even if that were true, why do you need us? You have manpower." Silas motioned to the armed guards. "And you still control a sizable number of ships."

Silas had doubts about Qilin Orzone's claims, even if they sounded reasonable. His father had been a fair and honest man in their dealings. Qilin meanwhile was a self-proclaimed outlaw, and Silas had seen many of his exploits firsthand.

"Look at him. He's an accountant, not a soldier," Marcus said, and even if Silas agreed, he knew insults weren't helpful. He gave Marcus a steely glance.

Orzone spread his arms as if to agree. "I am a businessman first and foremost. I can see the big picture and take all these disparate parts and create something new and exciting. That may include the duchess, the Pandora Fleet, or the young Lord Hayashi here." Hayashi seemed agitated that Orzone knew his name. "My father tried to do that once and nearly succeeded. I have since learned from his mistakes. While he was gentle and trusting, I am neither."

Orzone raised his hand without turning, and one of the guards handed him a digipad. He manipulated the device before handing it to Silas.

There on the screen, Silas saw several ships with the Lunar surface below. They were Dvorak's ships. He recognized the familiar hull of the Elysium easily. In the far distance were the remaining Lunese ships he had sent her to observe. Then he flipped to the next feed, and the camera panned out to reveal several other ships flanking Dvorak's. They had her surrounded.

"I don't show you this to intimidate you, High Commander. I only need you to understand my capabilities. This partnership can only thrive if it is built on mutual respect."

Silas handed the digipad to Marcus. "There would be nothing stopping us from destroying the docks, along with you and everyone else here. It would be over before you make your next move," Silas said harshly.

"Perhaps, but that is a waste for all of us. We're on the same side, even if you don't care to admit it. We waited to see what you would do before committing to the fight. Now I know you are as invested in success here as we are. Luna needs to be freed from the Republic's grip," Orzone said, adjusting his glasses again.

"However, Commander Higgins is right. I am no soldier. I command markets and manage logistics, hiring the greatest captains to lead my fleet. I ensure soldiers are paid and stomachs are full."

"So you want us to fight and die while you sit back and bathe in your riches, magnate?" Hayashi said.

There was a commotion at the door. A Pandora Fleet soldier was attempting to enter the room, while the Protean Company guardsmen and Pandora men-at-arms at the door began to scuffle over letting him pass.

Orzone motioned for his men to stand down, and Silas waited for his soldier to approach. He provided Silas with the information he already knew. More ships had arrived, and they were in a precarious situation. He sent the soldier off with orders to await his command or his death.

"You're not negotiating in good faith, Orzone," Silas said when the soldier was gone.

"You have guns trained on us here and on my fleet. I think it's reasonable to assume I would do the same. That you didn't consider I could do it is your mistake, not mine."

"I liked your father better," Marcus said, eyeing the man. Qilin's father had been a brilliant businessman and a sympathetic soul, but he was never adept at military strategy. Which made him a far easier adversary.

Orzone ignored Marcus. "Tell me, High Commander, how did you intend to pay your men once the Republic freezes the central bank and stops any payments to your fleet? How will you supply your ships, feed your men, refill munitions? I'm sure you realize you can only pillage so much before you make even more enemies than you have now."

Silas had considered this problem initially, but in his calculations, he had been relying heavily on the Duchess of Luna to be their main benefactor. Without that source of support, he wasn't sure what the alternate option was beyond going back to the Mercurians.

However, even if he could get his fleet back to them, what good would it do when he informed Duke Vardan that his daughter was dead. Orzone had caught them in a vulnerable position.

"You need me to be the face of your operation," Silas surmised from everything that had been said and not said. Orzone had spent his life in the shadows. The pirate king was an idea more than a person. What this cause needed for the long term was a tangible leader on the surface, leading troops, someone visible and well known who multiple factions could tolerate.

Orzone smiled. "A fair partnership I think."

"I won't be your puppet, no matter our history. We've come too far to abandon our own cause now." *I've come too far,* he thought. His guilt for the events of the Midnight Raids didn't erase the image of Catherine's charred body.

"Like I said, I'm a businessman, not a politician or dictator. Like you, I have no intention of ruling Luna. We both need a base of operations, and neither of us could truly conquer these unruly people. Even Lord Hayashi here could not garner the love of so many." Orzone's tone was conversational, and he seemed at ease despite the tension in the room.

Hayashi said, "You have interpreted my power and ability incorrectly."

Orzone ignored him, continuing to address Silas. "We both need the duchess more than we need each other. In her name, order can be restored to Luna. Then we will have a steady base to operate from, and we can all go back to our original mission."

Silas only paid the seething Hayashi passing notice. "What mission is that?" he said, arching an eyebrow.

"Making the eternal dream a reality. Rebuilding Luna, Mars, and the rest of the Solar System to the glory that once was. This time better and more equitable than it ever was before. The days of emperors and God are over, High Commander. Now we will usher in the era of man," Orzone said, his eyes mirroring the passion in his voice. He clearly believed what he was saying, or he was the greatest actor Silas had ever seen.

"He is a liar," Hayashi said openly beside him. "He will take what he wants and leave us to pay for it."

Silas had read about the eternal dream. Mostly in whispers through classified documents. Part of him was curious to know more, another part of him recoiled at the thought of man being placed above God.

"It sounds like you would replace the Republic with a new one under a different name and seek to destroy the church and nobility." Silas was not and had never been an Imperialist sympathizer. He never desired the imperial crown, despite his family's historic claim to it. Uprooting so many ancient systems would have dire consequences. Orzone's ideology didn't come without practical implications.

"I have no desire to destroy church or tradition, High Commander. I only wish to bring humanity into the future where it belongs. We have languished in our self-imposed exile for far too long. That said, we are still short of time. The duchess's life remains in danger. I need to know if we have an agreement." Orzone stretched out his arm to Silas.

Silas wished he was a better politician. What he did instead was use the knowledge he had as a duelist and soldier. Those skills made him adept at reading body language and patterns. He did that now to decide whether Orzone showed any signs of nervousness or betrayal.

He was unable to find any. He also weighed what immediate options he had. They had limited means to fight any longer. When he opted not to follow the Mercurians, he committed himself to this path.

Perhaps this was God's way of testing him again by bringing him to Orzone after all these years. A chance to make things right. The duchess also needed him, and that was a cause he would gladly take up for an old friend. He had many reasons to stay, and many reasons why he couldn't leave. He looked briefly at Marcus and Hayashi, but neither spoke.

Silas grasped the man's forearm firmly. "We have an agreement. At least for now."

Orzone exhaled, and his shoulders seemed to relax. Silas was glad to see he was not immune to the tension. Orzone spoke to the guards behind him. "Inform the captains to begin coordinating with the Pandora Fleet for dock arrangements and resupplies. We will provide them with all aid possible."

"Thank you," Silas said honestly. "Marcus, send a communication to our fleet." He turned to Orzone. "Now, what do you know about the duchess's whereabouts?"

"We have confirmed she is being held in the Selenean Palace by the Archbishop."

Hayashi added, "It makes sense he would take her there. It's heavily fortified, deep within loyalist territory."

Marcus turned off his comms and said, "Sounds like a trap. Even if we can march all the way there and somehow take the palace, why would he leave her alive?"

"The archbishop needs her like we do if he plans to rule. It's also possible he might only want a bargaining chip. We cannot say for sure yet," Orzone said.

Silas rubbed his chin. "The duchess has always been popular. Killing her would only inflame the populace further. It might also be his insurance policy to make it off the planet if things begin turning against him. How popular is this archbishop. It is still Ames, I believe?" Silas had never dealt much with the archbishop personally, so all he had to go on were vague recollections.

"He commands the respect of many and the fear of many more. With the failure of the duchess's coup attempt, his position is only stronger," Orzone said, and a smile came to his face. "However, that was before they knew of your resounding victory in orbit. If we can spread the right message quickly and make landfall, I think there is still hope."

Silas felt unconvinced. "We will need numbers to control any sizable territory. The archbishop has already had time to mobilize the Lunese army and Lunar Guard divisions."

Hayashi turned to face him. "If I can show my people I'm alive, we can turn at least some of the Lunese army to our side. There are many who were loyal to my father and the duchess. The archbishop made many enemies when he murdered my father and others within the council chambers. There are likely entire divisions willing to defect given an attractive option."

Silas wondered if what Hayashi said was true or merely his wishful thinking.

"There are a lot of factors to consider, and we can't do that here in an empty warehouse," Silas said, looking to Orzone. "Let us organize the fleet and take stock of our resources. When things are settled, come join us on the *Specter* to discuss our next moves. We will need more information on the manpower at your disposal."

He didn't expect Orzone to be forthcoming, but they had to try and collect as much information as they could anyway.

Orzone nodded. "I'm glad we were able to come to an agreement, High Commander. I will convene with my team and be in touch."

Silas clasped arms with Orzone and turned to leave, his party close behind.

"You go on ahead," Marcus said when they got back to their transport.

Silas gave him a questioning look.

"I'm going to stay to organize the crews when they arrive. I'll be back aboard once we get things settled."

Silas found it strange Marcus was volunteering for extra work, but he didn't want to question him in front of Hayashi. "Don't linger longer than you must." He motioned for several marines to remain behind with Marcus.

Marcus saluted and walked back into the facility.

Silas was glad the meeting had gone so well, and they avoided violence. He always found it helpful to at least have some direction to move toward. He only hoped it was the right one.

Hayashi meanwhile seemed elated at the prospect of reclaiming his home. Silas hadn't made him any promises, but they had few other leads to go on. They would need to make landfall somewhere, and that task alone would be incredibly difficult.

CHAPTER

19

Kaya

July, 4103 U.E.T. – Tilicho Lake, Earth

KAYA BRUSHED THE HAIR from her face and turned over in bed. She felt the familiar warmth of sunlight on her face and yawned. She thought about her strange dream and opened her eyes, searching for Victoria to tell her about it. Then she remembered where she was and sat up.

"Good morning, princess," Reina said, seated in a chair on the balcony. The chair's front legs were off the ground, and her back leaned against the frame of the open doorway. Her long black hair looked freshly washed, and she wore new clothing.

"I thought for a moment it was all a dream," Kaya said, rubbing at her face.

Reina crossed her arms over her chest, swinging her one leg absently. "It feels like it could be."

"They haven't come for us? I didn't expect to sleep this much."

"Servants came and left all of that," Reina said, indicating a table covered with breakfast foods, hard-boiled eggs, sliced meat, assorted fruit, bread and cheeses. There was enough to feed four times as many people. It all smelled quite good. Next to the food was a stack of clean clothing.

"I wish I knew what they were planning," she said, swinging her legs off the bed. Her body was sore and stiff from the crash the day before. "We need to get back to the *Rubah*."

"I'm not sure, but I've been watching for a while. It seems like they're preparing for something. I've seen a few transport ships come in."

Kaya stepped up to the balcony to join Reina. The estate spread out below her. It was smaller than the Alhazen Castle, but equally ornate. Flowers and gardens abounded, and the artificial light of the dome mimicked natural light with near-perfect precision. Beyond the dome were magnificent snow-covered peaks that reached into the sky.

"It's beautiful," she said.

"It's easy to see how it could be. When I was growing up, my parents used to tell me stories about Earth and how once even Luna had been made to look like it. Not only inside the massive domes but the entire moon. They said sometime after the fall of the empire the tools needed to maintain a thick atmosphere on Luna were lost, and now it's only a thin shadow of what it once was. Enough to support human life, but just barely."

Kaya listened quietly, leaning against the open doorway. Reina rarely spoke of her origins and even less about her family. "We might be able to get back to Luna soon."

Reina let the legs of the chair drop to the floor. "I left a long time ago for a reason. There's nothing left for me there now."

"Do you want to talk about it?" she prompted. Reina glared and she didn't push the subject.

"Is something else bothering you?" Kaya asked. Reina was normally calm and confident. An attribute she was often jealous of.

Reina said bitterly, "You mean besides the obvious? I'm worried about you Kaya, and I don't know how to get us out of this mess."

Kaya's mouth tightened as she tried to think of the right thing to say. Reina had called her by her name, and she seemed genuinely concerned. Maybe given the recent events it shouldn't shock her as much as it did, but she still found it surprising.

"Like you said, if they wanted to kill us, they would have. When we get back to the others, they will-"

"They won't know what to do either. Besides, I don't trust anyone else here but you, princess." Before she could thank her for the unusually kind words, Reina raised a finger. "You make horrible decisions, and you are very, very, annoying, but..."

Kaya wondered where she was going with this.

Raina continued, "You care, and that's more than I can say about most people. Whether it's the people of the slums or the Gaian survivors, you want to help them. You never ask about the costs, although that's probably because you grew up filthy rich."

Kaya frowned. She was becoming uncomfortable with the direction of the conversation and decided to throw it back to Reina. "With your posh Lunese accent, we probably have a lot in common, even if you try and hide it. Don't think I haven't noticed."

"Who's hiding? I've spent too much time with Martians." Reina stood up to lean over the balcony's railing. Kaya could see several groups of people moving around the estate, and then a new transport came into view. It landed in the distance behind one of the main buildings.

"Maybe we can steal one of those ships," Kaya said and then considered how little Reina enjoyed improvising.

"That would be suicide. No, we need to get more information first."

Kaya stepped out on the balcony to stand beside Reina at the railing. She leaned in close, assuming there were listening devices spying on them. "I was thinking about what you said about my mother. This will sound crazy."

Reina blinked. "That seems pretty typical for the last twenty-four hours."

"I don't think that was one of my ancestors in that painting. I think it *was* my mother."

Reina's eyebrows drew together. "Kaya..."

"I know. I'm not saying she's alive. I get that." She took a deep breath and ran her hand through her hair. "That picture they had up on the wall, I've carried around one like it for years. It's nearly identical."

"I could take a picture of you right now, and it would probably be nearly identical," Reina countered.

"It's not only that. The way the archduke looked at my blade. He recognized it."

Reina exhaled, "That still doesn't prove anything. It's your family blade, isn't it?"

"Do you remember when I asked Aelius about the Ageless Legion once? I drew the symbol on that paper, and he recognized it right away."

Reina's eyes narrowed as she remembered the exchange. "Okay…"

Kaya unzipped the front of her bodysuit and reached into one of the interior pockets, producing the folded note she still carried. She handed it to Reina. The note read simply,

Remember, you are stronger than you could ever imagine.
Be the light of the world.
Guide those who struggle in the darkness.
I love you.
Mom

At the bottom of the note was the Ageless Legion symbol marking the stationary.

Reina finished reading the note and handed it back to Kaya, who quickly tucked it away.

"I think she wanted me to have this symbol. She wanted me to know the ageless were real."

"Let's say I believe you and this all makes perfect sense. Which it doesn't. What does that mean for us now?" Reina looked receptive but noncommittal.

"I…I don't know, but it means there's much more going on than either of us know. We've all been lied to for a long time."

"I have a feeling that's an understatement, princess."

Kaya was hesitant to say much more, but she took a deep breath and continued, "Maybe she gave me this note so I would know she was still alive. Maybe this symbol is some kind of key or secret code."

Reina squinted. "This all seems excessively optimistic, even for you. You could show it to Leopold. Maybe it will mean something to him like you said."

"I want to wait until we know more." Kaya walked back to the table of food that had gone cold. She grabbed two large and perfect-looking yellow apples from a bowl and walked back to the balcony. She tossed one of the apples to Reina, who deftly caught it.

"We need to figure out who my mother is, or was, to him," she said, biting into the fruit. The taste caught her off guard. It was the most flavorful apple she had ever eaten. "We don't even know if my familial association is a good thing or not. He might have some blood feud with my family for all I know."

"I wish I knew how they made everything taste so good," Reina said after biting into her own apple. "Anyway, that will be hard with how little he's told us so far."

"Well, if he won't tell us, then we will need to find someone else who will. I have a suspicion Aelius is a good place to start."

"The prophet? Why him? I mean, he does tend to know a lot, but what makes you think he knows anything about the ageless or Earth?"

"Right before we crashed, I saw him whisper something to Captain Masoumi and Theodore. He seemed to know we could land here safely."

"There weren't many options left I think," Reina said, still skeptical.

"I don't have all the answers," she snapped, her frustration bleeding through. "But right after I woke you up to leave the bridge, Aelius looked right at me. He knew we were leaving but didn't try to stop us. I don't know what that means either, but I'm telling you he knows something."

"Alright, princess, relax. I'm on your side, but you know I hate a half-baked plan, but we aren't going to solve this now. You should go freshen up and eat more. It might be a long day. I'm worried they are up to something, and we're going to be at the center of it."

She sighed and took another bite of the apple. She also wondered what Theodore really knew. Looking back on recent events, she was sure he hadn't told her everything. What about her father? If it was true that her mother was one of the ageless, surely her father must be too? She thought maybe Aelius was working for them both. Maybe they sent him to watch over her and make sure she discovered the truth about the world.

"Thank you, Reina, for everything."

"Don't start with that. Let's get out of this new mess you got us into first."

"You're as much to blame as me."

"I'm not the one that dragged us out of the ship," Reina said, sitting back in the chair.

Kaya smiled to herself as she walked to the bathroom. Happy to have Reina by her side.

The bathroom was as ornately appointed as the rest of the room, but luckily the fixtures and their controls were generally familiar to her.

It was shocking that so little had changed in five hundred years. She would have expected some foreign and exotic time capsule, but instead she got something very similar to what she knew. Except where her world was dull and crumbling, the buildings here were fresh and vibrant, at least inside the energy dome. Then she realized she was the one who had been living in a time capsule.

Kaya stepped into the shower, enjoying the warmth of steaming water washing over her skin and hair. She rested her head against the tiled wall, letting the water cascade over her face. Her thoughts drifted to her life before all of this. She wondered if Victoria still thought of her at all. Then she thought of Hal and how she missed his companionship. The quiet moments she spent with him looking at the stars and imagining what life could be like if they could choose.

I need to make all this worth it.

Kaya thought someone had a plan for her, maybe her mother, father, or even Aelius. Either way, it all started with the eternal dream. She was beginning to see that now. Her mother had been telling her all this time that this future was coming. Kaya didn't know it had been so close.

Her mother taught her to be an independent thinker, compassionate, and a stalwart soldier in equal measure. Preparing her to lead one day and fight for her own future and the future of those who couldn't fight for themselves. Maybe her mother knew she would be in danger and that Kaya would have to pick up the pieces.

She turned off the water and took a deep breath as the last drops splashed to the floor. She reminded herself that what she wanted didn't matter right now. Nothing mattered beyond her mother's last commandment, "Guide those who struggle in the darkness." She used to think that meant people like Aron and the members of Prometheus who fought for a better life. Then it came to include all the coalition members aboard the *Rubah* who had no one else to fight for them. Now she included the poor people of Earth who toiled under grim and dreary conditions on her long list.

She only hoped she could figure out how to help them before she got stranded in the darkness of Earth herself. Not knowing how much time she had left; she didn't linger in the shower and made her way back to get dressed.

Kaya chose to wear the same bodysuit she had worn earlier under her exoarmor, instead of the clothing provided. She felt more at ease in something familiar. It also had a pocket for her mother's note, and a high collar to keep the Jiddi tree necklace close to her chest.

She did, however, take a pair of boots and a light orange sweater they had provided. It was made from a fine fabric, maybe even wool, and sported two large pockets in the front. The loose fit made it look particularly old-fashioned.

She looked ridiculous, but at least it would be warm and practical. Reina had decided to wear black slacks and a white blouse from the clothes provided. They were among the more normal-looking items.

Finally, Kaya arranged her hair into a long braid since she had no means to dry it. The servant returned shortly after she finished to lead them from the room.

She thought she would be more nervous as they marched off to do who knew what. Instead, she felt a sense of calm at the inevitability of it all. What was going to happen was going to happen. She could start getting nervous when she reached the first problem to overcome. Worrying now would only be wasted energy, she reminded herself.

Reina was scanning their surroundings, as the servant led them through the estate. "I think it bothers me more that they don't have us under any armed guard. They only sent one of their peasant workers."

"Where would we even go? Where do you think he's taking us?" Kaya said, looking from the servant to the fields where others toiled. They seemed happy and well-treated, but she hated that this was the most these people could hope to aspire to in life. "I don't see anyone here but farm workers."

"Whoever arrived in those transports must be tucked away on the other side of the compound," Reina said.

They took a winding path that led them through paved gardens and quiet pavilions. She realized quickly that the domed estate was substantially larger than she originally thought. Far larger than any private estate dome she had seen before.

After a few minutes, they reached a rise where she could look down on a beautiful blue lake, which was flanked by snow-covered mountains that reached up into the sky like the Republic's cathedrals. She could see the mountains spread out toward the horizon, before disappearing out of the dome and into the darkness beyond. The water looked crisp and inviting. It was so still that once she got closer, she could see the bottom.

"It's beautiful," she said as they passed, imagining what Eden must have looked like once.

Reina seemed more focused on figuring out what was going on. "Over there," she said, motioning to a flat area outside the energy dome.

Kaya looked to where she indicated and saw a collection of black-clad figures standing in a rough circle. They looked like the knights who had accompanied Leopold in the cavern. As they approached the edge of the dome, their guide stepped aside and motioned for them to continue through the gate. She stopped to take a deep breath.

Reina stepped up beside her. "Whatever happens next, I'm with you, princess."

She reached out to squeeze Reina's hand, and to her surprise she didn't pull away.

They stepped through the gate together, and the air immediately turned sour. She resisted an urge to cough from the particulate blowing around them in the breeze. It was dark outside the dome, and when she looked into the sky, she realized the sun was nowhere to be found. It was still night outside the dome.

"If I hadn't lost track of the time cycle weeks ago, I'd probably be more confused," Kaya quipped. She was trying to keep things light to hide her anxiety.

Outside, the gate was a stand of burning torches, and Reina grabbed one, using it to illuminate their path.

It felt a bit silly to use a flaming torch, but she thought maybe it was a way of rationing power resources. Except it could easily have been for theatrical purposes as well. When they got within sight of the group, she felt the latter was a more likely answer.

"Maybe they feel like they need to be imaginative," Reina said. "You know, to spice things up."

The paved path turned to gravel, and they continued walking toward the silent crowd. They stood arrayed as if in some ritual, with heavy hoods drawn over their heads. She got the uneasy feeling they were about to become the focus of their rite. She swallowed hard as the thought came to her for the first time that this could be some kind of sacrifice.

They parted as the pair approached, leaving them room to enter the center of their circle. It was snowing lightly, and the white flakes landed on her body before quickly melting, the melted snow leaving behind a trace of dust. She took some comfort that there was no bloody alter in sight.

Leopold stood in the center of the group, which contained a mix of men and women, some in armor, others in uniforms or formal attire. All of them were fit, and most stood as tall or even a foot taller than Kaya.

She could only make out some of their features in the torch light, but nearly all of them bore serious expressions. They also carried weapons, mostly spears that resembled lightning pikes but shorter and with a sharp point in place of a blade. Those closest to her also carried plasma blades on their hips.

"Sarding hell," Reina said. "I'm counting at least twenty."

"Thirty-three," Kaya said, closing the gap with Leopold. She stood defiantly in front of him, raising her chin so she could look directly into his sapphire eyes. Reina took a defensive position beside her.

Whispers reverberated through the crowd.

"You come to be judged and tested," Leopold said, and a cheer erupted. The cloaked onlookers slammed the butt of their spears into the ground, and Kaya shivered. She told herself it was only from the cold.

"Your judgment means nothing to me, but give me your test, and I will make light work of it," she responded.

Leopold looked content, and quiet murmurs emanated from the crowd. It was possible her words were taken unfavorably, or like the dowager empress, there were many others who didn't understand what she said and required translations.

Leopold took the hilt of her mother's plasma blade off his hip and raised it above his head. He spoke several words in the Imperial tongue, and the crowd cheered again.

"Who here will measure themselves against the descendent of Najm and daughter of House Vardan?" he repeated in the Standard tongue.

She watched the hilt in his hand, her anger rising at it being used as some kind of prop. Her mother had left it to her, and he had no business with it in his hand. He had no right to judge her.

Reina leaned in whispering, "You might want to take it down a notch, princess. This isn't a fight we can win."

"You don't need to do anything. I'm tired of hiding and running," she said, scanning the crowd to see who would accept the challenge. Since Leopold had taken her blade, Kaya assumed there would be some kind of competition, likely a duel. She was hardly a blade master, but she was proficient enough to at least put on a good show. They would see she wasn't some puffed up socialite and return the blade to her.

"Your Highness, I will fight the little fox," called a heavily accented voice from within the crowd. A mountain of a man with a large black beard stepped aside, making room for the speaker to pass.

She rankled at being referred to as little once again, even if the fox was her house's symbol. Then she got a good view of her challenger as he stepped into the light and questioned her bravado.

He looked to be youthful, but then again many of these people did. She had to remind herself most, if not all, were much older. The *larger* problem was that he was over a foot taller and twice as wide as she was. He was a younger version of the bearded mountain that stood beside him.

"You were saying, princess?" Reina offered.

God's bones.

"I, Lord Harald Alfson, son of Birger and Sigrid Alfson, will fight this Martian theist," he said, stepping forward to stand beside Kaya in front of Leopold. His accent was thick and gruff. The older giant, who must be his father, Birger, cheered enthusiastically.

She tried to ignore his condescending smirk and held her chin high. "I am no theist. I'm here to see the eternal dream become reality. Nothing else."

Leopold cocked his head. "A phrase I haven't heard in a long time. Now we will see if they are words on the wind or belief forged through experience."

Leopold motioned to one of his knights, who came forward with two spears, like the ones the others carried. The knight stabbed one into the snow-covered ground in front of each of them.

"Take your weapons and prepare yourselves," Leopold said, stepping back. Harald bowed and hefted the spear as if it were weightless and moved toward his father.

Kaya was left stunned. How was she supposed to fight this giant. Let alone with a weapon she had never used before.

Reina stepped forward toward Leopold, and his knights hefted their spears to stop her advance. Reina didn't blanch at the sharp points threatening to skewer her. "You can't seriously intend for her to fight that monster."

"The little fox said she is the keeper of this blade. That is a serious claim that cannot be made without proof. These are not toys that are given to children. They are earned through sweat and blood." Kaya was fighting to maintain her breath as he spoke. "Your lady can choose to yield now if she likes. It is her right."

Reina stepped back, and the knights lowered their spears. She pulled Kaya by the arm, out of earshot of the archduke. "You need to yield, Kaya. This isn't a game. Those aren't blunted training spears. You saw that, right? One good hit, and that giant *will* kill you. Do you understand?"

Kaya blinked to clear her vision.

"There's no shame in yielding. This isn't a duel between equals, Kaya." Reina silenced her before she could object. "No, you aren't equals, not in this. That man is ageless and has been fighting for longer than either of us have lived. These are new rules, and we aren't prepared to play their games. Let him take the sarding blade, and we can find another way to get it back. It isn't worth the risk."

Kaya swallowed hard. Her mother entrusted her with that blade. She couldn't let someone take it. Not like this. Not without even trying. "I need to fight him. If I yield, he might take our ship anyway, and there's no telling what will happen then. If I fight, we at least have a chance to have a say in what happens next," she said, but her voice felt like it was coming from outside her body. "Look at these people, Reina, all of them look like they were cut from solid tungsten and molded in supernovas. They will never respect or listen to me if I back down now."

Reina shook her angrily. "Stop thinking about your sarding pride for one second."

Kaya shook her head and put a hand on Reina's shoulder. She knew it wasn't only about the blade but also everything it represented. "This isn't for me. It's for our collective dreams. For yours, mine, and my mother's. The dreams of all those people back on the *Rubah*. For all the lost souls on this planet. If I don't fight for them, who will?"

Reina cursed again. "You won't be able to help them if you die here either! All over a stupid blade."

"It isn't about the blade. These people know how to fix the Earth. How to rebuild Eden. We need them, and that is worth everything," she said, holding back tears that welled in her eyes.

"The time is now, little fox. What do you choose?" Leopold asked as the others continued to stare at them. There was no shortage of snide expressions among the watchers. It seemed like they shared Reina's opinion of the outcome.

"I accept the challenge," she shouted, and her voice threatened to betray her. She walked with shaky legs to retrieve the spear from the ground and returned to stand beside Reina.

A mighty roar came from the crowd, and they slammed the butts of their spears into the ground once again. Harald walked forward into the center of the circle to meet her. He jabbed his spear into the ground and removed his shirt, tossing it aside. He flexed his mass of muscles, and she felt her resolve evaporating.

Then the crowd began to chant. "Sol Invictus! Sol Invictus!" Over and over.

Reina leaned in one last time to speak directly into her ear. Her expression transformed into one of anger and resolve. Her normal confidence returning.

"Give him sarding hell and do whatever it takes to win. You can do this." Reina gave her one last firm shove into the center of the circle.

Reina doesn't really mean that, does she?

Kaya wanted to win, but she wasn't sure if she was prepared or willing to do anything in the process. She had no desire to hurt or kill anyone. She hoped it wouldn't come to that.

Kaya

July, 4103 U.E.T. – Tilicho Lake, Earth

Breathe, breathe, she reminded herself as the cries of Sol Invictus drowned out her thoughts and the encouraging shouts from Reina.

She stepped forward toward the behemoth. Hefting the unfamiliar weapon in her hands. She had practiced with a dull spear on occasion with the Alhazen master-at-arms, but it was hardly a skill she had mastered. She was far more talented with a plasma blade, but that wasn't an option given to her for this. Then she remembered the guard in Trinity Square.

No, she couldn't think of that now. *Breathe, breathe.*

The spear was lighter than she expected, and the bare metal felt cool under her touch. It took her several moments to find the trigger points that would allow blue-coiled electricity to arc from the spear tip. She felt a lot like she was stumbling through the dark.

"Don't worry, little fox. This will be over very soon. I don't like to toy with my prey," Harald said once they were within striking distance of each other. His accent was thick, but she was able to understand him.

His words fanned the flames of her anger. She hadn't come all this way to get beaten by this brute.

"Don't confuse my youth with my strength." She hoped her delivery was convincing.

"You misunderstand, theist. It is only a name. Our name is a part of us, but we are not only the name. They call me little bear, but you can see I am quite large," he said, amused.

"Do all the ageless deal in empty platitudes?"

"No," he said with a large grin before jabbing out at her mid-section with his spear.

Kaya jumped back, only narrowly avoiding the strike. Harald laughed without pressing the attack. She could hear others in the crowd jeering at her. *So much for not toying with me,* she thought.

She returned with a strike of her own while he continued to laugh. He stood casual and relaxed as she jabbed out at his massive torso, both hands gripping the spear.

He dodged aside with a start, and his mirthful grin grew. "The little fox has claws!"

She stabbed out again, but he was paying attention this time and her attack was sloppy. He easily batted the spear aside with his own. Her momentum took her right past him as he stepped aside.

"And fangs!" he said with another laugh.

Harald spun lazily and used the sharp point of the spear to slice her left bicep. She grimaced at the pain. The wound was superficial but began to bleed heavily.

She felt her panic rising. This wasn't like fighting some childhood bully or even the unsuspecting guard she had killed in New Olympia. This was like her recent sparring match with Namtar. She was outclassed in almost every way. She had rarely if ever been outmatched in physical pursuits. Now it seemed to be happening on a daily basis.

She struck out again, swinging the spear in a wide arc. She swung high before quickly redirecting the strike to Harald's legs. As the spear point grazed the back of his thigh, she activated the electrical element. Electricity crackled as it burned into his leg, causing him to mutter something that must have been a curse in the Imperial tongue.

She didn't have a chance to celebrate her small victory. His glib expression vanished, and he slammed the butt of his spear around and into the side of her own thigh. The force was debilitating, and she cried out as the leg gave out from under her. He came in for another strike, and she somehow managed to deflect several of them before receiving several more cuts to her torso.

"Yield!" he shouted, looming over her.

She scrambled back, trying to get to her feet, but her leg didn't want to work. She felt trapped, like the time the brute Gram had grabbed her in the slums. Like then, she scrambled toward Reina for salvation. Harald didn't follow, but his mirth returned as she scurried away like a coward.

Her body ached from the wounds, and blood began coating the thin fabric of her exosuit liner and the borrowed sweater. Reina came to rush to her side, the concern obvious on her face. "You can yield," she whispered. "There's no shame in it."

"I...I can't."

"Then you better figure out a way to end this! I don't want to watch you die," Reina growled.

Kaya fought to catch her breath. Her mother wouldn't yield. Catherine didn't yield when they led her to the pyre. Aron didn't run to the ship when Trinity Square erupted into war. No, she couldn't yield either. All their sacrifices needed to matter. She needed to secure the help of these people.

Jimmy told her there was no turning back and that death would be her only escape. She had agreed to those terms. Gritting her teeth, she screamed, pushing herself up to her feet, using the long spear to steady herself.

Hefting the weapon, she charged at Harald again and swung with all the power she could muster. She channeled every ounce of fear, sadness, and pain into those strikes. One and then another. Again, and again. All the while releasing a manic scream that drowned out the jeers of the crowd.

The world became a daze, and she watched like a bystander outside her own body as she lashed out. Her blows landed on Harald one after another. He was sloppy at first in his defense and began to bleed from several wounds. He was forced to step back and realign himself against her onslaught.

Then the phase of the fight changed, and she could tell, even outside herself, that all her effort wouldn't matter. His form changed like the tide. He planted his feet, his massive body like a boulder in the snow, and swung out, possessed by some force she had never seen or experienced.

Although it felt like an eternity, she knew it had been merely seconds. She managed to deflect his first blow as she was pushed back, but then one hit after another landed, the strength of each increasing. First a slice to her arm, then another cut to the body, and then her hand buckled under the barrage. The butt of the spear rounded one last time to slam into the side of her head.

She landed in the snow face-first. The cold, icy surface embraced her throbbing wounds. She could see through cloudy vision the snow was turning red. She heard nothing but the rustle of the wind and torches. Wondering if perhaps *this* would be how it all ended. She had reflected far too many times lately on the end of her life. How many times could she dance with death before death finally won?

Reina came rushing to her side. "She yields! No more, you made your point!" she shouted, and Kaya tried to protest.

A roar passed overhead, the familiar sound of a transport ship approaching. She ignored it. Instead, she struggled to her knees. Reina offered her a hand up, but she waved her aside. She needed to do this herself.

Harald stood almost dumbfounded. Gone was the mocking smile, replaced instead with something more thoughtful. Even the crowd remained silent.

Reina remained by her side, although she raised the spear again in shaky hands. She would keep fighting. She was ready to see this through to the end. She charged again, but her balance left her, and she slipped in the snow, falling again to the ground.

She struggled to get up, rising to her knees as a familiar figure pushed through the crowd and stepped into the light. It was Namtar. He came and lifted her up from the ground before she could offer any protest. He held her easily in his arms, and she grudgingly leaned on him for stability.

He wore no armor and carried no weapons beyond a plasma blade at his hip. None of the assembled knights moved to stop him.

Namtar looked from her to Harald before turning his attention to Leopold, who came to join them in the fighting circle. "You shame yourselves with this display."

Leopold eyed Namtar wearily, and Harald looked to take a step back.

"The descendent of Najm agreed to the terms," Leopold said.

"This girl does not know your ways. You've dealt in bad faith," Namtar replied.

"I didn't know if what she said was true. She carried this blade and claimed a right to it," Leopold said, holding out her mother's blade. "Authority is not inherited. It is earned. You understand the law is clear in this regard."

Namtar considered that and nodded. "A child must be instructed before being expected to know. Look at her face and see the truth of her claims. Have you already forgotten your own laws?"

"Much has changed," Leopold said.

"This child is not the reason why. This isn't the path of justice. By my right under the Solar Charter, I challenge this preceding as unlawful and void. Let any who challenges my claim step forward and face me," Namtar shouted so all in the crowd could hear. He repeated himself in the Imperial tongue.

Kaya had no idea what was happening, but Leopold tightened his jaw. She thought he looked almost ashamed. No one came forward.

Leopold bowed his head slightly to Namtar. "If you had come forward, I would not have gone down this path. However, as is my lawful right, I will retain this blade until such a time it is earned through blood or trial."

Kaya was even more confused now, but Namtar nodded. Leopold came to stand in front of Kaya and placed a hand on her shoulder causing her to wince.

"This pain is temporary child. You showed spirit that is worthy of your ancestor. That Namtar stands by your side tells me everything I need to know about your origins. Rest now, and we will talk in the morning."

She tried to reply but couldn't. Harald approached next, a big toothy grin shining through his beard. "Little fox, your bravery is unquestioned. I will gladly fight beside you," he said before walking away. Then she heard another cry of Sol Invictus begin to ring out, and Namtar helped lead her back toward the estate, Reina following them.

"Did I win?" she muttered through the pulsing pain in her face. It felt like her eye was beginning to swell.

"No, princess, you lost. Very, very badly, but sarding hell it was amazing to watch. I didn't think you could move like that."

Kaya smiled as blood dripped from her nose and into her mouth. The warm copper taste left her thankful to be alive. Things could have gone so much worse. Kaya leaned into Namtar as he led her back toward the estate, and her legs got heavy.

He lowered her onto a bench in one of the delicate gardens they had passed through earlier. Back inside the dome, the artificial light erased the darkness of night and warmed her chilled skin. A fountain bubbled softly beside them. In her current state of confusion, the transition was especially jarring but welcome.

Servants came with a bowl of water and bandages, which they placed deferentially beside Namtar. He saw to dressing her wounds while she winced at the burning sensation from the multitude of cuts. Reina took up a worried position beside them.

The adrenaline subsided from her body, and Kaya slumped on the bench. The growing pain caught all her attention, but when the first wave passed, Kaya said to Namtar, "Why are you here?"

"I told you I would protect you."

Barely a day had gone by since he had said that. This seemed to go far beyond any casual sense of honor. "How did you even find us?"

"I followed you when you left the ship."

Kaya tried to think through how that might have been possible. She hadn't seen him following them at all. Reina's thoughtful expression confirmed she hadn't either, but then a more important question came to mind. "How did you find us once we boarded their ship?"

"I knew where to look."

His vague responses made her wonder if he had spent too much time with Aelius. "I guess it's obvious you're one of the ageless then?" she asked, and he nodded. His intervention during the fight had been proof enough. Yet casually mentioning the ageless still felt incredibly strange. "How many of you are there?"

He didn't answer, so she pressed him.

"There are many things I cannot answer for you, My Lady."

Kaya resisted the urge to strike him. He claimed to want to protect her but wouldn't give her any useful information so she could protect herself.

"Why didn't you stop us? Did you know the other ageless were out there?" Kaya asked.

"My job isn't to stop you. It is to keep you safe, My Lady," he said, turning to a rather deep wound on her thigh. His hands worked in practiced motions, and she wondered again how many secrets this man kept from her. "But, no, I didn't know they would be here. I haven't returned to Earth since the cataclysm."

"Isn't Leopold your emperor or archduke or something? Why would you confront him like that?" Her mind jumped from one thought to another. She wondered if dedication to the Solar Empire was as absolute as the dedication of many to the Republic.

"Maybe once, but my service to the gods has always come first."

Reina stood to confront him. "Why did they look at you like scared school children back there? Who are you really?"

"I am Namtar," he said as if there could be no other answer.

Kaya winced as he pressed on the largest gash. Through the pain, she grabbed his hand and made him look her in the eyes. "No more sarding riddles. No lies. Why are you here? Why are you protecting me?"

He paused. "I served your grandmother and your mother after her. Those ageless back there," he said, motioning to where they had come from, "they have long memories. They remember me and them. Oaths cannot be undone. They are not temporary things."

Leopold arrived unannounced, flanked by the older giant she identified as Harald's father, Birger. He held a bloody spear. Namtar bowed his head, but Kaya and Reina offered no such deference. This man had been ready to see her die for their ancient ritual.

"You are right to judge me," Leopold said to the women. "Namtar reminded me of who I was. I seem to have lost my way in the darkness." He looked off to some other time and place. "If you are serious about rebuilding the garden, then I will help you."

"There is nothing else more important to me," Kaya said.

He nodded. "I have sent an emissary to your ship while we prepare for the voyage."

"I told you it isn't my ship. It is my father's, and he left someone else in charge."

"Like I said before, it should be yours and will be yours," he said with a wink and turned to leave the garden.

"Wait!" she said, wincing as she tried to stand. Leopold stopped and turned back. "Where will we even go?"

"The sight of Namtar has given me hope that other ageless remain out there," he said motioning to the sky.

"No one believes the ageless even exist, and with the war going on we can't sail around wherever we want to find them."

"Then we will fight our way to the answers we need," he said, seemingly unbothered.

Birger grinned through his bushy beard. "What a grand adventure after so many years!"

Reina rolled her eyes. "Unless you're hiding an army somewhere, what are a few dozen of you supposed to do against the Republic's armies, the armies that already beat you once?"

Kaya worried Leopold would lash out at Reina for her snide comment, but he took it all in stride. "Do not worry, theist. We will have enough to accomplish our goal. You're right we can't yet fight a war, but we can still win many battles."

Birger echoed Leopold's confidence.

"Accomplish which goal exactly? I don't even know the first place to start," Kaya said, annoyed.

"We need to find one person in particular, Widukind. He will have the answers and tools we need to begin fixing things here. Then we can start to focus on the bigger picture."

Kaya remembered that name. Aelius had said he was the one who made her mother's plasma blade. He said Widukind was the greatest of all the ancient artificers.

"I think I might know where to start. Well, not me, but someone on our ship, Aelius." Reina looked at her, surprised.

Leopold's eyes narrowed, and he stepped closer. "Did you say Aelius?" A wildfire suddenly lit behind his eyes.

"Yes...why?" Kaya said cautiously. She realized she may have said too much. Was this her confirmation that Aelius was in fact ageless?

The fire burned out quickly, and he composed himself. "It's a familiar name. It's nothing. I have had your things gathered onto the transport. We will be leaving soon."

"Did you know an ageless by that name?" Kaya pressed. Considering the stoicism he had shown all this time, his reaction to the name stood out. Then again, Aelius always seemed to have that effect on others, she thought sarcastically.

"Once, but I thought he died here on Earth. A bad memory," Leopold said.

Kaya thought Aelius could be ageless, but she never suspected he could have come from Earth. Was that the source of his odd accent? "So not all the ageless are aligned in their beliefs?"

Birger grunted, and she took that as confirmation.

"Like anyone else, they differ in opinions and desires," Leopold confirmed. "You can trust any left here are loyal to me and the Empire."

Kaya hoped that was true. She would have no way to vet them otherwise. Before Leopold could turn to leave, she said, "I want my mother's blade back."

"That I cannot do. Namtar can explain why. Now we must prepare," Leopold said, not waiting for her to respond.

Birger however remained behind, still holding the bloody spear. He eyed Namtar warily before approaching.

"Harbinger," he said with a tentative nod to Namtar, before turning to Kaya. "Little fox, you fought with honor and bravery. Take this spear, coated in the blood of my only son. It is a worthy weapon and a worthier trophy," he said in a booming voice that matched his size, handing her the spear.

She took it slowly, unsure of what all this meant. Birger grinned and, seeming relieved, left.

"He honors you with this gift," Namtar said.

"I thought I was done with barbaric rituals," she said, sitting back down with a groan. Placing the bloody spear to the side. Namtar went back to working on her leg.

"There is much for you to learn of their ways."

"Don't you mean *your* ways?" Kaya asked.

"No," he said, tightening the last bandage.

Kaya winced. "How is that possible? Is it because you are a theist? You said you put your service to God first."

"Gods," Namtar corrected. "No, my gods are not yours or theirs, but that is not important. They call you theists because you speak Martian and lived under the rule of their enemy. The Republic placed God above the needs of man, and for that they were labelled theists. The Empire was not without its religion. Many of the church's beliefs were taken from imperial tradition."

Kaya had assumed they were simply atheists. "They let you maintain your own traditions?" There were those who kept their own ways in the Republic, secretly of course, but none in a position of influence she knew of. Doing so was an easy way to ensure your own execution.

"Yes, there were no prohibitions. It is why the Republic's church gained such influence before the great war."

Reina probed, "The giant called you 'Harbinger.' And the way they looked at you, they were frightened. You aren't one of them, are you? Not really, anyway."

Namtar stood and walked to rinse his hands in one of the fountains. The water ran red, and Kaya blanched at the reminder of how much blood she had lost.

"It's a very long story." There was a ritual quality to the way Namtar washed his hands that Kaya found mesmerizing.

"Would they really have killed me?" Kaya asked. She didn't want to die, but she saw now how close she might have been to that eventuality.

"Yes," he said, unequivocally. "If you did not yield, he would have been forced to."

She dropped her face into her hands and rubbed her eyes. "Seems extreme for a plasma blade. They don't have any shortage of them here. Does he think I stole it or something?"

"No, it is-"

"More complicated, yes, I get it. It's all anyone ever says to me."

"Not about theft," he finished without a hint of smugness. "The blades are rare and more than a weapon. They must be earned through trial or blood in light of the respect and authority that comes with carrying one. There is no greater honor within the Empire."

"What would have happened if I yielded?"

"You would have given up any titles and wealth to the victor," he said, returning to stand beside them. "Most would rather die than ruin their families and live with such shame."

"I would have had to kill him then?" Kaya said slowly.

Namtar agreed. "It is why these duels were so rare. There is much to lose for all involved. Instead, most blades were awarded through blood, by proving your prowess on the battlefield."

Kaya's breath quickened. "I'm glad you came when you did. Killing your own seems like such a waste."

"It isn't my way," Namtar reiterated. "I think Leopold assumed you were deceitful about your origins and your request for the blade gave him an opportunity to test his theory. However, he should have known the truth and stopped the proceeding when it was clear he had made a mistake. There are requirements for a lawful duel that were not met."

Reina sat down heavily beside her. "I guess when people live forever you need new ways to settle disputes or distribute wealth. You know, when that pesky parent lives longer than you'd like."

"Now you begin to understand," Namtar said, reaching to help Kaya up.

She took his hand, considering briefly how her mother might have earned her blade. There was a lot for her to learn if she was going to get it back, but she was determined to do what it took to earn their respect.

Kaya

July, 4103 U.E.T. – North America, Earth

THE TRANSPORT WAS FULL to bursting with people and supplies when they arrived. Only enough room had been made for the three of them to sit beside Leopold and several of his knights. It was clear they would have to make several trips back and forth to get everyone to the *Rubah*.

She sat holding the gifted spear. Reina had thankfully cleaned off the blood. Kaya was spinning it between her fingers, the point scratching a mark into the floor.

"I thought of another problem with your plan," Kaya said after a time. "If we don't return to my brother or the Pandora Fleet, how will we supply the vessel? The amount of food you all require will be a challenge, and that doesn't even include other supplies and expenses, like maintaining the *Rubah's* crew. They will already dislike being away from home for so long."

Reina added, "If we returned to either fleet, I doubt we would be allowed to leave again."

Kaya had considered that too.

Leopold smiled. "That part is easy, Lady Vardan." He motioned for his men to open one of the many boxes they loaded into the craft. When they did, they revealed a mountain of gold coins, ancient credit chips and other valuables.

"You see, we have the wealth of an empire and nowhere to spend it. Also, to your point, Captain Kwon, or is it Lady Kwon?" he said with a thoughtful tilt of his head. "In any event, I have no intention of being held anywhere against my will. We have been prisoners here long enough. Wouldn't you all agree?"

One of the female knights to his side, a broad-shouldered woman with a sour expression, growled her agreement.

There were so many new faces for Kaya to learn among the ageless. However, most of the ones she had met so far didn't speak her language, save for the few who hailed from Mars long ago or had spent extended time in the cities there. The Imperial tongue had been the language of the educated elite. Her language, the one she thought of as the Standard tongue, was the one used by theists and commoners.

The transport sped along like it had the day before, but this time she couldn't see the alien landscape of Earth. The sky was dark, and no stars shone through the heavy clouds to illuminate the ground below. The others seemed happy to sit in silence, so she did the same.

Kaya had expected the ageless to be some mythical group of godlike humans. Ancient philosopher kings who spouted wisdom and nobility in equal measure. Their behavior had quickly stripped her of that notion.

There were some who looked the part. The knights embodied the stoic ideal she had envisioned. Men and women with large statures and immaculate physiques who stared out at the world with knowing and confident eyes. Except their behavior had failed to live up to those lofty ideals. The knights made up the majority of the ageless she had seen so far, but they weren't the only ones.

There were others, physically unassuming and quite ordinary. They looked like dozens of men and women she had seen all her life in her father's service. There were others still who hid their slender frames behind heavy robes and studious expressions. They looked like professors and clerics she had met throughout her years at the Sanctum. Some appeared old and others young, and their individual characteristics varied wildly.

She distilled from all this what stood out to her the most. The fact that with limited exceptions, they looked like anyone and everyone. There was very little to distinguish them, and that thought sent her mind reeling. *Who else could be among the ageless?*

Her father was a prime suspect. She knew he had become Duke of Mercury only a short time before she was born. Before that, he had reportedly spent years on campaigns in the Far Coast. Maybe whoever left for the Far Coast all those years ago wasn't really her father. Instead, the real Mithridates al Vardan stayed hidden away, waiting patiently for her grandfather's death and his time to rule. She would have to think more about that. Then there were Theodore and of course Aelius. Two other people who always seemed to know so much about things no one was allowed to know.

Most of all, there was the open question of her mother and whether it was her or one of her ancestors that Leopold mentioned. If it was really her mother, then that meant maybe she was still alive.

"If you were in a spacecraft that exploded, would that be survivable?" she asked Leopold, and Reina turned with a worried expression. Kaya knew Reina wouldn't approve of this line of thinking, but she couldn't let the topic rest. Not yet.

To her surprise, Leopold considered the question. "Unprotected, probably not, at least not for long. That is a bit of a worst-case scenario. Along with decapitation of course."

Of course, she thought dryly.

"Why do you ask? Thinking of ways to get rid of us already?"

"No, only curiosity, but I'm surprised you would tell me your weaknesses so freely."

He shrugged, leaning back in his seat casually. "They are the same weaknesses as yours, Lady Kaya. Like I said before, we are ageless, not mythical creatures. What can kill you can kill me, but I will put up more of a fight. My body can heal much faster than yours, but it isn't instant magic. That is why catastrophic injuries can still be life-threatening in the right circumstances and take a long time to heal."

There wasn't any new hope for her to cling to in his words.

When they landed, she was relieved to see the *Rubah*, mostly how they left it. The array of mechanics she had expected to see repairing the ship were replaced with armed soldiers. It looked like a tense standoff between Imperial knights and Mercurian soldiers was already well underway. Kaya stepped quickly toward the crowd and saw Theodore in front of the gangway. He was staring down the Imperial she assumed was in charge.

When the Imperials, as Kaya thought to call them now, saw Leopold approaching, they parted to make room for their small party. Kaya shuffled to the front as fast as her wounds would allow.

"Theodore!" she shouted, and the man turned to her, his eyes a well of relief.

"Kaya! What's happened to you?" he said, looking her over quickly. Then his eyes turned to Leopold, and he froze. She had her first confirmation.

"You recognize me," Leopold said in the standard tongue.

"Yes, Your Highness, he said with a bow. I must admit I'm surprised to see you have survived all this time. That any of you have."

Kaya glowered at Theodore, but he refused to look at her.

Leopold switched to speaking Imperial.

"Theodore Parker," something, something, "Mithridates al Vardan…"

Kaya tried to follow. The names, however, were all she was able to pick out. Based on Leopold's initial surprise she could only assume he wanted to know who Theodore was. She surmised this meant the ageless were numerous enough to not all know each other.

Theodore's expression changed to one of deep concern. Then suddenly he nearly collapsed, and Kaya had to reach to steady him. Tears streamed down his face, and Kaya couldn't fathom why. "What did you say to him?" she demanded.

Leopold didn't answer, and most in the large crowd, save for the Imperials, seemed as much at a loss as her. Theodore's tears remained, but he was able to steady himself.

"What is it, Uncle?" she whispered, temporarily setting aside her anger at his continued lies.

"Something I have waited so long to admit to myself. I had held out hope my wife and children were still here somehow, alive and well. My hope was rekindled when I saw these knights arrive, but now I know it was for nothing."

Kaya didn't know what to say.

Leopold lowered his head as if in respect and spoke loudly. "From the sun we are born, and to the sun we return. Destined to be born again in a new era. There is no beginning and no end, only transition."

Kaya found the prayer surprisingly similar to something the clerics would say back in New Olympia.

A new cry wrung out, "Sol Invictus, Sol Invictus!"

Theodore steadied himself, his tears retreating.

"Thank you, Your Highness. It has been too long since I've heard that."

Leopold nodded. "Everyone will hear our battle cries again, I promise you, but first we must rebuild the garden. The Lady Vardan here has reminded me of that."

"Have you come to take my ship?" Theodore asked. "I am afraid I cannot allow that." He then switched back to speaking Imperial, and Kaya cursed. They were trying to cut her out yet again.

Kaya spoke over them, "We are only one ship and so very few. We cannot impact this war directly, but if we can rebuild the garden...what better way is there to give the people hope?"

Theodore turned to her. "Kaya...it isn't that-"

"Yes, it is that simple. We... I," she corrected herself, "am taking this ship." She paused, expecting Theodore to interrupt, but he remained quiet. "We are going to find Widukind and fix this planet," she said, confronting Theodore like she never had before, like an equal.

To her amazement, he didn't seem angry or even surprised. Instead, he looked her over then turned to Leopold, who didn't so much as blink. She wasn't sure what that meant but appreciated his silence in that moment. She wanted to stand on her own.

Theodore bowed his head. "The bridge is yours, Lady Kaya."

She paused again, this time looking for the trap. She didn't expect it would have been this easy. "Just like that?"

"It's been a short time but a long road to this point for you," Theodore said, a contemplative expression washing over him. Now she understood the tired look in his eyes she had noticed years earlier. "If you've convinced the archduke to stand by your side, then there is nothing more for me to stand in the way of. I have not forgotten my oaths."

She searched his face, looking into his eyes, but couldn't tell if there was some hidden meaning in them.

"Then let's end this standoff and get to it," she offered.

"Come, let us discuss on the bridge," Theodore said and turned to lead the party inside.

The ship was full of activity. Sailors moved purposefully with tools or parts in their hands. Kaya assumed they had been busy making repairs in her absence. She limped slightly as she followed Theodore.

"Are you alright?" he whispered beside her.

"Yes, I'll be okay," They would need to speak about a great many things after this, but for now she only wanted to stick to what was critical.

On the bridge, Captain Masoumi stood like a conductor in an opera, directing her crew to various tasks. She looked relieved to see Kaya. Aelius stood nearby studying one of the digiscreens. When he turned to see her, she thought he might have seemed pleased.

"Lady Kaya," the captain said in greeting. Then her eyes went wide as Leopold followed in behind her. Aelius showed no reaction at all.

Kaya was surprised when Captain Masoumi shouted for everyone to leave the bridge. It was obvious she sensed the immensity of what was happening, or was it that she knew who Leopold was? *Was this another confirmation, she thought? Was Captain Masoumi also ageless?*

Kaya was caught completely off guard when Leopold shoved past her and Reina like a thunderbolt. A harsh cry escaping his mouth as he tackled Aelius. Their bodies smashed violently to the ground as gasps erupted around the bridge. Kaya barely had time to blink, let alone process what to do.

Leopold had his mechanical hand firmly around Aelius's neck, but the prophet didn't struggle. He didn't even fight back.

"That's a twist," Reina said, and Kaya limped over to try and stop him, but Reina pulled her back. "Oh, let them sort this out a little longer."

Kaya shouted, "Both of you, cut it out!" She broke free of Reina's grasp and tried to insert herself in the melee. It was then that Namtar rushed forward and pulled Leopold off. He didn't try to press the attack again, but he teetered on the cusp of resuming violence.

Leopold shouted something at Aelius she didn't understand. Yet the prophet maintained his stoney facade. Barely looking fazed by the violent assault.

Aelius replied in the standard tongue, "Archduke Leopold, I am glad to see you well, and with two functioning arms."

Leopold had to be held back again, and Kaya wondered if that had been an attempt at sarcasm. Coming from Aelius it seemed impossible.

"How did you find a way off this planet?" Leopold shouted.

"It took many years, but eventually I had my chance when an intrepid pilot crash-landed on the surface with a suitable craft. I told you we needed to find Widukind, but you didn't wish to listen. I could not remain here indefinitely."

"If you knew where he was, why has this place remained a prison... Unless that was your plan all along, Oracle?"

Oracle, she wondered. A new title to add to his long list. For the first time, there was someone who seemed to know something about Aelius and was likewise willing to say it out loud.

"I told you long ago I did not. It was only recently that he was found and not even by me. My daughter was the one who finally found him and broke him free of the prison the Venatores kept him in,"

Kaya tried to keep up, but the conversation was going too quickly and contained too many new terms and information. Aelius had a daughter, but who was she, and why had Kaya never heard of her?

"The Venatores..." Leopold said under his breath as if he was trying to figure something out, and then he looked back to Kaya. Then his anger seemed to soften, and he switched back to speaking Imperial. "Semiramis" was the only word she caught, and her breath caught in her throat. She was beginning to piece it together.

Kaya rushed forward, taking Aelius by the collar of his robe. Theodore rushed to stop her, but Reina blocked his path.

"Who is your daughter? Tell me, Prophet," she yelled, shaking him.

His expression never changed as he uttered three simple soul-crushing words. "Semiramis, your mother."

Kaya thought there was no way her world could become anymore unhinged then it already was. Then his words shattered the door to pieces. Her legs buckled, and Reina rushed to hold her up. "That means..."

"I am your grandfather," Aelius said.

"I think I'm going to be sick," she said, and Reina led her to a nearby seat.

"She never knew," Leopold said to Aelius, returning to stand in front of him. When Aelius nodded, Leopold swung his mechanical arm, landing a wicked punch to his face. Aelius was knocked back by the blow, and she saw a small cut open above his eye. Oddly, it barely bled at all. Leopold didn't follow up his strike with another; instead, he turned to exit the room. No one tried to stop him from leaving.

Everyone was quiet, and it seemed like no one knew how to handle the situation. It was clear five hundred years of tension coupled with years of lies had come to a head for many of them, while they languished on a dead planet with no guarantees of escape. It all felt like a cruel cosmic joke. If she wasn't having a panic attack, she might have laughed.

Breathe, breathe, breathe, she thought. It seemed to be helping. None of this, as crazy as it was, could change her plan. She had made her commitment, and that was what mattered now. The people of this planet and the people of Mars and everywhere in the system. All those who had no means to fight for themselves.

"My...my mother found Widukind? Where is he?"

Aelius dabbed at the cut on his face with his bare finger, studying the drops of blood that came away. "On Triton at a hidden facility there."

"The rebellion on Triton, is that her doing? Is my mother still alive?" She had to ask. It was going to be the only thing on her mind for a while either way.

"Yes, she might be, but I have no confirmation."

Kaya rubbed at her face, and Reina looked shocked. It had been a challenging few days for all of them. It was a miracle they remained functional at all. She forced her mind to focus on their immediate problem.

"If Widukind is near Neptune, then that is where we need to go," she said. The fact that her mother might possibly be there only strengthened her desire to go. "My mother never died in that ship explosion, did she?"

"No, it was all by design," Aelius said, and Kaya looked from him to Theodore. She wondered how much each of them knew, how much they kept from her all this time.

Theodore stepped forward. "Kaya, I-"

"No, I'm not interested in hearing your excuses," she said, standing up. "You have lied to me most of all. Captain, will we be able to fly off this planet?"

"Yes, Milady. The repairs are nearly complete," Captain Masoumi said, bowing her head. Theodore ran a hand through his hair, and she could see him struggling to formulate a response.

"Good, let's see to the repairs and regroup to discuss details. The Imperials will begin gathering here, along with their supplies," she said, motioning for Reina to follow her, and Captain Masoumi nodded. Kaya walked toward where Leopold had gone. She was glad Aelius and the others didn't try to stop her. She didn't have the mental capacity to deal with them now.

Reina sped up to stand beside her. "I'm sorry, princess."

"You would think I would be happy or at least relieved," Kaya said.

"I wouldn't be hard on yourself. This is a sarding mess. I haven't spoken to my family in more than a decade, and it was for much less than this."

She turned to look at Reina as they made their way back out to the gangway. "Do you regret it? It's obvious they aren't a part of your life now, but do you wish they were?"

Reina looked away. "Sometimes I do, but every situation is different."

"That's all you're going to say, no extra advice?" Kaya asked, a bit surprised.

"Would you listen to me if I gave you any?" Reina said with a hint of exasperation.

"Maybe," she said sheepishly. "Depends on if it was good advice, I guess."

"Hear Theodore out when you're ready to speak to him. I'm not saying you need to forgive or forget but listen. He might have had as little choice as you do now, or he's truly a massive sard. Either way, you won't know which unless you hear him out."

"You know, I think I like it better when you're mean," Kaya said.

"Oh, sard off," Reina said, shoving her lightly to get her moving again.

"See, like that," Kaya said with a laugh. Her life was becoming quite a mess, but she had to try and laugh about it.

"Where are we going?" Reina asked as they neared the gangway.

"I'm going to go talk to Leopold. I want to find out what all that was about back there. Why don't you go find Rudra and check in with the other Coalition members? I'm sure many are frightened. We will also need to make room for the Imperials," Kaya said, trying to quickly think through the many problems they faced.

The stress of it, coupled with her personal problems, was starting to feel harder than the fight with Harald.

Reina nodded. "I'll check in soon."

Kaya found Leopold outside, a few dozen meters away from the *Rubah*. He was sitting on a large boulder, looking out over the landscape. She quietly climbed up and took a seat beside him; she didn't want to disturb his meditation, so she waited patiently until he was ready to speak.

"I have been wondering if I will miss this broken world. I have come to know this version of Earth for most of my life," Leopold said, staring up into the sky. The feint glow of dawn was beginning to bathe the ash covered ground.

In the low light, the ash could almost be confused for sand, and the soft orange glow reminded her of the end of the long night on Mercury. It was typically a time of celebration.

Kaya nodded solemnly, and he went on.

"I think in my soul I gave up a long time ago, settled into the routine that felt a lot like death. Now I'm terrified of the change. I'm afraid of stepping into a world I will no longer recognize. I have grown old here and forgot what it's like to feel the thrill of something new. I think once I became ageless, it was easy to lose sight of what life is about and become fixated on keeping things the same," he moved his metal arm in flowing arcs as he described his inner thoughts. "It makes me feel like a ghost returning to haunt my descendants, criticizing what they've done with their lives. It makes me wonder if I will be a good ghost."

"Why would you tell me any of this?" she asked, confused by his candidness.

"I would have told your mother if she were here. It felt right to tell you instead. I don't expect you to understand or offer advice, but I appreciate you listening," he said without looking at her. "It's probably better if you just listen."

Kaya tried not to feel insulted, but his words stung. "I don't think I've ever been afraid of change." Staying quiet wasn't one of her strengths.

"What are you afraid of?" he asked. His tone was curious and carried no judgment.

She pursed her lips. "My first instinct is to say failure, or letting everyone down, but I don't think that's true. I'm always willing to try. I think what I'm really afraid of is losing..." Kaya paused to collect her thoughts before speaking further.

Leopold chuckled. With a hint of condescension, he said, "We all like to win, but losing goes hand in hand with progress."

She shook her head. "No, not like that. I've failed at plenty of things. What I mean is, I'm afraid of losing the people and places that make me, me."

"We all lose those things eventually. I have lost both in droves. I'm still here, the same man as before," Leopold said, but his tone was softer now.

"Maybe, but can you say you never lost even a tiny fragment of yourself, who you were? Maybe you've only forgotten the part you lost," she said.

He harrumphed, "Recollecting what I've lost is one of my greatest past times."

She continued despite his sarcasm, "I think it's easy to lose those small pieces of yourself, the parts that grounds you and shows you how to live. The parts that make you, you and not a stranger to yourself," she said, thinking of her mother and father, Alhazen, and everything she left behind on Mercury. The feeling of loneliness and loss that came with being away from them. How she felt adrift in those feelings.

Leopold considered that. "Maybe those pieces aren't lost. Maybe they simply drift away, forcing you to go reach for them. Maybe that's all life really is, reaching out forever at the stray pieces and assembling them into something better and stronger than before. I don't think humans were ever meant to stay the same forever. What would be the point in that?"

"I hope you're right," she said, smiling weakly.

She looked at Leopold and thought for the first time since she had met him that he seemed himself. Not a caricature or an actor playing a role but the genuine person behind all the layers.

In the silence, she worked up the courage to press him for answers. "Who was my mother to you?" she asked finally.

"She was many things to many people," he said diplomatically.

"I want to know who she was to you. Everyone tells me they knew her, but then I realize the woman they knew is someone foreign to me."

"She was my father's closest advisor and Imperial Field Marshal of the Ageless Legion. She was the beating heart of our war effort," he paused, his voice softening. "To me, she was my teacher and most of all my friend. No one believed in the Eternal Dream as much as she did."

Kaya smiled. Her mother believed in that dream because she had seen it, lived it, made it hers. Kaya could only guess how hard it must have been to live in a world devoid of all that hope and promise. Then she began to wonder about all the lives her mother must have lived. It was still so unbelievable, even as abstract as it was.

Kaya said, "She always talked to me about the wonders of your age and of her dreams for the future. She wanted to see us return to that golden age. I only learned about the eternal dream recently, but I think she wanted to make it a reality again."

Leopold pursed his lips.

"What is it?"

He hesitated, perhaps searching for the right words. "I'm not sure it was ever a reality, although she and others certainly tried to make it one."

"But you didn't?"

Leopold clenched his jaw. "To my lasting shame, no. It always seemed a utopian fantasy to me. Maybe there's still a way to undo this mess and make it a reality, but for now, I don't see know." His answer wasn't satisfying, but at least it felt honest. That was more than Kaya could say about others she had dealt with lately.

They sat in silence as transport vessels began floating into view and landing near the *Rubah*, throwing up clouds of dust. It didn't take long before the area had become a miniature spaceport. She was surprised by how soldiers from the *Rubah's* crew were able to converse with the Imperials despite the language and cultural barriers. This might have been what it was like when ancient humans explored

Earth and discovered unknown neighbors. They would draw symbols in the sand and use universal hand gestures to communicate. It was a testament to the human spirit to identify its own and connect with them, no matter the time and place.

"From the way you attacked Aelius back there, I'm guessing we all have some history to work through," Kaya said, trying to gauge how volatile that particular relationship would be.

"I have been blaming him for all of this for a long time but seeing him again now makes me doubt my conclusions."

Kaya didn't understand. "What does Aelius have to do with the Iron Cage?"

"It was Aelius who pushed for it to be built and his acolyte Widukind who made it reality. It was built to guard against asteroids and other existential threats. My father supported the project, while your mother and I, among others, warned against it." Leopold's features returned to the rigid form she had come to associate with him. "When disaster came, it was easy for me to draw conclusions, but I must admit blowing up a planet while you remain on it seems especially nonsensical. Particularly for a man like Aelius, who values his life so highly."

Kaya never thought of Aelius as being reckless. Everything he did had a clear objective and logical choice behind it. That he was the force behind the Iron Cage to begin with surprised her, but it would explain how he knew a way around it. "If Aelius is responsible for the Iron Cage, why do we need Widukind? Couldn't we make Aelius provide you with what's needed?"

"Last time I saw him, he was searching for Widukind like the rest of us," Leopold said, scratching his chin. "I always believed they conspired together to create this disaster, but now I'm not sure. Maybe Aelius was trying to fix things all along."

"We can add finding the truth of what happened with the Iron Cage to our objectives," she offered, hopping off the large rock. She knew she would have to confront Aelius as well. He had been unwilling to share his secrets with her as a prophet, but maybe as her grandfather he would be more open. The thought felt foreign and uncomfortable. What she really wanted to do was find her mother and let *her* explain the truth.

Leopold nodded. "Will what I have told you impact our arrangement?" At first, she thought he might be joking with her, but, no, he was being serious.

"We all have history to unravel," she said, looking up at him.

"Your calmness is a model for my own behavior," he offered.

"Sarding hell, I'm barely holding it together," she said, trying not to laugh or cry. "On that note, I need to go start planning or I will collapse completely."

Leopold smirked. "Go, you're too young to be as depressing as me," he said, waving her away with his mechanical arm. The sight of it made her think of one other thing.

"How did you end up with a metal arm?" she said, thinking of what Aelius had said. She wondered if he had something to do with it.

"I got tired of replacing the original," he said without turning back to look at her. "Maybe one day I will tell you the tales."

Kaya blinked in amazement. He spoke so casually of losing his arm not only once but multiple times. She had a lot to learn and understand about the ways of the ageless.

Walking back to the ship, she tried to keep her mind focused on the most immediate problems. First and foremost was making room for everyone on board, making sure they all don't kill each other, and then getting off this planet safely.

Reina came to meet her on the gangway. "How's the archduke doing?"

Kaya looked back to see him still sitting on the same rock. "Hard to say. He's been through more than I can imagine. I'm guessing if he made it this far, he'll be okay."

"Not sure I would mind if he wanted to strangle the old man again," Reina said and then tried to back pedal.

"It's fine," Kaya said, stopping her. "He can say he's my grandfather, but that doesn't make it real to me. I know as much about him now as I did before that news. That is, he's a stranger to me."

"You still need to be careful of the archduke. I don't think he's cruel or malevolent, but there is a hardness to him I can't really explain," Reina said worriedly. "He may as well be an alien."

"I don't plan to let my guard down, but for now what choice do we have? It's not like I trust Aelius or Theodore any more than I trust Leopold. Everyone seems to have some secret agenda, but right now we need all of them."

"You might be mad at them, but don't forget they've done a lot to keep you safe up till now. Maybe more than either of us knows," Reina said, crossing her arms.

"How is Rudra and the others?" Kaya said, preferring to change the subject. She needed to keep her mind in the present.

"Calm for now but anxious to get off this planet. We'll need to figure out what we are telling people about the Imperials though."

She pulled Reina aside so they could make room for the soldiers and mechanics coming in and out with supplies. "We can't let any of this information leave the ship, which also means we can't go back to the Pandora Fleet."

"That makes sense. We'll have to come up with a cover story." Reina added in a whisper, "So it's to Neptune then?"

Kaya nodded, and then she had a thought. "Do you have any way to contact the fleet discreetly?"

Reina raised an eyebrow. "Maybe, why?"

"I don't fully trust everything that's going on. I think we need to let them know where we are going. But it should be too late for them to stop us by the time they know."

"It's risky, but I guess it could be worse if they think we're dead. There's no telling what chaos that news could cause. They might already assume we are honestly."

"We'll give the messengers a cover story, but I assume they will send someone after us when they can. I want a head start, but I don't want to be truly alone in the Far Coast. There's too much that can go wrong."

Reina rubbed her chin. "I guess maybe you were paying attention during all those meetings back with Prometheus."

Kaya exhaled and pushed past Reina. "Come on, I could use your help. You used to be a Pandora Fleet officer, right? I need to pick your brain about how to get a handle on all this madness. Then we need to talk to the captain about getting off this rock."

Silas

August, 4103 U.E.T. – *Specter*, Luna

THE HULL OF THE *Specter* shook rhythmically as the fleet unleashed their fury like ancient gods on those that displeased them.

Silas watched from the screens on the bridge as the guns fired and hit their targets on the surface. Energy domes surged, some crumbling under the onslaught, while other targets disappeared completely in brilliant flashes of light and flame. He didn't watch long enough to see the dust settle.

For the past two weeks, they had begun ramping up their operations on Luna and everything was proceeding brilliantly. They had secured the docks with the help of Orzone and his pirates, which gave them opportunities for limited resupplies and repairs.

Until they made landfall, they still had to contend with Lunese attempts to disrupt their orbital operations, but the enemy's ability to do so was decreasing.

There were many attempts to destroy the dockyards and orbiting vessels utilizing long-range weapons systems from the surface, but they never managed more than a handful of successful strikes. The fleet's missile defense systems were more than capable of defending the docks, but Silas knew they couldn't keep up with the near constant barrage indefinitely.

With their orbital superiority, the fleet was able to operate with relative impunity, but they didn't have enough ships to blockade the entire moon. All they could reliably do was control the docks and stop any larger ships from leaving the surface.

"We should have burned the whole sarding moon. Drop the thermos and be done with it," Lancaster said. He had been a vocal critic of their current plan and continued to suggest a more violent and permanent approach.

The *Specter* carried several large thermonuclear weapons, the kind that could turn a large target to glass. Weapons Silas had no intention of using.

"That isn't why we came here," Silas repeated, mostly for the benefit of the nearby crew. He wanted them to know they didn't come here as conquerors set on destruction. "Status on target vector?"

"Approaching launch window, T-minus one hour," the bridge officer replied. Silas flexed his armored hand, knowing it would be time soon enough for him to enter the fray, but for now he would wait and command.

As their formation orbited Luna, they had made it a point to target a specific array of cities and installations throughout the surface.

They started with the largest-known orbital guns and long-range rail guns before beginning their systematic assault on hostile military installations. They softened targets in diverse locations, which ate into their munitions store but worked well to hide their true target. They would rescue the duchess, but first they had to make landfall.

"Lancaster, you have the bridge."

"Aye, Your Grace, give them hell." The man still seemed annoyed but saluted before turning back to his screens. Silas could hear him shouting orders as he left the bridge.

He wasn't sure where Marcus had gone off to. He had become increasingly aloof in recent days, but Silas lacked the time to figure out what was going on. He felt confident Marcus would be there for the launch of their ground offensive, and that was good enough.

Silas decided weeks earlier that leading from the surface was the only way he would undertake any of this. He would not have men and women die under his command while he stayed tucked away in orbit. His honor would never allow it.

He stepped into the massive rear hangar bay, which served as one of the primary muster points for the ship. Men-at-arms snapped to attention as they saw him, and he could hear cries of "God wills it and Pandora eternal."

Some even called, "For the king!" as he passed.

He had tried to stop the spread of that last lunacy, but it hardly worked. It felt like the more he denied them, the louder they clamored for him to take up a crown.

General Taylor stood near the center of the formations, overseeing their organization. Unlike Lancaster, he had been an enthusiastic supporter of their plan to ally with the pirates and liberate Luna from the Republic forces. Taylor wanted to set the world on a better path as much as Silas did. In the past two weeks, he had become vital to the assembly of their ground forces and indispensable as one of his advisors.

So much so that Silas had found it necessary to promote him to General of the Pandora Fleet, a new rank to ensure no one questioned his command over the assembled forces. He was the most experienced and capable ground commander they had, and squabbles between officers now would only get men killed. That reality expedited the need to establish a new chain of command that worked in their current situation.

Hayashi stood beside Taylor, aiding in the organization of the units. As he knew the land best, he had volunteered to be amongst the first on the ground. As a result, Silas had given him the acting rank of colonel. He would retain that rank so long as he remained with the fleet, or a more formal restructuring could be completed.

"Your Grace," Taylor said with a bow as he approached. The senior command had tried to insist he take on the moniker of king, since the "lowly" rank of high commander would no longer suffice. However, he continued to voice his displeasure at the idea, and they eventually conceded to using his noble title as Duke of Mars.

That was enough for Silas to freely promote and lead both naval and army officers without question. Such as the Lunese generals and admirals who had joined their cause.

"General, Colonel," he said, saluting them both, "it seems the men are in order for the launch."

"They are, Your Grace. It's been hundreds of years since such a fearsome force was assembled in one place," Taylor said, his eyes full of pride. "When we studied this manner of warfare at the academy in New Olympia, I scoffed. I never in my life imagined those lessons would be useful."

Silas grinned. "I don't imagine any of us did. I hope you paid attention though." Then he added more quietly, "I hope we all did. Where's Marcus?"

"I haven't seen him yet, Your Grace," Taylor said.

It was very unlike Marcus, Silas thought, but maybe he was trying to find a snack for the ride down to the surface. "Has Bishop Vesivi completed his benediction?"

"Yes, final checks on gear are being completed now before the troops file into the drop pods."

"I haven't heard any contrary reports, so I assume the pods were in serviceable condition?" Silas said, watching as men and women checked weapons and organized their gear amongst their units.

"We had to clean out some cobwebs. Even found one that had been turned into a secret lounge full of commandeered booze, but they are serviceable," Taylor said.

"The spirits or the drop pods?" he asked with a raised eyebrow.

Taylor laughed. "When we return from the surface, we can find out together, My Liege." Silas grabbed his forearm and truly hoped they would get the chance.

"I don't think anyone wants to hear me give anymore speeches, so I will keep this brief. Who has volunteered for the vanguard?" Silas said.

"The 1st Battalion of the 3rd Pandora Infantry Brigade came forward. It seemed fitting I honor their request," Taylor said solemnly.

Silas nodded. "I expected the Cloud Splitters would be the ones to volunteer for the vanguard, but I couldn't in good faith assign them myself. It seems like we will be continuing the theme of resurrecting old traditions. There is one more that I think deserves a revival. Where is the battalion forming?"

"This way, Your Grace," Taylor said, pointing across the hangar bay.

Silas made his way to the indicated location with Taylor and Hayashi close behind him. The Cloud Splitters had earned their battalion's nickname for being the first to split the clouds of Venus and make landfall during the Great Solar War.

They had earned immortal glory at the cost of one of the highest casualty counts of the entire war. Although the scale was admittedly different, Silas anticipated the results would be similar here.

Grizzled veterans shouted, and soldiers snapped into position, standing tightly at attention as he passed. He studied their faces, maintaining his own neutral expression. The vast majority were little more than children, save for the sergeants with their scarred and tired faces or the occasional officer in their standard-issue gray exoarmor. In reality, most of the officers were only marginally older than the troops they led.

The knights of his force, the officers who stood at the front of their formations were the only ones who wore exoarmor. Most chose to carry lightning pikes and rifles, with ceramic blades at their hips. Only a very small minority carried plasma blades.

The rest of the troops carried rifles and wore basic ballistic resistant vests and helmets. At best their body armor would stop small arms fire. They would all carry enough gear to survive the initial forty-eight hours of the invasion. After that, they would either be dead or resupplied.

The Republic's military doctrine had always called for overwhelming numbers, followed by reinforcing any success. It was expected the casualties would be high amongst the men-at-arms, but the officers, in their superior equipment, could rally survivors. He wouldn't send his men into the meat grinder unnecessarily, but this type of operation necessitated a high level of risk.

Silas stopped in front of Major Thompson, the commanding officer of the Cloud Splitter Battalion. She was a middle-aged woman with a stern expression and an iron will. Her hair was cut short to her scalp, and her face was tattooed with intricate geometric designs. An Armanic tradition from deep on the ice moons of the Far Coast.

He saluted. "Major, we honor the bravery and strength of your unit. You will throw open the gates, and we shall be the flood that brings new life to this land."

"God wills it!" she shouted, fire in her eyes. Her accent was thick, her voice commanding. The formation behind her cried out, "Pandora eternal!"

Energy coursed along his skin, and he felt the familiar allure of combat. The romantic ideal that sat far removed from the bloody reality.

He stepped away from the major to address the rest of the formation, looking from one youthful face to the next. He raised his voice so those in the back could hear. "Who among you will carry our colors first onto this new world. Plant the flag that will lead your brothers and sisters to victory?"

He let his words hang in the air. No matter how much they weakened the surface, the drop pods were made to be light, cheap, and fast. That meant if they were hit, the chance for survival was almost nonexistent. This was especially true for the first among them and the average soldiers strapped inside who wore no exoarmor.

When Silas thought he might need to repeat himself, a soft voice called out, "I will, sir."

"Step forward soldier," he said, searching for the source of the voice.

A young man, likely younger than his nephew Henry, stepped out in front of him. His face looked innocent and hopeful. He wore a field medic's pouch on his thigh. His skin was pale white, and he looked to be from the Far Coast. Silas said a silent prayer for this poor child.

"What is your name, soldier?"

"Corporal Jordan Smith, sir," the boy said, his eyes locked forward. Silas could see his body trembling slightly, but he felt no criticism. Any man or woman brave enough to step forward deserved every ounce of his respect.

"You're Lunese, Corporal Smith?" Silas said, a bit surprised by the accent that wasn't what he expected.

"Yes, sir," the boy said nervously. "Well, I was born on Enceladus, sir," he added quickly.

Silas gave him a reassuring smile. "Today we will all become Lunese, no matter where we were born. We will all embrace this land as if it were our own and see it set on the correct path. The honorable and Godly path," he said, motioning to an aid who handed him a folded bundle of cloth. "Hold out your hands."

The boy held out shaky hands, and Silas placed the bundle into them. "This is the flag of our fleet and my personal banner. Corporal Smith, I entrust you to fly them proudly once landfall is made," he said, raising his voice. "Do you swear it?"

The boy paused, looking down at the bundle and then back to Silas. "I...I swear it, Sir. Pandora eternal, for the king!" he shouted. His eyes gleamed brightly, and the others behind him took up the cheer.

Silas reached into a compartment of his exoarmor for one last item, a gold pin with the Pandora Fleet emblem on it. He pinned it to the boy's uniform.

"Let this mark you as the first and bravest to step foot on this foreign land. May your torch guide us all through the darkness," he said, using the ancient words. He stepped back and saluted, expecting to never see the boy again.

As the cheers raged on, an alarm sounded signaling they were in position to begin the initial drop. At his direction, Major Thompson shouted commands, and troops began filing down the tight tunnels that would lead them into their drop pods. Silas returned to where Taylor and Hayashi stood issuing their own commands. Marcus had arrived at some point and stood with them, appearing armored and ready.

"Everything okay?" he asked when he saw Marcus.

"Yeah, all good."

Silas thought he sounded off but didn't have time to question it now.

"Your Grace, we're still clear for the agreed upon targets in the city of Lassell. Once initial landfall is established, I will follow behind with the bulk of our forces. From there, we will surround the Bishop of Lassel's estate, and you and the remainder of the troops can descend," Taylor said.

"Good, thank you, General. Colonel Hayashi, I'll need you to remain by my side. I will need your knowledge of the local bishop's palace and its layout."

"Yes, Your Grace. My family estate is not far from it, and I have visited on many occasions."

"Good, if no one has anything else, let us prepare for launch. May God be with you. Malum contineri debet," he said, embracing Taylor's forearm.

Taylor grinned widely. "Hopefully the next time I see you I will be sitting on the bishop's throne, drinking his finest whisky."

Silas returned Taylor's enthusiasm, but Marcus remained oddly quiet. "God wills it. Let us spread the light."

Taylor left with his men to begin boarding their own transport craft. Silas used a digipad one of his aids handed him to watch as the first pods departed from the *Specter*.

The Cloud Splitters had an unenviable but vital job of establishing a safe landing zone. Their intel on the Lunese ground forces was limited to what their sensors, cameras, and Hayashi could provide. He only prayed the information was good enough to avoid catastrophe.

The command team had concluded the city of Lassell was not likely to be considered a prime target and would therefore be less defended. However, less defended on a moon that supported billions of souls was relative. There would still be an array of anti-air defenses and enemy troops on the ground. But if they could gain a foothold in Lassell, they could begin their march to the archbishop's castle on the Selenean Summit.

They were thousands against millions, and all the orbital guns in the nine worlds wouldn't completely even those odds. Not if they wanted to keep the moon habitable, he thought dryly.

The screen displayed dozens of different camera angles as the pods began dropping into the Lunese atmosphere. The screen flashed red and bright as the pods burned through the denser layers, before their velocity slowed and the moon's gravity reeled them into the surface. Anti-air batteries on the surface began firing as they came into range, and he was forced to switch camera feeds several times as pods were blown to pieces.

The fleet's guns returned the favor by raining fire on the gun batteries that revealed themselves. Then the parachutes began to deploy, one and then another. In several long moments, the drop pods began making landfall like barnacles on an ancient sea beast. Soldiers crawled out to meet the enemy, which was scrambling to react.

From what he could see, it looked like their decision had been the correct one. The enemy didn't anticipate Lassell would be their target and had left it lightly defended. The soldiers who successfully landed sent their success back to the fleet, and those close enough to hear the news cheered wildly.

Silas handed off the digipad and motioned to Marcus and Hayashi. "Come on, let's prepare for launch. We need to be amongst our men for this."

He heard the siren song of battle calling and didn't want to be left behind. This was the beginning of creating the new world God had entrusted to him, and he needed to be there for it.

CHAPTER

23

Silas

August, 4103 U.E.T. – Lassell, Luna

Silas's heart raced as he saw his men-at-arms bravely surmount the fortifications of the palace. The Lunese managed to rally and put up a strong fight for hours as the fleet's pods continued to land. He didn't know how costly the initial landing had been, but they had been successful in establishing a foothold.

Silas dropped with the rear guard, which included the armored units and mobile artillery. They didn't have enough of this equipment to risk any of it in the initial assault, but thankfully the majority had made it to the surface intact. For the sake of safety, Silas had also arrived aboard a small corvette that would serve as their mobile command station. The vessel dropped them now in a large landing pad outside the bishop's estate.

What had struck Silas the most was that Marcus had spent the entire trip without eating a single thing. Instead, he seemed to go through the motions as if in a dream. Silas resolved to speak with him when they had a moment, but the events of the past several weeks hadn't provided an opportunity. His focus was his mission, and that had taken all his attention.

The estate was surrounded by large, manicured gardens that stretched out for several acres. There was even a pond in one of the many small craters that defined the Lunese surface. Scorched ground and lifeless bodies could be seen all around from the battle that had concluded as they arrived. Several large hover tanks positioned themselves in the middle of the garden, pointed at the estate.

"This way," Hayashi said, signaling for their small assault team to follow.

In the distance, Silas saw his troops pouring into the main entrance to search for any surviving enemy combatants and most of all for the local bishop. The bishop was the official leader of the city of Lassell, so capturing him was a priority.

Entering the building, Silas drew his plasma blade, anticipating the close quarters. They rushed as a team toward the sound of gunfire. They found a small cluster of white and gold armored Frumentarii knights that had a unit of their men pinned down.

Silas didn't hesitate as he ran them down, his blade in front of him. His armor's shield sparked brilliantly as they fired at him ineffectively with their rifles. They had been prepared to fight regular soldiers, not a squad of equally armored knights.

Silas slammed into the first, throwing him to the ground as he spun around in a wide arc with his blade. He heard the plasma slam into the enemy's shield, and he held it there as it overheated the mechanism.

Hayashi meanwhile came to his side with his ceramic blade drawn. He slashed out with a series of quick and precise strikes that pierced the other knight's shield, slicing into his armor.

Marcus came into the room last, but by the time he did, the small cluster of guards had been overwhelmed and dispatched. Silas was impressed by Hayashi's fighting ability and welcomed a strong swordsman by his side.

The guards had been protecting an ornate-looking door. They moved into position, and Silas motioned to Marcus to open it. The door swung open, and Hayashi moved in first, followed by Silas. They raised their blades, ready to continue the fight, but then lowered them when it was clear there was no immediate threat.

"By God's Bones," Silas said, dismayed by what he saw.

"I believe this is, or perhaps was, the bishop's son. A symptom of the disease," Hayashi said, stepping from the room. His face was painted with disgust.

In the room was a large, cushioned bed covered in plush pillows and expensive sheets. In the center was a young man lying beside his courtesans. Strewn between their unconscious bodies were copious amounts of empty bottles and the remnants of what looked like nectar cartridges. Their world was crumbling around them, and this was how they chose to approach it. The thought sickened him.

Silas motioned to a pair of his soldiers that entered behind them. "See if they are breathing. If they are, secure them with the others."

"I can sort out this mess," Marcus offered. "Make sure no one wastes a potentially useful prisoner."

Silas hesitated but then nodded. He wanted Marcus by his side, but with his current sluggish state he was of limited use. "Find us once they're secured."

Marcus saluted, and Silas left with Hayashi and the rest of their squad to find the bishop. He assumed they wouldn't be far away, but he relied on Hayashi to lead him through the corridor of rooms. It was obvious that Hayashi had been here before, and he moved with the purpose of someone who had an unsettled score. Silas had mused from the beginning that this bishop may have been among those who plotted against Hayashi's father and by extension the duchess.

Although the estate grounds were large, there wasn't much fight left in its occupants. By the time they had stormed the inner wall and subdued the few Frumentarii knights who remained, the regular soldiers surrendered. They understandably didn't want to throw away their lives in a fight they couldn't win.

In the end, the city had fallen in as little as a few hours, but it had taken weeks of planning. Not to mention the element of surprise. Even with their success, he had no delusions. They couldn't take and hold much more than this one city without the support of the Lunese military. At least now they had proven they could win.

His soldiers saluted or cheered as he strode through the hall. It appeared the fighting had stopped. He sent a message to the forward units, requesting a status update.

The cool voice of Major Thompson replied, "All clear, sir. We have the objective, main audience chamber."

Silas was elated that for once an operation had gone smoothly. It felt like a lifetime since he could say that, and he reached out to slap Marcus on the shoulder out of habit, instead hitting Hayashi before realizing his mistake. Silas played it off.

He only heard sporadic gunshots in the distance, so he retracted his helmet and snuffed his blade. Hayashi did the same, sheathing his ceramic blade.

"You've won the first of many victories, Lord Beckett," Hayashi said, smiling as they passed through a covered promenade, broken glass and stonework crunching under their boots.

"The men have won it, by the grace of God. I had very little to do with it."

"Then you must have guided God's hand to the proper place."

"I didn't take you for such a theist," Silas said with a grin.

"I think you may have converted me, Your Grace. The audience chamber is this way,"

They entered the grand room and found the bishop, a robust and round man, standing defiantly before his silvery throne. His bodyguards were dead at his feet, and Major Thompson stood holding her lightning pike to his throat.

The bishop became animated as Silas approached, his arms waving wildly. His long beard made him resemble an ancient prophet from old Earth. "My Lord, it's not too late to repent your sins and seek forgiveness from God and his servants in this world. You have fallen victim to false prophets and lies from the devil himself, but-"

"Silence," Silas commanded. "You're not here to speak for God but for yourself and the people of this city you have betrayed."

The bishop stammered, "I have remained loyal to God and his voice and hand in this world. Through them, I have led my flock toward their future salvation in the Celestial City."

Hayashi stepped forward to confront the man. "My father came to you with plans to repair one of our mid district's water systems. Do you remember what you told him?"

"I don't see what that has to do with any of this," the bishop said, his face flushing.

Silas nodded, and Major Thompson pressed the blade of her pike closer to his throat. "Answer, cleric."

"I...I do not recall," the bishop said, sheepishly.

"Then let me refresh your memory. You refused to allow the manufacture of the necessary equipment. Do you remember now why you did that?" Hayashi continued, as no response came, "I suspect you don't, since these occurrences were so frequent. You stated that if the machinery broke, it was because the people of that district have fallen out of God's favor. That they would have to pray for their water to be fixed. That you could only do as God directed and no more. All while you sat comfortably in your palace, benefiting from their toils."

"We must all pray for God's blessing," the bishop said, attempting to seem apologetic.

"Tens of thousands died during the outbreaks of illness that followed. All because you chose not to act," Hayashi snarled, drawing his ceramic blade.

"It was God's will! Our resources are limited and must be saved for people worthy of God's love."

Silas stepped forward. "That's enough." He put a hand on Hayashi's shoulder and pulled him back and waved Major Thompson aside. "Do you not deny these allegations, Bishop?"

"I was only following God's command," he said, spreading his hands with a bowed head.

Silas had known too many bishops like this man. Men and women more concerned with maintaining their own lives than improving the lives of others. They paid lip service to God while lounging in their palaces and partaking in every vice imaginable.

"The shepherd does not expect his sheep to wait for the rain," he said angrily. "You had a chance to help these people but failed to do so. You had another chance now to repent your own sins before me and God, but again you have failed to show any remorse."

"You have come as a conqueror and an apostate. Only my heavenly brothers and sisters who sit above me may legally judge my actions. I have always acted within the law," the bishop added, and Silas shook his head.

The bishop was right that he was the one in breach of the law, but the law was unjust to the people it served. It went against the laws of nature, and therefore God, that so many would die for the benefit of so few.

He looked for Marcus again, looking for his guidance but only found Hayashi grinning menacingly. Then Silas's mind turned to the image of Catherine burning in Trinity Square and the fiery angel that had come to visit him. He knew what he had been sent here to do, even if he disliked it.

"I have come with my own heavenly edict. Only from the ash can something new be born," he said, recalling the angel that had visited him. He didn't long for violence, but the choice was no longer his.

The bishop's eyes went wide as realization began to hit him.

"My Lord, you misunderstood. If only we can discuss this further and come to some suitable arrangements. I can provide funding and manpower to facilitate your campaign and-"

"No bishop, *you* misunderstand. This is not a business transaction. I'm not here out of greed, and you have already proven no desire to help the people you claim to serve. There is no more room in this world for people who claim superiority but add no value. Colonel Hayashi, is there a main square in the city?"

"Yes, Your Grace. It's not far away."

The bishop dropped to his knees. Ugly tears streamed from his face as he fully realized his precarious position. Silas looked down at him in disgust, not only for the man but also for himself.

That there had been a time Silas thought men like these could lead and shape the world. He had stood back and helped them remain in power all these years, and that made him equally guilty. He only hoped now he could begin to set things right.

"Take the bishop and see to the arrangements for his execution," Silas said.

Hayashi didn't hesitate in hauling the man up by the collar of his robes.

"Please, Your Grace. I demand a trial, as is my right by law."

"The laws of the Republic no longer hold sway here," he said coldly.

"Then I demand amnesty. You say you are a man of God. Why then succumb to the ancient and evil ways of the Empire? I have never heard anyone suggest Lord Beckett was an imperialist."

Silas paused, eyeing the man. He was clever to raise this point, because it was one Silas could not easily refute. What he was doing now was exactly what the clergy had warned against for centuries and why they worked so diligently to dismantle the nobility. Except Silas knew he wasn't here for his own prestige or power. He was here because God demanded it.

"Hollow accusations from a hollow man. We are the torch in the darkness, Bishop. Now you can turn your prayers to lighting the path for your soul. Take him away," Silas said and turned to leave the room, no longer listening to the man's pleas.

In another life, he might have offered amnesty, but not now. Diana was dead, and his daughter was lying near death aboard the *Specter*. He didn't blame the regular people of Luna for any of that. Instead, he blamed men and women like this bishop and himself for allowing these callous practices to continue.

His joy at their victory was quickly overshadowed by this grim new reality. Silas wondered, not for the first time, if he could see this through to the end. If he could fulfill the mission God had entrusted to him. Hearing the bishop's screams as they dragged him toward the city square, he thought the answer might be no.

Kaya

August, 4103 U.E.T. – *Rubah,* Earth

KAYA RECEIVED A CRASH course on military organization from Reina, but it was a grain of sand on the beach of things she didn't understand.

She tried to remember everything her parents and tutors had ever taught her about civil administration and logistics, but she was no less overwhelmed. There were hundreds of problems to solve, and she had foolishly inserted herself as the person to solve them.

It was exactly what she wanted, control, but it came at the cost of having to make decisions that impacted hundreds of others. They had taken to using the conference room adjacent to the bridge to host these regular planning meetings. They were down to the final details now, and Kaya was anxious to move to the next stage of their mission.

Leopold spoke from the opposite end of the large table. "In total, there will be approximately four hundred ageless knights who will be accompanying me on our mission. In addition to all their equipment and supplies. The rest will remain here to manage the local populations."

Kaya had been amazed to find out the true extent of life left on Earth. There were dozens of large domed estates and hundreds of predominantly underground bunker communities, as Leopold called them.

The captain looked at Leopold apprehensively. "I don't know that we can support so many."

"What is the main issue stopping us? We can find space in the hangar bays and common areas to temporarily house the extra people," Kaya offered.

"It's a long way to Neptune," Reina said, studying the array of charts and graphs spread out on the table. "It's going to be hard enough to keep the regular crew calm for such a long journey. Without adding in that most of these people had never stepped foot on a space craft up until a few weeks ago."

"It isn't even that, although you are absolutely correct," Captain Masoumi said. "The ageless will come with their own expectations and their own unique needs. They are like locusts in a field. They will consume everything if we're not careful."

Kaya looked at Leopold, who seemed annoyed at being compared to an insect but offered no rebuttal.

Kaya adjusted her hair while she thought. She couldn't leave without them, that much was obvious. So they would either need to try their best to deal with the problems that arise or come up with a novel solution. "You've been able to keep yourself, Theodore, and who knows how many other ageless here all these years."

Kaya hadn't been surprised when it was revealed Captain Masoumi was among the ageless. If there were others on board from what she thought of as her old life, she wasn't yet aware.

Captain Masoumi flicked through a stack of papers before finding what she was looking for and handing it to Kaya. It was a projection of their estimated food consumption. "We were only a few people with an otherwise small crew. It was hardly much of a strain, all things considered. If we're committed to bringing four hundred or more ageless, that will nearly double our normal crew size. Adding in the Coalition members...maybe we need to consider leaving some of them behind. They would be safe here until we can come back for them."

"No," Kaya said flatly. "I will not abandon these people here on a dead planet. Not after everything they've done for us, for me." She had plenty of apprehensions about her role as their leader. It was a role she didn't ask for, but if they insisted on her to do it, she wouldn't betray their trust.

Theodore leaned forward in his chair. "Captain, can we physically take off from the surface here with the weight we are carrying?"

The captain looked to be making some calculations in her head. "We don't have the final totals, but I think so. It is within the margin for wartime specs.

The *Rubah* was originally designed to launch from Earth's surface, which is lucky for us. Although, I don't see how that helps us solve any of the other problems. Unless we plan to leave people with the Pandora Fleet instead."

Kaya agreed that most of what had happened did seem incredibly lucky, but she was losing faith in the power of luck. There were far too many coincidences that pointed to an unseen hand that was guiding recent events. Now the real question was whether that hand belonged to God or someone else. Like a certain prophet, maybe. At her request, Aelius had not been included in their meetings.

"No, we can't leave anyone with the fleet. The stories they would tell will create havoc. I hate to agree with Aelius, but he's right that the people aren't ready for this news. At least not all at once," Kaya said.

Theodore said, "I agree with Lady Kaya. There is no benefit in us leaving so many people behind to create confusion. We need to keep our departure from Earth a secret for as long as possible."

Leopold had remained largely silent throughout the day's discussion. Maybe out of preference or some desire to allow Kaya and the others the freedom to take charge. Now he sat with a bit of a bemused expression.

"Do you have something to add, Your Highness," Kaya asked.

"I find it amusing that I went from commanding fleets of dreadnoughts to playing castaway on a rickety old antique. No offense," Leopold said to Captain Masoumi with a charismatic smirk. "That said, we have enough gold and credit chips in our treasury to rebuild an armada. Surely there is still somewhere between here and Neptune where we can purchase additional vessels. Unless the world is further gone than you've let on."

They all looked at Leopold, and no one seemed to have a response. It was a simple solution, but she hadn't considered it at all. If the others had, they never brought it up.

Leopold held his arms out wide. "Must be why they left me in charge. I am full of great ideas." He began tapping his mechanical fingers on the table as he was oft to do.

"We can't exactly keep a low profile while throwing around that kind of wealth. Not to mention ships this size can't be freely bought and sold without government approval," Reina said.

"Maybe we need to steal one," Kaya offered.

Leopold waved dismissively. "I trust you very smart and capable people will be able to sort all of that out. There is something more important and immediate we need to discuss."

Kaya subconsciously tensed at the prospect of new secrets being revealed. If she didn't have a heart condition before all of this, she would surely have one before it was all over.

"Aelius said Widukind was being held by the Venatores before your mother freed him. What do we know about their current capabilities?"

Kaya looked at Reina, hoping she would have some idea of what he was talking about. Kaya had heard Aelius use that word but had no idea what it meant. Reina didn't seem to know either. With Aelius not in the room, they turned to look at Theodore and the captain.

Theodore said, "This is the first time I am hearing of them in a very, very long time. I always assumed they dissolved as an organization after the Great Purge."

Masoumi shrugged. "I haven't heard any recent mention of them either. The idea that they're back is...unsettling. I was finally getting used to not constantly looking over my shoulder."

"Maybe you can explain to the rest of us who or what the Venatores are?" Kaya asked, leaning forward.

"Traitors who abandoned the Empire and turned to hunting ageless for the theists," Leopold said, his disgust obvious.

"They were the foundation of the original Frumentarii," Theodore added.

"So they were...are ageless?" Kaya said, correcting herself. If they were ageless, it was possible they were still alive.

"The original Venatores were, but I haven't heard of one being seen anywhere in centuries at least. News of something like that would have traveled fast through our small circle," Theodore said.

"How many could they possibly be? Is this something we even need to worry about?" Kaya looked at Reina. It felt like a small thing considering all their other problems, but when she looked at the faces of the ageless, they all seemed genuinely concerned. Surely the 400 ageless with them would be enough to handle a few Frumentarii bounty hunters.

"Maybe it isn't," Leopold offered with a wave of his hand. "I've been gone a long time, and maybe they aren't what they once were."

"If they were murderers and cowards, then not much has changed," Kaya said.

Leopold smirked. "That might be true of the Frumentarii you described to me, but the original organization, from which the Venatores originated, were the elite of the elite. Chosen for their strength, valor, and intelligence above everything else. They served the Empire for generations and distinguished themselves during the Great War."

Kaya's face scrunched. "I'm not sure I understand. You make it sound like they would be valuable allies."

Leopold seemed to consider that. "No, I'm afraid not."

Theodore spoke, as if he was navigating a field of land mines. "When the Emperor decided to invest so heavily in the Sanctuary ark project it created a rift among the nobility. Particularly between forces like the Venatores who had been on the front lines of the conflict for a very long time."

Kaya looked at Leopold clenching his jaw. Even now this seemed like a sour subject for him. "So what happened?"

"They were the first to switch sides. Given how embedded they were in the Imperial culture and hierarchy, they made exceptional ageless hunters for the fledgling Republic," Theodore said, looking uneasily at Leopold.

Kaya knew she wouldn't understand all this history anytime soon, but she got the idea. The Venatores were angry and dangerous and would happily kill them. Well, they would have to get in line, she supposed. They had a long list of enemies who wanted them dead now.

"Let's compile what we know and see what else we can squeeze out of Aelius. Maybe that's a good job for you, Your Highness," Kaya said before imagining Leopold strangling him for a second time. "Or maybe we can have someone else talk to him first."

"That might be best," Leopold said as if reading her mind.

Kaya stood from the table, and the others minus Leopold followed. The formality of it was still jarring. She held no formal title, position, or military rank, but they treated her with the deference her father would normally receive. "Captain, let me know as soon as we're ready for the final checklists and launch procedure."

Captain Masoumi saluted, "The best launch window will be here in the next day or so. I plan for us to be ready then."

"Good, I'll be in my quarters if I'm needed. Reina, walk with me please," Kaya said, leaving the room and making her way toward the small room she continued to call her own.

Theodore had offered for her to take the main cabin on the ship, but she had opted on keeping this one. It was small but large enough for her and Reina to share comfortably. The truth was she spent so little time in her quarters that it hardly mattered.

Besides, she enjoyed filling the large suite Theodore occupied with Leopold and his retinue. They had to make use of what space they could so everyone had to share.

"You needed something, princess?" Reina said, stepping beside her.

"Yes, so many things, but I'm losing track of where to even start."

"One step at a time, according to the plan."

"What if I'd rather run off the ship and live with the bunker people. Their lives seem so simple and peaceful," she said, carelessly.

Reina looked confused. "Peaceful? How do you figure that? Even if they don't fight each other with swords and spears..."

Reina raised a finger for emphasis. "But I'm sure they probably do mind you. They still fight things like hunger and thirst, like the people in the slums back on Mars. War comes in many forms, and all of us struggle. Don't ever think your pain is worse than another person's because it seems more complex. Dying in a ditch from hunger is a slow and painful process. Much more so than a blade to the chest. To suffer through life knowing that is a possibility takes a kind of bravery and strength neither of us knows anything about."

Kaya felt embarrassed that she had suggested anything of the sort. "Well, hopefully we don't all die trying to get off this dusty rock. First, we need to hope this overstuffed holiday fowl can fly and then hope Aelius and Captain Masoumi can find the opening in the Iron Cage a second time. Very simple." Kaya swiped her badge to open the door to their room.

"Well, we also need to go meet with Rudra and the Coalition members. Give them a pep talk before things get bumpy again. We can also give them the option to stay here if they prefer, but I doubt many will take that offer."

Kaya sniffed her shirt as she stepped into the doorway. "Let me change, and I'll meet you there. I think I've been in the same clothes for a couple days now."

"I thought I smelled something ripe," Reina said, scrunching her nose. Kaya slammed the door in her face.

A knock came a few minutes later.

Maybe it was time to find a new room and not tell anyone where it was.

She opened the door and after finding Theodore standing there began closing it.

"We really need to talk," he said, putting his foot in the door.

"If it's about our mission, you can go through Reina. I have nothing else to discuss with you directly."

"You have every right to be angry."

"Then let me continue to be and step aside," she said, glaring.

"I have been in an impossible position, but everything I have done has been for your family, for you. There are more things you need to know before they are used against you."

There were always more secrets. She stepped aside to let him into the room. "You have ten minutes." She closed the door behind him.

"You know I've always been loyal to your father and mother."

She crossed her arms. "So you say."

Theodore exhaled sharply. "Everything I did was at their command. From the moment we left Mercury I was tasked with keeping you safe, and I have done that to the best of my ability."

"The coalition kept me safe. *I* kept myself safe."

"And it was me and this vessel that got you off Mars, but I didn't come here to duel with you over who did more. I only want to highlight that I am on your side."

"Then you shouldn't have lied to me all this time and continue to lie to me now," she said, turning her back on him. Her eyes began to tear, and she didn't want him to see that.

"This secret was more than my own. It was a secret of a generation, of thousands. Speaking it into the world puts us all in great danger. You can't fathom the complexity of our situation, the costs of keeping our identities a secret," Theodore said pleadingly.

"Surely if these Venatores are real, there would be ageless within the Republic ranks. They must have known you existed."

Theodore put his hand on her shoulder and turned her back around. "Undoubtedly there are, but we don't all know each other's identities. Some ageless joined the Republic early on out of belief in their dogma. Others like me joined when we had no other choice but death. Then there are others existing even more on the fringes."

"I don't think I can take anymore history lessons," she said regaining control of her emotions.

"What you need to understand is that most of us have been living cyclical lives based on our visible age, coming out like hibernating bears when the season suits us. Hiding away while our natural born children, like you, take over for a generation. We have waited many years for the right time to reemerge together now."

"So, this revolution, all of it has always been the plan?" she asked and then thought of something else. "Wait, you said natural born children, like me."

"Yes, that is exactly what I'm saying. It was your mother's plan. It always has been."

"Why didn't you mention my brother?" she said, and her heartbeat quickened again.

Theodore hesitated.

Kaya sat down on the bed, her legs feeling weak. "He isn't my brother, is he?"

There was a long pause. "No. I wasn't supposed to tell you that, but one day you will say the wrong thing and Leopold will hear of Tiberius al Vardan. It is better you are prepared when he does."

"He already knows I have a brother," she said, confused.

"And he believes you, which is why he is unconcerned. The name Tiberius is quite common, but the Tiberius I am talking about he would assume is dead, since no one has mentioned him."

"You aren't making any sense," she said, shaking her head.

"Tiberius al Vardan is your grandfather, Kaya. He was the last one left leading the Empire before its collapse."

"No...no, that can't be right. He was always there. We grew up together."

Kaya was in total disbelief. Aelius had been one blow already, but this one threatened to hurt her so much more.

"Was he though? Do you ever remember him being there outside of your teenage years? What about how he was always absent in some academy or away visiting a distant relative? After everything you've seen here, you know what I am saying is true. Even if you don't want to believe it."

Kaya combed her memories and realized he was right. Tiberius *had* always been away. When he *was* there, he always clashed with their parents. He always seemed separate from them somehow. It also certainly accounted for his typically odd behavior and sudden display of military skill.

"But he's so young. The rest of you at least look to be twice his age or more."

Theodore nodded. "Yes, that is true. His is an unusual case. There were rules in place for when someone could attain agelessness. Whenever it was done, it would lock in that person's physical age forever. These rules were put in place for practical and...ethical reasons, but your great grandfather broke with this tradition when it came to Tiberius."

Theodore sat beside her on the bed. "Or more likely Tiberius found a way to break this rule himself. No one is quite sure, but it mostly backfired. He was mocked incessantly for his apparent youth. He even gained the moniker of the boy who would be emperor, although at the time the Vardan's had no direct path to the throne."

"This is all too much to take in right now," she said, trying to steady her breathing.

"I can only imagine," he said, placing a hand over hers. "Take the time you need. I think we will have the luxury of it for a while. I would also keep this information to yourself for now. Even this much I wasn't supposed to share with you."

Kaya nodded. "Why would Leopold be unhappy to hear he is alive?"

"That is another history lesson, but suffice to say they have never been allies. That Tiberius was the last one standing and lost the war will not enamor Leopold to him either. I also have my own concerns," Theodore said, hesitating to elaborate.

"Tell me. It can't possibly make this any worse."

"I don't want to color your view of him with my own suspicions. What I will say is that Tiberius has always been loyal to himself above everything else. That is the only thing any of us can be sure of," Theodore said softly.

Kaya smiled.

"That makes you happy?"

"I don't know, but it does mean he was at least honest about that much. It certainly sounds like the Tiberius I've always known."

Theodore chuckled bitterly. "I guess that's true."

"Well, we have our own mission for now. Then we can worry about what comes next," Kaya said bravely.

Theodore nodded, standing up from the bed to leave. "I agree. Thank you for listening to me. I need to go see to our final preparations. It will be hectic here soon. You should try and get some rest if you can."

"One more thing," she said, reaching out an arm to stop him from leaving. He paused at the door.

"Does my father know my mother could still be alive?"

"None of us have had contact with her since the day of the accident. We all hoped she was out there somewhere, but, no, he didn't know. That was by design. When we heard about events on Triton, we suspected it was her but haven't known for sure."

"Should we try and send word to him?" she asked.

Theodore shook his head. "No, it is better that news remains a secret. Especially until we know for sure. They both knew what this path would entail before they ever set foot down it."

Kaya stood up, adjusting her clothes. "Thank you," she said reluctantly.

Theodore bowed his head. "We will get through this together. This is only the beginning."

Kaya smiled kindly as he left. She didn't know if Theodore would be her guide out of this purgatory, she floundered in. Maybe it would be Reina, Leopold, or someone else, or maybe even all of them. She couldn't deny that they understood the darkness they faced far better than she did.

Except maybe she didn't need a guide at all. She had taken up her position as their leader after all. Wasn't it her job to show *them* the way? Kaya sighed as she felt the pressure of everyone's needs bearing down on her. She never considered that manifesting her mother's dream and making it a reality would mean personally protecting the hopes and dreams of so many people.

Friends and strangers alike looked at her for answers, and she pretended to know what they were. Hoping they wouldn't realize she was a fraud.

Breathe, she reminded herself.

"One step at a time. One day at a time," she said out loud. She reminded herself that she had fought the Praefectus Frumentario, explored a dead planet, and even fought toe to toe with an ageless giant. She had survived all of it.

No, that wasn't totally right. Silas had fought the Praefectus, and she had tried to help. Reina explored the dead world right by her side. Neither of their steps outpacing the other's. She had faced the giant alone, but Namtar had saved her from her own ignorance.

As much as she had done, others had also done a lot to get them, to get her, to this point. Kaya had only accomplished anything at all because of the help of those around her.

That was the point she had been missing all this time. She wasn't in this alone. She didn't have to have all the answers to every problem. Theodore was right. They would get through this together because there was no other way. All their individual skills would be needed, now more than ever.

Kaya took another deep breath. The ship's air smelled fresher than it had a moment before. Her feet felt lighter. She paused before opening the door, a line from scripture coming to her mind. It felt fitting for the moment, even if she didn't believe in a divine power.

"We will move ever forward into this, a new dawn," she said and kissed the Jiddi tree pendant that hung around her neck. "The fires of the righteous will light the path, and evil will cower before the light." Her vow, sealed with an oath. An oath to the garden, to the citizens of the Solar System, and to her mother's Eternal Dream.

Kaya made her way to meet Reina, firm in her purpose and brave in the face of the uncertainty that came next. She would do the best she could and keep her oath. It was all any of them could do, and their best was needed, if they had any chance of success. Any chance of building a new world.

ARON

August, 4103 U.E.T. – Nia Tholus, Mars

GWEN THREW ANOTHER STONE across the deep blue water. "Do you think he'll show up?" she asked, finding her next victim. It was a smooth orange rock with specks of black and white minerals. She threw it effortlessly, and it skipped nearly twenty times across the surface.

Aron was impressed. He was hardly able to get a stone to skip at all. "They said they would, so I don't see why not."

Jimmy was standing nearby on the patio, his large arms crossed on his chest. He looked especially pensive.

Their party had settled into a large, posh, and most importantly empty estate on the coast of Nia Tholus. The property overlooked the Marineris Channel, which eventually flowed into the Bay of Chryse and the Acidalian Sea beyond. Tall pines rustled in the breeze, giving the property a cozy atmosphere. It didn't look like the kind of place the leaders of a rebellion and a psychopath would be meeting.

"How is it you found this place?" Aron asked.

Jimmy kept his eyes on the landscape. The sun was dropping below the horizon, casting a warm blue glow over the water. "Good intel."

Aron wasn't convinced. This was a remote place he had never even heard of. Full of the rich and elite of Mars who hid here like mice, hoping the war never came to them. Aron had never left New Olympia before, but he welcomed the opportunity to see more of his home planet now. If he was going to die young, he'd at least like to make the most of the time he had.

The estates in Nia Tholus were stately and spread out, maximizing privacy and security. It was unlikely to ever be a direct target because there wasn't enough here to justify the expense of the munitions, making it a great meeting location. For the same reasons, it wasn't a place that would be heavily surveilled by Republic Forces.

"This is your house, isn't it?" Aron said, using his hand to block the waning sunlight.

Jimmy didn't shy away from the light, although he probably should have with his fare features. "I never get tired of seeing the sun rise and set. When I was growing up, the sun was so far away it was barely more than a distant dream. About as big a speck in the sky as Phobos over there."

"That sounds like a yes," Aron confirmed.

"Sarding hell. If I'd known the fleet pension would be this nice, I would have told you all to sard off and stayed with the Republic," Gwen said.

Aron laughed, but then he thought she might be serious. He would have expected Jimmy to chuckle too, but he didn't seem to be in the mood. Aron wasn't entirely sure why he had been included in this mission, but he was happy to be there. He owed Jimmy now as much as he owed Kaya, so he would do everything he could to pay them back.

Gwen walked back from the shore to stand with Aron and Jimmy. Only the three of them had come to represent Prometheus, along with a small number of guards. "We should have brought more men. This place is bigger than you said."

"The amount of men will suffice. It's going to have to. We don't have many to spare anymore. We're already spread so thin," Jimmy said under his breath. "Anyway, this is a good place to hide but a bad place to escape from," Jimmy said, still staring out at the water.

"I never met the Father, but from what you've both said, he's a lunatic, isn't he?" Gwen asked.

Aron said, "Yeah, I don't think he's suicidal, but he'll gladly send others to die for him."

No one really knew how this meeting would go. The Father, as the leader of the Children of Men was called, was an unpredictable man. No, that didn't really do him justice, Aron thought. He was an agent of chaos that could be as easily measured and controlled as water in the ocean.

Aron went on, "But like I've said, the problem isn't only him. It's his generals too. In some ways, they are worse than he is."

Gwen said, "Another reason we shouldn't have traveled so light."

Jimmy shook his head. "We couldn't spare any more men if we wanted to. The Republic is moving in on our position in the canyon. They found it too sarding fast," Jimmy said, his anger showing.

"The Republic has millions of soldiers to throw at the problem, but they can't be everywhere forever," Gwen offered.

"No, but they can be in enough places to cripple our operations for generations. This is why we need the Children's help. They have enough manpower to make a difference. Turn the tide like they did in New Olympia during the execution," Jimmy said, growing grim. "The problem, like always, is the price they will ask for the privilege of their services."

Aron wondered what Jimmy might have promised them before but decided not to ask.

All the disparate cells of the Prometheus group were spread around the planet and beyond. Their distance and secrecy were boons that worked to keep them safe. However, the isolation also meant they were unable to mount a unified defense or win any decisive victories. So Aron understood what Jimmy meant. Unfortunately, none of the other Coalition groups on Mars had manpower like Prometheus and the Children.

Aron felt apprehensive. He had finally gotten away from the Father thanks to Kaya, and he had no desire to associate with him again. The Father wouldn't offer anything out of the goodness of his heart or some desire for the greater good. Those weren't things the man cared about, and Aron had told Jimmy as much.

"Yes, I know how you both feel," Jimmy said in the silence. "No one hates that psychopath more than me, but we're stuck. Horribly stuck."

One of the guards came out of the house and informed Jimmy their guests had arrived. Turning to Gwen and Aron, he said, "Let me do the talking and keep your eyes open. They're going to try and unsettle you. Don't let them."

Aron tensed. "On his own the Father is not so bad, but hopefully he left his generals behind. They make my skin crawl."

Jimmy agreed. "I've only met them in person once before, but it was once too many."

Gwen rolled her eyes. "I don't know what could be so scary, but I'll keep you boys safe."

Inside, the three of them took their places at the dining room table. It was large enough to seat twelve, but they were expecting far fewer. They took seats at the center of one side, leaving the other side for the Children. A pair of guards, armored and holding rifles, stood on either side of the room. Pitchers of water and small plates of fruit and cheese were arranged in the center of the table.

Aron fidgeted in his seat. He appreciated being included but struggled with how to handle the situation. Gwen and Jimmy seemed like they were carved from stone. Their sharp features and stern expressions left no doubt they were in command of the room. Aron felt more like a boy with a mop who wandered into the wrong office while the adults were speaking.

The first to enter the room were two guards wearing the blue burnished exoarmor of Republican Guardsmen. Aron couldn't see their faces through the visors of their helmets, but they looked authentic.

Then came the first of the three people Aron dreaded seeing again. She was a tall and fit woman wearing a lacy black dress. Her long black hair hung loosely on her shoulders. Her lips were painted black to match her dress, and her eyes were heavily shadowed. Aron's breathing quickened at the sight of her, Skotadi.

A man by the name of Fos in a golden suit came next. His many chains and bracelets rattled as they reflected brilliantly in the low light of the room. His hair was slicked back in a posh style, and his skin was smooth and unblemished. He looked to be about forty, but Aron suspected he was older.

"Yes, hello, you glorious little rabble rousers. What a fine evening," the golden man said with a flourish.

Skotadi and Fos embodied darkness and light in their own ways and served as the Father's generals. Aron had only met them both once before, but that meeting was enough for the memory to stick with him. What Fos embodied in cheer and charisma, Skotadi replaced with malice and dread. Jimmy and Gwen looked blankly at the two.

Finally, the Father arrived. He wore a simple white robe with no adornments. His head was shaved bald, giving him an appearance not entirely unlike Aelius, albeit older. Once he entered the room, the three of them took their seats.

Jimmy said, "Don't you tire of the theatrics, Falak?"

The father smiled broadly. "Please, call me Father." He then turned to look directly at Aron. "And you, child, how nice to see you again."

"I would sooner rip out my own fingernails," Jimmy said eyeing the man. Aron had to force himself not to look away.

Skotadi hissed, "You will show respect."

"I know you have better manners than that, Commander. Be a good chap and apologize," Fos cooed.

"This isn't your temple of maniacs, and I'll do as I please. I came for business, not a performance," Jimmy said, crossing his arms across his chest. Aron had questioned once if Jimmy truly disliked the Children, but those thoughts were gone now.

The Father giggled like a child. "Yes, but how joyous that would be to watch! Maybe after we're done, you can pluck one or two out. For fun, of course." The father's smile was one of the most terrifying things Aron had ever seen. The madness in his eyes was obvious to see for anyone with half a brain cell. Yet he somehow amassed an immense and loyal following.

Jimmy ignored his psychotic babbling. "The Republic forces are burning their way through the valley. If they make it into the deep canyons, it will put all our operations at jeopardy."

"Yes...how dreadful," Fos said.

The Father added. "Good thing our homes aren't in the canyons, isn't it?"

"What a blessing indeed," Fos shouted, feigning relief.

Aron was ashamed to think he ever got mixed up with the Children. Although most of their members weren't quite so unhinged, at least outwardly. He should have acknowledged the writing on the wall from the beginning. When they realized his skill with machinery and electronics, they put him to work assembling bombs and other weapons.

Even if he hadn't really had much choice, it ate at him to think most of those were used to bomb innocent civilians. The children claimed they used the bombing of high-district cafes to mask their attacks on Republic positions and breed paranoia. Their tactics may have been effective, but it always felt wrong to Aron. Now he told himself if they hadn't of had Clara captive, he would have found a way to leave. He hoped that was true.

Jimmy pressed on through their mockery. "You waste your time bombing civilians when you could be helping us win this war."

"Wasting time?" the Father said, holding a hand to his chest. "No, no. We are sowing seeds that will grow into brilliant trees. Or maybe not," he said, cackling again. "I don't really care about gardening or trees. I simply go where nature and my children direct. Ever the obedient servant."

Aron found his choice of words interesting. Was he saying someone else was in charge of the Children, not him?

"Have you always been this much of a nutter?" Gwen said, breaking her silence.

Skotadi hissed.

"Does your dog have any other tricks?" Gwen asked, eyeing Skotadi. Fos began to laugh, evidently thinking it was a great joke.

The Father smiled. "Oh indeed…I'm sure she would be happy to show you, child. What beautiful music you could make together."

Aron had heard rumors about Skotadi's abilities with a blade.

Jimmy took a deep breath. "Let me be a little clearer. If the Republic destroys our facilities, the guns and equipment your men have been using will dry up, and they will come for you next."

The Father sat back tilting his head. "Yours aren't the only weapons we buy, you know. Last week, we took our own little army depot," he said, motioning to the blue armored soldiers. "It is *you* who needs *me*, and what a treat that is. The delectable morsel mother nature has given me for my most loyal service."

"Last time I checked, we were on the same side," Jimmy said.

"Of course, but like in nature, there is always competition." The Father looked squarely at Aron. "Like when you took this little scrap of meat right from my mouth. That was very thoughtless of you."

Aron looked at Jimmy, unable to hide his surprise. This entire time he was under the impression the Children agreed willingly to let him leave.

Jimmy seemed unfazed. "The boy wanted to go, so I helped him out. He was free to leave, wasn't he? Besides, I left you a lovely little apartment in payment."

The Father turned back to Jimmy and scowled. "We both know the child is worth more than a dusty old apartment. Ultimately, he's the reason I'm here at all, but I'm sure you know that. It's likely why you had him contact me in the first place."

Skotadi leaned in, her palms on the table. "I will have what is owed."

Gwen scowled. "Leave these clowns to their circus. We don't need 'em."

Fos cooed in his sing-song voice, "That's where you're wrong, little birdy. You need us because we'll do what you cannot. What you *will* not. We are the monsters under the bed and in the closet. The darkness that consumes the world and the light that recreates it. The winds that blow-"

"Yeah, yeah, we get it," Jimmy interrupted.

"Do you, Commander? Who burned the capital while you rescued your old friends and let them escape?" The Father didn't wait for a response. "It was *me*. My children bled and died so that yours could live. Are your children worth more than mine? You were supposed to collect prisoners, but my cells are empty."

"Very empty," Skotadi emphasized.

Jimmy smoothed his beard. "Targets got away. It was a hectic day, but you still got the war you wanted."

Aron tried to keep up and balance these new details against what he had been told. Had the plan originally been to hand over the people they were rescuing to the Children? He felt confident that had never been Jimmy's plan, but still.

The Father waved dismissively. "I want to rid the world of its useless and contrived institutions. War is one part of that."

"Sounds like you should move to the slums," Gwen surmised.

Fos scoffed, "Such small-minded thinking. That is hardly the natural order of things. First, we must eliminate the ones who have stunted our progress. The Republic and its church, the nobility, and their schemes, even the trappings of the dead empire that came before. All of it, worthless. The slums are only a pale shadow of the natural beauty that will emerge from the canvas."

Jimmy looked to be barely containing his temper. "We need coordinated strikes on armed enemy forces. Not blown-up dance clubs in the capital."

"And I needed clergy and nobles in my prison, but we don't always get what we want I suppose," The Father said.

"Did you come here just to mock me?" Jimmy said, leaning across the table.

"No, although it's quite fun, isn't it?" he said with a laugh. "But no...I came here because I was so very curious. I didn't expect you to meet with me personally. Then I realized who the message came from, and it was an opportunity I couldn't pass up." The Father pulled a data chip from somewhere inside his robes and slid it across the table to Aron, who made no move to grab it.

Jimmy watched it slide and said, "What's this?"

"A proposition. Load it up on your digipad. I promise it's harmless."

Jimmy looked like he was about to say no, but Aron grabbed the data chip. "We'll be OK," he said, knowing they couldn't corrupt his personal device so easily.

He saw an array of folders and files on the data chip. He opened one folder at random and saw designs for devices that were totally foreign to him. Some looked like they could be weapons but then others looked something like rad scrubbers and water purification tools, but he wasn't certain.

"What are all these for, and where did you get them? I've never seen any devices like these." Aron tried flicking through as many files as he could, but Skotadi snatched away his device before he could dig too deeply. Perhaps sensing what he was trying to do. She removed the data chip and threw it back to him. He hoped it had been enough time for his software to make copies.

The Father smiled, his arm held wide. "Those aren't for you, child, but they could be. My proposition is that you come back and work for me on building these. You'll learn things you never thought possible and help us accomplish our real mission of rebuilding the world. In exchange, Prometheus will get the soldiers they desire."

Jimmy and Gwen tensed.

"It's a fair price," Fos said, his golden bracelets jangling as he laced his fingers behind his head.

Aron's heart rate quickened, and he considered his options. Clara was already safe, but for how long? He was curious about the technology he saw in the designs, but at that moment he was more interested in the continued safety of his friends. If he could secure that safety, he was willing to pay the any price. Even if it meant working again for these shameful fiends.

"No deal," Jimmy said before Aron could speak. He felt some relief at Jimmy's quick response.

The Father seemed to expect that answer and quickly said, "Then you give us the little princess you have locked away in that dungeon of yours. To cover your previous debts and as credit for the future."

Surely the Father already knew Kaya was gone. Unless he meant Victoria, but how would the Father even know she was with Prometheus. Then Aron panicked as he remembered how Jacob had accosted him, and his own slip of the tongue. Was he the one who gave it away, or had Jacob figured it out on his own? He was ex Frumentarii after all.

Aron didn't know what the Father would want with Victoria, but knew it couldn't be anything good. He didn't want her or anyone to go through that to protect him. He didn't want to be a coward.

"I...I can go if it will keep everyone else safe," he said, trying to put on a brave face. Jimmy looked his way, but his expression didn't change.

"I'm fresh out of princesses. What I have are guns, food, and other supplies. Same as before."

The Father sighed, sitting back in his chair. "You know, when you stole that information about Hex's location, I thought you may have come over to my way of thinking. You know, making a move for yourself. It's what

I would expect from someone like you but then...well, you really were a disappointment. You let lesser animals redirect you on a different path."

Jimmy stood abruptly, and the guards in the room tensed. "This was a mistake. I should have known there was no negotiating with you. I think it's best we go our own ways," he said, motioning to the door.

Fos smirked. "Already folding again so quickly. Tsk, tsk. Come, Father, I'm thoroughly bored. If we aren't going to kill them, we could shine our light elsewhere."

The three of them stood to leave.

"Yes, of course, child," the Father said, taking Fos and Skotadi in his arms. "The commander will be coming back to us soon. There's no need to purge them... yet. He's only playing hard to get. Think of what you could achieve, unburdened by your artificial chains."

Jimmy crossed his arms. "Think of what you could accomplish if you focused on the real enemy. Any coward can kill children and noncombatants."

Skotadi swiftly drew a plasma blade she had concealed behind her back. She brandished the hot plasma at Jimmy's throat, and the Prometheus guards jumped forward, guns leveled. "Speak ill of the Father again, and I will gut you."

Jimmy stood calm and firm. "Try it and none of you will leave here alive. I came here with a fair offer to work together. If you're intent on playing your games, you can do it without me. Taking over an understaffed equipment depot won't make you soldiers. You're cowards hiding in the shadows," Jimmy said, not shying away from the blade.

The Father gently caressed Skotadi's cheek. "Come, child, there will be time for your fun. I'd hate for you to spoil your appetite on such poor-quality sport."

Skotadi reluctantly snuffed her blade, and the Father turned back to Jimmy. "If you want my help, the price can only be paid in blood, my little pheasant. The blood you owe me and haven't delivered. Give me that, and I will swoop in to shelter you beneath my wings. If not, I will watch everything you built crumble. Both will give me equal pleasure. Goodbye, Commander, for now."

When they had left, Jimmy sat heavily back in his seat. "Follow them out and sweep the property once they're gone," he said to the guards still in the room. They quickly saluted and left.

"I would have gone with them," Aron said, breaking the silence.

Jimmy looked equal parts proud and sad. "I know, kid. It's brave of you, but I don't like using people as bargaining chips. Besides, we couldn't trust him to keep up his end once he got what he wanted."

Gwen said, "I don't even understand what he wants most. What was on that data chip?"

Aron said, "I'm not sure. I only got a quick look."

Gwen cursed. "Could have been useful for figuring out what they're playing at. Some kind of super weapon maybe? They don't strike me as the tech types though."

Aron shook his head and turned to his digipad. "I have no idea, but they might not be gone forever. I have a custom program that creates copies of my files continuously. It's helpful when you are working through multiple iterations of new designs." He swiped through several menus and grinned. "Yeah, we got them. I'll need to work on breaking into them. I think I can manage that with enough time."

Gwen slapped him on the back. "I guess it makes sense why they would want you for that kind of job. What it doesn't explain is why they care about the girl or how they knew we had her."

Jimmy scratched his beard. "I'm not sure either. Aron mentioned Jacob was asking about her, so we can investigate that. Otherwise, that lunatic enjoys the perversion of murdering clergy and nobles to demonstrate his own power. It might be that simple. During the Ashen Sunset, we stopped him from getting a truly noteworthy prize. Maybe that had an impact on his reputation among his own people."

"Would any of them even care? Those closest to him jump at his every word as if he was God," Aron offered. "Although, the Father did make it sound like he might be taking orders from someone else. It could make sense now that I think about it. No one ever knew where he and his generals lived. There could be someone else out there calling the shots."

Jimmy shook his head. "I don't know. There might be, but either way he still seems to be in charge. Which is also why I think his generals would gladly stab him in the throat if they thought they could get away with it. When you indoctrinate your followers with a belief that might makes right, it's only a matter of time until someone thinks they are bigger and scarier."

Gwen grunted. "He's a waste of time. Another charlatan."

"Maybe, but he commands many more men than I do. They're willing to do anything he asks, and he cares very little about their lives. I don't need to explain how dangerous that makes them."

"Would have been better if you never dealt with the Children at all," Aron said.

"Forgotten your own history so soon?" Jimmy asked accusingly. "I wouldn't spend a single moment with that monster if I didn't think it was my only choice."

Aron exhaled sharply. He hadn't meant to insult Jimmy, only voice his frustration with the situation. He knew it was easy to run out of options. "What now then? Give him what he wants?"

"No," Jimmy said sharply. "There's no easy way out once you make a deal with a devil like him. We'll have to figure out another way to win."

"Reminds me of the neighborhood bosses back in the slums. They'd steal some food from a mid-district truck and pass it around before draping some old metal around their heads, calling themselves kings," Gwen said. "People would follow them for a while after that."

"Then what?" Aron asked.

Gwen shrugged. "Eventually they wouldn't be able to keep pulling off the same trick, and their people would turn on them. They didn't usually last long after that."

Aron hoped something like that could work now.

Jimmy walked to a small cabinet and pulled out a set of glasses and a bottle of some brown liquid. "It's a shit situation, has been for a while now. Have you had whisky before, kid? Not the stuff they make in rusty drums for cleaning. The real thing?"

Aron shook his head.

"Good, you're in for a treat then. We have some time to kill before we can leave. Need to make sure they can't follow us," Jimmy said, and Gwen grinned, grabbing the bottle, and taking it outside.

"Come on. If there's anything I learned in the Fleet, it's to enjoy the quiet times when you get 'em," she said, turning back to look at them. Jimmy wrapped his thick arm around Aron's shoulders and led him outside to join her.

Aron couldn't help but smile, wishing Clara could have been there too, along with Reina and Kaya. He knew Clara was safe back at the base, but he looked up at the sky and hoped the others were too.

CHAPTER

26

Henry

September, 4103 U.E.T. - Chryse, Mars

"Captain Beckett, we have 'em on the run," one of Henry's lieutenants transmitted.

"Follow them. We want to push them into the old city center. Don't let any escape, we need prisoners," he replied.

The operation was going according to plan, and soon these people would surrender, and proper order could be restored. This was his first command since he was cleared for duty. The injuries he sustained fighting the berserker on Deimos had finally healed. Although physical and mental scars remained.

Chryse was a dense and compact city, nestled on the coast of its namesake, the Bay of Chryse. Following the deadly events in the capital that they had come to call "the incident," Chryse had chosen unwisely to declare its support for the rebels. Which led to it becoming an epicenter for anti-Coalition operations.

Margot spoke from beside him at the command vehicle. She was looking out over the hood at the city street beyond. "Can we join them in the fight? Feels like a waste to stay back here."

"Soon, Lieutenant Palmona. As company commander, my first job is to direct the operation. If you would prefer to command a platoon of your own, simply say the word, and I'll find a new second in command," Henry said, while he surveyed the battlefield. His personal squad had taken up a defensive position around them, using the armored vehicles as a protective barrier.

Following the capital incident, Henry was assigned to a division of the Republican Guard, where he would aid with the pacification of Mars. The senior command even decided to promote him to captain, even though he had only recently graduated from the academy.

It felt like a hollow gesture when he had done so little to earn it. His crowning achievement had been surviving. Then he also considered it may have been because they lacked enough competent officers given the surge in recruitment and deployments. They had to fill spots where they could.

"I was only asking," Margot said sheepishly. Henry didn't consider Margot a coward, but she lacked the drive to lead others. She was a follower through and through. So he found her useful as a second but only in so far as she could follow his orders. If it ever came time for her to lead in his place, it was unlikely to end well for anyone.

The Republic had labeled Henry a hero when they learned he had killed his traitorous aunt. The stories went on to highlight how he bested a berserker and personally captured Hex. His growing status only made Margot cling to him more as the next best option following the death of her beloved Boniface.

Henry felt no pride in the label. He wasn't a hero in any sense of the word. He had fought the berserker alone, that was true, but it left him bleeding and crippled on the floor, while Boniface and Zhou rushed in to finish the job with Hex.

On the day of the incident, his physicians had loaded him so full of pain medication, that he was little more than a zombie standing on that stage. His aunt's death was an accident, but they didn't care. He never held any ill will toward her, even if his father did. He struck out with his blade on instinct and regretted what happened the moment he realized his mistake.

The Republic leadership was committed to finding any whisper of victory they could glean from the aftermath of such a tremendous failure. So they didn't let the facts of the matter get in their way.

"I can't believe they're still fighting, even with all the losses," Margot said, her arms crossed. She was standing lazily against the door of the command vehicle. Margot hadn't seen fighting like he had on Deimos. To her, this was all still a distant game.

Henry could believe why they were still fighting. He had seen men and women on Deimos blow themselves up rather than be captured. That was the power of real, deep-seeded belief. His own belief that one day things would improve kept him moving. A belief that his life could go back to the kind of happiness he so briefly had with Kaya.

He appreciated that she accepted him for who he was on the surface. Kaya was the only person in his life he had ever met who wanted nothing from him, besides his company. She accepted what he told her and didn't dig any deeper. She seemed content to have a connection that didn't go beyond the surface or threaten her own illusions of the world. Which was fine for him.

"There isn't much they can do to win, but it will be a long campaign. The surrounding land is naturally isolated, and there are plenty of places to hide. I want prisoners, because without them we will have a hard time finding the Coalition's base of operations," he said.

Margot shrugged. "I hope all of this will be over before the holidays. It will be, right? I always love being home on Venus for the holidays."

If Henry hadn't expected her ignorance, he would have laughed. None of them were going to see a peaceful holiday for a long time. He had read the histories, studied old wars, and knew there would be no end in sight.

After he saw his aunt die, and the Pandora fleet firing on New Olympia, he knew, like everyone else who opened their eyes, that the world would never be the same. *He* would never be the same.

"Come on, we're moving forward. It looks like the resistance is softening," Henry said. The sound of explosions in the distance was becoming more sporadic, and he could see his troops were making steady progress into the city.

It felt strange to think of them as *his* troops, but they were under his command. At first, they had been reluctant to follow him, but then they had won their first skirmish with the Coalition, and then their second, and after the fourth they no longer questioned him.

The city center was densely packed with moderately tall buildings. They were originally built to maximize the space underneath the old energy dome that would have protected them. That dome had been removed centuries earlier when the atmosphere was tamed, and the limits of the city expanded rapidly.

He checked the hilt of his plasma blade at his hip and hefted his rifle. Deploying the helmet of his blue burnished exoarmor he shouted, "With me!" to his squad, and they fell in behind him. Margot was sure to keep especially close. "Remember, we want prisoners. Don't shoot unless you have to."

He didn't want to kill these people. He knew they were victims in all of this, but his job was to subdue this region, and he would need information to do it. If he could find the sources of unrest, maybe he could secure peace for the majority at the cost of only a few.

They stepped deeper into the narrow city streets, two people, side by side, following behind their armored command vehicle. He scanned each building looking for signs of the enemy but only saw blank and haunting faces staring back at him from doorways and windows. They were civilians, unarmed save for their disapproving stares. These people didn't regard him as a hero, and he agreed with them.

"Search every home," he ordered. "Confiscate any weapons and detain anyone suspicious."

His troops fanned out, making their way down the empty street. They searched homes and businesses in teams of four. Contraband weapons were passed to waiting troops outside who would stockpile everything for destruction or redistribution to Republic forces.

Those found with weapons were bound at the wrists and sent outside, where their heads were covered with thin cloth. They would be executed eventually, but not before being paraded on digiscreens as a warning to others.

Out of the corner of his vision, Henry noticed a glint and instinctively dove behind their armored vehicle. He moved just in time, as a bullet pinged off the vehicle's metal plates.

"Take cover, sniper!" he shouted, and his troops moved into action.

Save for Margot, who rushed beside him, covering her head with her arms. "Where are they?" she cried.

"Northwest building. We need to separate," he said to her. They were the only two people in exoarmor and were likely to draw the most fire.

Margot hesitated.

"God's bones, you need to move!" he said in his private comms to Margot.

"I...I don't think I can," she said, remaining still.

Henry cursed again and moved his head around the corner of the vehicle. Before he got a clear look, another shot ricocheted off the vehicle. Sarding hell, he was lucky the sniper was a bad shot.

A lightly armored sergeant slid to his side, shoving between Henry and Margot. "Sorry, Lieutenant," she said and removed her helmet. "I saw 'em up in the top-right window, maybe 250 meters. Are you a good shot, Cap?"

"Probably not as good as you are, Sergeant," Henry said honestly, taken a bit back by the initiative of this soldier. In any event, he was skilled with a blade, but a rifle was not his strength. He had seen the flash but wouldn't have been able to guess the distance without the sensors in his helmet.

"Alright, guess you get to hold the helmet then. Here," she said, tossing it to him. "Hold it out when I say so."

He hesitated at being given commands by this sergeant he didn't know. She looked several years older than he was, with dark-brown hair pulled tightly behind her head. A single blue line was tattooed diagonally across her face. Her eyes were light gray, and her skin nearly matched them. She looked like an Armanic from the Far Coast but spoke with a Lunese accent.

The sergeant slid under the vehicle and shimmied into position. "Alright, Cap, on you," she said.

He put the helmet onto the end of his armored gauntlet but then thought better of it. He grabbed Margot's rifle, as she still seemed unable to use it. If the sniper had the proper ammunition and managed to hit his mark, the exoarmor wouldn't do much to stop the bullet. He preferred to keep his hand if he could. So Henry placed the helmet on top of the rifle.

"Alright, on three, Sergeant, one...two..." On three, he raised the helmet out over the edge of the vehicle.

As expected, another shot flew, and the helmet was flung into the air. The sniper had finally hit his mark, but then another, closer, shot rang out.

"Target down," the sergeant called from under the vehicle. "Mind giving me a yank, Cap?"

Henry was a little shocked, but then he took a look around the corner, and no more shots came. He pulled on her leg, helping drag her out from under the vehicle. The added power of his armor made it quite easy.

She stood up, dusting herself off. "Don't suppose my helmet made it?"

Henry looked over to where it sat dented nearby. "We'll have to find you a new one. That was a hell of a shot. Hang back with the transport until we can get you some new gear."

The sergeant frowned. "If it's all the same to you, Cap, I'd rather stick around. I'm a better shot than anyone else here."

Henry couldn't argue with that. "What's your name, soldier?"

"Sergeant Smith, sir. Arabella Smith."

Henry smiled. Even now, amidst the violence and covered in dust and dirt, he couldn't ignore her exotic beauty. He had to force himself to refocus on the mission at hand.

"Margot, see to the men out here," he said, handing her back her rifle. "Alright, Sergeant, stick with me. Let's investigate the home that sniper was shooting from. There might be some useful evidence."

Normally Margot would have been the one in his position, but she was quickly proving she wasn't cut out for the battlefield.

Margot gave him a look and cleared her throat. "Yes, of course." Anger was evident on her face as she looked at Sergeant Smith and back to him.

Henry didn't have time to deal with her pettiness now, so he turned his back on her. His squad approached the target building, encountering no additional resistance. Several soldiers entered first while others set up a perimeter.

The building was an average-sized residential dwelling with multiple floors. Its windows were blown out and the facade was scorched from the initial bombardment of the city. When he entered, there was dust strewn about the room, and building debris littered the floor. A young woman sat in a chair under gunpoint holding a baby wrapped in an equally dusty blanket. Her eyes were wide, and she looked to be in shock.

Henry got between the soldier and the woman, forcing him to lower the weapon. "You can watch her without holding a gun to her head."

"We found him," called another soldier from above. Henry listened as they dragged something heavy down the stairs. *Dear God*, he thought painfully.

Henry wanted to stop them, but a moment later they emerged on the main floor dragging the body of the sniper. His head was slumped, revealing the exit wound from the shot that had killed him. Despite the gore, Henry could see he was young like the woman and assumed it was her husband.

The woman's scream confirmed his thought.

"Shut up!" the soldier guarding her yelled.

Henry shouted back, "Get him outside, and keep searching the home for weapons. Sergeant Smith, with me." The soldiers complied with his commands.

Henry grabbed the hysterical woman, moving her forcefully into an adjacent room, away from the body and blood-streaked floor. Sergeant Smith followed behind to keep guard, her face unreadable.

Henry whispered into the sergeant's ear, "Block the door."

Sergeant Smith took up a position in the doorway where she could keep others out while observing Henry. "Yes, sir." She held her rifle defensively.

He directed the woman to an empty chair. She had stopped screaming, but then the baby took over her cry. He tried to talk over the noise.

"Your husband committed treason. You understand that, right? You will be arrested as a conspirator unless you can provide us with names of his accomplices. Do you understand? Where did he get the rifle?" Henry said forcefully. He wanted to give her an opportunity to make it out of this.

The woman stared at him with a glassy expression. He wasn't sure if she heard him at all. Even the baby's cries didn't rouse her from her stupor.

These were not situations that the academy had prepared him for. He heard his father's voice in his head, telling him this woman was nothing but a scourge on their planet. He pushed his voice aside.

Henry couldn't fail on his first command. His father wouldn't tolerate the failure, and he subconsciously twitched at the thought. He shook the woman by the arm, hoping to make her responsive.

"Please," he whispered. "For your baby, tell me."

The woman's shock turned to disgust, and she pulled her arm away.

It was then he heard a communication through his helmet comms. "Captain Beckett, status report," ordered his commander.

Henry moved back from the woman, and she stood up, taking the opportunity to move toward the closed window. Sergeant Smith raised her rifle to stop her, looking from her to Henry for guidance.

Sarding hell, he thought, panicking. He held up his hand to stop the sergeant.

"Major Devi, we're pushing to secure the city center. Resistance has broken," Henry said, trying to maintain a steady voice.

"Good, good," the major replied. "Now we will break their spirit. Give the order, torch the city."

Henry clenched his jaw tighter. The major was casually ordering the death of thousands from the safety of his command vessel hovering miles away.

"Sir, they're beaten. We have prisoners..." Henry emphasized, looking back to the young mother.

Major Devi scoffed, "Look into their eyes, Captain, and tell me those heathens are welcoming you with open arms. Kill the prisoners and return to the command ship. Their lies of desperation are worthless to us."

Henry felt like he was overheating inside his armor. Even if Major Devi was right, it didn't matter. No one welcomed conquerors, and that was surely what these people saw them as.

"Sir...they're beaten," he pleaded.

"Are you disobeying a direct order, Captain?"

Henry ignored the communication and walked up to the window smashing it with the gauntleted fist of his armor.

"What are you doing, Cap?" Sergeant Smith asked hesitantly.

Henry looked out the window and saw that the alley beyond was empty. He looked to the woman and then back to Sergeant Smith. "I believe the prisoner got away," he said loudly. He was taking a risk, but it felt right. The major's angry voice echoed in his helmet.

Sergeant Smith stared at him before turning around to exit the room. "Yeah, this room's clear."

The woman clutched her baby tighter, her eyes softening from the disgust they held a moment earlier. She nodded to them and climbed out of the window.

Henry knew her odds weren't good. The rest of their forces would capture her running, or she would die in the fires he didn't think he could stop. All Henry knew was that he wouldn't be the one to light them, come what may.

They returned to their caravan, and Henry saw the decision was taken away from him like he expected. In the street, a line of prisoners were being systematically executed. While other's began throwing incendiary devices into open doors and windows. Anyone who ran from the structures was likewise shot down.

Margot stood nearby; her face buried in a digiscreen. She didn't look at the bodies.

Henry walked up beside her, trying to hide his true feelings.

"Major Devi says he has been trying to reach you," Margot said when she saw him.

"Comms are dead," he said flatly.

"Don't worry, I took care of it. Can we go now?" she asked, still not looking back.

He walked toward the command vehicle. "No. Now you need to stay until the job is done. Sergeant Smith, take me back to the command ship."

"Yes, sir," Sergeant Smith said, entering the driver's seat.

Margot stepped forward. "What do you mean? I already gave the order. I'm your second in command. I need to be with you, not...here." He could see her face reddening through the visor of her helmet.

Henry got into the vehicle and said, "You gave the order, and now you will see it through." He closed the door.

Sergeant Smith made a quick turn and drove them back toward the hovering command ship in the distance.

"I trust-"

"Don't worry about it, Cap," Sergeant Smith said, not taking her eyes off the road.

Henry nodded, considering if he could trust her to keep quiet about what happened. With what he knew would come next, he decided he would have to trust her because he had no other option.

☼

When they arrived at the command ship, it was a hub of activity. Soldiers were loading back onboard at a surprising pace, and when he looked back at the city, he could see why. Perhaps looking back was his first mistake. Residential towers were beginning to burn like torches, and smoke rose in large billowing plumes as gas lines ruptured and fed the infernos.

When he turned to board the vessel, he saw Smith transfixed by the view. "You look like you want to say something, Sergeant," Henry said.

"I wish none of this ever happened. Sorry, Captain," she said, moving to join him on the gangway.

"Death is a part of life. A steppingstone on our path to the Celestial City. I only hope all of this serves a purpose in the end." He wasn't sure why he said this out loud. Maybe his own ambivalence about his predicament or some sense of kinship with the sergeant. Except, what could he possibly have in common with her?

"They're dead, Cap. Dead as dead can be. There's no deeper meaning. They were in the wrong place at the wrong time, and the universe told them to sard off."

He didn't have any platitudes at the ready to contend with her assertion.

Once on board, he was summoned to the bridge, where Major Devi waited for him. He had Sergeant Smith remain by his side as an escort. He would have to come up with some official function for her as an aid. Given what she knew, he had no intention of letting her out of his sight.

The major looked furious as Henry entered the room. He moved to stand in front of the man and offered a smart salute. The sergeant took a position off to the side with the other guards.

"Major," Henry said.

The major moved to stand within an inch of him. "Our young lordling hero has come back to join us."

Henry stared forward, and the major was forced to look up at him. He was at least ten years Henry's senior. A short man with a dark complexion who spoke with a thick Mercurian accent.

"Why are you here, Beckett, and not seeing to your command? Your troops are still in the field, are they not?"

"I had comm trouble, sir, and was not able to receive your command. When I found Lieutenant Palmona, she informed me that you were trying to reach me. I left her to fulfill your orders while I returned here to contact you," Henry said, offering his fabricated version of events.

"You didn't think to simply use another soldier's comm device?" the major said, obviously annoyed.

"The situation was under control, sir. I thought my presence would be more useful here." He lied again.

Henry wanted no part in a massacre. He understood maintaining order. Laws were the backbone of society, but he took no pleasure in the death of thousands, who as Smith put it were in the wrong place at the wrong time.

The major spoke softly but deliberately. "Do you think you can do as you please because of who your father is? Well, your father isn't here, and the chain of command exists for a reason. If you were anyone else, I could have shot you where you stand for dereliction of duty."

So that was what this was all about. Combating nepotism while securing his own authority. Henry supposed he shouldn't have been surprised.

"The consequences of my actions are my own, Major. If I have failed in my duty, I accept my punishment under the law." Henry wanted to get this over with. He would rather take whatever punishment came to him then live knowing he lit the first torch.

The major snorted. "We will see how long that bravery lasts. You're in luck that we received new intel and sending you back to New Olympia isn't practical."

"I live to serve," Henry said instinctively. He didn't know what that new intel could be, but it also didn't matter. He would go where he was told to go because it was the only choice he had.

"I'm sure," the major drawled. "However, that doesn't mean you will escape punishment completely. Remove your armor, Captain."

It was going to be the lash then. How uninventive.

Henry didn't hesitate in removing his armor while the others on the bridge, including the major, looked on expectantly. They wanted to see the young Lord Beckett brought low to elevate their own egos. They wanted to see him cry out, to beg for his father's aid, but they wouldn't get their wish.

Major Devi called for the whip, and his face was full of glee, like a child eager to open a gift.

When his armor was removed, Henry didn't hesitate to pull back the top half of his thin bodysuit layer. When he did, the room went quiet, like he knew that it would. He turned his back on the major and dropped to his knees on the cool metal floor and lowered his head, as if in prayer. Although he didn't pray, because he would be alone in this, like he always had been. God had never answered his prayers before, so he saw no reason it would happen now.

He knew they were staring at the scars that covered his back. Not only the fresh ones from his fight with the berserker, but the old ones too. Deep burns and gashes nearly as old as he was. They were the legacy of his father's instruction and love.

"Captain Henry Beckett," the major said, the fervor in his voice gone. "I find you guilty of negligence in the performance of your duty. By the power invested in me by God, through his voice, I sentence you to thirty lashes."

Henry didn't move, simply breathed. Thirty lashes wouldn't be enough to break him. Then it began, and the room remained silent, save for the crack of the whip.

One, two, three... And on they went. He never cried out, because his father wouldn't stop if he had. He closed his eyes, but not to hide his tears. Those had dried up until he was a hollow shell of who he used to be. He closed his eyes so he could disappear into the darkness, away from the judgment and the pain.

Twenty-two, twenty-three... The lash struck again and again, but he remained in his void. Content with the familiar comfort of the dark.

Then it was...over. He felt an arm under his own and opened his eyes wearily. Had he fallen asleep?

"I got you, Cap," called the voice of Sergeant Smith. He followed it out of the darkness.

"Sergeant...thank you," he said, rising to his feet.

He turned back to see the major staring with a look of disbelief. Henry turned to stand at attention and salute the man.

The major returned the salute, any sign of mirth was gone. "See that he gets to the med bay, Sergeant."

Smith assured the major she would and led him from the bridge. Henry didn't need the support to walk, but he appreciated having the kind face greeting him from the darkness.

His scars were typically something he hid from the world, but now everyone would know about them soon. On the very few occasions anyone had seen them, he said it was from a childhood accident. A trip and fall into a fireplace. He never knew if anyone believed him. He was fairly certain Kaya never had.

"What happens now, Cap" Smith asked.

"We do our duty."

CHAPTER
27

SILAS REMAINED ON THE surface of Luna far longer than he would have liked. Even with its green spaces and lakes, Luna was a place that didn't suit him. He found the people difficult to deal with and the landscape grim and off putting.

He never thought there were so many shades of gray. The dreary landscape was made worse by the multitude of craters that cast long and ominous shadows over everything. It was no wonder to him that the population of this world was as ornery as it was.

After the fall of Lassell, the city became their central operation point. Hayashi had graciously volunteered his family's estate to act as the fleet's forward command and operating base, since the structure was largely undamaged in the fighting. The same could not be said of the bishop's estate.

Although travel between orbit and their new base was largely secure, the risk and expense of frequent travel back and forth was avoided. This meant he was spending more time on the surface of Luna than he had anywhere else in years. It had been refreshing at first, but now he longed for the intimate comfort of the *Specter*. All its familiar vibrations and clanks.

While Taylor and Hayashi were actively commanding the military operations, Silas remained behind to organize the city. At first, he bristled at the thought of abandoning the front line, but he took quickly to his new role. He knew it was the most appropriate place for him to be until the campaign got further along.

He also did admirably negotiating treaties with neighboring municipalities and the military commanders who had taken control of them. As Orzone and Hayashi had predicted, there were many who were willing to abandon the archbishop's cause.

Silas stood on a balcony, overlooking the city. Marcus and Bishop Vesivi stood beside him. Bishop Vesivi was the highest-ranking clergyman they had in the fleet, so he was a logical choice to interface with the ecclesiastical elements on Luna.

With a set of binoculars, Silas was able to see the main square of the city, far in the distance. A large group was beginning to form around a man who stood on top of a small ladder. Silas had seen enough of these public displays by clerics and would-be prophets to know something was brewing. He lowered the lenses and frowned.

"Your Grace, should we send a team to silence this assembly?" Vesivi asked.

Silas turned to Marcus. "Do we have an audio feed?"

"So, you can decide if we should silence them?"

"No." Silas was nearing his limit with Marcus and his obstinance in recent weeks. "All citizens have retained the right to peacefully assemble, even under martial law. I want to understand the sentiment of the people."

"A wise position, Your Grace," Vesivi said, and Marcus scoffed while he pulled up the audio feed on his digipad. They had established a connection to the local security systems and could now easily use them to their advantage.

Silas raised the binoculars back to his eyes. Focusing on the speaking man as the audio clicked on. The man's white robes were disheveled, but he looked like a cleric. Perhaps one that had been cast out from his church once the fleet had taken over.

"You clamor for this alien king of Mars to lead you, but only through God can you find salvation," he intoned, and the crowd booed.

The cleric's eyes were wide with passion, and he waved his arms enthusiastically. "This evil and traitorous king of mars will defile the land and take your children off to war on alien soil. While you're gone, he will usurp your property and leave you alone and broken to fend for yourselves. God, however, would never abandon you. Unless you choose this path of darkness and villainy!"

Most of the crowd shouted expletives in condemnation, but there were others who in their silence seemed to agree. This was a divided populace, even here on Luna where anti-theist sentiment was common.

The man continued through the heckling of the crowd. "Your would-be king has reached up to heaven, but his hands will be severed before they grasp a sliver of the divine. God has already given us his voice and hand in this world and will not allow another to usurp them!"

This seemed to be a step too far for the crowd. They lashed out at the man with fists and feet. They knocked him from his perch and violently assaulted him in their fervor. The security forces moved quickly to break up the assembly once the violence began, but not before several more people were dragged into the fray. Speech would be tolerated, but he had given strict orders for violence to be quashed quickly.

Marcus clicked off the audio and Silas lowered the binoculars.

"You shouldn't let these loyalists continue to speak unfettered, Your Grace," Vesivi said.

"If we silence them, we're no better than the Republic we're fighting, cleric. Not every citizen will drop their beliefs so easily," Marcus said.

"My belief in God is unchanged, Commander," Vesivi said, looking intently at Marcus. "Lord Beckett, the duke and soon to be king of Mars and all the nine worlds, has been appointed by God. He has been successful because God has led and protected us on his behalf. I'm smart enough to not stand in the way of divine will."

Silas had never sought power for its own sake, but the words of Vesivi, his crew, the Lunese citizens, and the divine edict he had received left him questioning. Perhaps he *had* been divinely ordained to lead the people of the Republic out of the darkness.

"Let's move back inside. It's almost time," he said, stepping past the men.

They took their seats at a large conference table. Aids came in with stacks of reports they placed in front of him. They would typically ambush him the second he became stationary enough to review and sign off on a host of different documents.

"Your Grace, the meeting is ready," another aid said, before placing yet another folder on the growing pile in front of him.

"Patch them in," he said, turning to look at the large digiscreen on the far wall.

Marcus sat at the table absently swiping at a digipad. Silas noticed he was still looking increasingly haggard. He had heavy bags under his eyes, and his face was taking on a perpetually tired look. The baked goods on the table remained untouched.

Captain Lancaster, along with the other assembled fleet captains, were on the screen to the left, with Orzone and his staff on the dockyards to the right. Taylor connected last from his forward operating base near the edge of the Selenean Plain.

"General, how goes the front?" Silas said, opening the conversation. Taylor had been on the front line of the campaign since the beginning and had done an admirable job by all accounts.

"Our forces continue to make progress, but it's becoming slow going. We have hit more intense resistance as we get closer to the archbishop's capital. The influx of soldiers and materials has been sufficient, but we could certainly make use of more," Taylor said.

With the help of Orzone and his intermediaries they were able to secure even more support from farther-away bishops and nobles. That left the bulk of the Pandora Fleet force, combined with the rebellious might of Luna, to cut a direct path for the archbishop's capital on the Selenean Summit.

Orzone was the first to speak when Taylor had finished his report. "We've seen all the defections we are likely to attain. From here it will be hard fighting to the archbishop's palace."

"What do you know about war, pirate?" Lancaster said sarcastically. "I've been saying since the beginning we should have turned the moon to glass and left. There's nothing here worth the lives lost."

Marcus's head jerked up. "You shut your sarding mouth. Good men and women are fighting and dying while you sit in orbit. You know even less than Orzone."

Orzone remained neutral, as he always did. Personal insults never seemed to bother the man.

"Enough!" Silas snapped. He was tired of the bickering. "Everyone is doing their part. Our goal remains to free Duchess Engstrom and restore order to Luna. Only then can we sail for Mars."

"She's probably already dead," Lancaster said, tightening his lips.

"I said enough," Silas repeated.

Orzone and Taylor seemed more annoyed than enflamed by the outburst. Marcus slumped noisily back in his chair, and Silas was left wondering yet again about his wellbeing. Marcus wouldn't even make eye contact with him.

"Orzone, what's the status of your communications with the patriarchs?" Silas asked, changing the subject.

"No updates. One remains staunchly committed to our cause, while the other has remained aligned with the archbishop," the man said, adjusting his glasses.

Early on, Silas had hoped to use the senior church leaders to sidestep the archbishop and garner support from local bishops. A plan that had largely worked. Luna, based on its size, had two senior clerics, a patriarch and matriarch who served as the next line of administration below the archbishop.

"Any chance for a meeting to convince the holdout to join our cause?" Silas asked.

Orzone shook his head. "I wouldn't count on it. The matriarch's appointment was thanks entirely to the archbishop. It is unlikely she will abandon him now. Although we have some leverage we will continue to apply. As the campaign continues, she may become more amenable."

Silas didn't ask what Orzone had in mind because he knew the man wouldn't tell him anyway. He also lacked the time to become intimately involved in anymore schemes or plans. He had to trust the people he surrounded himself with were working toward the same goals he was.

"Very good, keep me apprised. Captain Lancaster, how are repairs going with the fleet, particularly our newly acquired carrier ship?"

"The *Specter* has been our focus on repairs, but it's been slow going since the largest berth on the docks is reserved for the carrier. I won't bring up my problems with that again," Lancaster started.

Silas would have preferred to see the *Specter* take priority also, but he was trying to think ahead. They would need a functional carrier most of all for an extended campaign.

Orzone interrupted, "My dock crews have been hard at work on the carrier, despite Lancaster's unwillingness to provide additional support. It's a far larger vessel than anything currently in your fleet, and it's also significantly more damaged from the battle." Orzone spoke in a calm and steady tone, while Lancaster seethed openly.

"Our crews will continue to focus on our fleet until they are fully operational. We don't have the manpower to repair the ships we already have, let alone repair and crew such a large vessel." Lancaster was growing redder with each word. "I'm not helping your pirates create a ship capable of matching our own."

Lancaster struggled with the idea of working outside the tightly formed circle of the Pandora Fleet. Even more than Silas, it was all he knew, but unlike Silas he wasn't curious in the least about the outside world. He made it clear he had no desire to see other worlds or rebuild a crumbling empire.

Marcus scowled. "Those pirates could have already destroyed us. You shouldn't forget that, Captain." If Lancaster had been able to reach through the screen, he might have, based on the icy look he gave Marcus.

Silas sighed. "I can only repeat myself so many times. We must focus on finding solutions to our issues if we're going to have any hope of long-term success. Orzone, provide Marcus with your needs, and we will see about acquiring crews from the surface. There are many workers displaced by the conflict that could be useful on the docks."

"Your Grace, we don't need more potential security concerns," Lancaster said.

Marcus interjected. "You mean you don't want to be replaced."

Lancaster scoffed. "As if anyone here could match me. I just don't want to be stabbed in my sleep by some upstart brigand. We have no way to vet so many people or keep an eye on them."

Taylor cleared his throat. "The Lunese have proven to be vital comrades and assets on the ground. There's no reason they couldn't be equally so in orbit."

"They can be used for basic tasks until such a time as they are vetted for more sensitive projects. In any event, it will free my men to continue work on vital systems," Orzone said.

Silas nodded. "Yes, I like that idea. General, assign an officer to the task of directing displaced labor to the dockyards. Perhaps one of Lord Hayashi's noble cousins," he said with a wave of his hand. He would let others figure out who was best for the task.

Taylor saluted in the affirmative. The others offered no more complaints.

"The last agenda item, the Mercurians. What have we heard?" Silas said, directing the question to Lancaster.

"The first update arrived this morning from Lord Vardan's fleet. The relays remain down, so we're sending regular couriers until a time when reliable and secure long-range communication can be established."

Silas rubbed his chin. "Did they ask after the *Rubah* and its crew?" They had cut off the search after several weeks turned up nothing. The engineers thought it likely the ship crashed into the Earth based on its last-known telemetry.

"They did, Your Grace, but we mistakenly forgot to provide their correspondence with the outbound courier. I think we may have bought ourselves at least a little time before the next one arrives," Lancaster said dryly.

"Understood." This was a problem Silas could only ignore for a little while longer. He hoped by the time he was forced to answer he would have the support of Luna at his back.

"Very well, I'm sure we are all eager to get back to our duties. Pandora eternal," he said with a salute.

Silas waited until the video feed ended to dismiss his staff, including Vesivi, before turning to Marcus. "Care to explain what the hell that was all about?"

"I don't trust that sarding bastard, Lancaster. The cleric is almost worse with how badly he's trying to angle for his own position."

Silas shook his head. "What are you talking about? Lancaster has been with the Fleet longer than both of us. He has done as much as anyone to get us this far."

Marcus glared at him. "If you have it figured out, then why the sarding hell are you asking me?" he said, rising from his chair.

"Because you're my friend and family."

Marcus laughed. "Yeah, okay. Well, speaking of family, I can tell you Diana didn't die so that self-important asshole could play admiral of the fleet at the expense of the people on Luna."

"You don't need to remind me of what Diana would want," he replied angrily. "Lancaster is keeping my daughter safe, along with all of us here."

"Until he decides to shatter the moon, and then what? You know what, never mind. Come talk to me when you're ready to open your eyes," he said, storming out of the room.

Silas considered going after him, but then he saw the stack of files on the table. There was still too much work to be done, and he couldn't shirk from his duty, so he stayed seated and called the staff back into the room.

He seemed to be one of the only people here who could keep this fractured group together and working toward a common goal. He was the common piece linking all the different factions together. Perhaps it was thanks to God that they listened to him and from this divine authority that he pulled his legitimacy to rule. He would have to pray for guidance.

The day continued in the same fashion with an endless stream of conversations and requests that left him exhausted. He found the constant grind of administration wore him down more than battle did, and he envied Taylor.

He had left Mr. Beach on the *Specter* to keep him apprised of Catherine's condition, along with any other rumors he was able to ascertain. Even if Marcus didn't think so, he wasn't completely oblivious to the machinations of those around him. He had been navigating them his entire life. Mr. Beach was both competent and invisible, which made him an asset aboard the ship.

The absence of Mr. Beach, however, left him feeling quite alone. Normally he would at least have Marcus by his side, but now his friend had been more aloof than ever, and he barely saw him. Attempts to speak to him, had been met with anger and condescension. Up till now, he thought Marcus only desired some space, so that was what Silas gave him. Now he worried things were more serious than he originally realized.

When his eyes ached and he could no longer read the words on a page, Silas left the office. His shoulders throbbed from being hunched over a desk, and he had no desire to sit anywhere else, so he went to the estate's gym. He spent the better part of an hour working through sword forms and lifting weights, but it didn't make much difference. The comfort and joy he got from hours of sword training as a youth provided no comfort now.

He continued to train because of how important it was to his survival, but he tired of the violence. He went through the motions but took no joy in it. He would have preferred to visit Catherine and sit with her, but he knew a trip to orbit wasn't possible. Soon he would have to move to the front and join Taylor for the next major push of their campaign.

As competent as Taylor was, he knew he would need to be there to make quick decisions and stave off disagreements. Except, the question of Marcus still gnawed at him, and he was having trouble ignoring it any longer. He placed the weights back on the rack and left the gym.

Silas went to the small apartment where Marcus was staying not far from his own. He was hoping his friend had cooled off enough to have a reasonable conversation. There was a guard stationed at the end of the hallway who informed him Marcus was in his room when asked. Silas knocked once out of curtesy, but when no answer came, he entered.

The main room was a mess, discarded bed linens on the sofa, clothing and food containers strewn around. The furniture was covered with unknown stains, and the large digiscreen on the wall sported a large crack that resembled a spider web. The curtains were drawn tight, and only slivers of light came in from the illuminated gardens. The scene put Silas on edge, and he wondered if drifters had made it onto the estate somehow.

"Marcus, where are you?" he asked into the gloomy space, before finding the light switch. No answer came. With the light on, it was obvious no one had been in to clean for the entire time they had been on Luna.

The apartment was small. With a single bedroom, flanked by a common space and bathroom. He investigated the bathroom first but found nothing besides more trash. Marcus had always been messier than himself, but he had graduated from the same military academy in New Olympia.

It was impossible to make it through that experience without at least a measure of respect for cleanliness and order. This apartment resembled the slums of Tiyas, more than the room of a military commander. Silas saw visions of Marcus fighting off an intruder and lying bloody and injured somewhere nearby.

"Marcus," he called again, making his way toward the bedroom. He moved his hand toward the hilt of his blade out of habit. "Are you in here?"

A muffled groan escaped from the bedroom, and he rushed to investigate. Silas had his blade drawn but quickly saw there was no need. There on the bed, the sweaty and twitching form of Marcus was lying. What stopped him from rushing to his friend's side were the empty liquor bottles beside him. Then his eyes went to the nectar cartridge on the nightstand. His heart twisting at seeing his best and oldest friend succumb to such demons.

He found a half-full beverage and used it to douse Marcus. "God's bones! What the sarding hell is going on?" he shouted with his eyes still closed. His speech was slow and slurred. "I said I don't want any cleaning or anything sarding else. Now go away." He buried his face back into his pillows.

Silas pulled him upright and struck him across the face with his open palm.

Marcus opened his eyes with a snarl and shoved Silas away as recognition came back to him. "Look who finally showed up. I figured it would take even longer than this."

"Watch your tone with me," he said, picking up the nectar cartridge and stepping back. "What the sarding hell is this? God's bones! When did you suddenly become so weak?"

"Still not weak enough. I haven't brought myself to use it," Marcus said, rubbing his temples.

Silas seethed and threw the cartridge against the wall. It shattered, spilling its sickly liquid onto the wall. "Do you want to die, is that it?"

Marcus looked at him with distant and sunken eyes. He looked like a shadow of himself. "What difference would it make now? You have your new sycophants and don't need me. Let me die peacefully, and you can shoot my body into the Earth with the others."

"Why?" It was all he could force himself to say. He wanted to strike Marcus again, but he didn't understand what was happening.

"I have nothing left."

"You have everything. Your career, your family."

Marcus scoffed. "My career means little to me, and my family died with Diana. She was all I had."

That statement hit Silas like an unexpected knife to the back. "You've always been a brother to me. More than my own flesh and blood."

"I thought so too. Then all of this happened and, well, I felt like a sarding fool for believing it. I've always been here for *you* Silas, not my career. You took it for granted," Marcus said, moving on shaking legs out of the bedroom. He stumbled to a small bar, where he grabbed a new bottle of liquor. He took a deep swig before sitting on the sofa.

Silas scrunched his brow and followed Marcus out of the bedroom. "What are you talking about, Marcus?"

"In all these weeks, you haven't come to ask me how I'm doing. Sure, you came to check on business, but that was to cover your own ass. It wasn't about me. I don't think you understand, Silas. Diana was everything I had left."

"I feel her loss as much as you do," he said angrily. "She was everything to me too."

Marcus waved the bottle in his hand, pointing accusingly. "Was she? Then why did you abandon her all those years, along with Cat and everyone else, including me? The only things you truly hold on to are God and guilt. It was your downfall once, and you still won't listen."

Silas clenched his fist. Marcus was right—he wasn't going to listen to this abuse from an addict. "You would need to be here to listen in the first place. For weeks, you've been a memory of yourself. Now you're what, jealous that others are rising above you?"

"You're so predictable." Marcus shook his head, a sad smile on his face. "You know before the trial ended. When we were discussing the Tenebris protocol, Lancaster came to me. He wanted to see if I was prepared to move forward, even without you."

"He was taking precautions. That isn't unreasonable."

"Yeah, or maybe he was preparing to take your place. I told you I don't trust him. Vesivi isn't much better. I was in favor of this king business when I knew you hated the idea. Now I'm not so sure."

Silas was only half listening. He didn't believe Marcus hadn't used the nectar, given his nonsensical rambling. It was an obvious symptom of the narcotics. "Now I know where this sudden paranoia of yours is coming from. Why stay if you hate me so much?"

Marcus took another swig. "The same reason you kept going after the trial. I kept fighting for you and everyone else here. I thought my desire for revenge would fuel me. It did at first, but now even that feels empty."

"Nothing has changed. Our mission is still to protect these people and retake what was stolen from us," he said adamantly.

Marcus got up and walked to stand in front of him. "I can't bring back Diana. I don't have anything else left on Mars to take back. Protecting these people is all I have left, but if people like Lancaster get their way, nothing I do will matter. We'll have a new leader and the same problems. This isn't the world Diana talked about building or the world Cat was willing to die for."

"Get yourself and this place cleaned up before I see you next. I'm going to arrange for a physician to come and supervise you," Silas said.

Out of respect for Diana, he would do that much for Marcus. He hoped this was a simple indiscretion that could be rectified before his addiction got out of control, although he couldn't help but look at Marcus differently.

"Is that an order, or are you asking as my brother?"

"Whichever gets you to listen," Silas said bitterly. "I have plenty of soldiers, but I've already disowned one brother. I have no desire to prematurely lose my last one." The words hurt to utter. He put them into the world, in hopes they could coax the old Marcus back from the darkness.

Marcus took a deep breath and leaned over to place his liquor bottle on the table. As he did so, a piece of paper fell from his pocket.

Marcus tried to snatch it up but was too slow in his current state. Silas took a step back and uncrumpled the note. Written there were only two short sentences.

Gaia is alive and well. Not free of me yet darling,
but see you in a while. Off to visit some moons. -R.K.

"What in God's name is this?" Silas asked, holding out the paper.

"I got it from one of my birdies back on the *Specter*," Marcus said, standing to snatch the note away.

"Recently?" Silas asked and then considered the initials. "Is this supposed to be from Reina?"

"It's her handwriting," Marcus slurred. He moved back to the sofa as he seemed on the verge of falling asleep. "Came through a private channel. Something from when we used to see each other," he said with a scowl. "Transport landed on the *Specter*."

"Why would Lancaster not tell us?"

Marcus shrugged as he closed his eyes.

Silas wondered what the note even meant. "Is Gaia code for something?"

"Nope," Marcus drawled as he sank further into the sofa.

"Did your source say where the transport came from?" His only response was silence. A moment later, Marcus began to snore loudly. *Sarding hell.*

Silas didn't understand why Lancaster wouldn't report something like this. Had the Mercurians decided to return to their own fleet? Then again, what was the mention of visiting moons? There were no safe moons to visit this side of the asteroid belt. Was Reina referring to Earth? No, that wouldn't make any sense. He concluded it must be some kind of code that Marcus failed to remember in his current state.

His mind went next to what ulterior motives Lancaster might have to deceive him, but he came up empty. Then he wondered if Marcus's paranoia was beginning to rub off on him. He would have to consider these details further. However, in the meantime he had more tangible problems to attend to.

CHAPTER

28

Aron's party had arrived back at the old mining facility a few days after the meeting with the Children. Jimmy led them back using a circuitous route to ensure they weren't followed. Unfortunately, they couldn't trust the Children to help them, and they couldn't rule out what they might do to actively work against them.

It was late afternoon when they arrived, and Jimmy told them to get some rest. It was a long trip, and they could all use it. Except, Aron really didn't feel like being alone.

First, he tried to find Clara. When he got to the infirmary, she seemed to have her hands full assisting Dame Heather. Not wanting to disturb her he moved on to the hangar bay.

There he saw Seb sitting in the cockpit of their new Falcon. They had gotten it fully assembled a couple weeks prior, and in his absence, Seb had continued testing the Falcon's complex systems. It was a lot of work but needed to be done before they could let anyone attempt to fly it.

When he saw Seb was too distracted with his new toy, Aron decided to move on. He found Demitri in the communication room hunched over the desk. Aron startled him as he entered the small room.

"Sorry, didn't mean to sneak up on you," he said.

Demitri jumped back, trying to look casual. "Oh, welcome back. Didn't expect you so soon."

"Got back a little while ago. Did I miss anything, or were you too busy napping?" he chided.

Demitri laughed awkwardly. "No, all quiet. I must have zoned out for a minute there."

Aron nodded. "Need me to switch places with you for a while? I don't mind."

"No, that's okay. I'll be fine."

Aron appraised him and decided he seemed alright. He was only there to listen for anything unusual. Even if Demitri fell asleep, an incoming transmission should easily wake him up. "Alright, I'll try and have someone bring you coffee."

Demitri nodded and went back to staring at the console. So, Aron left. For someone surrounded by people he felt awfully lonely.

He didn't want to be rejected for a fourth time, so he went to his small room. Except, he disliked spending time in the tiny room. If he was a bat or a mushroom, he might have loved it, but it made for a bad place to sit and read.

With a sigh, he went to the broken board he used as a shelf. There he had his small collection of books. He scanned the shelf for something to read. Most were technical books on various topics, but there were also a couple of Milton Krane adventure books. He ignored those. He wasn't in the mood for Far Coast swashbuckling.

His eyes settled finally on the books he had taken from the Boundless Library with Kaya. The back of his head throbbed slightly at the memory, and he smiled. It felt like a lifetime ago, even if it had only been a few months. *Actually, closer to a year now,* he corrected himself.

The books gave him an idea, so he grabbed them both. One was titled *A Reflection on the Past: Hope in the Face of Chaos* and the other *The Rise and Fall of the American Empire.* For good measure, he grabbed a dusty old copy of the *Holy Scripture* he had found while cleaning out the room.

He found Jimmy and Gwen outside in the common area speaking with some of the others. Jimmy waved him over.

"Already back to studying, kid?" Jimmy asked, scratching his beard.

"Everything else seems to be sorted out for now, and it's too early for sleep. Where are you guys headed?" he replied.

"We have some business to sort out before the patrols get back tomorrow. Then we'll have a lot of work to do."

"So much for all of us getting rest," Aron said.

"I've always been a workaholic." Jimmy motioned to the books under his arm. "Lot of books for one person."

Aron shrugged. "I was thinking I'd bring them for the professor. If you don't mind," he added quickly.

Jimmy looked dubious. "The professor, eh? Only her?"

Aron nodded, hoping Jimmy wouldn't press the issue.

"Alright, go talk to her if you want. She's in my office. In about two hours, come meet us in the mess hall."

"Thanks, Jimmy."

Jimmy leaned in close and whispered. "I may be old, but I remember what it's like to be young. Victoria may not be a prisoner per say, but she also isn't free to go. We don't know how dangerous she might be."

Aron wasn't surprised Jimmy saw through his attempt at secrecy. He knew Jimmy had left the professor in charge of Victoria, so Aron assumed it would be his best way to see her. "She seems more scared than anything else. Why are we even keeping her here?" he said, matching Jimmy's whisper.

"She's safer here than out there, and letting her go will endanger us, especially now that the Children want her for something we haven't figured out. There's also always a chance she'll come around to our way of thinking and help us. I don't know," Jimmy said, and Aron thought he was being honest.

"I'll let you know if I learn anything," Aron said.

"Thanks, kid, but don't get too attached."

Aron nodded and went to Jimmy's quarters. Aron wasn't entirely sure why he had really come to see Victoria, but he was drawn to her. Not only for her looks, although she was beautiful, but to try and make her feel better. He saw the lost look in her eyes and instantly recognized it.

He knew what it felt like to be on the outside looking in. He also knew what it was like not to have your family around when you needed them most. The others might not care about those things, but he did.

Inside the room, he found Victoria and the professor seated on opposite sofas. Victoria was lying lazily, with Argos curled up beside her. She was casually scratching behind his ears. She still wore her cleric's robes, but they were clean and mended.

Elyna was busy writing in a notebook but stopped when Aron entered the room. She looked at him suspiciously.

"I come in peace," he quipped and instantly felt his cheeks reddening.

Victoria turned to look at him, propping herself up on one elbow. Elyna continued to stare.

"I uh, brought some books. Thought you might want something new to read," he said, holding the stack out like an offering.

Elyna stood up gracefully, setting her notebook on the coffee table. She swiped the books from him while Victoria sat up, swinging her legs off the sofa. Argos yipped when he was forced to move.

"They're probably pretty rare," he said, trying to fill the silence.

Elyna looked over the titles and raised her eyebrows. "Where did you find these, child?"

"The Boundless Library Archives. Well, the *Holy Scripture* I found here. I thought Victoria might want it," he said, looking to her.

"You're the reason Kaya disappeared, aren't you? I suspected as much, but Jimmy wouldn't tell me. The fact you have this book in your possession tells me everything I need to know." Elyna pulled the book on the American Empire aside and tossed it onto the table beside her notebook.

Aron tensed at the sudden accusation.

Victoria stood, her fists balled. "Did Kaya send you here? Where is she hiding?"

Aron raised his hands defensively. "Wow, everyone, relax. I didn't do anything to anyone, and Kaya isn't even on this planet. She left with the rest of the Mercurians after the Ashen Sunset."

"Kaya disappeared after I sent her to the Boundless Library to get that book," Elyna said, motioning to the sofa. "I don't think it's a coincidence you're here now with it. I don't believe in coincidence."

Aron frowned. "I thought she was looking for this one, something about an eternal dream. I don't know much else about it." He held up the other book to her.

Elyna snatched it from him.

"It's in another-"

"Yes, it's in another language. I'm aware," Elyna said, studying the book before tossing it onto the table with the other one. "What I want to know is why you have these books instead of Kaya. You said *you* got them from the Boundless Library."

Aron felt like he had stepped into a thief's ambush in a dark alleyway. "I was there to retrieve the same book."

"On the same day, at the same time? Who sent you?" Elyna's questions came quickly, and Aron had no idea what cliff she was leading him toward.

"Kaya told me once about the eternal dream, when she first got to Mars. I mentioned it later to my old employer..." He hesitated. "I was with the Children once but not anymore," he said, waving his hands for emphasis. "I guess it meant something to him because he sent me to the library to look for the book."

Elyna seemed to consider that. "But why on that particular day?"

Aron shrugged. "Maybe for the same reason you sent her that day. I actually got to it first and would have left before I even knew she was there."

"Why didn't you?"

"She found me first. Well, she kidnapped me really," he said.

Elyna laughed. "I actually believe you, but that still doesn't answer my question," she seemed to be speaking out loud to herself. "The children aren't as careless as people think they are. If you were sent on that day, it was because they knew something. Maybe *you* knew something." She studied him more closely.

Victoria rustled on the sofa, and they both turned to look at her. For a moment, Aron had forgotten she was there at all. Elyna turned to her dramatically. "What do you know?"

Victoria stuttered. "Me? Nothing!"

Elyna closed in on her. "Tell me. Now."

Aron pursed his lips. "Are you some Frumentarii agent? Can't we talk about this calmly?" He was a bit surprised by her sudden aggression. It was a lot coming from a Sanctum professor.

Victoria turned to look at Aron. Elyna grabbed her under the chin and turned her head back. "Don't look at him! Tell me what you know about this."

"I..." Victoria's eyes began to well up as if she were going to cry. Elyna slapped her.

"Cut that out," Elyna said, and Aron moved to defend Victoria but was stopped by an outstretched arm. "You, stay over there. She knows what she's trying to do, and it isn't going to work on me. She also knows why you were sent into that library."

Victoria grimaced and huffed but she raised her hands in defeat. "OK, God's bones, woman. Did you really need to hit me?"

Elyna stepped back, crossing her arms, and waited expectantly.

Victoria started hesitantly. "I saw the pass you gave Kaya for the Boundless Library Archives. She left it sitting on her desk, and I looked at it."

Aron relaxed, more interested in where Victoria's story was going.

"She left it out where anyone could see?" Elyna asked.

"We were roommates, and I may have looked through her papers. I saw her looking at something when she came in, and she looked so happy. I was curious why," Victoria admitted.

Aron interjected. "Why didn't you ask her what was going on?"

"We weren't speaking much," Victoria offered. "Besides, she lied to me before, and I knew if I asked that she would lie again."

Elyna waved dismissively. "So you went digging through her things and found the library pass. Then what? Who did you tell? Were you working with the Children?"

Victoria looked alarmed. "The who? What! No, absolutely not. I..."

"You what?" Aron asked, anxiously.

"Well, I might have mentioned it to Headmistress Blaiset. No one else!"

Elyna squinted, raising a finger to her lips, as if she were deep in thought. She went to pick up her journal and flipped through several pages before settling on some specific note. "Ah-ha."

"Are you sure you aren't a spy?" Aron asked, shaking his head.

"I'm just a historian who cares about the truth."

She was more frightening than any history professor Aron had ever met.

Victoria looked confused. "Why would Head Mistress Blaiset care at all? Are you saying she was working with the Children of Men?"

"I didn't consider it before, but it does make sense. I always knew she was up to something but didn't know what. It's why I stayed so close to her on the last day of the trial. I didn't think she would be an innocent bystander," Elyna said, sitting back on the sofa as if nothing had happened.

Victoria's said angrily, "You were spying on me? Did you know Kaya would be there? Were you planning to kidnap me?"

Elyna opened her notebook and began writing. "Spying is a strong word. I was...watching, in case. When you spotted Kaya in that hallway and decided to start bleating like a sheep, I had to get involved." She spoke casually, without looking up from her journal.

Aron wasn't sure what they were talking about. He assumed it must have been events that happened when he and Kaya got separated.

Victoria put her head between her palms. "This is all giving me a headache."

"Welcome to the study of history, child. The twists and turns are enough to give anyone a migraine."

"So, uh, can I take a seat?" he asked tentatively. He wasn't sure if the professor was done toying with them.

"Yes, be quiet, I need time to think about this," Elyna said dismissively. He still didn't know what to make of her odd behavior, but he was glad she seemed placated.

Aron approached the sofa, and Victoria moved over to make space. However, Argos insisted on sitting between them. He handed her the copy of the *Holy Scripture* he had brought for her. She took it gently.

"Here, before my own headache gets worse. I thought you might find some comfort in it," he said.

Victoria seemed put off by the condition of the book and held it aloft so it wouldn't touch her newly cleaned robes. "Thank you," she said politely.

He shook his head, thinking back to the events of the Ashen Sunset. "I don't know where you found Kaya, but it wasn't where she was supposed to be. We had a plan, but she didn't follow it. Looking back, I don't think she ever planned to follow it."

Victoria laughed bitterly, placing the book down on the coffee table. "That sounds like her. She always had her own agenda she would neglect to tell you about."

Aron chuckled. "She told me a little bit about what happened that brought you guys here. I'm sorry about that."

Victoria's face contorted, and he considered he might have brought up the wrong topic. "Yes, well, sympathy won't get me back home to Venus. Not that any of you care about that. Kaya never cared either."

Aron sighed. "I'm still sorry. I know what it's like to be away from home. At least you know your home is still there waiting for you."

"If I ever leave here," Victoria said, looking on the verge of tears again.

"Jimmy is a man of his word. I was his prisoner once, and now look at me. He'll treat you fairly if you do the same."

Victoria seemed to be listening. "Alright," she said softly.

"For what it's worth, I think Kaya did care, but she isn't good at showing it and is even worse at letting people in. I think she has good intentions though," he said, reflecting on his own relationship with Kaya. It was a common bond they had, and he didn't see the harm in using it to bridge the social gap between them.

"I think that's why I hate her even more. She should know better. We were like sisters growing up, and then her mother died, and everything changed," Victoria said sadly. "It's like she went away on a trip and came back a different person. I'm not sure why I'm even telling you any of this. I'm sure you don't care."

Elyna continued to write in her journal, seemingly unaware or uninterested in their conversation.

"When I share a story, it's to not feel alone, I think. Once someone else knows my story, then it's like they're with me. We all want someone by our side in the darkness," he said.

Victoria nodded and scratched behind Argos's ears. He barked to signal his approval.

Elyna cleared her throat. "This is all very touching, but if you plan to keep chatting, can you move to one of the other rooms? I have some research to get to," she said, opening the book on American history.

Victoria looked smugly at the professor. "I'm sure you'll be asleep from boredom soon. History is a worthless subject, especially at a time like now."

Aron thought Victoria might be trying to bait the older woman into an argument.

"There is much to gain from history if you know where to look. You need to have the vision to see the forest for the trees," Elyna said.

Aron looked at his comm device to check the time. He had plenty but decided it was a good excuse to see himself out and avoid another confrontation. "Jimmy wanted to see me, so I need to get going anyway. Maybe we can talk some other time soon."

Elyna waved him away, and Victoria nodded. She didn't smile, but Aron thought she might have seemed less hostile than before. He thought that was good enough and stepped out of the room.

CHAPTER

29

September, 4103 U.E.T. – Echus Canyon, Mars

Aron didn't leave Jimmy's quarters feeling any less lonely than he was when he entered. He had a headache and was stuck wondering who else had secrets hidden away. All because no one bothered to ask the right questions.

At least Jimmy wanted to meet in the mess hall. His stomach growled, and he knew he could use something to eat. As he walked, he noticed the facility was busier than normal. No one seemed particularly panicked, but at the same time many of them wouldn't look him in the eye. What was odder was as he got closer to the mess hall, which was centrally located, the activity thinned out to exceptionally low levels.

In the corridor that led to the mess hall, he saw a lone figure posted before a bend. Aron wouldn't have noticed the man normally. He looked like dozens of others who lived and worked within the facility. He noticed now because the hallway was empty save for the two of them, and when he came into view, the man vanished. Not in a phantasmic way. In a generally suspicious kind of way.

Aron wasn't much of a spy, but he could identify odd behavior when he saw it. He considered turning back to find someone to inform, but he didn't even know who he would tell. Jimmy and Gwen were supposed to be up ahead in the mess hall. Were they in trouble? He wasn't sure, but he felt a sense of urgency to find out.

Hurrying down the hall he noticed a broom leaning against the wall and grabbed it. It wouldn't make for much of a weapon, but it made him feel better to carry it. He stopped at the corner, looking back at the way he came. He hoped someone else might appear who could offer him aid, but he was still alone.

He took a deep breath and steeled himself before turning the corner. He held the broom defensively like he did as a child, pretending it was a plasma blade. Luckily, there were no enemy legions to greet him, and he relaxed his shoulders.

"Where the sarding hell is everyone?" he said to no one.

His improvised blade held tightly at the ready, he approached the mess hall. Normally the doors would be left open, welcoming you with delicious smells and a generally festive atmosphere. Now they were closed and didn't open automatically when he walked up. Aron looked at the control panel for answers. He tapped through several screens to manually override the door.

Moving to the side, he hit the open button. His broom held firm. The door opened with a swoosh, and then...nothing happened. The lights were off, and he considered leaving all over again. He reached for the switches inside the door but hitting them didn't do anything.

He wanted to leave, to turn around and run back to Jimmy's office. He had absolutely no desire to step into the darkness of the room, but if the lights were broken, he felt an obligation to fix them.

"Sarding hell, why is it always me?"

Aron entered the room tentatively. It was dark, save for a soft light that came in from the hallway and the indicator lights of various equipment. He knew the main control panel was in the far corner of the room because he had spent several days repairing faulty wiring a few weeks earlier.

He had barely crossed into the darkness when the door closed behind him. He tried to dart back toward it, swinging the broom wildly at the invisible enemies he pictured all around him. He was alarmed when he hit something and heard a groan.

He kept swinging, but then something wrapped its arms around him, and he screamed. He couldn't see anything, but a hood came down over his head anyway.

"Let go of me!" he cried, but no response came.

Then his feet came off the ground, and he was carried a short distance and tossed into a chair. He continued to kick and cry out, but no rescue came. He struggled against what felt like multiple people, but he wasn't strong enough to overpower them. They bound his arms and legs to the chair easily.

His body shook, and he panted from the exertion of trying to fight back. He had no idea what was happening or where Jimmy and Gwen might be. Had they finally been betrayed? Was all their planning and hard work ultimately for nothing?

A modulated voice intoned, "You will answer our questions, and maybe you will live. Where are the other Prometheus cells hiding?"

He didn't answer, not out of bravery but out of fear. He tried to open his mouth, to plead for his life, but nothing came out. He was stuck rigid.

For his efforts, he got a bucket of water dumped on his face.

"Tell us," the unnatural voice repeated.

Aron didn't want to die a coward. Even if that was what he was. He didn't want to die because Clara needed him, and the others. If he told whoever this is what they wanted to know, maybe they would protect them. He debated with himself but knew it was all a lie. He would have to protect the ones he loved himself.

"No," Aron said shakily. Then he waited for what came next. The answer was another bucket of water.

He spat and coughed, trying to breathe through the waterlogged cloth that stuck to his face.

"Bring the pliers," the unnatural voice said. "Maybe that will loosen his tongue."

A gruff voice cackled, and Aron felt his resolve slipping. He flinched as he heard metal clank on a table a moment later. The pliers, he thought as they doused him with another bucket of water.

"Tell us," the voice repeated. He felt someone grab his hand. He began to shake but didn't waver. He couldn't waver. They stretched out his fingers, and he felt the cold metal on his skin as the tool clamped down on his fingernail.

"I...I can't. I won't," he repeated through shaky breaths. He was hyperventilating under the waterlogged hood. He tensed, waiting for the pain he knew was coming.

Instead, he heard laughing and saw a bright light as the hood was pulled off his head. His eyes struggled to adjust to the change. There were roughly a dozen faces looking at him.

"I told you he wouldn't break that easy," Gwen said like a proud mother.

"Yeah, yeah, take yer fifty credits," one of Jimmy's other lieutenants said, handing them to Gwen.

Aron blinked, trying to clear the water from his eyes. "What the sarding hell is going on?" he said, struggling to catch his breath. "I thought I was about to die."

Jimmy stepped into his field of view, a big grin shining through his bushy beard. "Sorry, kid, not yet, but you did really good."

"Good at what?" he said, struggling against his bindings. "Can you untie me? Were you really going to pull out my fingernails? Sarding hell!"

Jimmy shook his head dismissively. "That's hardly my style. I'm here to offer you something much better than torture, but I wanted to make sure you had the...authentic initiation experience. Even if times are especially chaotic."

Aron raised an eyebrow. "That's a really low bar you're setting."

Jimmy waved another man over. He was old and grizzled. His pale skin had the feint outline of geometric blue tattoos. Aron recognized him as one of the supply clerks but didn't know his name. The man pulled out a long knife as he approached, and Aron tensed.

"Now you need to make a choice," Jimmy said, beginning to pace in front of him. The others in the room watched on with stern or bemused expressions. "I know you didn't come to us by choice at first, but you stayed when you didn't have to. Now you continue to stay loyal, even when put to the test."

The old man took the knife and cut open the sleeve of Aron's shirt. "Wow, what is that for?" he shouted, trying to watch the knife while also keeping up with Jimmy.

"I don't have a long fancy speech, but I like you, kid. You've done good, and I think you can keep doing good. I was talking with the others, and we all agree we should make you an official member of the Prometheus Group. What do you say?"

Aron blinked and then relaxed. The old man pulled up a chair beside him and unrolled a bundle on the table. It contained some kind of device and what looked like bottles of ink.

"Why do you want me? I'm no soldier."

"Not every soldier carries a gun, but we can work on that. Probably a better idea than having you rely on a broomstick," Jimmy said, and a laugh erupted from the room.

Aron felt his face growing red.

"Don't let 'em rib ya too much," Gwen said, moving up beside him. "You looked pretty threatening when you came in here, broom stick swinging wildly."

Aron tried to gather his confidence. "Really?"

The room erupted into more laughter. "Nah, not really but I've seen you do braver things," Gwen said, becoming more serious. "A lot of people here owe you their lives, and even more who made it off planet back in Trinity Square."

The room erupted with a cheer, and Aron felt like he had emotional whiplash. "I mean, yeah, of course I'm staying, but, uh, why am I *still* tied to a chair?"

"In case," Jimmy said matter-of-factly.

"In case of what?"

Gwen clapped him on the shoulder. "Better not to think of that." He could hear snickering behind him but still felt some apprehension. No one moved to remove his bindings.

"Have you gotten any tattoos before?" Jimmy asked.

Aron shook his head in the negative.

The old man began wiping down the blank area on his forearm.

Jimmy's smile broadened. "Where I come from, they're a great honor, and I'm happy the crossed torches will be your first. Now, grit your teeth, and when it's over, we'll celebrate."

The small crowd raised their drinks, and the old man diligently began his work. Aron didn't have time to contemplate what was about to happen before the needle pierced his skin. It was a sharp prickly sensation but much less painful than he imagined.

A smile came unconsciously to his lips as he looked at the faces around him. Men and women he had grown to know and respect over the last year since Kaya abducted him. Someone else might have been mad about this strange turn of events, but not him. For the first time since his parents died, he felt like he had a home and a way to keep Clara safe.

A tear welled up in his eye, but he held it back. It was a happy tear, but he still wanted to appear strong and resilient amongst these alpha types. Really, he was glad to be there and to be included for once.

This was something else he would have to thank Kaya for, if he ever saw her again. She had changed his life in more ways than one, and she probably didn't even know it.

The old man finished the outline of the crossed torches on his forearm and began shading the design in blacks and grays. He was a talented artist with steady hands, despite his age.

"The fire burns toward your hand, so you can always light the way," Jimmy said, and Aron nodded. He hoped he could live up to Jimmy's lofty ideals and what the Prometheus Group represented.

When the tattoo was done, he admired it with a sense of pride and a chuckle for how much his mother would have hated it. He didn't think the tattoo would improve his ordinary appearance, but maybe it was a good start.

Gwen sliced the bindings holding him to the chair. He scratched his nose. "Oh man, I needed to do that so bad." He let out a long sigh.

Gwen laughed and handed him a cup of something that smelled a lot like paint thinner. The smell was much worse than the whisky they had drank back in Nia Tholus. He looked around at the dozens of other faces in the room and realized he only really knew a third of them.

"Lot of new faces tonight," he said to Gwen.

She turned to scan the room herself. "Yeah, patrols haven't come back yet, and we didn't want you to have an empty party. Recruited who we could on short notice."

Aron smiled. "Thanks for all of this, truly."

He watched as Jimmy spoke to the old man cheerfully. Aron wasn't surprised that Jimmy would be close with one of the few other people from the Far Coast within Prometheus.

"I'm surprised you haven't gotten your own torches yet," he said.

Gwen studied her arm that had a Pandora Fleet tattoo. Her other arm had a series of small tattoos, but there was enough space for a Prometheus insignia. "Jimmy offered, but I'm not out of the fleet yet. I should have retired when he did years ago," she said wistfully.

"Why didn't you?" he asked.

Gwen laughed bitterly. "I thought I'd do a few easy years and pad my account. Look how that sarding turned out. Anyway, that's not what we're here for tonight." She took a long swig of her drink.

Aron raised his cup to his lips and then paused. Looking past Jimmy something...off caught his eye. While some of the men and women drank deeply, others sipped or were pretending to drink all together. He had seen that trick before. The Children used it to drug magnates and politicians to lure them out of their fancy bars.

"Gwen, put the drink down," he whispered.

Gwen looked at him suspiciously but paused, sniffing at her cup subtly.

As he turned to look, the central alarm began to blare. It was an old mining alarm that shrilled awfully. As if they had been waiting for that signal, several people in the room lashed out violently. Their cups turned to cudgels as they grabbed whatever bottle or utensil they could wield as a weapon.

Aron panicked and grabbed the broom he had abandoned close by. It wasn't much, but it offered him some comfort in the chaos of the moment. He had no idea what was going on and even less idea of what to do about it.

Gwen only hesitated briefly before diving on Jimmy, knocking him to the ground as a gunshot rang out. The old man was knocked over in the process, and it likely saved his life, as a bullet struck the table where he had been standing. They flipped the table as a makeshift barricade.

Aron dove behind another table and likewise flipped it over. He looked toward the exit and saw it wasn't very far away. He wanted to make a move for it, but he was blocked by a pair of men fighting for control of a pistol. So he hid and watched.

Jimmy shouted for those he knew to rally with him. Standing up, he drew the pistol at his hip. He fired several shots into a nearby woman before charging forward. Aron had never seen Jimmy fight, but it was obvious he had seen a brawl or two. He leveled a sickening punch with his left fist into another man who tried to stop him before unloading several more shots at targets Aron couldn't see.

Luckily none of their assailants wore armor, and only a few carried guns. It looked like they were winning easily, but then several people doubled over clutching their stomachs. Some wretched while others collapsed. The fight began to turn against them as their side suffered from the poisoned beverage.

The old man drew his long knife and charged forward. He stabbed an unsuspecting assailant under the armpit, driving the long blade into his heart. Then the old man shifted, diving onto another pistol-wielding target like a man half his age. He stabbed wildly into his chest then released a war cry, his arms held high, before enemy gunfire ripped through him, and he slumped.

Gwen slid in beside Aron and pulled him to his feet. "Time to go," she said, firing several shots with her pistol from behind the table.

"What, what's going on?" he said.

Jimmy dispatched the last of the obvious enemies. He spared a moment to check the old man's pulse before he came up beside them cursing. By Aron's quick count, it looked like at least seven people were dead, several more wounded. "We need to initiate the evacuation protocol."

Aron tried to catch his breath. If the enemy was already inside, how would they even get everyone out? "I think it's the Children."

"Are you sure?" Jimmy asked.

"Yeah, I think so. I know they like to use poison," he said, glad that he hadn't taken a drink. Except then he thought of Gwen.

Jimmy grabbed Aron's face, forcing him to focus. "Kid, I need you to get to the comms room and notify the other facilities. We've been infiltrated. Trust no one else."

"How...I," Aron stumbled over his words. "I need to get my sister. Get her out of here."

"I'll get her, kid. Gwen, go with him. Grab the professor and the girl. We'll meet back at the evac point in the main garage. I need to see who we have left and get everyone moving in different directions," Jimmy said. Gwen nodded her acknowledgement, and he took off, not waiting for Aron's confirmation.

"Where is he going?" Aron asked.

"To try and salvage whatever he can of his organization. I told him it was a risk letting so many people in here. Sarding hell, these academy drones never listen. Come on, we have work to do," Gwen said, pulling him along behind her.

In the hallway, Gwen stopped at a storage locker and punched in her code. She grabbed a rifle for herself and held out a pistol to Aron. "Can I trust you not to shoot your own foot?"

Aron swallowed, gripping the broomstick tighter. "I...I hope so," he said, before dropping the stick and taking the gun.

"Keep your finger off the trigger, and only point it at something you want dead. Got it?" Gwen groaned, grasping at her stomach.

"Are you OK?" Aron asked, concerned.

"Will take more than some third-rate poison to get me. The slums aren't easy on your stomach. Come on."

Gwen seemed to be struggling, but Aron followed her because she knew what to do and he didn't. Without a console at his disposal, he was as good as useless. At least the corridors were largely empty, and it seemed like people had already begun scattering to the deeper tunnels. From there, they would follow predetermined paths out into the canyons and toward secondary Prometheus facilities. All this left Aron hopeful.

Gwen held up a hand before they stepped into the communal space outside Jimmy's quarters. "Two outside the door. Wait here."

Aron was going to object but thought better of it and stayed where he was. He held the pistol defensively, surprised by its weight. He didn't look but heard the rapid gunfire and prayed Gwen wasn't on the receiving end.

"All clear," she called. Aron followed in quickly, but Gwen had already moved into Jimmy's office. He rushed in after her and was stopped in his tracks.

"Let the girl go!" Gwen shouted, her rifle held up at the ready.

Aron instinctively raised the pistol, his hands shaking. Inside the room,

Jacob had his arm wrapped around Victoria, his own gun pressed to her head. His yellow-stained teeth were visible as he grinned maniacally. Professor Moreau was lying on the ground beside him, her hands and feet bound. She seemed to still be breathing.

"Sard off. They're both mine. My gifts to the Father!" Jacob shouted back. His yellow eyes were crazed. Aron scanned the room and saw a spilled glass of liquid on the table and then noticed the stains on the professor's clothes. Victoria was sobbing uncontrollably, and Argos barked furiously from behind a closed door.

"That ain't happening, you crazy bastard," Gwen replied, stepping forward.

Jacob pulled Victoria closer. "Not one more step!"

Aron considered taking a shot but knew he was more likely to hit Victoria. He kept scanning the room hoping for an answer. Then he noticed the professor's eyes were open, and she was squirming her way closer to Jacob.

"You don't want to do this. What does it accomplish?" Aron said. His voice was more confident than his shaking hands. "You can be better than this."

"I've seen both sides. The Frumentarii abandoned me after everything I did for them. Jimmy cast me aside to run his dirty errands while he favored weaklings like you," Jacob said, spitting in his direction. "The Father realizes what really matters. He-"

Elyna kicked Jacob behind the knee. The unexpected strike caused his leg to buckle. As he stumbled, he pulled Victoria directly into Gwen's line of fire, blocking any clear shot. With a curse, Gwen tossed aside her rifle and dove toward the three writhing bodies. They quickly became tangled in a mess of limbs and robes.

Elyna swung her bound fists down onto Jacob's head as Gwen fought for control of his gun, while Victoria tried to get away. Aron moved closer, to grab Victoria by the arms and pull her to safety. Jacob struck Gwen several times in the side before she was able to bite his wrist. He let out a scream and released his grip on the gun. Gwen grabbed the gun and pressed it into Jacob's chest and shouted for Elyna to back off.

Aron pulled Victorias head away just in time as several shots rang out. He turned back to see Jacob's lifeless body slumped on the professor. Gwen got to her feet with a huff and helped Elyna untangle herself from the body.

"Nice job," Elyna said. "Glad you showed up when you did."

"How are you still moving around?" Aron asked. It looked like her glass had been mostly empty. Even Gwen was struggling, and she only had one swig of whatever poison the Children had employed.

"I only had a sip before I realized what it was," Elyna said, before changing the subject. "Let that dog out of there. We need to get moving."

Aron moved to let Argos out once Victoria looked stable enough on her own. He barked excitedly at the sight of him and Victoria.

They threw a few supplies into bags before rushing out into the corridors and toward the rally point.

"Where are you taking me?" Victoria said as Elyna led her by the arm behind them.

"We're all getting out of here," Gwen responded.

"It'll be okay. we have a plan," Aron tried to reassure.

Victoria huffed. "You already told me I would be safe, and then that monster held a gun to my head!" She started crying.

Elyna must have clamped down on her arm because Victoria suddenly let out a squeal. "Be silent, child. I don't know how that miscreant managed to poison me, but if it weren't for that, this would be a non-issue. Now be quiet. The less attention we attract, the better."

"Looks like most people have already gone deeper," Aron observed. The corridors were empty save for occasionally strewn objects. They didn't encounter any resistance and saw only limited evidence of struggle. "The Children must not have had many people inside."

"I think the poison was their main play, and then they would move their forces in," Gwen said. "Stay sharp. Main garage is up ahead."

"We aren't going through the tunnels with everyone else?" Elyna asked. She sounded apprehensive.

"Most will get out through the tunnels, but some of us need to go this way to throw off the search and buy the others time. Then we'll try to follow overland or fall back into the tunnels. Either way, we need to get Aron to the comms office first," Gwen said.

Elyna seemed satisfied with the response, but Victoria looked panicked.

They found the main garage deserted. Even the Falcon was missing, and

Seb was nowhere to be seen. Aron wondered how the two events were connected. The door to the comms office was closed, which was unusual. Normally they kept it open because it was so warped it would be difficult to open. He thought maybe Demitri or Seb had thrown it closed in their rush to leave.

Gwen said, "Hurry and do what you need to. We'll keep an eye out for anyone unfriendly. You have until Jimmy shows up."

Aron walked over to the office door and tried to open it, but it didn't budge. He yanked on the handle harder, but still nothing.

Aron was about to call Gwen over, but then he heard Demitri's voice over the intercom system.

"I have you locked out," he said. "Get out of here. Help is coming."

"What, what are you talking about Demitri. Let me in. I need to warn the others," Aron shouted back.

"What's he talking about?" Gwen asked.

"I have no idea, Demitri! By God's bones, open the sarding door," Aron shouted, kicking the heavy metal door to no effect. "Sarding hell that hurt."

Jimmy arrived moments later, a small group at his back that included the berserkers. He looked anxiously for Clara before realizing where she was. She sat on the back of the largest berserker, her skinny arms clinging tightly around its neck. "Clara!" Aron cried. He ran toward her but stopped when he saw a new arrival.

Coming from the main entrance, strode a black-clad figure. She looked like a carrion bird, descending from her perch. Her murder of crows following closely behind. It was Skotadi.

Gwen raised her rifle and opened fire on the woman, but the bullets ricocheted harmlessly. She appeared unarmored but must have been wearing some kind of personal energy shield Aron had never seen before. "Tisk, tisk, tisk. Is that how you greet your betters? I told you I would have what is owed." She sneered venomously. "Time to return these halls to darkness. What do you say?"

Skotadi motioned for her troops to fan out. There was only half a dozen of them, but they created a competent roadblock to their exit.

"Demitri, let me in. You don't want to side with these lunatics!" Aron said, slamming on the door again. He wanted to be anywhere but in a room with that woman again.

Skotadi cooed, "Oh, he isn't one of mine. Seems like you picked up some new strays."

Jimmy stepped forward to meet her. "I don't care how many spies you have here. The people and equipment are already gone. There's nothing for you to take, no one for you to capture. Your plan was for nothing."

Skotadi cackled. "Nothing, yes! Nothing is all there is. All there ever will be." She stepped forward, and the berserkers moved to intersect her movements. Clara hopped from the leaders back to stand behind the others.

"Your mistake is assuming I want anything at all. You can go run and hide. In fact, I hope you do." Skotadi continued to close the gap, unconcerned with the berserkers. "I'm here for the thrill of the hunt. I don't care about your little operation."

"We'll stop you. *I* will stop you. I won't let your madness infect this planet," Jimmy said, matching her stare. He moved his hand to rest on the grip of his pistol. Aron knew it wouldn't do much against whatever shielding technology she had. Based on her confidence, Skotadi knew the same thing.

"Oh, my little birdie. I don't care about this little planet either. It was here before you and will be after. You're a blink of an eye to its history. Now, should I give you a head start?" she said, her lips curling into a sick smile.

The large berserker who had been carrying Clara stepped forward, moving Jimmy aside. He stood nearly eight feet tall with mechanical legs and arms. What flesh was left on his body was covered in heavy iron plates. His face was hidden behind a heavy-looking helmet. A menacing red glow emanated from the eye slits as he hefted a large iron blade.

Skotadi grinned broader. "I haven't fought one of your kind in a while." She took a step back, drawing the hilt of a plasma blade and kindling it.

Aron abandoned the door and rushed over to stand with Clara, who was holding Argos tightly, alongside the others. Skotadi's troopers didn't try to stop him, and she began her dance with the berserker chief.

ACT
3

Henry

September, 4103 U.E.T. – Echus Canyon, Mars

THE INTEL THEY RECEIVED proved to be accurate, and Republic forces were easily able to locate the Coalition facility deep in Echus Canyon. Henry was impressed by how well they had hidden it. If it wasn't for their informant, it may have been months or even years before they found it.

"Captain, their scouts have been located and eliminated. The road is open," said Lieutenant Tabat, the leader of their scouting party.

"Good, any word on that Falcon?" Henry asked. They had seen one flying rapidly overhead in irregular motions.

"Not sure, sir. It isn't responding to our hail. Maybe a damaged ship or lost pilot."

Henry issued his orders. He couldn't do much but relay the information. Lost Falcons weren't his concern. "Secure the entrance and send patrols to secure the surrounding area. Sergeant Smith, bring up the vehicle. We're going forward."

"Yes, sir."

He had remained near the command ship while he awaited news from his scouts. Waiting for good intel was prudent, but leading from the rear was something his father would do. He chose now to do the opposite.

The skin on his back chaffed, and he needed something to distract himself from the discomfort. His wounds had mostly healed, but the scabs still routinely broke open as he moved. It was painful but not the worst he had ever suffered. He used it as fuel to keep himself moving.

The command ship had set down in a flat section of land, so additional supplies could be unloaded. The major and ship's commander anticipated it would be a protracted operation to root the Coalition out of their deep caves. As a result, they were prepared to set up a siege while the surrounding region was pacified.

What they didn't mention to anyone else was their informant suggested this could be the heart of the Coalition's resistance in this region. So his superiors very predictably wanted to be the first to establish a presence here. That way they could secure the greatest rewards.

Henry entered the vehicle when Smith pulled up. A small detachment of soldiers joined them in the vehicle, and more would follow on foot.

When they got close to the entrance, he was surprised by the lack of resistance. In fact, he didn't hear any gunfire at all. No stray projectiles pinging off their vehicle or the vibrations of heavy artillery.

"Lieutenant, do you have eyes on the enemy?" Henry asked through his comms.

"No, sir. It's been quiet like this since we found it. Seems almost abandoned."

"Sergeant, bring us as far as the road will take us," he said, considering his next move. At worst, it was a trap or, perhaps equally bad they were already gone. It wouldn't be the first empty facility he had raided in the few short months of campaigning.

The vehicle screeched to a halt, and they stepped out. He could see the large roadway, sloping down to a large hangar bay in the canyon wall. There were fresh vehicle tracks in the soil, so he knew something had come through recently.

"Lieutenant, keep watch out here. I'm going to go investigate."

"Sir, perhaps I should go instead?" Lieutenant Tabat countered. He seemed uncomfortable with the idea but knew it was his duty to say so.

"No, remain here and inform me if you see anything," Henry reiterated. He was itching to move. To forget about the ache in his back and the scheming of his superiors. At least in the moment of action he felt like he had purpose.

He moved with Sergeant Smith and another half-dozen soldiers toward the entrance. He was the only one in exoarmor and chose to take the lead position. Another way he would differentiate himself from his father.

The main door was already open, and Henry led them inside. He noted the explosive residue near the entrance. Someone had beat them here.

"Looks all clear," Sergeant Smith said, scanning the large open space.

Henry used his helmet optics to scan the room but found no noticeable heat signatures. The room was empty, but it did look like it had been occupied recently. There was fresh mud on the concrete floor, tracked in from the outside. Abandoned beverages and other supplies were strewn around haphazardly.

At the far end of the room was a tunnel leading deeper into the facility. The tunnel was large enough for vehicles to descend and would have been used generations ago to transport people and equipment deeper into the mines.

Henry motioned for his team to keep moving. They only made it halfway down to the next level before he heard a very familiar sound.

Henry held up his fist. "Something is up ahead. Be ready," he said calmly. Stowing his rifle on his back, he drew the hilt of his plasma blade. Kindling it, he continued forward. The plasma formed in the straight shape of a longsword, its faint glow lighting the way like a torch.

It was a relic from before the time of chaos that had remained in the Beckett family for generations. He had received it as a gift from his father on his graduation from the academy. Except he felt like he owed more to the blade and its memory than to his father.

When the large room beyond the tunnel came into view, he stopped, but not by choice. It was as if an invisible hand had tethered him to the ground. The sight of not one but multiple berserkers ahead sending a chill down his aching spine. Memories of Deimos washing over him.

Bullets began raining down on him from other enemies in the tunnel he hadn't even noticed. The projectiles collided harmlessly with the energy shield of his armor, but he was still unable to move, his attention locked on the berserkers and a woman in black fighting them. She wielded a plasma blade but wasn't one of theirs. Henry was even more amazed she wasn't wearing armor.

It took Sergeant Smith braving the gunfire to pull him to the side to get his body working again. He instinctively snuffed his blade as his men shuffled around him. They were using his armored body as a shield as they hastily erected a barrier and returned fire.

"They're fighting each other," Smith said. "Do we wait and see who wins?"

Henry wasn't sure. He had to get another look.

He rose up from behind the barricade, his troops providing covering fire. Using his helmet's optics, he could more clearly see the far end of the large room. There was another group there firing back at the soldiers who were shooting at his position. They looked like a ragtag group of soldiers and civilians. The berserkers who had been protecting the civilians rushed forward when the other troops were distracted to decimate their ranks.

Henry shivered at how easily they tore through their enemies, but they kept a healthy distance from the woman in black. It seemed like only one of the berserkers was confident in their ability to fight her. Henry was content to watch them tear each other apart, and then he saw, huddled in the back of the group, a mess of bright golden curls.

God's bones, it's Victoria, but why is she here?

"Stay back here and only target the soldiers in black. We want the others alive," Henry ordered.

"What about the berserkers and that mad woman?" Sergeant Smith asked, her concern evident.

"Leave them to me."

Henry darted out from the safety of their position, rekindling his blade. The group must have sensed his plan to help because they stopped firing at him.

He quickly approached the two dueling bodies. It was like watching molten rock collide with a tempestuous ocean. She was tall but thin, especially compared to this mountain of a berserker. It was far larger than the one Henry had previously fought. Yet she held her ground, dodging and deflecting blows with ease, uncaring that the loose fabric of her dress would offer no protection if she were struck.

Henry hesitated again, unsure of how to enter the maelstrom without being swept away. On Deimos, he had been pressed forward when Zhou commanded it in his cowardice, and Boniface was content to watch. He struggled to make the choice for himself.

The woman disengaged with the berserker, jumping back to land near him like a cat. She gave him a contemptuous snarl before swinging out with a savage blow to his torso.

Henry had to hold the hilt of his blade with two hands to absorb the blow without falling backward.

"Another tyro, what a pity," the woman cooed. She didn't even appear to be out of breath.

Henry attempted a series of attacks, which she effortlessly blocked. The berserker attempted the same with similar results and gained several new wounds in the process.

Henry swung out again hoping to catch her when her back was turned. He feinted left and then right before his blade danced forward in a high sweeping strike toward her head. It was a challenging maneuver to sell to a skilled opponent, but it was the best he had.

The woman didn't fall for the feints, but she respected them enough to reposition. In the process, the berserker rejoined the fight, and she was forced into a difficult position to defend from. The berserker's heavy iron blade looked like it would slam into her hip but instead slid down an invisible shield that shimmered under the impact.

She brought up her blade to deflect Henry's and counterattacked with her own wide arch that he was too slow to block. Her blade made his armor's shield flicker, and he was pushed back, stumbling. If she didn't have to defend against the berserker, he would have been easily overwhelmed.

In his panic, Henry looked back at his men and saw the soldiers in black were nearly dead to a man. "Fire on the woman in black. She has a shield. Overload it!" he shouted through his comms.

A moment later, heavy fire from their rail rifles rang out, peppering the woman's shield. It held firm, but she backed off her assault on the berserker. She looked back at her decimated troops and shouted with a gleeful expression, "I guess the hunt doesn't end today, my little birdies. See you soon."

For good measure, the woman plowed forward directly through Henry, slamming him back to the ground. She ran up the tunnel toward his troops and sliced through several with her blade before disappearing. The berserker took up a defensive position but didn't chase.

"Hold your fire," Henry shouted and held up his blade defensively as he got to his feet.

The ragtag group likewise stopped shooting.

"Lady Victoria, is that you?" he shouted, and Victoria shot up at the mention of her name.

"Yes, yes! Get me out-" She was cut off by an older woman who held a hand over her mouth. She appeared vaguely familiar, but Henry couldn't place her.

"Release the Lady Victoria and no one else needs to die."

A large muscular man with a beard shouted back, "Who the sarding hell are you?"

"Captain Beckett of the Republican Guard. The facility is surrounded. Throw down your weapons and we can resolve this peacefully."

"Not happening, kid. You throw down yours," the man replied, and the berserkers who had stood back began to move closer. Everyone tensed as the two parties came together in the vaulted room.

"I have a full company of men outside these tunnels. One call, and they'll be here," Henry said, his blade still held ready. He had no desire to fight another berserker, let alone several.

The bearded man held up one of his arms, a Pandora Fleet insignia emblazoned clearly on his pale skin. "Your uncle is fighting with us. Why aren't you?"

Henry frowned. "My uncle is dead."

"You've been lied to."

"No, it's you who are lying now," Henry retorted. The man looked vaguely familiar, but he couldn't place him.

"It's true. I saw Lord Beckett leave with the Mercurians. With Kaya al Vardan," said another young man. He was skinny and wore a mechanics' uniform. He didn't look like anyone Henry would expect to know that kind of information.

"You know Lady Kaya even less than you know my uncle. My uncle died alongside my cousin. Kaya has been dead for months, but you would already know that since it was the Coalition that killed her," he said.

"Sir, I have a clear shot at the bearded guy," Sergeant Smith whispered beside him. Henry knew she could make the shot. Then they could make a run for it and blow the tunnels. It was a bad gamble.

The mechanic continued, "They're both alive, and I know you too, Hal." Henry was surprised to hear his nickname uttered. There were very few who ever called him that. "I know Kaya is alive because I spent every day with her after she left the Sanctum. I even went with her to find you before the Ashen Sunset. Kaya wanted you to join her."

"Convenient that she never found me," Henry said.

"Oh, she found you alright, but you were walking arm and arm with Lady Victoria."

That wasn't what he expected to hear. "You...you pried some details from Lady Victoria for this pathetic game of yours. You have no idea what you're talking about."

Victoria broke free of the older woman and shouted, "Hal, I never told them anything. I swear it!" The woman got control of her again. Knowing Victoria's uncooperative personality, her outburst felt genuine.

"How could we have known you of all people would walk in here and now?" the bearded man added.

Henry was receiving too much information.

"What am I doing, Cap?" Smith repeated.

God's bones. "Stand down, Sergeant. All of you, lower your weapons." A few soldiers hesitated. "That's an order!"

The berserkers eased slightly, and the bearded man lowered his own pistol. He then motioned for the rest of his party to do the same.

Henry retracted his helmet and snuffed his blade but kept the hilt in his hand. "Let's say I believe you, then what? There's no winning this. Surely you all know that."

"You know the Pandora Fleet and the Mercurians are still fighting. The resistance on Deimos, Titan, and the rest of the Coalition spread throughout the Solar System. It's far from over. We're just starting, kid," the bearded man said.

Mercury was a small planet, but with the help of the Pandora Fleet, they had crushed the Martian fleet in their own orbit. Although his father had gone to Deimos, and Henry knew that cause was lost for the Coalition. Then again, Henry thought his own cause was lost up until this very moment. A thin lifeline was being thrown to him. but the cord rested precariously on a razor's edge.

"You were in the Pandora Fleet?" he asked the bearded man.

"I was your uncle's aid-de-camp for many years, Commander James Torres. I've been retired for a while, but I remember you," the man said, stepping forward, and Henry was able to get a closer look. "You came with your father aboard the *Specter*, when you were a little boy. I took you on a tour of the ship while your father and uncle dealt with meetings."

Henry's mind scavenged his memories, but it didn't take long for the recollection to return. It had been one of very few happy memories from those years.

The commander continued, "I took you to go see the Falcons, but you didn't care to sit in one. You found a better distraction."

Henry knew what he was talking about. An orange tabby cat had snuck aboard, and he found it sleeping in a bundle of coiled fuel hoses. He was far more interested in playing with the cat than the aircraft.

"Whatever happened to that dog?" he asked.

"You mean the cat." The commander smiled. "I took care of him for a while, but I always felt like he belonged to the ship, not me. So, when I left, I gave the responsibility of caring for him to my successor."

Henry laughed sharply. "Marcus? I'm sure he loved that."

The commander nodded with a sly grin.

Henry began to relax, but the others remained tense, likely waiting to see what came of their odd exchange.

A crackly voice spoke over the room's intercom. "Captain, don't believe them. You need to get us out of here." The voice was full of panic.

Henry frowned, looking up at the speaker. "Who's that?"

The commander let out a heavy sigh. "My mole and your informant, I think."

Henry turned to his remaining men, Sergeant Smith, and a half-dozen others. Some he recognized. "I won't deny anyone of their agency. Decide now where your loyalty lies."

"I'm loyal, sir! Get me out of this room," blared the same voice over the intercom.

Sergeant Smith raised her rifle without hesitation toward their own people, firing several shots into two of the men. They collapsed, lifeless.

"They would have betrayed us before we even left the tunnel," she said, anticipating his question.

Henry stared.

The other soldiers looked from Smith to him.

One of the younger women with a deeply pitted face said quickly, "My mum got sick, and they wouldn't give me leave to visit before she died. I've no loyalty to them. They ain't ever done much fer me."

One of the older men said, "My boy is with the Pandora Fleet. I'd like a chance to see him again one day." The rest added their feelings, while another man made the sign of the star and cross. Henry thought that man would abide by their judgment and hope it never landed on himself. In other words, the man would do what he had always done living under the Republic's rule.

The intercom went silent, and Henry turned back to the Coalition members, or whoever they were. "Commander, I will count the man behind that door as one of yours, but how many more are there? We have very little time if we plan to make a move. The senior command has already sent word for reinforcements."

"Call me Jimmy," the bearded man said, snapping his finger to one of the berserkers and pointing toward the nearby door. "Everyone else has already gone deep. It's only us now."

The berserker moved quickly, slamming its metal fist into the door. Its hand easily pierced the metal, and it peeled the door off its hinges like the lid of a can.

The berserker was too big to enter the small room easily, so a stocky woman went in his place. She came out dragging a skinny man by the collar, depositing him roughly amongst the others.

Jimmy spoke, "Aron, get on the comms and warn the others. Start with Deimos. They need to know what's coming their way. Then send the distress signal to everyone. It's time to shelter in place until this storm passes."

The man in the mechanic jumpsuit, who must have been Aron, nodded. He looked grimly at the skinny man cowering on the floor but continued to his assigned task.

"Elyna, why don't you join him in the comm room with Clara and

Lady Victoria?" Jimmy said. That was when Henry noticed a young girl clutching at the neck of a shaggy dog.

He thought she was clutching at the dog for comfort, but on closer examination he thought she was the one doing the comforting. The girl looked like she wanted to protest, but a nod from an older woman wearing a hospitaller uniform convinced her to cooperate.

Henry approached Jimmy, leaving Sergeant Smith and the others to stand guard. Henry was surprised no one else had rushed in yet, but he was happy to accept whatever luck came his way.

Jimmy looked down at the cowering man, clearly disgusted. "I'm disappointed in you, Demitri."

Henry didn't interrupt because it wasn't his place.

"The fleet abandoned me here. Why should I stay loyal if they haven't?" he shouted angrily.

The older stocky woman interjected, "You forget I came down with the fleet too. I'm still here doing what it takes to finish the mission. That's what you signed up for, remember? Face the darkness without fear and stay steadfast in your duty to safeguard the realms of man."

Henry recognized the line from the Pandora Fleet oath of service.

"I didn't want to spend the rest of my life living in a cave," Demitri said through tears. "Please, let me go. I won't say anything to anyone."

"You killed millions with this stunt of yours. You know that, right? I trusted you, let you in, gave you everything. I must assume you already told them everything you know or will as soon as you get the chance. I have my own oaths to keep to these people. So, no, I can't let you go," Jimmy said, and Henry didn't think he took any pleasure in this.

"The Children would have come anyway. I didn't have anything to do with that!" Demitri pleaded.

So the other group was the Children of Men, interesting. Henry had assumed the Coalition was more homogenous than this. It seemed like they were dealing with their own civil war as well. It made Henry wonder if he was making the right choice.

Jimmy let out a long sigh. "Maybe, but we would have been better prepared to deal with one problem instead of two. You abandoned your fellows and left me with no choice. Make your peace with God, and maybe your Celestial City will be waiting for you. Goodbye, Demitri."

"Please Jimmy, I-"

Jimmy raised his pistol and fired several shots into Demitri's chest. He holstered his pistol and turned to Henry. "You said the command ship is nearby. Is it a standard corvette-class starship? Is it fully crewed?"

Henry spared the body only a brief glance. "Yes, but the majority of the men-at-arms are on the ground on operations." He could see where Jimmy was going with his line of questioning. "But even if we take the ship, then what?"

Jimmy rubbed his beard. "We'll have to make it off the surface and into orbit. If we play this smart, we might be able to do that before they know what's going on."

"If we can take the command ship quietly, maybe. The Martian defense fleet is thin on ships right now, and most are deployed to Deimos." Henry scrunched his brow. "I don't know anything about piloting a ship that large, and obviously I can't guarantee how cooperative the crew will be."

Jimmy smiled and motioned to the berserkers. "They can be very persuasive, but leave the flying to me, kid. I had command of my own ship before you were even born. Your job is to get us to the bridge."

"I think I can do that if I bring you in as prisoners, but I can't think of any way to hide them," he said, motioning to the berserkers. Henry could see how they might be useful, but he would feel more comfortable without them around at all.

"They can follow at a distance," Jimmy said, and the big berserker lowered his head as if in agreement. The ominous red glow emanating from the eye slots of his helmet only added to his fearsome appearance.

Henry felt a shiver run up his spine. Up close, he could see the creature had numerous wounds, where metal didn't cover its skin. Many of the wounds looked quite painful and even its metal limbs looked dented and worn. There were fresh cuts and dents next to old ones where rust and grime had settled in. He wondered if the beast had ever known anything but violence.

Aron came back to join them, his eyes lingering on Demitri's still form. "I... I got the messages out and trashed the equipment."

Jimmy pulled Aron's face away from the body. "Good, we need to go. Any word on Sebastian?"

Aron shook his head in the negative.

"Sarding hell, OK. Everyone, grab what weapons you can, but keep them hidden," Jimmy instructed his people.

"Make it appear your hands are bound, and I'll lead you in. When I give the signal, we will have to move quickly to take control of the vessel and lock it down," Henry explained.

Aron spoke up, "Get me to a control panel on board and I'll be able to do that."

"Alright, then we have a plan. Forward unto glory," Henry said.

His men took up the call behind him, but Jimmy's group seemed far more apprehensive.

CHAPTER

31

Aron

September, 4103 U.E.T. – Echus Canyon, Mars

Aron tried to steady his breathing. He told himself it was to be strong for Clara, but he knew if he didn't, he would collapse where he stood.

His hands were held loosely with twine in front of him, and he stepped slowly along behind the others. They expected heavy resistance when they left the main tunnel, but they only found eviscerated bodies. The guards Henry had left behind were no match for Skotadi in her haste to get away. Except that wasn't what left Aron queasy. It was the image of Demitri lying lifeless on the concrete.

He had only known Demitri for a few months, but the pain of his betrayal and the pain of his death left him shaken. He didn't want to think of Jimmy as cruel. Then he reminded himself that Demitri had betrayed them. What happened was justice, not cruelty. Or was it?

Then his eyes drifted to Clara, and he knew what really mattered. They had to survive, and for that to happen they had to protect their own, no matter what. He also wondered if Clara would forgive them for leaving Argos behind. She had been understandably furious, but there was no way for them to conceal a canine prisoner. He would also have to thank Dame Heather for keeping Clara safe until Jimmy had found them.

"The ship is another three kilometers or so ahead. I see more patrols in the distance, so stay alert," Henry said as he rode along beside them in his vehicle.

Aron was glad they weren't being shot at, but he would have preferred to not have to walk so far. His thoughts weren't making for pleasant company.

"Chin up, kid," Jimmy said, walking up beside him. "I don't like this any more than you."

Aron didn't want to look at him, but Jimmy had gone for Clara like he said, and that mattered more to him than anything else. "We could have gone into the tunnels with the others," Aron said, turning reluctantly to look at him.

"Skotadi and her goons would have caught up to us. Then we'd all be dead. You, me and the thousands of others in the tunnels. At least now they might make it to one of the other facilities. It's about giving them a fighting chance."

"What if we die trying to take this ship? Even if we make it into orbit, then what? We abandon them?"

Jimmy tensed, and Aron suspected he struck the wrong nerve.

"This has been my life's work, for longer than you've been alive. Don't think I want to throw it all away for nothing," Jimmy snapped. "But Prometheus is more than this facility. More than this planet. More than me. It's an idea, and that idea is bigger than any of us."

"I believe in your dream, like I believed in Kaya's." Aron hesitated, trying to find the right words. "But this keeps going so wrong. I don't know that I'm cut out for any of it."

Jimmy softened. "Take a deep breath, kid. You've handled it better than most people would. Besides, all any of us can do is the best we can with the gifts given to us by our creator."

"I never thought you were very devout," Aron said.

Jimmy shrugged. "Growing up on the ice, there wasn't much else to bring you comfort but a promise of something better."

"You've been away from the ice for a long time, haven't you? Does it still bring you comfort?" Aron asked honestly.

Jimmy considered his question. "Sometimes, but then I realized only humans can tackle problems on a human scale. That's why we have the gifts we have, to make changes and mold the world. If I had waited for God to do it for me, I'd already be buried deep in a crevasse."

Aron agreed with Jimmy but prayed anyway. He prayed for guidance from his parents and from God. He thought maybe one of them could intercede on his and Clara's behalf. He was practical and wouldn't be so proud as to cast aside divine assistance.

He hedged his bets and mouthed the words before making the sign of the star and cross. They would need as much help as they could get. Then he palmed at his side to confirm the pistol Gwen had given him was still there.

He had no plans to use it, but he felt better knowing he would have a chance to defend himself at least. Jimmy was right. If they didn't take things into their own hands, they would have already been dead. Demitri betrayed them, and if he had succeeded, Clara and everyone else including himself would have been captured and executed.

Jimmy chuckled. "Good strategy, kid. Never know what you will need when."

"What if Henry betrays us?" he asked.

"I don't think he will. I think he needs this as much as we do," Jimmy said.

"How can you be so sure?"

"Call it a hunch," Jimmy said, and they continued their march in silence.

After a time, the command ship—as Henry had called it—came into view. Aron hadn't seen many starships up close, but this one appeared much like he expected. It was roughly one hundred meters long and twenty meters high, with visible rail gun batteries on the sides. It was much smaller than the ship the Mercurians had left New Olympia on, but it seemed capable.

Henry drove his vehicle toward the stern of the ship where a large ramp was lowered. Soldiers were milling around moving crates of equipment, while others erected perimeter defenses.

"Welcome back, Captain. We heard some chaos on the radio. Glad you made it," a soldier called out to Henry as their procession joined him at the ramp. His soldiers put on a good show of pushing their party along.

"We were hit hard. What's the status of the others, Sergeant?" Henry asked the man.

"Main force is unloaded and setting up camp below the rise. The major was looking for you. Even sent a party out after you."

"They didn't make it," Henry replied coolly. "But we have others who require aid coming down the road. Go see to them while I update the major and take these prisoners aboard."

"Yes, sir," the soldier said, saluting. He hurried away, gathering a few of the others nearby to continue down the road.

Aron knew the berserkers were hidden somewhere behind them and would wait for an opening before joining them aboard. They all agreed they would have the least amount of trouble fighting their way on if needed.

The ship was only sparsely occupied, and most gave them a wide berth as they were led onboard. The large cargo space at the rear of the ship was empty, save for a few troops that ignored them as they passed.

The brig was nearby, and they headed in that direction. When they arrived Henry led them inside, closing the door behind them.

"Sir, I, uh, don't know if we have space for so many. Major said no prisoners," the soldier in charge said, eyeing the large group. Meanwhile, the spacious cells sat empty.

"Sorry, mate, change of plans," Jimmy said before slamming his forehead into the man's face. The guard stumbled back, falling onto his desk. He struggled for his weapon, but Jimmy was on him quickly. He broke the loose twine off his wrists and grabbed the soldier's head before slamming it into the table one more time.

Gwen drew a hidden pistol from her pants and held it at the other guard, who promptly put up her hands. "Drop yer weapon and get in the cell."

The woman complied while Henry and the others dragged the unconscious man into the cell to join his comrade.

Aron searched the room looking for a control console but didn't find anything suitable. "Nothing here I can use. I need something connected to the main ships systems."

"We'll need to take the bridge then before anyone notices these two. Can you secure this room at least?" Henry asked.

Aron nodded. "That should be easy enough."

"Lady Victoria and the others should stay here. We can move more stealthily as a small group," Henry said.

Aron was ready to voice his disagreement.

"He's right," Jimmy said. "Elyna and Dame Heather can keep an eye on Clara with the others."

Aron reluctantly agreed. He didn't want to put her in harm's way anymore than needed. He also didn't want her to see what he knew would come next. There were only so many peaceful ways to capture a warship.

They hastily said their goodbyes, and Aron followed Jimmy, Gwen, Henry, and the soldiers out of the room. On the way out, he manipulated the door controls to lock out anyone who wasn't him. It would buy them time, but it wasn't a foolproof solution. He hoped it was enough.

"This way," Henry said, leading them toward the bridge.

The corridors were mostly empty with only the occasional support personnel passing through. Those they couldn't avoid moved aside and saluted as Henry passed. Except a lone female that turned the corner up ahead of them and stopped in her tracks. She wore the uniform of an officer and had dirty blonde hair.

"Henry, what's going on?" she said, approaching slowly. The soldiers raised their rifles in unison. The woman snarled, putting her finger up accusingly. "You will all lower your weapons at once! I order it!"

"Lieutenant Palmona, step aside," Henry said, closing in on her. She put a shaky hand on the pistol at her hip. "I'm still armored. Think this through, Margot."

"What's going on?" the woman asked, her confusion evident.

"We're taking the ship. You can either help us or step aside," Henry said. "You need to decide now."

"On whose authority?" she stammered.

"My own, as Viscount Henry Beckett, Lord of Tyrrhena," Henry said confidently. When his father had taken the mantle of Duke, he saw fit to pass his old title to Henry. He would use it to his advantage if he could.

"What about your father the duke? I don't understand."

"My uncle is the rightful Duke of Mars. Now decide, Lady Palmona. Will you serve or will you die?"

Aron blanched at his ultimatum. The Henry Kaya had described was sensitive and caring, but this man was none of those things.

"I... Yes, My Lord, how can I serve?" Lady Palmona said, lowering her head.

"Gather soldiers you can trust and prepare the crew for a departure. Don't tell them anything more than that. If anyone tries to stop you or becomes suspicious, silence them." Henry put a hand on her shoulder. "Where is the major?"

Lady Palmona looked nervous, but her expression calmed at his touch. "He was in the bridge last I saw."

"Good, go. We will catch up soon."

Lady Palmona smiled weakly and saluted before running off.

"Can we trust her?" Jimmy asked.

Henry turned to Jimmy. "I don't know, but I don't think she will actively try to stop us. The bridge is up ahead. There'll be guards out front, and we'll need to move quickly. Is everyone ready?"

Everyone nodded while keeping their eyes peeled for any other newcomers. Aron had very little to do with the fighting, but his palms became sweaty at the prospect.

Jimmy slapped Aron on the shoulder. "You got this, kid. Be ready. I'm going to need your help to take control of this ship."

Aron swallowed hard and nodded. He drew the pistol on his hip, holding it in shaky hands.

"Sergeant Smith, take point," Henry said, waving them forward.

With another soldier by her side, Sergeant Smith turned the corner. Aron heard the gunshots but thankfully didn't see anything. He was pulled forward by the intensity of the moment and Gwen by his side. It was like he was experiencing all of it from a distance, like he had during that first operation, months ago. Except there was something about the narrow space of the warship that made this feel much more personal.

They flowed forward, and he was trapped in the wave, tumbling through space. They rushed past the bodies of the two guards and into the bridge. Gwen and Sergeant Smith opened fire into the limited resistance as the crew was caught off guard. Several more soldiers dropped to the floor dead or dying and others surrendered as the room fell silent.

Inside the bridge, Aron was overwhelmed with new sights and sounds. He had never seen the bridge of a warship, and the multitude of screens and consoles was overwhelming. He didn't think he had ever seen so much tech assembled in one place. It was so much more than he imagined it would be. His excitement momentarily overcame his fear.

Jimmy and Henry approached the man who looked to be in charge. They stood side by side, and Aron wasn't sure what would happen now.

Henry said, "Major Devi, the vessel is ours by right of conquest under God. Do you yield your sword?"

The major placed his hand on the hilt of a ceramic blade at his hip. "Has the lash gone to your brain? It's no matter. Your father can deal with you when I send you back to him. Arrest them!" he shouted to the remaining crew on the bridge.

Gwen and the others raised their rifles, and the remaining crew was largely unarmed and didn't move. They knew they didn't stand a chance.

"Major, I'm giving you a chance to surrender honorably as per the Fundamental Law of the Republic."

The major laughed. "Captain." Aron thought he seemed disgusted by the word. "No army officer has surrendered a ship in a dozen generations. I don't plan to be the first to break that streak. Least of all to you. I spent twenty years clawing my way into this position, and some noble upstart isn't going to replace me."

Major Devi drew his blade, and Aron tensed. Henry, however, held his ground. "Although I have no doubt I could best you, Major. The claim is not on my behalf but his," Henry said, motioning a hand toward Jimmy.

"And who the sarding hell are you?" Devi snarled.

"Commander Torres of the Pandora Fleet and loyal confidant of the true Duke of Mars, Silas Beckett," Jimmy said with a flourish that reminded Aron of a courtly digiscreen romance. Jimmy was enjoying this a little too much.

"How noble of you to follow a ghost, but I'm happy to send you to join him. Prepare yourself, and let's end this ridiculous business," Major Devi said.

Henry moved aside to make room for the pair, but not before holding out the hilt of his plasma blade.

Jimmy looked at it absently but waved him away and scratched his beard. Then he made a show of stretching dramatically. Aron didn't think Jimmy would be so relaxed if he wasn't confident in his ability to beat the man.

Aron was focused on the unfolding scene, but something caught his attention. Out of the corner of his eye, he saw one of the soldiers trying to discretely type into a control console.

Aron rushed over, raising his pistol threateningly. "Hey, cut that out."

The soldier spoke while he continued typing. "I'm making routine adjustments to the life control systems. We don't want anything overheating."

"Sard off, I know what you're doing." Aron had spent enough time in the comms room to recognize a message being sent. "I said cut it out!" He brandished the gun closer, his hand continued to shake, and it wasn't having the desired effect.

"Move out of the way, Aron," Gwen shouted, but Aron didn't back away.

"No, you'll hit the controls! God's bones." He held the gun up one more time, intent on using it. Except he couldn't bring himself to shoot, so he swung the gun like a cudgel and hit the man over the head. He cursed before slumping out of his seat. Aron hit him one more time for good measure.

Gwen rushed over, and Aron jumped into the now empty seat and cursed. "Uh, Jimmy, you might want to hurry this along." The signal had gone out and responses were already coming in.

"Copy that, kid."

Aron looked back long enough to see the major swing out at Jimmy with his blade. Jimmy danced back and drew his pistol, shooting the man several times.

The room went silent, and they all stared at him.

Jimmy shrugged. "I was never very good with a sword. Besides, the Fundamental Law only applies to Republic citizens. We're pirates now, aren't we?"

After a long moment, Henry said, "Yes...I guess we are. The bridge is yours, Commander. What are your orders?"

Jimmy sported a big boyish grin. He was certainly proud of himself, Aron thought and returned to the console. He began the necessary work to access the ship's systems.

Jimmy clicked on the ship's main comms. "All crew, all crew. This is Commander Torres of the Pandora Fleet. I have taken control of this vessel, and all aboard have been conscripted to the Fleet. If you're a coward, I suggest you find the nearest exit."

Jimmy paused. "All of you brave enough to fight for a better future, I commend you. Ready the ship for immediate departure. Pandora eternal."

The bridge crew, either out of fear or bravery, returned to their seats and began to do as instructed. Aron watched the various digiscreens to ensure they were all doing what they should be.

The truth was he only half understood what most of them were doing but they didn't know that. So he played the part and looked for anything that seemed wildly out of place. Satisfied with what he saw he turned his attention to the security systems and was able to see the berserkers fight their way aboard the vessel, followed not far behind by a furry companion. Aron smiled at the sight.

"Everyone's onboard, Jimmy," Aron said, turning around.

"Close the hangar door and lock down everything. I don't want anyone able to move compartments until we're off this rock," Jimmy said.

Aron did as he was told. Another member of the bridge crew informed Jimmy the engines were ready for launch. Luckily, the ship wasn't very large by starship standards and wouldn't take long to get airborne.

"Alright, I suggest everyone find a seat and strap yourself to it," Jimmy said excitedly.

Aron fumbled with the belt at his seat. He had no idea what to expect, but he was terrified. He knew space travel was a common thing, but not for people like him. He wasn't meant to travel to the stars or visit moons. He wasn't meant for a life of adventure, but somehow it had found and embraced him.

Unsure of what to do, he held on tightly to the sides of his seat with white knuckles. The ship began to shake, and he thought it might be normal. He looked to the faces beside him for guidance on what to feel. Everyone appeared calm, so he concluded everything was still operating routinely.

"Commander, launch initiated. Fifty meters and climbing," one of the crew members relayed.

The shaking began to increase, followed by the sound of alarms and flashing red lights on the screen in front of him.

God's bones, this is not normal.

"Commander, Falcons inbound," another crew member said calmly.

Aron could see from the gauge they had already climbed over a thousand meters. He reluctantly loosened his grip on the seat and flicked through menus on the digiscreen until he found what he was looking for. "Looks like only two. Wait, three!" Aron shouted over the rising noise.

Jimmy replied confidently. "Remain on course. Auxiliary power to shields."

Aron studied the scans of the enemy ships and paled slightly. "Uh, Jimmy. If these were heavy falcons, would that be a problem?" Aron didn't have a lot of intimate knowledge of starships, but he did know the heavy falcons were bigger and carried much larger missiles. He also knew that starships were most vulnerable when they launched because only a fraction of the ship's power could be diverted to its shields.

"Sarding hell," Jimmy muttered, his confidence slipping. "Let's hope we still have some gunners on board."

Aron turned back to the video feed, his body tense. He had the screen up long enough to see a blinding white flash envelope the digiscreen. The entire ship rocked violently, and he struggled to stay at the console.

"Shields thirty percent, Commander," a panicked crew member called.

The video stream was restored, and Aron could watch as the surface of Mars drifted away. The Falcons were still tailing them, and the gunner's shots continued to miss.

Aron prayed for a miracle while trying to find some way to help. He was looking for a way to eke out more power from the shields, but he was unfamiliar with the systems. A wrong choice could doom them, so he watched and trusted in the others.

The miracle came when the third falcon closed the gap. It was flying erratically, like its pilot was struggling to keep up. "I think one of the Falcons has been hit!" Aron relayed to the others.

"No, now its shooting at the others. God's bones!" Aron shouted, watching the first of the two heavy Falcons take a direct hit. It left a trail of thick black smoke as it fell back to the Martian surface.

A brief thought hit him, but he quickly dismissed it. No, it couldn't be.

Then the remaining heavy Falcon took a direct hit from the ship's guns, the gunner's finally finding their mark. They began to fire on the remaining Falcon, which dove away in a less than elegant maneuver.

"Tell the gunner's to standdown! Someone get me a comm line to that Falcon," Aron said to no one in particular. He assumed the crew would know how to accomplish that faster than he could. He was right because in a moment he heard an unlikely voice from his console.

"I thought you chaps might need a hand," Seb said, and Aron grinned. Of course it would be Seb.

"Great job, mate, but I think you need to work on your precision. I think I could maneuver a tractor more gracefully," Aron joked. It was of course amazing he was able to do what he did at all, but he did look like a drunk in a simulator doing it.

"I told my father all that time I spent in the simulator was good for something. Be a sport and let me in now."

"Follow along, and we will advise when the hangar is open," Aron said, and Seb acknowledged. He could see him flying nearby in the video feed. The Falcon had a much easier time transitioning into space.

"Sarding hell, that kid is crazy," Jimmy said.

"Commander, we are into the upper atmosphere. No more sign of pursuit," a crewmember called.

"Aron, plot us a course into interplanetary space. Avoid any ships larger than our own," Jimmy said, stretching in his chair. The shaking lessened dramatically as the warship broke into the upper atmosphere.

Aron looked back one last time at the video feed. He could start to see the curve of the planet now, and the feeling left him queasy. It was all too much for one day. He unbuckled himself quickly and darted for the nearest trash bin and heaved the contents of his stomach.

Gwen left her seat and slapped him on the back. "You'll get used to that part. It's worse on smaller ships like this."

Aron coughed and wiped his mouth with his sleeve. "It's crazy to think this ship is a small one. I've never been on anything bigger than a basic transport before."

"You're in for a real treat, I think," she said, offering him a rare smile.

Henry stood from his seat. "If we avoid Deimos, we should be able to get away before anyone knows to follow us. My father went there personally with the bulk of the remaining fleet."

Jimmy grimaced. Aron could tell he was thinking of the forces still resisting there.

"I wish we could help them, Commander, but if we try, it will be the last thing we do. We can't fight real warships with this dingy," Henry said.

Jimmy nodded grimly. "All of our recent information on the resistance ships has been local. Do you know where the Pandora and Mercurian fleets went?"

"Last I heard they were split between Luna and Venus."

"Any idea who was where?" Jimmy asked.

Henry shook his head. "If my father knew, he didn't tell me. Maybe because he didn't want me to find out my uncle was still alive."

Jimmy seemed to consider, and after a long pause he said, "Set the shortest course for Luna."

"Why Luna?" Aron asked.

"I've known Silas for a long time. If those were his two choices, he would pick Luna."

"How can you be so sure?" Henry said.

"Luna has the largest dockyards on this side of the belt. He has a large fleet that undoubtedly needs service and supplies. I would assume the Mercurians were more interested in securing their closer neighbors on Venus. It's a logical choice. On a personal note, Silas also has a much closer relationship with Duchess Engstrom," Jimmy said confidently.

When no one raised any other objections, Aron rejoined the other techs at the consoles to set their new course. When he began entering the information and realized how long the trip would be, his stomach sank. Panic washed over him as he thought of floating in space for over a month. It was difficult to keep his emotions in check, but he tried to focus on the task at hand.

Then they heard a scratching at the door, and Aron smiled. He had almost forgotten. Gwen held her rifle up defensively toward the door, but Aron rushed over to open it. Before it was even fully open a ball of fur rushed and jumped on him. Argos was panting heavily, licking his face. In that short moment, his fears were erased.

"Maybe one day it'll be me he runs to," Jimmy lamented nearby.

CHAPTER

32

Silas

October, 4103 U.E.T. – Lassell, Luna

The bottomless stacks of requisition forms and action reports flowed to and from Silas's desk like the endless march of time. There were no greater guarantees in his life than death, taxes, and paperwork. He handed another signed stack to one of his aids who quickly carried them off.

Silas took the moment of peace to stretch his aching neck before returning to read the next document in his pile.

"Your Grace, if you have a moment, I hoped to speak with you," Vesivi said when they were alone in his office.

"What is it, Bishop?" Silas said, looking up from the report he was reading. Taylor's progress had been stalled for weeks now on the Selenean Plain. Despite their orbital advantage, they were not making much progress in taking the archbishop's capital.

"I understand Mr. Orzone has been facilitating negotiations with Matriarch Soubirous. I wanted to highlight that she is a shrewd woman."

"That seems true, but that is hardly surprising given her status within the clergy," he said, thinking back to his recent conversations with her. The Matriarchs and Patriarchs of the Solar System numbered less than a hundred. This small number of positions presupposed whoever attained them would have a high level of skill and ability, at least in politics if nothing else. "Do you have a specific concern?"

"I'm afraid she'll ask for too much and offer very little in return. Her goal may be to delay our campaign while they have time to regroup and gather additional reinforcements," Vesivi said, his arms crossed. The voluminous sleeves of his robes partially obscured the file folder in his hands.

"You don't need to worry yourself with military concerns. They are well taken care of. Do you know the Matriarch personally?" Silas wondered why he was taking a sudden interest in military affairs.

"Yes, Your Grace, I studied with her at the Sanctum a long time ago."

"Are you saying I shouldn't trust her, Bishop?" he said, setting down his pen and leaning back in the chair. If Marcus had been in the room, he would be telling him not to trust any of the clerics.

"No, Your Grace, I only mean to say I could be of service to you during meetings with the clergy. I know them in a way no one else on your council does." Then he added quickly, "I like to think my advice has been valuable to you in the campaign so far, beyond only matters of the divine."

Silas would often speak with the bishop about theology. At least prior to his recent vision. Occasionally they would even speak of family and other things. However, now with his new edict Silas felt like it was his task alone to carry out, but he offered a reassurance anyway.

"Yes, of course, Bishop. I welcome your council."

Vesivi bowed his head in acknowledgement. "Very good, Your Grace. I have also prepared here a document detailing the proposed structure for the new Reformed Church of God." He handed Silas the folder he had been holding.

Silas frowned. "I have no desire to make a new church."

"Nor do I, but in my extensive discussions with the local bishops and magistrates it has become clear that reforms are required. The church and by extension the Republic, in its historical form, is heavily reliant on executive power held by the leading clergy in New Olympia. Without that connection, many functions go unfilled, and many more decisions go unmade."

Silas was tired of these endless complications. There were still men and women manning their governmental posts, but many were unable to fulfill their duties properly. Although high-value and sensitive documents remained in physical printed formats, the software used in day-to-day administration no longer worked.

Access to many databases was lost, and even verifying identities had become quite difficult after the Republic shut down long-range communications and locked down servers.

Their techs and engineers had been working hard to establish connections and crack into digital data vaults, but the progress was slow. Fighting the physical war was already difficult enough and left very few resources to fight a digital war at the same time.

Silas opened the folder and flipped through several pages until he stopped at a graphic showing a proposed organizational structure. At the top was himself, and in small print was the title of King of Mars. Directly below was a new role, the Voice of the King, followed by roles and titles he was already familiar with. A mixture of ecclesiastical, noble, and civil positions.

"The clergy would no longer sit separate and above the rest of the government?" he asked, trying to discern what the intention was. He had made it very clear from the beginning he had no desire to eliminate the church. His personal desires aside, it was a practical impossibility, and he would quickly be thrown on a pyre for seriously suggesting it.

Vesivi shook his head dramatically. "Quite the opposite, Your Grace. The church and state would become one. Instead of a Vox and Manus, there would be a divinely appointed king and his messengers, the Voice of the King first among them. Meanwhile, worldly advice would stem from the Assembly of Lords and matters of the divine might be debated amongst the council of bishops, but both would hold equal authority. Ultimately all issues would fall to the divinely appointed ruler for arbitration if a consensus could not be met."

Silas looked over the document again briefly before putting it aside. "I will consider your proposal, but let me ask, do you envision that this... Voice of the King would be a cleric, nobleman, or perhaps neither?"

Vesivi spread his arms in a coy manner. "This is of course up for debate, but in an effort not to stray fully from the old ways...I think a cleric would make the most sense."

Silas nodded. "I'll take some time to review the rest of your proposal. It's unlikely much or any of it could be implemented prior to the conclusion of this campaign."

"That is to be expected, but these things take time to plan, and with our victory being a foregone conclusion, I see no reason to further delay these discussions."

Silas tightened his jaw. "Victory is far from a foregone conclusion, Bishop. There are many Lunese who have enjoyed positions of comfort under the Republic's banner and have no stomach for change. Convincing them will be a slow and difficult process."

"I am a man of God, not war," Vesivi said, looking up to the sky. "But as scripture teaches, the wicked must be cleansed in fire to protect the faithful. Absolution can only be achieved through fire and blood."

Silas knew the teachings. Even with his heavenly edict, the thought of cleansing fire sickened him. He wanted there to be another way to rebuild the world, but the angelic presence looming over him made him reluctant to speak his feelings out loud.

"Yes, of course, but the ones leading this apostasy are my focus. They are the ones who have access to the truth but still reject it. The ignorant should not be held to the same standard," he said.

Vesivi nodded gravely. "As you say, Your Grace. The clergy I've assembled will continue to spread the word of our divine revolution. There are many who come to see the truth every day."

Silas looked down at his watch. "I'm pressed for time, but I wanted to ask, have you had any word on Marcus's progress?"

Silas had requested Vesivi keep an eye on his ongoing treatment. Mostly because he had no one else he trusted to do it and because he struggled with doing it himself, Marcus's choices had been weighing heavily on him, and he found it hard to be too closely involved.

The bishop's face turned to one of concern. "He has followed your orders, Your Grace, but I still have my worries."

"Is he not recovering well?" he asked to gauge Vesivi's response. From the physician's report, it seemed like everything was normal from a medical perspective. They also didn't find any nectar in his system, confirming what Marcus had said. Silas however still had his doubts.

"I'm not a hospitaller, but it's well known that the long-term effects of even a little nectar can be quite unpredictable. I know he is family, so I understand your desire to see him well. I share it myself," he said, placing his hand over his heart. "I only worry that he could fall into bouts of delusion or paranoia that might put your person or our operation at risk."

Silas didn't blindly trust Vesivi. Silas had his own doubts about his motivations, but the bishop wasn't saying anything he hadn't thought of himself. Silas had always disdained those who abused nectar and other narcotics. He had trouble seeing the abuse as anything but a lack of discipline and a personal shortcoming.

The fact it was Marcus only made things worse. It was his love for the man that made him question his position. He knew Marcus was strong and disciplined, at least when he wanted to be. Silas had never doubted his ability or trustworthiness before now, but he was still struggling to be empathetic.

"Have faith no single person will be put in a position to undermine our efforts here. Our objective is clearly presented before us, and anyone who stands in the way of that divinely appointed path will be set aside." He stood up from his chair to stretch. "Now... If that's all, I need to see to my next meeting." The physicians had told him he needed to spend more time moving, particularly in the low gravity of Luna, to maintain his fitness.

Vesivi bowed. "Of course, Your Grace."

Silas moved to stand before the large glass windows as the sun shone down onto the gardens below. Vesivi left quietly behind him, and he contemplated his next moves.

It seemed that God was determined to see him become a politician even though he had no gifts for it. His ability as a commander had gotten him to the highest position his station would allow, but he lacked the scheming mind men like his brother Simon used to push even higher.

One of his aids brought him a fresh cup of coffee. Holding it, he felt a slight tremor in his left hand.

Maybe I've already had enough coffee for one day, he thought absently, stretching his fingers.

He would continue to improve at playing this political game because he had to but wished the next major offensive would come sooner. He would rather be in the field, focusing his energy and attention on the military campaign that he understood far better.

Orzone arrived not long after with Marcus by his side. Orzone wore a well-tailored suit and seemed calm and maybe even happy despite the circumstances. Silas appreciated how easily he navigated the chaos and paperwork. Marcus looked neat, and although he still had bags under his eyes, he seemed more energetic than he had in weeks.

"Mr. Orzone, Marcus," he said with a nod to each man.

He still felt uncomfortable with the situation between himself and Marcus, but he wanted to maintain what normality he could. If not for the sake of their relationship than for the sake of others watching.

"Your Grace, a pleasure to see you in person and without the other talking heads."

"I appreciate you making time for the journey. I know you must be as busy as I am."

Marcus took a seat, but not before grabbing a bag of pretzels from the cart in the corner of the room. "Don't let him fool you. When I got to the dockyard, he was busy closing a deal on a new estate."

Orzone shrugged. "Busy is a normal state of being for me. As for the estate, well...it's the cost of choosing the wrong side in this war." He smiled.

"We may need to assign some new monitors to keep an eye on your accounts. I have a feeling we are being horribly overcharged for everything from missiles to ration packs." Silas was only partially joking.

"By overcharged, you mean not charged at all. My companies are taking horrible losses to support the war effort," Orzone said, taking his own seat. He pulled a tobacco case from his jacket pocket. "Do you mind if I smoke?"

Silas waved him on and took his own seat behind the large desk. "We appreciate the line of credit, but I worry what the bill might look like when everything comes due with interest."

Marcus loudly opened the bag of pretzels. "It'll probably be equal to the cost of rebuilding a moon, that can't be too much right?" he said glibly.

Orzone spread his arms, smoke trailing off into the room from his lit cigarette. "A fair market rate, no more and no less," he said, blowing smoke toward the ceiling. "Would you like one? I apologize I didn't ask, but I know sailors usually don't smoke."

"Fire and starships don't mix well. Thousands of sailors smoking in a small, enclosed vessel is even more problematic," Silas said. "But let's get started. I know we have a lot to discuss."

Orzone crossed his legs. "We've made some strides at maximizing the output of the dockyards. The influx of workers from the surface has been a big help, although coordination with the fleet has continued to be a challenge," he summarized. "The *Specter* takes the supplies we send without argument but offers little cooperation on other matters."

Silas considered his options and saw Marcus shaking his head. He knew Marcus had something to say about Lancaster but was holding his tongue. "Direct your inquiries to Captain Dvorak aboard the Elysium for now. She should be able to coordinate what you need until Captain Lancaster becomes more available. How goes repairs to the captured carrier ship?"

"Slow, right now we lack the excess resources for a project of that scale. Basic hull repairs are the best we can do for now. Available factories have been converted to the production of munitions, vehicles, and other supplies for war." Orzone pulled a data chip from his jacket pocket and handed it to Silas. "This has a summary of the current production capabilities. Additional manufacturing facilities are coming online as we work out terms and management concerns with prospective magnates and the local authorities."

Silas worried about how little he understood of what Orzone was doing but also knew he had no one else with the expertise or local knowledge do it. In all his years within the Republic military, he never had to overly concern himself with the economics of war. He submitted budgets of course, but the actual business of it all had always been handled by ecclesiastical leaders, magnates, and their clerks.

Orzone took another puff of his cigarette. "Working with the banks has been problematic, but the longer they remain disconnected from Mars, the more accommodating they've become with offering lines of credit. So for now we have the funding we need to continue paying the soldiers and our suppliers."

"Maybe you can see about slipping in a raise for some of us," Marcus said.

Orzone smiled. "Maybe once profits improve."

"You better hope we win," Silas said, lacing his fingers on the desk. "I'll have my logistics officers go over this. I trust any details can be worked out with them."

Orzone nodded. "One other note is that industrial shipping traffic has begun to decline in the last two months since the beginning of your campaign."

"Is it something we should be concerned about?" Silas asked.

Orzone looked thoughtful. "Yes, in a broad sense. Luna needs raw materials to feed its factories. Traditionally raw materials flow out of the asteroid belt and to our factories depending on orbital patterns. Now, it looks like most of the traffic is being diverted to Mars or elsewhere."

"Well, we can continue to monitor. Once things become more secure perhaps, we can extend our security patrols to entice more commerce. Is there enough material in reserve for the time being?"

"Yes, Your Grace. I merely wanted to make you aware of the situation. There have even been some suggestions in the past of scavenging Earth for what is needed, but that would require dealing with the Iron Cage."

Silas grunted. "That is a complex problem for another lifetime maybe. Thank you for the report. Assuming there are no more pressing financial concerns, I would rather talk about the matriarch. What have you found out?"

Orzone motioned to one of the aids in the room for an ash tray. "The matriarch is aiding the archbishop in everything short of manpower. She has kept what forces remain hers close to home in the cities of her region on the light side of the moon."

Silas rubbed his chin. "She has the people and equipment to influence the war, maybe even turn things to one side or the other. You likely know her better. Is she waiting to side with the winner or eliminate whoever is left?"

Orzone took another puff of the cigarette while he and Marcus both looked at him appraisingly. "I think that depends on who is left. If the duchess comes out of this alive, likely the former. If not, well, I don't think she'll side with foreign invaders."

"We've tried to negotiate for the duchess's release through official channels, but that has unsurprisingly been a nonstarter," Silas said. "She's part of the archbishop's end goals somehow. Were you able to find out much more about her exact whereabouts?"

"Well, she's still alive," Orzone said.

"And locked away in a tower at the far end of a dark and dangerous forest," Marcus added.

"Something like that. My sources say she's being kept in the old fortress of the Selenean Summit, the Archbishop's capital city."

"I probably could have told you that," Marcus said.

Orzone pinched his nose. "The information is a bit more specific than that. I'm summarizing for the sake of time and security."

"Do your sources go by the name of Prometheus or maybe Hermes by any chance?" Silas asked suspiciously.

Orzone shrugged. "Do you want secrets or solutions? Revealing the first jeopardizes the latter."

Silas waved dismissively. "Would it be possible to extricate her?"

Orzone paused. The expression on his face said he had been considering this question himself. However, Marcus was the one who answered. "I can get her out of there. I've led these kind of extraction missions before. Small assault team, in and out before they even know we're there."

Silas had to stop himself from instantly saying no. Under normal circumstances, he wouldn't send away his closest advisor and friend, but these were no longer normal circumstances. They had far too many roles to fill and limited resources with which to fill them. However, then there was the question of trust. Trust that he was now forced to question.

Silas eyed Marcus to see if his face held any madness brought on by the nectar. "It's too risky."

Leaning forward, Marcus let out a heavy breath. "The way I see it, it's too risky not to try. For now, the archbishop still sees a way out of this. Once we have his city surrounded, how long will it be before he gets angry or desperate. He'll kill the duchess when we leave him with no other choice."

Silas knew he was right. The duchess was popular and influential, so it made sense to keep her alive while the prospect of ruling Luna was still in play. However, with no path to victory, she was at best a bargaining chip to get himself off the moon and at worst, a liability if kept alive.

He looked at Orzone. "Do you have a team that is up to the task? I can't spare much for such a low-probability mission." He wanted to emphasize how bad of an idea he thought this was. It wasn't quite a suicide mission, but it was very unlikely they would ever get anywhere close to the duchess.

"Yes. The Protean Company is up to the task. With Marcus, a few of your best marines, and some transport equipment, I think there's an opportunity here," Orzone said, evidently not sharing any of Silas's pessimism.

Silas looked at Marcus again but saw no madness in his eyes. He also saw no signs that Marcus would back down from this next questionable decision. *If this is how he wants to earn his absolution, then so be it,* he thought.

"See to it then," Silas said, trying to hide his apprehension. "We'll proceed with our larger plans to assault the Selenean Summit in tandem with your operation. With some luck, they'll be distracted enough that you can slip in undetected."

"I won't let you down," Marcus said in a deathly serious tone.

Silas considered if he was making the wrong choice in sending Marcus away. Marcus was experienced enough to see the risk for himself, but maybe he was looking for Silas to stop him. For his oldest friend to embrace him instead of sending him away like a pariah. It was possible, but Silas didn't offer him a way out. Above almost everything, Silas believed in personal accountability, and he knew Marcus had to reckon with the choices that led him to this point.

"Understand there's very little support we can offer if things go awry," Silas said, as if Marcus were any other soldier

Marcus saluted formally. "Evil must be contained," he said, reciting the fleet's motto.

"God wills it," Silas replied and considered how Marcus was taking his cold response in stride. "With that settled, we can discuss preparations for the coming siege and how this operation could work into our plans. There are many moving parts to coordinate but we have them cornered."

Orzone nodded. "I will summon the Protean Company captain. He should be part of this conversation."

Silas agreed and called in one of his aids. "Lieutenant, send a message to the senior command. We will meet shortly." There were too many things in motion now to second guess his choices. He had a heavenly edict to fulfill and obligations to his troops and the people of Luna to win this fight as quickly as possible. That also meant he had to consider every possible path to victory. He only hoped his goals of preservation over destruction proved to be the correct path.

Aron

October, 4103 U.E.T. – *MRG-739*, Interplanetary Space

THE FOOD IN THE MESS was delicious, and Aron was glad the cooks hadn't been part of the crew that abandoned ship before their hasty departure. He was able to eat his fill of noodles, dried meat, and compressed veggie cakes. At first, he was shocked that no one stopped him from retrieving a second or third helping.

They lost some sailors to defections, but a surprisingly large number remained onboard. Aron had only spoken to a few of them, but they seemed to fall into one of two camps. There were those who had personal grievances against the Republic and those who didn't see a difference in who they served. The latter group only wanted to be paid and fed.

No matter the reasons they gave, Gwen had set to work vetting them to the best of their ability. It was a far from perfect system. As they settled into their month-long journey, there were frequent fights between the original crew members and the Prometheus contingent.

Jimmy decided maintaining military discipline would be the best cure for the chaos, and it did help. Each group was forced to learn from each other, and through their collaboration they found common ground. Jimmy also repeated regularly that routine was the best cure for everyone's anxiety onboard a starship.

Aron tried to take that advice to heart and buried himself in his work. He had a lot to learn about starships and a short window of time. The more he learned, the more he would be able to help when the time eventually came for him to be useful. He even started a basic physical training regimen with Gwen. She insisted soggy noodles had no place aboard her vessel. Aron avoided asking her when it became *her* vessel.

Argos barked sharply from below the table. "Yes, OK," Aron said and broke off a piece of his veggie cake, tossing it under the table. It disappeared almost immediately.

Aron had taken to space travel faster than he expected but much slower than Clara. Maybe it was his sister's youth that gave her the flexibility to adapt to an ever-changing landscape so easily, although he supposed she probably didn't remember much about their old home anymore. Clara was young when their parents died.

He tried his best to make up for it, but the life he provided for her wasn't what his parents would have wanted for them. Aron took solace in knowing he had kept her safe. That was the most important thing.

He knew she was with Dame Heather now in the ship's small infirmary, likely tending to the wounded or, worse, the berserkers. The beasts had acquired a fair number of injuries in the escape from Mars, and there was no one save the two of them willing to help.

Clara had tried to explain to Aron why it was so difficult to treat the berserkers. The challenge, she explained, was the tangled collection of wires and tissue fused together with metal and bone. It was all interconnected in a way that was difficult to understand and made isolating the issue nearly impossible.

She had gone on incessantly about it like Aron would about fluid mechanics or astronautics. She explained what Dame Heather had taught her and her own ideas on how the berserkers came to be the way they were. He wanted to return her excitement but couldn't see past her safety. To him, they were dangerous beasts, or maybe even machines—it didn't matter. He didn't think they were capable of rational thought beyond fulfilling basic needs. Which didn't make them human.

"Are you still worrying about her?" Jimmy said, taking a seat across from him.

Jimmy had already heard Aron complain a dozen times about the berserkers and his fears. "How can I not? You know how dangerous this all is. Are you not eating?"

"No, I came to get you, but you can finish eating first." Jimmy helped himself to a chunk of his veggie cake. He grimaced at the taste. "Anyway, it's natural to worry, but you aren't her father. Even if you were, you need to let Clara choose her own path."

"That's easy for you to say. What if she chooses the wrong one, then what?" Aron said, stabbing at his food. He wasn't very hungry anymore.

Jimmy shrugged as he chewed. "Then you'll be there to help her sort it out, but she won't learn anything if you stand over her shoulder.

"Are you speaking from experience?" he asked delicately. Jimmy had never talked about his family, and Aron assumed that was on purpose.

"If she always thinks you will disapprove, then you'll be the last one to know anything about her life. Be supportive, and she'll come to you first. Then you can watch for the things she doesn't have the perspective to see and guide her accordingly," Jimmy said, and Aron assumed he was in fact talking from experience.

"That already sounds like what I'm doing. I'm older. I've seen things, learned things, she knows nothing about. I can protect her," Aron said defensively.

"No. You're deciding what she can and can't do to make yourself feel better. Let me ask you this, kid. Why did you study to become an engineer?" Jimmy said, leaning closer.

"My father was an engineer, and his mother before him," he said without thinking.

"Okay, and what was Clara going to study before all this happened?"

"Engineering, of course."

"Was that her decision? Did you ever consider that maybe she had no interest in engineering?" Jimmy said, eyeing him accusingly.

"Well, no, I guess not," he admitted. "It's our family tradition. It's what we're good at."

"It's what *you* are good at. Have you seen the way she is with the injured and sick? You probably haven't because you were too busy focusing on Justinian and his companions." Jimmy paused with a sarcastic smirk. "Like I suspected, you don't even know who I'm talking about, do you? This is why everyone needs to make their own decisions. We all have a unique perspective, but we need others too, because sometimes we miss things."

Aron was confused by what he was talking about. Then it dawned on him. Clara had told him the berserkers had names. She may have even told him what they were, but he likely never listened. "Are you talking about the berserkers?"

"I knew you were sharp. Figured that out pretty quick." Jimmy leaned back.

"You're talking about being objective. They're objectively dangerous. Did you see the big one, er Justinian or whatever, fight Skotadi? It was terrifying."

"Are they fearsome? Yes, absolutely, but they haven't harmed any of us. They follow directions and never avoid doing what's necessary. I won't pretend they don't make me uneasy," Jimmy said with a shrug. "But I think there's more to them then the stories people scare their children with. Your sister realized that too. I never knew they had names until Clara came. They just appeared one day with Hex and never left."

"What did Clara have to do with it?" Aron asked, unsure of what he meant.

Jimmy laughed, shaking his head in disbelief. "I didn't even think they could speak. They never said a word to me, only grunts and nods. Then one day your sister went up and asked the biggest one for his name. That's how I know it's Justinian. No fear, pure curiosity." Jimmy seemed almost wistful. "She has a special gift."

Aron would have to think about what Jimmy said. He thought there was some truth to it, but he also wondered if Clara was just naive. "So did you learn where they came from...Justinian and them?"

Jimmy shook his head. "It turns out they still aren't much for words. Anyway, I came here for a reason. We need to get back to the bridge."

"I didn't finish eating," Aron said, looking down at his mostly untouched food.

"I'm doing you a favor. Trust me. Food in the service was never known for being delicious," Jimmy said, standing up. He grabbed the tray and set it down on the floor for Argos.

"I thought it was good," Aron said hesitantly.

☼

Jimmy, Aron, Henry, and Gwen crammed into the small office attached to the bridge. It was a small space reserved for the commanding officer of the vessel to conduct day-to-day business. So it wasn't particularly large or spacious. If they had invited one more person, they would have had to stand shoulder to shoulder to fit.

"Couldn't we have used the actual conference room?" Aron asked. The heat felt stifling with so many bodies in such a small space.

Jimmy looked up from the chart on the table. "No, we haven't had time to finish sweeping the ship. If the major was even mildly competent, he would have taken measures to disable any listening devices in his own rooms."

"We're weeks away from Mars. What does that matter now? Besides, the relays are down anyway, remember?" Aron pressed.

"This is war, and information is everything. If it were only us, maybe it wouldn't matter much," Jimmy said, waving a pen in his hand for emphasis. "They wouldn't spare the resources to chase us, but with him and Lady Victoria on board, the math changes," Jimmy said, motioning absently to Henry. "I'm sure his father will want him back."

Henry's face tightened at the mention of his father, and Aron wondered if he was regretting his decision to leave. Aron didn't necessarily distrust Henry; Kaya had spoken well of him after all, but he was still suspicious. It seemed to him like Henry had too much to lose by coming with them and almost nothing to gain.

"So what's the plan then? Find the Pandora Fleet and whatever Prometheus members we can on Luna and go back to support Deimos?" Aron surmised based mostly on conversations he had overheard in the past weeks. There were some who wanted to focus on helping their allies on Deimos and others who already considered them dead and gone.

"Maybe," Jimmy said rubbing his chin. "Although I feel for our allies on Deimos, there may not be much we can do for them."

"My father was tasked with recapturing it, but they don't want to destroy it. The industries there are too valuable to the war effort," Henry said. "The docks aren't as large as others, but they're still capable of building and deploying warships if set to the task."

"I don't know that I like the odds of a bunch of seneschals and paper pushers against the Martian and Republican Guard," Gwen said.

"They're playing it smart and positioned themselves well. If they lose, the Republic also loses," Jimmy said. "Besides, they aren't all paper pushers. Most of the seneschals served before they took their posts."

Gwen looked dubious. "Served in some command office, you mean."

Jimmy sighed. "It is what it is now. We need to hope they win. What's left of Prometheus on Mars will be deep underground, and we likely won't have news for a long time."

"There was more than the facility I saw left?" Henry asked.

"Yes, many more. On other planets also. This loss will hurt our capabilities, but it's far from a death blow," Jimmy said adamantly.

Aron only had some idea of how large the Prometheus Group really was. Little clues he pieced together from reports and his work on the comms network. However, they all knew the emergency directive if things collapsed. They would go to ground, cease all operations, and await further instructions in the future. It was a choice of last resort, but it was where they were now.

"I don't think we can trust the Children not to stir up more trouble. Things seemed personal for Skotadi," Aron said.

Jimmy looked dismissive. "No, we can't, but the Children are a problem for everyone. You saw how they killed the Republic soldiers as easily as they killed ours. We'll need to figure out what their agenda is but right now, we need to worry about our own next steps."

Aron wondered about that too. Skotadi came personally to their facility, and he didn't think it was because Jimmy had rejected their offer. She was there for something or someone. So Aron felt confident there was more to it.

"Getting to my uncle is our best option. We can link up with his forces and then together retake Mars," Henry said confidently.

"Assuming he wants to retake Mars at all. What about the Mercurians? They came to help us," Aron said.

Jimmy looked up from the table. "Silas will want to help us. The Beckett family has ruled the planet for hundreds of years and is the rightful duke. Throwing that away now would go against every fiber of his body. He yearns for tradition and is above all an honorable man."

Aron was dubious, but Gwen nodded her agreement. "He's a noble sard. No offense," she said, turning to Henry, "but he's a good man. Always cared about his people."

"Alright, so if that's all true, what's the problem?" Aron asked. He wasn't sure why they were still discussing any of this at all. "We tell him his nephew is here, and he lets us into his fleet?"

Henry lowered his eyes, rubbing his forehead. Aron slumped into his chair, feeling extremely out of place. Gwen gave him a reassuring nod, but he didn't like feeling so clueless. He would rather stay in the engine room, where it was too loud to talk to anyone. So he never had to worry about saying something awkward.

Jimmy offered some context. "Well, we don't have much information. The few transmissions we had from passing ships were mixed. Some made it sound like it was an active war zone on Luna, others like any fighting was already over. I normally assume the truth is somewhere in the middle."

"The last report I saw regarding Luna," Henry said, "the archbishop had everything under control. There was only some minor unrest left to deal with. If you're right and my uncle is still alive, then that was likely a lie."

"That's my thought too. Which means best case, it's still a war zone. Hopefully one where the Pandora Fleet is winning." Jimmy turned to Aron. "How long could we stay operational if we aren't able to refuel at Luna?"

Aron did some quick calculations in his head of their fuel reserves and usage. "Maybe two to three weeks, maximum. We burned a lot of fuel exiting the Martian atmosphere. The fuel load was kept light to minimize weight while operating in the atmosphere. So we're nowhere near full potential."

"That doesn't leave us with much of a choice," Jimmy said thoughtfully. "We need to link up with the fleet or whatever's left of it. Some might remember my name, but I think it's better we leave mention of Henry out of it."

"Assuming they haven't changed them, I have security codes that should get us safely into their formation," Gwen added. "They won't get us much further though."

Jimmy nodded. "I can take care of that part. We need them not to blow us to pieces before we can talk to someone with some knowledge."

"How do we explain our motley crew and the Republican Guard vessel?" Henry asked.

Jimmy smirked. "Leave that to me, kid. Like I said, we don't need a great plan. It needs to be good enough to get us in the door. From there, we get to Silas, and the rest should be much easier."

Henry and Gwen nodded their understanding.

"What do you need me to do?" Aron asked, still wondering why he had been invited.

"You're our engineering officer. I'm going to need you to look the part. Gwen thinks she can whip you into shape with the time we have left. It will be easier that way."

Aron's stomach twisted. Every time he'd gone undercover, it had ended badly. Maybe not because of him, but he was obviously bad luck. "What does that matter if we're able to get into the fleet?"

"They might try to transfer civilians somewhere else, or at least kick out anyone without plausible credentials." Jimmy leaned back in his chair and crossed his arms. "They don't know you like I do, and I want to keep you close until Silas is standing in front of us. If we get into trouble, you'll be more useful than anyone else."

Aron was a bit surprised by such a bold statement. "I don't even know how to fight."

"You know how to operate controls, ship systems and a host of other things none of us here can fathom."

Aron already felt overwhelmed. Jimmy was expecting him to be proficient in things he had never once considered. He swallowed hard. "This is my first time in space. I don't know anything about this ship. I know even less about a floating city like the *Specter*."

Jimmy looked unconcerned. "Keep learning what you can. I trust you'll be able to figure it out. You have a better mind for these things than I've ever seen."

Aron took a deep breath and switched topics. "What about my sister and the other non-fighters? The berserkers?" If the wrong person saw those monsters, it wouldn't matter what any of them said. At least Henry seemed equally concerned.

"I'm going to need you to figure out a way to hide them on board. It's better they aren't found during any initial scans or visual sweeps," Jimmy said, like it was the easiest job in the world to hide a half-dozen bodies the size of horses.

Aron wondered what the rest of them would be doing while he solved all their problems. The room felt very hot, and he was sweating profusely. "I'll think of something."

He used to think he wanted adventure or a change of scenery. Now that he had it, he wanted to go back to his familiar corner of the library. "Anything else then?" Aron said, looking at each of them.

Henry and Gwen didn't have anything to add. Jimmy had already gone back to looking at the charts but looked up as if he remembered something. "Yes, actually," he shuffled a few papers before handing a small slip to Aron.

"What's this?" he asked.

"The new name of our ship."

Aron read the paper. "Titan."

Henry said, "A good name, I think."

Aron looked at them blankly.

Jimmy said, "It's bad luck for a ship to only have a number designation. So I'll need you to update the logs and systems. We're going to need all the luck we can get."

Aron took the paper and sighed at having yet another task.

"Anyway, we all have plenty to prepare. Let's get to it," Jimmy said, dismissing them.

SILAS

NOVEMBER, 4103 U.E.T. – SELENEAN SUMMIT, LUNA

THEIR PLANNING HAD BEEN meticulous. The fleet bombarded the city's shields while Silas watched from the edge of a distant rise. The missiles exploded in brilliant technicolor displays but by design, did little actual damage.

The bombs were mostly a distraction to keep the enemy's anti-air defenses busy while they moved their troops and armored units into position under the cover of Falcon squadrons. Although the open plains and craters of Luna were largely terraformed, the cities were still very compartmentalized. A legacy of the time when all the lunar cities were relegated to domes.

Lines of hover tanks moved in intricate formations on the flat plain that led to the edge of the city on the slopes of the Selenean Summit. Nestled in the center of the city, high on the mountain, was the archbishop's castle.

Through his binoculars, Silas watched clusters of their troops following closely behind the armored units. Falcons strafed overhead, ready to provide covering fire, but so far, they hadn't met much resistance beyond land mines and other traps.

"Status check," Silas sent on his private comms line to Marcus, who had left days earlier with the Protean Company contingent to undertake the secret rescue mission. Silas initially had his misgivings but was ultimately convinced the plan was sound.

"In position. Give the signal when you start lighting the place up," Marcus replied from somewhere deep in the castle's utility tunnels.

Silas replied simply with, "Stand by." Although he wanted to say more.

He was worried about Marcus. This was the first time they had operated separately for nearly a decade. His worry for his oldest friend drowned out his pain and anger at Marcus's betrayal of his trust. When Marcus returned, they would have to talk through it, but for now they both had work to do.

"General Taylor, bring me the city, so we can return it to the people," he said confidently on the open comm line. As much for his own men as for the enemy.

Silas wanted the archbishop to know he was there, and he wanted his troops to understand his intention. He would take this city whole and return it to the rule of the duchess and the Lunese people.

"Copy that, Lord Beckett. God wills it," Taylor replied. The formations began their crawl forward toward the city. He knew the initial assault would be bloody, but it was what the situation demanded. If the Lunese wanted their city back, they would have to bleed for it and most seemed willing to.

Silas lowered the binoculars and checked his armor was in order. He noticed Hayashi fidgeting beside him. "We'll join the fight soon enough," he said, trying to anticipate the young man's thoughts.

"We could level the city and begin anew. We can't proceed into the future with this cancerous patch left behind," Hayashi said, mirroring words Lancaster and others had said before. It was clear not everyone agreed with his more measured approach to warfare, and Lancaster's cancerous attitude was spreading.

"We're committed to our path and will see it through," Silas said before turning to Major Thompson, who had previously been the commanding officer of the Cloud Splitters. "Major, gather our team. We will join the assault."

Major Thompson had taken Marcus's place in his absence. Her tattooed face bore fresh scars from the Lunese campaign, which added to her intimidating presence. Her ability, years of service, and loyalty made her a logical choice.

She returned promptly with the squad that would accompany them to the surface.

Silas knew from his vision that he couldn't leave all the fighting to others. He needed to be here personally to see the Lunese who would not bend, delivered into God's hands.

Major Thompson saluted. "We are ready."

They began loading into a waiting transport ship that would take them from the rear command to the front lines. Hayashi seemed reluctant to go with them.

"Perhaps you would like me to remain behind to aid in coordination in your absence?" Hayashi asked, and Silas was surprised. Hayashi had never shied away from combat in the last several months he knew him.

"No, it's better that a Lunese native stands beside me on the battlefield, same as before. The people need to see we are united in our cause," he said, putting a hand on his shoulder. "Now isn't the time to lose our nerve."

Silas turned to enter the waiting transport, the nerves he always felt before a mission returning. What was new was that his hand began to shake.

Hayashi seemed to notice. "Are you well, Your Grace?"

"Quite," he said curtly.

As they were beginning to load into the craft, a lieutenant approached, handing him a comm device. Silas looked at it suspiciously before pressing it to his ear.

"I can hear your breathing, so I assume you're listening," said Orzone in his posh voice. "The Proteans are in position, but I have heard some rumors that concern me."

"It's a bit late for any of that," Silas said, stepping off the ship and walking to what passed for a quiet corner of the hangar bay. "Has our operation been discovered?"

"No, everything seems to be continuing smoothly, but I'm not as confident about your fleet."

"What about them?" Silas didn't hide the annoyance in his voice.

"Lancaster is repositioning vessels. I'm familiar enough with orbital combat to know what he's doing. It looks like there's a plan for a larger assault. I tried to contact Captain Dvorak, but she's gone silent. What do you know about that?" Orzone said coolly. "Given past events, you can understand why right now, on the eve of victory I have my reservations. I would hate to see your history with my family repeat itself."

Silas felt his blood rise and his hand continued to shake as he clutched the comms device. "Everyone will stick to the plan," he said through gritted teeth. He had made it clear from the very beginning that the orbital bombardment was meant to be little more than a distraction. Meanwhile, their ground forces and the extraction team led by Marcus would accomplish their real mission.

"I certainly hope so, but I will have my own ships on alert. I'll not repeat my father's mistakes," Orzone said, and the line went dead.

Silas cursed and considered smashing the comms device but thought better of the display. Orzone's paranoia threatened to undo them, now on the brink of a new dawn.

Major Thompson approached cautiously. "My lord, we're ready on your command," she said, hefting her lightning pike.

Silas placed the comm device in a compartment of his armor and followed her. As he loaded back into the transport, he grabbed his twitching hand to steady it. Orzone had sowed new doubt into his mind, and he was struggling to find the truth. So he did the only thing he knew to do. He prayed.

The battlefield was teetering on the edge of madness when they arrived. They were a fair distance back from the heaviest fighting, but even here the rattle of heavy machine guns and artillery fire rang out nearby. Exploding missiles and detonating land mines likewise shook the ground around them.

Silas watched from his new vantage as buildings were cleared one by one and medics rushed in to treat injured soldiers. He had given orders for them to treat any victims they found, regardless of affiliation. He was happy to see that the Lunese troops were following his orders.

Major Thompson motioned their unit forward toward a command vehicle where a dirt-covered captain stood issuing commands.

"Captain," Silas said through the short-range comms of his armor. "What's the status? Where's General Taylor?"

The woman looked confused by their sudden appearance. On closer inspection, her armor was heavily burned and damaged. He considered she may have been hit by a mine.

"My...my lord," the captain said, surprised, "we've hit fierce resistance. The enemy is heavily intrenched. The general took the main force forward personally to break their line." Silas cursed, hoping Taylor wasn't trying to die a hero.

A large mortar round exploded somewhere nearby, showering them all with dirt and broken concrete. The captain twitched momentarily before going back to relaying her orders, his presence there forgotten.

Major Thompson grabbed him by the arm. "Time to move!" she shouted, pulling him into a nearby office building for cover.

"We need to find the General. He was supposed to be here," Silas said, activating his comms device. "Taylor, where the sarding hell are you?"

There was a long delay before a crackling communication came through. "Your Grace..." He breathed heavily, straining. "I needed to take matters into my own hands if we're going to break the bastards. You wanted a city, and I plan to deliver it. I left Brigadier General Oceanus in command." There was another pause as a series of loud explosions detonated near Taylor. "Now if your highness will leave me to it," he said tersely and cut off the comms.

"Sarding hell," Silas muttered. They were all far too old to be playing heroes. "Let's find Oceanus."

Hayashi spoke from beside him, "What we need to do is unleash the orbital guns and level the city before we all die here."

Silas didn't want to have this conversation again. "You might appreciate an opportunity to rid yourself of rivals Lord Hayashi, but our goal remains the same. This is war, and war is messy. I suggest you find your nerve," he said, slamming an armored fist against Hayashi's chest. Silas noticed as he did that several of their soldiers twitched, as if they meant to defend the man.

Before he could process the implication of what he saw, the building shook as it was rocked by another missile strike. Followed by the familiar sound of Falcons and heavy Falcon bombers strafing the ground nearby, delivering their deadly counterattack.

While he was distracted, Major Thompson had pulled up a map in her helmet display, taking only a moment to study it. "A larger contingent of our forces are this way," she said, leading them back out of the building deeper into the fighting.

Silas nodded for her to lead on, turning away from Hayashi. Their small force followed closely behind as they navigated the chaotic streets and buildings of the outer city districts.

He kept his rifle at the ready but only had to fire a few shots. His squad was more than capable of handling what light resistance they encountered as they followed a trail of bloodshed toward their forces.

They came upon a small cluster of soldiers, who fired on them when they came around a corner. "I can't tell if they're ours," Major Thompson said, trying to get the unit on their short-range comms. "They aren't responding, and I can't see any blue armbands."

They hadn't had enough time to retrofit all the new Lunese soldiers with proper tags, so the displays of their exoarmor didn't provide them with useful targeting data. Silas had to make a quick decision. "Light them up. We need to get to the command dome."

Major Thompson didn't hesitate. She threw a grenade around the corner and led the charge toward the enemy barricade. The lightly armored troops of their squad following closely behind for safety.

Silas moved around the corner to provide covering fire and watched as she plowed into the enemy line, her lightning pike twirling effortlessly through the enemy. The Armani people of the ice moons were well known for their fighting prowess, and Major Thompson did her people proud.

In a few moments, it was over, and Silas was able to approach.

At first, Silas saw what he expected to see, wounded soldiers slumped behind broken barricades and burned-out vehicles. He moved a piece of debris to better see one of the soldier's bodies and noticed the band on his arm, under the dirt and grime he could tell it had been blue. These had been their own soldiers, or at least soldiers pretending to be.

"Saboteurs?" Major Thompson asked from beside him but he had no reply.

Silas scanned the scene for additional clues, but what he wasn't prepared to see was the neat row of civilians lying face down in the gutters. There were nearly a dozen bodies of men, women, and even children, their blood running into drains that should have only collected rainwater.

"God's bones," he said, offering the deceased a simple prayer as he made the sign of the star and cross. Silas had given no orders that would lead to this and couldn't imagine Taylor had either.

He wanted to think anyone who had seen the horrors of the Midnight Raids would never choose to give an order like those again, but he knew better than to be so naive. He had to get to the front and find whoever was responsible for this new horror.

"The people of this region can't be trusted. It's no loss," Hayashi said coldly.

Gunshots rang out near their feet and forced them to keep moving. God had tasked him with preparing the ground for a new future by cleansing it through his righteous fire, but not like this. He knew God to be firm and demanding in his judgment, but never cruel. Innocents were supposed to be led by hand to the light, not meet such brutal ends.

"Fleet command, this is Firebird. Status report," Silas sent through his comms.

No response came.

"Fleet command, I repeat, this is Firebird. Status report, over."

There was only more silence. *Why is no one responding to me?*

"Marcus, do you copy?" he sent on their private comm line.

"Copy that," responded a whispering voice. "It's been sarding quiet for a while on the comm line. I was starting to worry about you," Marcus said.

"Stay sharp. Not sure what's going on with our comms. One of the arrays must have gotten damaged."

"Copy that," Marcus replied, and Silas continued moving forward with the team. His concern was growing, but from his vantage on the surface he had a limited perspective. He knew it had been a risk coming here personally, but at the time it seemed worth taking.

They finally saw a mobile energy dome in the distance and moved in that direction. They sent a message ahead to make sure they weren't confused as the enemy. Thankfully any resistance disappeared as they got closer to the command dome. They could see large groups of soldiers retreating from the front lines in the distance.

Silas and his team were ushered promptly through the defensive perimeter despite the chaos. The young officers seemed to be struggling to direct the flow of soldiers as they passed by. The command setup was easily located in the center of the temporary energy dome that crackled occasionally under sporadic fire.

"General Oceanus!" he shouted over the noise, his helmet retracted. Men and women hurried around them on any number of tasks. His blood was running hot, and he wanted answers to what the sarding hell was going on. "I want a status report, *now.*"

The general looked up from a map displayed on a large digiscreen. He looked surprised to see Silas there beside him. "Oh, Your Grace. How are you here so quickly?"

"It would have been much quicker if my escort would have been where I expected it to be."

The general looked even more confused. "I had sent an escort to meet you when Lord Taylor advanced, but then I received new orders."

Silas moved in close. "What new orders, General?"

"To recall our forces from the city center. That's why I'm surprised to see you here," General Oceanus said with some hesitation. "I was told you were no longer coming."

"General, the plan was always for me to be a part of the assault, which is already well underway and going according to plan. Why would I order a retreat?" Silas reiterated.

The general looked to be formulating an answer, but it became unnecessary as the familiar sound of rockets crashing into the city's exterior dome began to ring out in the distance.

Dear God, what is happening?

"What of the civilian population?" Silas asked.

General Oceanus shrugged. "Left to fend for themselves. The order came to leave them and take no prisoners."

Silas felt sick. "You would abandon your own people so easily?"

"These aren't our people," Hayashi answered. "The theists don't deserve to share this moon with us any longer." The general didn't look like he disagreed.

"Get me a comm line to the *Specter*," Silas said forcefully, and the general motioned to one of his officers to comply. His mind raced to come up with a reasonable answer for why Lancaster would have begun bombing the city.

The young engineer replied, "Connection is down, General."

"Repair it then!" Oceanus shouted back and looked from Silas to Hayashi. He was surely trying to make his own assessment of what was going on.

"We need to get out of here," Major Thompson whispered into his ear. "I don't like the look of this."

Silas cursed. The missile launches were quickly becoming more intense, and any thought that this had been an accident washed away with the mushroom clouds blooming over the dome. He knew he didn't have much time to try and stop what was happening.

He remembered the device Orzone had given him and stepped away from the group. Pulling it out, he quickly entered the proper code.

"You better have a good explanation for why you would betray me now," Orzone said before the device beeped more than once.

"Orzone, what is going on? My comms have been down for the last hour," he said, trying to hide the panic he was beginning to feel. He had to shout to hear himself over the explosions in the distance.

"Are you on the surface?" Orzone said in disbelief. "Lancaster is unleashing hell on the city. No one in the fleet is responding to me, but..."

Silas stopped listening as he heard a ceramic blade being drawn behind him, his trained ears parsing the sound from all the rest.

"Drop the device," Hayashi said forcefully as he turned around. Major Thompson rushed to stand between them, her lightning pike at the ready.

"What are you doing?" Silas asked, lowering the device from his ear.

"What I should have done a long time ago. Silas Beckett, your authority is no longer recognized here. By my own authority invested in me by ancient imperial charter to my family, I'm relieving you of command and placing you under arrest." Hayashi stood tall and proud as he delivered his message.

The soldiers who accompanied them this far fanned out to support him. *So they were his men all along,* Silas thought. He should have anticipated this. Others tried to warn him, but he was so focused on his end goals that he had missed the signs of betrayal yet again.

Silas could see Oceanus reaching for the hilt of his ceramic blade but wasn't sure who he meant to strike with it. Only Major Thompson still seemed to be squarely on his side.

"Lower your weapon, and we can return to the *Specter* and discuss all of this," Silas said, trying to reason with the boy. There was still too much at stake. Not only Taylor and the success of their mission, but Marcus was deep within the city that was at this very moment being shelled to oblivion. Then he thought of Catherine back aboard the *Specter* and almost unraveled. *If they hurt her, I will have them skinned alive.*

"No. As I said, you're under arrest," Hayashi repeated and motioned for two of his soldiers to take him into custody.

Major Thompson stabbed out with her lightning pike at the first soldier who approached. The blade bit deep into his lightly armored chest, and he collapsed almost instantly.

Oceanus looked from Silas to the dead man and then to Hayashi. Silas had served with Oceanus some decades earlier. Now he waited to see which way the wind would blow. Without the generals' help, he knew they were unlikely to make it out of the situation alive.

"Take the duke into custody," Oceanus said to his own officers. The fully armored soldiers approached more cautiously with their weapons ready. "Go peacefully and we can sort this out when the battle is over."

"I will die with you now, Your Grace," Major Thompson said without hesitation. For the people of the ice moons, death in battle was preferable to failure. A worthy end to the story of their lives.

He appreciated her strength and honor, but in this moment he had more to gain from being prudent, unless God already decided he had failed in his mission and was to be discarded for good. If that was the case, then it didn't matter what he chose to do now. So he tried to do what felt right.

"This isn't the end," Silas said and motioned for Thompson to lower her pike.

Hayashi tilted his head, and the knights moved in to secure them both in shackles designed specifically for armored prisoners. His heart began to beat faster at the restriction placed on his body.

"You should have listened to your own commanders, Your Grace. You have your own hubris to blame for this. The duchess was always destined to die so new and fresh leadership could be installed," Hayashi said, walking beside him as they were lead away to a nearby transport. "Then you could have sailed back to Mars with your fleet and your daughter, but no, that wasn't enough for you."

Silas thought back to when he had first met the boy, trying to figure out where he had gone wrong in trusting him. "You know the situation was always bigger than that."

Hayashi shrugged. "Perhaps, but Luna was still never going to accept a foreign king, least of all you. My father always thought Duchess Engstrom was the answer to Luna's future, but she turned out to be even easier to defeat."

Silas could feel his skin prickle at that. "It was you who betrayed them. Now you'll betray the archbishop and what, take it all for yourself?"

Hayashi stopped in front of the transport ships entrance and turned to smile at Silas. "No, I'm not so bold, but I will take what is owed to me for my years of loyal service to the Frumentarii." Then he motioned for Silas to enter the ship.

Silas was seeing a theme of what loyal service to the Frumentarii looked like. It seemed like they had been working on dismantling the nobility from the inside out. "All for the small price of murdering your father and betraying your fellows."

Hayashi flinched slightly. "I tried to warn him, but he chose not to listen. We're all responsible for the path we choose to take." In that, Silas agreed with him, and he planned to hold Hayashi responsible. "But I would worry less about me and more about answering for your own failures."

Silas felt no need to defend his choices against Hayashi. "When we return to the *Specter,* you will watch your plan unravel. Lancaster and the others won't follow you."

Hayashi laughed and the pit in his stomach grew. "Who do you think came to me in the first place? I was ready to be your loyal lap dog for as long as I needed to be, but then Lancaster came to me with a better offer."

The transport ship's door closed with only the two of them, Major Thompson, and a few guards inside. The noise of their acceleration silenced everyone for a moment, and Silas choked down the bile rising in his throat. *Marcus had been right all along.*

Hayashi continued, "At first, I didn't believe him, but over time I saw how you sided time and again with Orzone and knew Lancaster was right. Yours wouldn't be a future either of us wanted."

Silas stopped listening. Without Lancaster, Marcus, the fleet, without Taylor and the army...what did he have? Nothing except Catherine, but she was still unconscious aboard the *Specter*. He was going to lose even more than he did on the day of the execution.

His hand trembled uncontrollably inside the gauntlet of his armor. He had lost and, in the process, betrayed Diana's memory, his daughter, his closest friends, and even God.

CHAPTER
35

Silas and Major Thompson were stripped of their armor and weapons inside the transport. Silas wanted to fight, to lash out at those around him, but he was only one man against dozens. Even with Major Thompson, it wouldn't be enough.

He appreciated that many of the regular soldiers seemed put off by what they were ordered to do, but they didn't try to help them.

He didn't blame any of them for not wanting to put themselves in the middle of a power struggle, one he should have seen coming but chose to ignore. He kept making the same mistakes despite the outcomes. His recent experience should have been the wake-up call he needed, and perhaps he thought it was, but the present circumstances said otherwise.

Now Orzone would think he was betrayed, and there was no telling how he would retaliate. Marcus was likely to be abandoned in the lion's den that was the archbishop's castle. Now he hoped the domes of the Selenean Summit could resist the fleet's bombardment. Then at least Marcus would have a chance at survival.

"This all could have been avoided," Hayashi said from his seat across from Silas.

"Yes, if you had any honor," Silas replied, regaining his composure. He wouldn't let traitorous cowards lower his own dignity. He was the Duke of Mars and would act like it until the end.

Hayashi scoffed. "There is no honor here."

"The Lunese are honorable people, but then there are those like you who give the rest a bad name. You could have helped change the world."

"Change the world? By what, returning the same duchess to power who kneeled to the clergy? By ceding authority to the magnates and their profiteering? I say there was no change to be had with your same tired system."

"You're smart enough to know the duchess had as much choice as any of us. Even when my daughter's trial and the ensuing conflict provided an opportunity for change, you abandoned her. Along with your own family. That is the move of a coward."

"I took a risk, because if I hadn't, I would have lost everything. The duchess was too weak to see this through, and my father was a fool to trust her," Hayashi said dismissively.

"You mean she favored other allies more. Like Orzone and his forces?" Silas prodded. He would use the man's vanity against him if he could. "Do you chafe at the idea that a commoner could be your superior?"

"They lack the pedigree and disposition of those like us. They think they're our equals, but they lack the innate ability to lead," Hayashi said confidently.

"Orzone assembled a fleet, gained noble patrons, and avoided capture for decades. I would say that is ability of the highest order. What have you accomplished besides stealing your father's legacy instead of building your own?"

Hayashi glared at him.

Silas shook his head. "You doomed millions to a life of decay and senseless toil, all so you could elevate your own position. This is why the Solar Empire lost the war so long ago. Do you actually think you'll wear a ducal crown?" He narrowed his eyes. "Who was it that promised it to you, Lancaster, the archbishop?"

Hayashi raised his chin and swallowed.

Silas blew air from his nostrils. "How long before your benefactor tires of you and chooses a new person to back? We all think we're irreplaceable until suddenly the floor falls out from under us."

Hayashi didn't respond.

Silas leaned back into the seat.

The real question now was why Hayashi hadn't killed him out in the field. If he had died in combat, they could have easily replaced him and gone on with whatever direction they chose. With him still alive, there was the chance the rest of the fleet wouldn't follow them.

Hayashi may have been able to handpick followers to do his bidding on the Lunese surface, but once they reached the *Specter*, Silas would regain the advantage. Surely Hayashi, Lancaster, and whoever might be involved in this plot knew that. It was a dangerous proposition for them, and Silas needed to learn their endgame.

When the docking procedure began, Hayashi handed him a digipad. Silas took it and almost crushed it immediately when he saw what was displayed. He understood now at least how they planned to keep him in line. "What have you done to her?" he snarled, tossing the device across the room in disgust.

"Your daughter is safe, for now. What you see there in the pouch connected to the intravenous line is enough narcotics to stop the heart of a berserker."

Silas tried to steady his breathing. "Why?"

Hayashi said cruelly. "We need to make sure you understood she wouldn't be coming back a second time. The hospitallers won't be able to fix this."

Silas stood up to charge the man.

"Uh, uh, uh," Hayashi said, holding up a finger and his own digipad. "Do it, and I deliver the drugs. Do anything I don't like, and I'll do it. If anything at all happens to me, it'll still be the end of your precious daughter. Do you understand?"

"What is it you want?" he choked out through his anger.

"For now, your obedience. We won't put you in chains through the corridors, but we also can't allow you an opportunity to rally your supporters," Hayashi toyed with the digipad in his hand.

"In any case, your most outspoken allies have already been reassigned to cells or the void of space," Hayashi said, and Silas began to understand what their plan was.

"You need me to issue the orders to destroy the moon," Silas said flatly. His chest ached, and he was finding it harder to breathe. They wanted him to betray his own people, the ones who had put all their trust into following him this far. Along with all the people he convinced to follow him. He would be their devil. He needed to find a way out of this, but they had Catherine, and that made him pause. He didn't want to betray her again.

Hayashi looked him in the eye. Silas had never thought of him as a cruel man, and even now he wasn't sure that was the right word for him. He didn't have the wild energy he saw in his brother's eyes. Hayashi took no pleasure in his suffering, but he would turn a blind eye to it for his own gain.

"You want to kill billions of your own people?" Silas asked, trying to steady himself.

"I don't want to destroy the entire moon. Only the portion that can no longer be redeemed."

"Look out the window at Earth," Silas said, motioning aggressively with his hand. "You would do the same thing now to even half a moon?"

"The atmosphere is thin, and most of the population that matters lives within the domed cities. Collateral damage will be minimal," Hayashi said calmly. He seemed to have already done the mental gymnastics necessary to ease his conscience.

"I won't be a part of this perverse exercise," Silas emphasized.

Hayashi motioned again with the digipad. "We'll see about that. All we want are the launch codes for the thermonuclear arsenal."

Silas ran through a brief inventory in his mind. There were four thermonuclear devices capable of doing what they suggested on board. He also realized that without Vice Admiral Zhou, who had yet to be replaced before the trial, there was no one else who possessed the codes to use them. There would be someone back in New Olympia of course, but not here and now.

"Do we have an understanding, Lord Beckett?" Hayashi reiterated.

They needed him because without him they could do nothing. At least he thought they couldn't. If they had a way to override the codes, surely they would have done it already. "Take me to Lancaster," Silas replied, never breaking the man's stare.

"I will take that as a yes. I hope you don't plan to beg, Lord Beckett. It would be beneath your dignity."

No, he wouldn't beg. He would find a way to tear them limb from limb. "I said take me to Lancaster. I'm done talking to a spineless coward."

Silas watched the man's eyes blaze with anger as he led Silas roughly from the transport. That was until others were in sight and he was forced to play the part of the loyal soldier. Silas was pleased to get this small victory. Even if it was petty. Major Thompson meanwhile was taken somewhere else, likely the brig, he thought.

They moved through the familiar halls of the *Specter,* and Silas pretended as much as a man like him could pretend. Anyone who saw him would know he was angry but wouldn't know why. Although they might assume it had something to do with the campaign.

Crew members saluted as he passed, and he at least took the time to acknowledge each soldier. These men and women had sacrificed everything for him, and he owed them so much more than he was giving.

Silas considered how easily he could slip away amongst the crew. He knew he could overpower Hayashi and then hide amongst the nest of corridors and rooms he knew better than nearly anyone. Except they had Catherine and who knew how many others. He would be condemning them to death and be no closer to a real plan. He could get away, but then what?

That thought turned into wishing he could speak to Marcus and devise a solution. The two of them had always made a good team, and Silas realized now how much of a fool he was to push him away. If he had left Marcus aboard the *Specter*, he doubted Lancaster could have executed his quiet mutiny.

Again, he prayed for guidance. Silas thought he had already deciphered the prophecy the angel had given him, but he knew now he had misunderstood the message. If he had been chosen by God, it was for a different reason than he originally thought. He tried to be an arbiter of God's justice, but here he was, a prisoner once again. Perhaps it was only a test of his devotion to his faith.

Silas looked back at the device in Hayashi's hand, and then the door that led to the bridge in the distance. This would probably be the best chance he had to get away, but it felt cowardly to take it.

Even if he tried, Hayashi was still fully armed and armored, making his chances of overpowering him unlikely. Silas was a skilled fighter, but Hayashi was still well trained, and he was severely disadvantaged. Even if he got away, there were thousands of personnel on board who could easily give him up if they chose to.

It was ultimately too risky of a proposition.

Silas continued forward and walked through the door and onto the bridge. He eyed the guards who stood watch and noticed they weren't the usual people. On the bridge, familiar faces were replaced with new ones he recognized but hadn't seen in a long time.

They were veterans from his youth. Hard and grizzled men and women like Lancaster who Silas had looked up to. Soldiers he had tried to model himself after in the beginning of his career. He eventually replaced them when given command after they became excessively complacent and callous in their old age. They were allergic to change and had little compassion for the people they claimed to protect.

Silas would never blame anyone else for the things he did during the Midnight Raids. He made his own choices that led to that grim history, but when he became high commander of the fleet, he equated those crimes with people like these. Not directly but intellectually he saw the callousness bred in them as one of the root causes for their brutality. From then on, he tried to develop a new ideal for the fleet based on honor, faith, and compassion.

Lancaster stood beside his captain's chair watching the digiscreens intently. The *Specter's* heavy rail guns continued their assault on the Selenean Summit. Silas walked up beside the man he had once considered family and scanned the screens for himself. Hayashi remained back by the doorway.

Neither of them spoke for a long time. Silas seethed internally at the betrayal but tried to maintain his stoic demeanor. He wondered only briefly if Lancaster felt any regret for the path he was choosing now. He assumed the man likely didn't. Lancaster was decisive and single-minded in his desires. Silas noticed Orzone's smaller fleet clustering around the dockyards and the captured carrier ship defensively.

Silas broke the silence. "You know you can't maintain this assault indefinitely without Orzone's armaments."

Lancaster nodded. His expression was neutral. "That's why we need the launch codes, High Commander. We need to end this now. Orzone and his allies will fall into line after that."

"Why now, after all this time? The war has been an enormous success," Silas pressed. Maybe there could be a peaceful resolution.

"We didn't fight in Martian orbit to slowly bleed to death on Luna."

"*We are winning*, Lancaster. Release my daughter, and we can move on from this folly."

The old, grizzled man shook his head. "I don't have many years left, but I intend to spend them in my home. Every day spent here is another day I will miss with my family. I'll leave what's left for Hayashi, and he can do what he wants with it. The rest of us will sail back home to Mars. I made a mistake thinking you could win this fight."

Silas tried an appeal to reason. "Returning to Mars was always the plan, but with support and infrastructure behind us instead of burning flotsam. Going alone like you're suggesting is suicide. Did Bishop Vesivi convince you to take this path, the Mercurians?" Silas said, remembering the warnings Marcus had tried to give him.

Lancaster looked back at Hayashi and lowered his voice. "No, your pet priest tried to stop us but failed. Your brother on the other hand... He will welcome me back with open arms."

"My brother? How is Simon involved in this?" Silas asked, unable to hide his surprise.

"While you were away on the surface, he sent an emissary," Lancaster said with a satisfied expression. *How much more information had been kept from him?* "So we will sail home, and when Mars is secured, I will retire. The Republic and Mercurians can fight over whatever is left of Luna. It makes no difference to me."

"My brother is a man who murdered his own father and watched his niece burn," Silas said in disbelief. "This is the devil you've decided to deal with."

"I'm not as stupid as you think. I'm returning with a fleet while they're busy fighting the Mercurians over Venus. I'll be able to bargain a better deal."

Silas narrowed his eyes. "You're going to sell me to my brother?"

Lancaster shook his head. "No, he wants you dead actually."

Silas let out a sarcastic laugh. Why was he not surprised? "The Mercurians will come for me."

Lancaster smiled. "I don't think so. When I informed them of your failure here and the death of their precious flower, Lady Kaya, they were quick to send orders for our departure from this place under my command. I was instructed to bring you in to face justice. You should be honored. The bidding for your bones is competitive."

"You're walking a knife's edge trying to play both sides. They know that game better than you could ever hope to," Silas said honestly. Lancaster was very much out of his depth.

Lancaster said bitterly, "I'm not surprised you have no faith in me."

Silas's jaw tensed. "You betrayed a lifetime of camaraderie and the lives of billions on Luna because you were homesick and jealous?"

"Your brother and Lord Vardan assured me there would be rewards for loyal service. There will be Baronies left abandoned by traitorous rebels. I'll finish this last mission, and my family will be secure for generations to come. It doesn't even matter which side wins. I don't expect you to understand the value of that," Lancaster said accusingly.

"What of your honor? Your oath?" Silas said, digging his eyes into the man.

Lancaster moved his face within inches of his own and pressed a finger into Silas's chest. "What have my oaths or our friendship earned me? I won the battle over Mars, while you prostrated yourself before the Vox. Again, I won over Luna when you were lying delirious in a sick bed from that explosion. *I* did that, not you or the others, but *me*!"

"The Mercurians won over Mars, as much as the other dozen captains and thousands of marines who fought in the battle. Luna was no different. Your skill was important, but it wasn't the only factor," Silas countered.

"You say that, but then I'm still wearing the same captain's insignia as everyone else," Lancaster said, angrily, indicating the golden eagles pinned to his lapels.

Silas let out a breath and shook his head. It was the same story for nearly everyone. Their honor was for sale for titles and empty promises. "I won't give you what you want. I won't let you do this."

Lancaster sighed heavily and turned to stare off at the monitors. He couldn't even look Silas in the eye now. "You know we have Catherine. Give us what we want or-"

Silas didn't have his blade, so he pulled back his arm and drove his fist into Lancaster's face. It struck with a resounding crunch as he felt the man's face buckle. At the mention of his daughter, he lost what composure he had left. This worm didn't deserve to utter her name.

"By God's bones, I will see you all burn!" Silas screamed as he jumped onto Lancaster and struck him several more times before jumping back to defend himself.

Hayashi rushed forward, having grabbed a lightning pike from one of the guards. He swung out at Silas, the coiled electricity only narrowly missing its mark.

Lancaster meanwhile rolled on the floor, moaning and spitting blood. The remaining bridge crew moved to block the exit.

Silas dodged the blade of the spear and managed to strike Hayashi's face before he was able to raise his helmet. With the helmet up and the exoarmor fully activated, Silas had no more soft targets. He tried to move past Hayashi, rolling to the ground and out of his guard. He avoided another strike of his pike and managed to barrel over the bridge crew, making it to the door controls.

It was then that he felt the shock of the electricity coil through his body. He gasped for breath as the air left his lungs, and he felt like he had been kicked by a berserker. He fell to the ground convulsing, and Hayashi moved to stand over him, the digipad in his hand.

He retracted his helmet as Silas struggled to catch his breath. "I warned you, Lord Beckett."

Hayashi pressed the trigger on the device.

Henry

November, 4103 U.E.T. - *Titan*, Great Cislunar Plane

Henry watched on the cameras as a Falcon flew in formation beside the *Titan* to escort them. They had arrived within patrol distance of Luna and were quickly spotted by the Pandora Fleet's scouts. What knowledge they were able to gain from the sparse traffic leaving the moon was enough to convince them the fleet was still largely in control.

The commander of the escort came in on the comms. "Vessel *Titan*, you're outside approved navigation channels and entering restricted space. State your name and intentions. Over."

"Follow the script," Jimmy said to Aron.

Aron cleared his throat before activating the comm line. "This is vessel *Titan* of the Pandora Fleet. Providing security codes now. We must speak with the high command at the first opportunity. Lives depend on it."

"Standby for verification."

"I don't think they're going to buy it," Aron said nervously.

Henry appreciated how Aron looked the part in his new engineering officer uniform. Gwen had found one that miraculously fit amongst the previous crews' things. Although Henry mused it wasn't that miraculous, as the tech sorts tended to be rather gangly.

Jimmy put up a comforting hand. "The security credentials are authentic. This is the easy part."

"Vessel *Titan*, follow us. Providing telemetry now for the *Specter*. You're assigned to port C14 for docking. Deactivate all weapons systems and lower shields to ten percent. Over."

"Should we actually lower our shields?" Aron said, looking back to Jimmy.

"Do it. It's standard procedure for docking to a capital ship like the *Specter*."

Henry added. "A direct hit from the guns on a ship that size could pulverize us with or without our shields."

Jimmy whistled his agreement.

The large displays on the bridge were set to an exterior view, creating the effect of a forward-facing window. Now they could all see up ahead the hulking form of the *Specter*. Henry had visited the ship before as a child, so it held no special mystique, but its size was still impressive. Meanwhile, Aron gaped openly at the immensity of it. It wasn't until they got even closer that they could see the large starboard canons firing toward the Lunese surface.

"Maybe this was a bad idea," Aron said.

"We knew this was an active war zone. Let's be thankful they aren't firing at us," Henry said.

They had cleared the ship of anyone they didn't feel they could trust the week before, launching them back toward Mars along the established shipping lanes in one of the escape pods. Knowing they would get picked up by a passerby eventually. Henry was glad for that mercy; he had seen enough executions recently.

Now they numbered less than thirty crew, which proved to be barely enough to operate the vessel effectively. Henry was impressed by Aron's ability to keep all the unfamiliar systems running smoothly in the absence of many experts.

"Approaching now for docking procedure," Aron said with only a hint of hesitation. "Seb, get ready to take the controls."

Henry turned to look at Seb, the son of a young magnate who turned revolutionary. He was well cultured if not a little peculiar, but he and Aron seemed to get along well.

The *Titan's* original pilot had been off the ship at the time they captured it. Then the secondary pilot was let go with the others in the escape pod. That left Seb, somehow, as their next most capable pilot. At least he had something of a talent for it.

"Slow and steady, kid," Jimmy said. The large man seemed unconcerned and sat back in his command chair. Henry assumed he had worked with many young pilots over the course of his career.

"Wouldn't want you to accidentally crash into one of the greatest warships that ever existed," Gwen said dryly. Gwen had likely spent a good amount of her career heckling young pilots.

Henry stifled a laugh. He found the banter good for his nerves.

"Seriously, can you guys be sarding quiet and let him concentrate?" Aron scolded. "No, not you," he said to the bridge crew. "Give me distances, come on!"

The screens switched to a view of the docking port on the starboard side of the vessel. Henry tightened his grip on his own seat. It looked like such a small target from his perspective.

"Twenty meters and closing. Approach speed one meter per second. Sir," the technician added hastily at the end. "Ten meters and closing."

"Seb, hands off. Standby for contact and capture," Aron said.

"Copy, one meter, hands off," Seb replied smoothly.

Henry worried they would slam hard into the designated port, but then he could see short blasts of air as the electronics took over directing the final docking procedure. The entire ship shook gently as they made physical contact.

"Soft capture confirmed," Aron relayed to the crew of the *Specter*.

"Vessel *Titan*, soft capture retraction underway. Standby for hard capture."

Aron let out a heavy sigh.

"Good job chap," Seb said, extending a fist to Aron who returned the gesture.

"Can I go to bed now?" Aron said, wiping his forehead.

Jimmy stood up from his chair. "Now the hard part starts. Aron, Gwen, Henry with me. The rest of you know where you belong. Forward unto glory," he said, marching toward the exit.

By tradition, as commander of the ship, Jimmy would be allowed a small escort while everyone else remained onboard the vessel. They had settled on having Sergeant Smith and Seb stay behind to monitor things. They all knew the ship wouldn't be going anywhere without clearance anyway.

Their small group formed up at the gangway waiting for the doors to click open. None of them wore armor as was customary, instead opting for standard military uniforms. Only Gwen's uniform bore Pandora Fleet insignia since it was still her original clothing. The rest of them had acquired suitable Republican Guard uniforms from the ship's stores. They'd left the original names and patches in place.

"If you're the religious sort, now might be a good time to pray," Jimmy said.

Henry took a deep breath and made the sign of the star and cross. There was always the possibility they would be shot on sight. Henry had left his plasma blade behind, lest it raise unusual suspicions. They didn't want to use his name and origin unless it became immediately useful, so he wore a ceramic blade he found onboard. The weapon wasn't his preference, but he was competent in its use. The others carried pistols on their hips.

"It's been an honor and a pleasure," Henry said, only partially joking.

"Wish I could say the same," Gwen quipped, and Jimmy laughed.

"Can you all stop sarding talking like that?" Aron said as the doors began to click and clank open.

"You get used to it," Henry said softly, his body tensing more with each passing second. When the door fully opened and no gunshots rang out, he was able to relax slightly.

An armed guard stepped forward to meet them. They held their guns firmly but pointed downward. "By God's bones, it was supposed to be an easy day. Who the sarding hell are you lot?" a middle-aged petty officer said gruffly.

Jimmy stepped forward to speak for them. "Commander Torres, Pandora Fleet, recently returned from the dead. We need an audience with the high commander right away. There's a lot at stake."

The man looked Jimmy over and then the rest of them. "Yeah, and I need an audience with the Vox to talk about my itchy balls. Let me guess, you lost yer credentials too?"

Jimmy reached into his pocket, and the guards tensed. He put up a hand to calm them down and slowly pulled out a piece of paper. "No credentials, we lost them in our escape from Mars. We were left behind when the fleet retreated. I have my security codes here though."

The man took the paper with a raised eyebrow. "Take these and forward them to the lieutenant," he said, handing the paper to one of the sailors. Then he turned back to Jimmy. "How'd you end up with the guardsman ship?"

"They weren't making full use of it, so we decided to take it off their hands," Jimmy said, and the man laughed.

"Serves the bastards right. Hope you gave 'em hell, Commander."

"Aye, we did. What about the fleet here? Looks like you guys got on well. We haven't had much news."

The man beamed with pride. "The Lunese tried to double-cross us like the pirates they are, but we trounced 'em easy. Now they'll regret it when their moon is melted. Am I right?" the man said with a laugh.

Henry ignored the banter. Scanning the hangar bay, he saw the House Beckett banner hanging on the wall but noticed it looked different. "What's with the crown on the banner?" he asked, and Jimmy shot him a look.

"After the battle, the crew got together and decided we didn't want any leader besides the high commander. The King of Mars."

Henry wanted to ask a follow up question but was interrupted when the sailor returned a few moments later.

The sailor spoke softly to the petty officer, "Lieutenant says he can't get through to the bridge, so put them in detention for now."

"Something wrong, Petty Officer?" Jimmy asked.

"Sorry, Commander, looks like the brass are busy with the invasion and all that. Gonna have to take you into holding for now." He turned back to his squad. "Lock down their vessel, no one in or out."

"Is that really necessary?" Jimmy muttered.

"Afraid so, you know the rules, but if you want to resist, I don't mind. It's been a little boring up here lately," the man said with a big yellow grin.

Jimmy seemed to consider his options before nodding to Henry and the others. Soldiers came forward to confiscate their weapons.

"You'll get these back once they clear you."

"And when might that be? Call the lieutenant back and have him come talk to me. I can set this straight right now," Jimmy said.

"Sorry, Commander. You might normally call the shots, but for now no one knows who you are. Might be a frumentarii agent for all we know. Is that what ya are?"

Jimmy stretched his neck, obviously exasperated.

The petty officer grinned again. "So are you going to go quietly, big guy?"

Jimmy raised his hands innocently. "I promise to behave. I know the way if you want us to head over there on our own."

"Nice try, frumi," he said, attaching plastic restraints to Jimmy's wrists. Soldiers came to do the same to the rest of them.

Henry noticed Aron looked increasingly nervous. The petty officer said to Aron, "First time being captured?"

"I wish I could say it was," Aron said, and the man laughed even louder.

They were led deeper into the vessel under armed guard. Henry felt calm despite the uncertainty of the situation. His conscience was aligned with his actions, and the feeling left him lighter than normal. He smiled thinking of Kaya and what she would have thought of all this. He guessed she would have loved the adventure.

He hoped she was okay wherever she was and prayed he would get a chance to speak to her again at some point. Aron had said she came for him but left because of Victoria. It was true Victoria had come to him after she left, but it was out of worry for her friend and not romance. At least that was what she told him.

"In ya go, single file," the petty officer said, stopping in front of a large door. Another set of guards followed the small group inside.

Through the door was a smaller room with a single desk manned by a serious-looking sergeant. "Where'd you find this lot?"

"Some drifters from Mars. Lieutenant wants them held until they can be vetted," the petty officer said lazily.

"Where am I supposed to put them? Running out of space over here," the sergeant replied.

"Put 'em in the reserve cell. I'll go check with the lieutenant and come back for 'em. See ya soon, Commander." The petty officer saluted Jimmy and left them in the care of the remaining soldiers.

The sergeant let out a long sigh and scratched his head, before making some notes in his logbook. "Name, rank, affiliation, and ID number."

They went one by one providing the information, which was only partially fabricated in the case of Aron and himself. Then they were led into the next room, which was much larger and lined with glass and steel-clad holding cells.

He was immediately struck by the number of people in the cells, many of whom wore Pandora Fleet uniforms. Jimmy noticed the same thing.

"Why are all these soldiers locked up in here, Sergeant?" Jimmy asked.

"Potential Republic spies," he said casually and led them to the last empty cell. It would be a small space for all of them to squeeze into.

"Get inside, and I'll cut your bindings once you're in there," the sergeant said, but Jimmy paused. He was looking at the cell across from theirs. In it was an old man who looked familiar, but Henry couldn't place him.

"What are you waiting for? Inside, now!" the sergeant repeated. He tried to shove Jimmy, but he didn't have the strength to move the larger man. The guards moved forward with their weapons.

Jimmy looked over to the rest of them and said, "Remember what I said before about the plan? Well, forget all of it!" and he proceeded to headbutt the sergeant.

Henry's training kicked in, and he charged the nearest guard who had a rifle. Gwen moved to attack the other, but not before pushing Aron to the ground and out of the way.

Henry stomped on the top of the man's foot. The soldier cried out in pain, and Henry used his bound hands as a cudgel, swinging down with as much force as he could muster. The soldier fell to the floor, and Henry grabbed his rifle.

Jimmy gave the sergeant one more swift kick before dragging his limp body into the open cell. "Get the bodies in here for now. Aron, get the other cells open."

Henry turned to see Gwen on the ground hovering over the last fallen soldier having dispatched him with his own knife. She was breathing heavily. "Care to tell us what that was?" She turned to look where Jimmy was pointing in the other cell. "Mr. Beach? Captain Dvorak? What the sarding hell are you two doing in here?"

Gwen used the bloody knife to cut all their bindings.

Aron jumped into action once Gwen released his hands. He began searching the sergeant's body, presumably for a clearance card. Meanwhile Henry helped Gwen move the bodies. Henry still had no idea who the occupants of the other cells were, but a few moments later Aron had the door open.

"Commander Torres," the old man said. "I have no idea how you're here, but your timing is impeccable."

The woman, Captain Dvorak looked furious. "Get the rest of these cells open," she shouted at Aron, who nearly tripped over himself to comply. "Lancaster is trying to stage a mutiny, but there might still be time to stop him."

"Sarding hell, where is he now?" Gwen asked.

The old man answered. "We don't know, but they have Catherine also. We need to get to her first. She should still be in the medical bay."

Henry wasn't sure he heard that properly. "Catherine Beckett? Do you mean my cousin is alive?"

"Yes, but not for long if we tarry any longer," the man said.

Henry was doubly surprised the old man seemed to know who he was. Then it dawned on him. "You're my uncle's valet, aren't you?"

"Yes, I'm Mr. Beach," the man said.

"Is my uncle dead then?" Henry was trying to understand why else this man would have been locked away.

"The duke was still alive last I saw him, but we shouldn't waste any more time. He might not be for long," Mr. Beach said anxiously.

Jimmy asked hurriedly, "Do you know if Silas is on board?"

Mr. Beach nodded vigorously. "Yes, I saw them take him off a shuttle with my own eyes, but I was careless, and they caught me spying where I shouldn't have been."

"They were smart enough to know how much trouble you could cause," Jimmy said with a sly expression.

Aron began opening the other cells and out of each one flowed dozens of angry soldiers who looked keen on retribution.

Jimmy ran his hand through his beard. "Alright, Captain Dvorak, can you and the others start looking for the high commander? We can go for

Lady Catherine and then regroup at the bridge. If neither of us finds him before that, then that's where he's likely to be. It's the most secure place on the ship."

The captain grabbed a pair of comm devices from the unconscious soldiers. "Yes, but let's take these," she said, handing one to Jimmy, who passed it off to Aron.

"Do what you have to, but we should try to avoid any large-scale violence. It's better we find them before any alarms go off and everyone's on high alert," Jimmy said.

"I don't intend to burn the ship, but there's a few individuals I might consider. Good luck, Commander. Pandora eternal! With me!" Captain Dvorak shouted and ran off at the head of her angry horde.

Henry said to Jimmy, "Alright, lead the way."

Mr. Beach stepped past him, taking the lead. "Try to keep up, My Lord."

"You heard the man," Jimmy said and followed, Gwen closely behind. Aron was distracted fiddling with a digipad he had retrieved. So Henry gave him a motivating push toward the door.

CHAPTER
37

SILAS KNEW HIS BODY was broken. His arms and legs were tied tightly to the table, an improvised rack. His naked body bare for their violence.

The lash cracked again on his back, but no cries escaped his lips. He had receded deep into his mind. To a place without the pain of this world. Willing his soul to the Celestial City.

"For through the mercy of God, may I bask in the light," he shouted.

Crack.

"Glorious God, show me your eternal beauty and welcome me to your kingdom!"

Crack.

"You will give us the codes, or you'll never be reunited with your daughter in the afterlife. You will be cast into Eden as a ruined and broken thing. Destined to shamble amongst the traitorous rabble for eternity," Hayashi shouted back, but it only vaguely registered. Then he saw Hayashi raise the whip yet again.

Crack

"For even if my distance is great, your eternal light burns with the fire of an infinite sun. Its rays are your angels, descended to guide us through the darkness. I will follow even the faintest light to your glory!" Silas shouted again, repeating scripture and through it finding his strength.

Crack.

Silas no longer felt the lash and gave them his bloody smile. He belonged to God now, and there was nothing more to be said. He would endure this trial and be welcomed home as a martyr. What was a temporary moment of agony for an eternity of peace.

"Enough," Lancaster called. "He's more stubborn than a mule. Try something else."

Silas could hear Hayashi panting from the exertion. "We can cast him into the darkness now and let the engineers figure it out. We've wasted enough time."

"There's no rush, My Lord. Orzone isn't contesting us, and the archbishop is stuck in his castle. We have time to continue in unison with the engineers. We can always stop if they figure it out first. There's still one more thing we can try." Lancaster leaned in closer to Silas's ear. "You know I don't enjoy this. I wouldn't have killed your daughter if it was up to me. Tell us what we want to know and this all ends. Quick and painless."

"The faithful will reject the will of serpents. They will cast fire into the darkness and burn away shadows. For evil cannot abide the light."

Lancaster sighed and turned back to Hayashi. "Do it."

Silas closed his eyes, and there he could see the brilliant glow. Feel the heat as it wafted over him. He would see his wife and daughter soon, and the thought exhilarated him. He felt a pang of guilt that he couldn't rescue the people of Luna or Mars, but he had tried. Now in his final moments he would use his strength to resist.

The familiar glow of a plasma blade burned through the fire of his mind and his bloody eyelids. He opened and saw Hayashi standing menacingly over him with Silas's own blade. The man didn't deserve to wield such a fine weapon. Silas spit blood and phlegm toward him.

Hayashi easily dodged the assault and laughed bitterly. "If the love of your daughter wasn't enough to keep you in line, perhaps the loss of your limbs one by one might be. This is your last chance, Lord Beckett. I've been asking nicely."

Silas tried to steady his breathing. "I've no need of hands or feet in the kingdom of heaven."

"So be it," Hayashi said and stepped closer.

"I will face the darkness without fear and stay steadfast in my duty to safeguard the realms of man," Silas said, echoing the oath of the Pandora Fleet.

"Your God has abandoned you, along with your fleet," Hayashi said, but he didn't listen.

Silas didn't look away from the blade. He would meet his trial with as much strength as he could muster. Catherine didn't avoid the flames when given the chance. He owed her memory that much and more. She was brave beyond measure.

Hayashi moved the plasma over his right hand, above the wrist. His sword hand. He allowed the blade to hover there as he looked Silas in the eyes. Silas felt the hairs singe on his arm but didn't look away.

Hayashi pressed down slowly.

The blade passed through flesh and bone with ease, and Silas cried out then. His body wouldn't allow for anything else, and he screamed as the pain erupted in his arms. It took only a moment, but the pain continued unabated.

Silas heard a faint *thunk*. Opening his eyes, he was faced with the grizzly image of the ruined stump where his hand should have been.

Lancaster said, "Let's give him a moment to consider his next decision."

Silas felt Lancaster's hand pat him on the shoulder as he panted, struggling to get himself under control.

Hayashi snuffed the blade and clipped it to his own belt. "I never had the luxury of owning one myself. I'll be sure to tell everyone about how I came to possess yours. Think hard now, Lord Beckett. We'll be back soon."

CHAPTER

38

Aron

November, 4103 U.E.T. - *Specter*, Great Cislunar Plane

THE HORDE OF PRISONERS that left ahead of them looked committed to burning a path of destruction despite what the captain had
said. When Aron's group stepped out of the brig, the pair of guards who
had been stationed outside the doors were lying bloody and unmoving.

"Try to act like you belong here. We'll never make it anywhere if we try
to fight our way. There are thousands of sailors on this ship," Jimmy said.

Aron thought that sounded perfectly fine to him. No one else offered
any complaints.

The old man led them confidently through the halls and Aron was
happy for it. Jimmy and Henry hadn't exaggerated when they said the
Specter was more of a small city than a ship. The maze of corridors quickly
overwhelmed Aron's senses.

"These hallways go on forever," Aron muttered.

"Keep your heads up and follow me. Don't let anyone question your
presence here," Mr. Beach said.

"I'm as lost as you are," Henry said.

Jimmy tried to reassure them. "Stay close to the rest of us, and you'll be
fine. The rest of us have spent a large chunk of our lives on this ship."

Mr. Beach shushed them. "Keep your voices down. We're almost at Lord
Beckett's quarters. I doubt he's there, but I need to retrieve something."

Luckily, they didn't encounter any resistance through the corridors.
Either some combination of Mr. Beach or their uniforms meant some gave
them strange looks, but no one stopped to molest them.

Mr. Beach stopped at a large pair of doors. "In here," he said, scanning his security card. There was a beep, but the door didn't open. "It seems they've locked me out."

Aron pressed forward while the others stood guard. "Here, let me see," he said, moving to the door controls. "I need a knife or something."

Gwen held out the bloody knife she had used to kill the guard, and he grimaced. "It's this or nothing."

Aron took it reluctantly and used it to pop open the control panel. He connected his pilfered digipad to the controls and began typing. He looked nervously down the corridors.

"You focus on that. Leave lookout to us," Gwen said.

It was taking him longer than usual to find his bearings with the new system and lacking his normal equipment. Aron couldn't resist turning his head as a small group of soldiers turned down their corridor. Aron tensed.

"Keep going," Gwen mumbled.

Aron turned back to the screen but heard their steps getting closer behind him.

"Hey, that's a restricted area!" shouted one of the soldiers.

Gwen was going to raise her rifle, but Mr. Beach pulled her back and stepped forward. "I simply lost my security card. I found the only available engineer I could to help me back in," Mr. Beach said, affecting an old and decrepit manner.

Aron tried clumsily to hide the bloody knife in his pocket and almost dropped it in the process.

"Oh, Mr. Beach, I didn't see you there. Of course, sir. Anything we can do to help?" the soldier said, moving closer to them. Aron tried to appear inconspicuous and returned to his work.

"Oh, no, that's okay. Go about your business, I should be all sorted out in a moment," Mr. Beach said, almost in unison with the door sliding open. "There we are. Thank you for your help."

The soldier narrowed his eyes at Aron. "I think you might have cut your hand, sir."

Aron tensed. "I what?" he asked.

The soldier looked more confused. "On your hand, it's bloody."

Aron looked down at his hand, his eyes going wide. "Oh yeah, a small cut from opening this panel. I'll get it checked out."

"Must be pretty bad with all that blood. I can look if you want. I have my med pouch. Save you some paperwork," the soldier said with a grin.

Jimmy stepped in. "That's okay, Ensign. We can send him along shortly. We're in a hurry."

"Yes, sir, sorry you had to experience the inconvenience as a guest on the ship." Then the soldier turned to Mr. Beach. "You need to be more careful with your credentials. We don't want them falling into the wrong hands. Especially these days." He sounded like someone speaking to their forgetful grandfather.

Aron thought the soldiers saw the Republican Guard uniforms and assumed they were guests of Lord Beckett.

"Yes, of course, first and last time it will ever happen to me. Now please don't let an old man hold you up from your service."

The soldiers saluted and went on their way. Aron let out a sigh and they moved into the suite, the door closing behind them. Gwen and Henry went to search the attached rooms.

"All clear," Gwen said, coming back into the main entry space.

Mr. Beach left and returned with a bundle under his arm wrapped in a cloth.

"What's that?" Jimmy asked.

"Some tools we might need. The medical bay isn't far from this side of the ship."

They rushed from the room as quickly as they arrived. Their pace was too quick for Aron to think of anything beyond keeping up. He wondered how the old man managed to do it. He would have to ask Gwen to increase their training regime.

They only made it a short distance down the corridor before alarms began to sound. They paused in their tracks.

Captain Dvorak came in on their comm device. "Commander, we have the armory secured and are beginning our sweep. I don't think most of the crew has any idea what's going on."

"Good, let's keep it that way. Let them think this is a drill," Jimmy replied and then said to the others, "Come on, we need to hurry."

The pace increased even more, but they were able to blend in with the sailors and marines who began to stream past them in waves. Everyone seemed to be heading somewhere and nowhere all at once. His ignorance of the ship and its inner workings left him with no clues as to what they were trying to do.

The med bay turned out to be close like Mr. Beach had said, but they were forced to fight their way inside. The handful of guards were caught unawares, and they were easily able to make entry. Aron trailed in beside Mr. Beach in the rear. Neither of them seemed interested in engaging in close-quarters combat.

The hospitaller physicians and support staff put their hands up, making no moves to stop them. Jimmy approached a man in plain medical fatigues, save for a silver oak leaf on one collar and the mark of the hospitaller's on the other. "Where is she, Knight Commander?"

The man didn't hesitate. He knew exactly why they were there. "Last door on the left. Two guards inside. They wouldn't let us anywhere close to her."

Jimmy signaled Henry and Gwen to push forward.

The physician kept his hands raised and spoke smoothly. "Can my people see to the wounded?"

Aron was surprised by his ability to stay calm with guns in his face and dead bodies on the ground.

Jimmy nodded. "We'll be out of your way in a moment. You can put your hands down."

The knight commander saluted. "I don't know what their plan was, but I had nothing to do with it. I owe the high commander quite a lot."

"We all do. That's why we won't let them get away with this."

The man inclined his head and motioned for his people to tend to the newly injured soldiers. They didn't hesitate in rushing forward, taking only an extra moment to disarm their patients before treating them. The scene brought Clara to mind, her own calmness in the face of similar violence standing out to him. It took a special kind of person to do this job, but it was a vital and honorable one.

There were several more gunshots followed by an all-clear from Henry. Mr. Beach hurried into the room, and Aron followed, unsure of where he would be of the most use.

There in a bed was a slender woman. Maybe a bit older than himself and Henry. She was secured at the hands and feet to the bed by thick straps that Henry was hurriedly cutting away. She had several needles connected to her arm and neck. They were connected to sacks containing some green liquid Aron couldn't identify. Her face was taut with anger or pain, and she strained against the restraints moving the entire bed in the process. Henry tried to work faster but the woman's flailing made his work difficult.

Jimmy came up behind him as Mr. Beach slammed some kind of syringe cartridge into her leg.

"Was that nectar?" Jimmy asked.

"Yes, it'll help her wake up and fight whatever they were giving her," Mr. Beach said, pulling the lines from her neck and arm, the sickly green fluid leaking out onto the floor.

"Since when does nectar help anyone?" Aron asked, but then the thrashing settled. Her breathing steadied, and Henry was able to finish cutting the restraints. It had worked almost like magic.

Aron looked at Jimmy, but he seemed equally surprised.

Mr. Beach gave her a gentle shake. "Lady Catherine."

Aron pushed forward to get a better look. This was the infamous Hex. He had seen the news footage from the trial like everyone else, but he had also watched her burn in Trinity Square, but here she was. Risen from the dead.

Wispy brown hair clung to the sweat on her brow. Her skin looked pink and delicate, like a freshly healed wound, but beyond that there were no major signs of injury. A few months shouldn't have been enough time for her injuries to heal. He was no physician, but it didn't seem possible at all. Henry and Gwen shared in his disbelief.

The woman's eyes suddenly opened. A vibrant brown, or no, maybe amber. They were like sunbeams in their intensity.

"Charles…" she said hoarsely.

Gwen quickly found a bottle of water and helped her drink from it. Catherine drank deeply and coughed.

"Where am I?" Catherine said before looking to the gaggle of people staring at her, the bloody pools on the floor, and finally the bullet holes on the wall beside her. "Okay, someone give me the quick version. Who are all of you, and what's going on? Jimmy, is that you?" She shook her head as if to clear it and raised a finger to her temple. "Sarding hell, it actually worked, didn't it? Can someone shut off that blazing noise?"

Aron shook himself and hurried to the nearest console. He had managed to tune out the alarm in all the excitement. "I'm on it!"

Jimmy spoke quickly in the background. "It's been four months, and you're in orbit over Luna. You started a war, and your father has been fighting it. However, he's been betrayed and needs our help. They were using you as a pawn for his obedience. Now that you're rescued, we can go and get our revenge."

"That was perfectly succinct, thanks. Someone have a blade for me?" Catherine said, throwing off her blanket. She adjusted her plain blue hospital gown before kicking her legs off the side of the bed.

The beeping stopped, and Aron turned around to rejoin the conversation.

"Sarding hell, thank you. Worse torture than the flames, that blazing bell."

Aron's eyes widened. *This woman might be a lunatic.*

Mr. Beach unwrapped the bundle in his arms, revealing a red and gold plasma blade hilt. Aron could see it had some kind of design etched into the metal but not what it was of. To his untrained eye, it looked very ornate and expensive.

"Where did you find this? This isn't one of my father's," she said.

"An old family heirloom," Mr. Beach said.

"How did you come to possess it? You know what? Never mind." Catherine took the blade, testing its heft with a grin. "Alright, let's do this. Move aside."

She ripped the myriad of wires and tubes connected to her body with a grimace. Aron was forced to look away out of decency and, truth be told, for fear of heaving. He didn't have a temperament for these types of things.

"Should my head be pounding this bad?"

Mr. Beach said, "The drugs they give you are still in your system. It'll take some time for them to wear off. For now, the nectar is what's keeping you going."

"Nectar? God's bones." Catherine part hopped and part fell out of the bed, her legs buckling under her. Henry was there quickly to catch her. "Oh, okay, I'm good." She grunted and stood straighter.

Her legs were still shaking, but she was able to walk.

Mr. Beach said, "The headache should pass in a little while."

"Let's get you some clothes," Jimmy said.

Catherine nodded to Mr. Beach, adjusting her simple blue hospital gown. "Do we know where my father is?"

"The bridge is our best guess," Henry said.

"Then that is where we're going. You can update me on who our enemies are on the way," she said and strode from the room.

Her steps got more confident as she moved. She walked barefoot, taking no care to avoid the bloody puddle. She strode confidently as if she were fully armored. Her hair was nearly shoulder length, and the brown looked especially vibrant against her freshly healed skin. Aron thought she looked almost otherworldly.

Gwen handed her a discarded uniform she had found in an adjacent room, and Catherine dressed quickly while Mr. Beach explained the situation in more detail. She and the others seemed to understand what he said but Aron was unfamiliar with the names and people involved. It wasn't long before they were back moving through the ship.

With the alarms quieted, the corridors had calmed, at least until Catherine came into view. Some soldiers merely stepped aside. Others bowed their heads deferentially, while others wept openly or threw themselves to the ground in supplication. None tried to stop them.

Catherine took it in stride with a slight look of bewilderment at what was transpiring. Aron knew from his time in the tunnels of Echus Canyon how much the people idealized Catherine and the persona of Hex. They saw her as a martyr, but he thought seeing her alive might be creating a new narrative. Now she was becoming something more, a seraph, sent by God. He had heard similar whispers in the tunnels of Mars.

Everyone grew up with the stories from scripture, about the judgment of God's angels. How they would be born from fire and pass their judgment on the land. Aron wasn't ready to make that leap, but he could appreciate where these people must have been coming from. If he wasn't already so suspicious of the bigger picture, maybe he would feel the same.

Many of these soldiers may have doubted it also, but it was better to give an angel deference and find out they were merely human than the other way around. Aron made the sign of the star and cross for good measure.

Perhaps hearing the commotion, a man in bishops' robes marched toward them from the far end of the corridor. They readied themselves for a confrontation, but when the man got closer, he threw himself to the ground with the others. His head down and eyes averted.

"Our lady of the dawn, I welcome your judgment and offer my loyal service, under the eyes of God and man. Command me and your will shall be done," the bishop said loudly. Any who were left standing in the corridor kneeled and bowed their heads.

Catherine looked back at Jimmy and the others as if to ask what to do now. "Where is my father? Do you know, Bishop?"

The bishop kept his forehead pressed to the floor. "The heathens took him to the bridge. I was gathering the righteous to go and rescue him."

"I'm on my way there now," Catherine said, reaching down to yank the man upright. "Captain Dvorak is securing the vessel. Aid her."

The bishop's eyes went wide at being touched, and he scrambled upright. "Yes, My Lady, it will be as you say! God wills it!"

Catherine nodded and they were off.

"Someone get me to the bridge before there's one more sarding interruption. I haven't even had my coffee yet," Catherine said, and Jimmy laughed.

Aron's frame of reference was limited when it came to how nobility was meant to act. He had never known any other nobles personally besides Kaya, and he always assumed she was a bit atypical. However, seeing Catherine now, he wasn't sure they weren't all this way.

SILAS

NOVEMBER, 4103 U.E.T. - *SPECTER*, GREAT CISLUNAR PLANE

THE SHIP'S ALARMS BLARED, and Silas smiled through swollen lips. He knew it hadn't been a long time since his ordeal began, even if at times it felt like eternity. Yet God was delivering him now from his torture.

Lancaster rushed from the room. "What's going on?" he shouted at the crew.

Hayashi rushed out to join him, leaving the door to his prison open. He also noticed the familiar vibration of the heavy rail guns firing on Luna had stopped.

Silas tried to bite at the rope binding his good hand to the table, but from his restricted position, it was a useless exercise.

"Send units to stop them, now!" Lancaster shouted angrily, and Silas grinned wider. God's army had come to answer his prayers.

Silas shouted back, as loud as his voice would allow, "For when the day of judgment comes, it will be heralded by trumpets and flame. Those in the Celestial City will hear the cries and arrive to welcome the coming dawn. The faithful will rejoice, and devils will be cast into the sun, never to see eternal life."

"Sir, no one is responding to our calls. Sir, uh..." a crewman said.

"What the sarding hell do you mean? Where are they?" Lancaster shouted back to the stammering soldier.

"De-dead, sir," the crewman said, the shock in his voice evident. "They've all escaped."

Silas laughed a sick and twisted laugh. His prayers were answered, and he welcomed the coming storm. Hayashi and Lancaster shouted at one another, unable to form a cohesive plan. Then the alarm stopped, and the room went silent.

The calm in the eye of the storm.

Silas continued his prayers. "We will all appear before the judgment of his angels and receive sentence for what was done with the body, whether good or evil."

"Shut him up!" Lancaster shouted.

Hayashi came back to strike Silas across the face. "Silence! The only one facing judgment here is you."

"I welcome my judgment before God, but do you, or you?" Silas said to each of them.

"Where are our soldiers?" Lancaster pressed his crew.

Silence was the only reply.

"You've both lost before you even began. I was touched by God's messenger with a purpose, and it's been served. You won't get your codes, and you'll face the consequences of your betrayal."

"I'll not die a groveling dog like you, Beckett. Lieutenant, set the destruction protocol," Lancaster said. "This is *my* ship, and I will stay with it to the end."

Silas couldn't see the lieutenant, but no response came to Lancaster's request. The protocol was a last resort, a holdover from the Great Solar war when rebuilding ships was preferable to allowing them to fall into enemy hands. As captain of the ship, Lancaster had access to the proper credentials.

"Have you lost your mind?" Hayashi said, kindling Silas's plasma blade and pointing it at Lancaster.

Lancaster spoke to the crewman. "I've already entered the verification code. Initiate the sequence, Lieutenant, and make for the escape pods. Your service here is no longer required."

Perhaps it was the prospect of an escape, a way out when death had been nearly guaranteed, that willed the lieutenant to follow that command.

Silas laughed. He had endured, and he had won. He would answer for his own sins soon, but he was prepared for that. He would make his penance in the darkness, and in time he would see Catherine and Diana again.

"Stop the sequence, now!" Hayashi shouted, holding the plasma to Lancaster's throat.

Silas craned his neck to see Lancaster's resigned expression.

"Not that I would, but I can't stop this now. It would take another valid code to override the sequence. If you intend to die honorably, I'd prefer your silence. If not, please leave my bridge, you're running out of time to get to the escape pods," Lancaster said, unfazed by the blade at his neck. Hayashi stood stunned as Lancaster moved to cut Silas's bindings.

Hayashi pivoted to point the blade at Silas. "Turn it off! Turn it off now!"

Silas struggled to move with his bindings free. Every movement hurt as dried blood ripped from shallow and deep wounds, leaving him dizzy.

Hayashi snuffed the blade and came to help Silas. Hayashi half carried and half dragged him out onto the bridge and toward a console. "You need to disable this now!" Hayashi said in a panic. "Go, do it!"

"No use asking him. We had his credentials revoked before we even brought him back to the *Specter*. That was your idea, if I remember correctly," Lancaster said, moving to sit in his captain's chair.

Hayashi was stunned and let Silas slip from his arms. He looked around the bridge for someone else who could do what he asked, but the room was empty save for them. He was out of options. "How...how much time do we have to escape?"

Lancaster looked at his watch. "Maybe about twenty minutes, which is plenty of time to find an escape pod but likely not enough to escape the blast radius."

Silas leaned against the console. He began to slip and tried to catch himself but made the mistake of reaching out with his missing hand. He grasped nothing and went crashing to the ground in new agony. He panted, trying to catch his breath as he rolled bloody and naked on the ground.

"It'll be over soon," Lancaster said, turning the large screens to a scene of Luna and space beyond.

Silas regained his senses and looked at the pair. Lancaster sat stoically staring into the distance, and Hayashi looked prepared to run him through with Silas's plasma blade. Silas would have done it himself if he had the strength to move.

Hayashi raised the blade, prepared to strike but paused when the door to the bridge opened. Hayashi turned the blade toward the doorway and Lancaster shook his head.

Silas looked up and was gifted with a scene of clarity and radiance. One of God's angels had returned to him, but it wasn't the visage of life and death. It was... No, it couldn't be.

"You should be dead," Lancaster said dryly.

"Turns out I'm pretty hard to kill," Catherine said, kindling her plasma blade as she approached. She turned her head, scanning the room, and found him. Her sarcastic smirk changing to one of pain and anger.

Silas never thought he would see her again. Despite the glimmer of hope and his endless prayers, he didn't think this was possible. He didn't think he had earned another such miracle, but then he had his vision and thought maybe that was the final test. He thought he had failed that test too, but maybe now he had one last chance.

Lancaster drew his pistol and pointed it at Silas's head. Hayashi held his stolen plasma blade kindled at the ready.

"You will all pay for this" Catherine snarled.

"Yes, all of us. The self-destruct is set. None of us are leaving here alive, so why don't we relax and accept the inevitable?" Lancaster said.

Silas watched as more people streamed in behind Catherine. It was... No, it wasn't possible. Henry, Jimmy, Gwen, and others he recognized, the boy who controlled the shields on mars so they could escape. Surely it was all a dream, and he was already passing to the next world to greet his friends again.

"Aron! On the console now!" Jimmy shouted.

Lancaster turned the gun on the boy, who paused. "I wouldn't do that."

Jimmy stepped in to protect him by blocking Lancaster's shot. "He can't shoot us both. Do your work."

Lancaster smirked. "Commander Torres, where have you been hiding all these years."

Henry stepped forward, drawing a ceramic blade. "You're outnumbered and outmaneuvered."

"Let my father go, and there is a way we all leave here alive," Catherine added through clenched teeth.

"No, there's no coming back from this. Your engineer will need another code, and there's no one here to provide it." Lancaster spoke to Henry. "If only you showed up a little sooner to help me, Henry. Curious that you're standing with them after your father offered me a place at his side."

"I've rejected my father. My place is here," Henry said, and Silas respected his resolve, despite the pain his presence dredged up.

Lancaster looked down at Silas, holding the gun to his head. "It's a shame your nephew didn't feel that way before he killed your wife."

Catherine looked to Silas. "What is he talking about?"

Lancaster snickered. "I'm sorry, sweetheart, but your mother's dead. Your cousin there killed her while you burned or was that even you?" he said questioningly.

"It was an accident," Henry hurriedly said. "I regret it every day."

Silas struggled to speak. "Henry is telling the truth. Let him shoot me. I'm ready. Save the people of Luna and Mars."

"You did all of this for my uncle?" Catherine asked, taking another step forward. She was within striking distance now. Hayashi moved slightly more to his left.

"He was only a tool. I did it for myself and what I was owed. I gave my life for this Republic, and what do I have to show for it?"

She took one more half step. "More than billions of others, and less than you could have achieved on our side." Catherine followed Hayashi's blade and then looked at Silas's stubbed arm. "I don't know how you got my father's blade, but I would drop it."

Hayashi repositioned slightly but he didn't lower the blade. "Take Lancaster and let me go. This was all his plan."

The room was near silent, with only Aron's furious tapping at the console echoing through the space. Silas closed his eyes and took a deep breath. When he opened them again, he looked at Catherine and no longer saw her as his daughter or as Hex. He saw an angel once more, and he finally understood. God had put the truth in front of him, but he failed to listen.

He was not the one chosen by God to lead the people. It was Catherine. It had always been Catherine. God had chosen her, led her to the

Coalition, and then saved her from the flames. She was born again from the ashes to protect the righteous and judge the wicked. She was the Ashen Dawn.

Silas didn't need to think about what to do next. He was where he was in that moment for one divine purpose. He used what strength he could dredge up from the depths of his soul and launched himself at Lancaster. The gun fired close to his head, leaving his ear ringing.

Catherine moved past him in a blur. She struck out at Hayashi, who only briefly defended her blows before tripping backward. He tried to block as he stumbled, but his movement was clumsy and no match for his daughter's expertise. She swiped out easily, severing his arm from his body. The hilt of the plasma blade rolled to the floor, and she pressed forward as he collapsed to the ground.

Silas continued to claw at Lancaster for control of the gun. The pain was excruciating, but his purpose was singular. He would protect his daughter with his dying breath, his last act in this human realm. Silas managed to wrestle Lancaster to the ground and used his good hand to keep the gun away.

Lancaster was a skilled captain, but so many years on board a starship hadn't kept his fighting skills sharp. Silas used that to his advantage, as he pressed his mangled forearm to Lancaster's throat. Years of pain and frustration flowed out in his final moment. He smashed through the dam he had created to hold back those flood waters.

Silas pressed his face to Lancaster's, baring his teeth and letting loose a primal, crazed scream. There was terror in the man's eyes as he watched his doom. Silas knew this devil would not defeat him, *could not*, defeat him. With the light of heaven at his back he was more powerful than the darkness. He pressed, and pressed, until he felt the last breath escape his lungs and the fire in his heart cooled.

"Dad...dad!"

Silas had collapsed on top of Lancaster's still body.

"Dad," Catherine whispered into his ear. "It's over. We did it."

Silas turned onto his back, and Catherine pulled him away from Lancaster's body. He gazed up at his daughter. A halo of golden light hung on her head, and he smiled. "No, you did it. You believed when others wouldn't. When I wouldn't."

She returned his smile and tears welled in her eyes. "I'm glad you finally decided to fight with me."

"I couldn't deny you a third time," he said, weeping with her.

"You were always stubborn, but I was hoping you didn't take the bit about burying our bones together literally."

Catherine smiled broadly, and only the pain stifled his own laugh. She took after her mother and the Higgins brand of sarcasm. The thought made him think of Marcus and the others.

"Taylor, Marcus, we need to reach them," he said, his tone serious.

She turned to Jimmy, who had come up beside her. "We'll do our best. Aron, give me good news!" Jimmy shouted to the boy at the console.

"I got it. By God's bones, I did it," the boy said through his own nervous laughter.

Henry came to aid Silas to sit up. His touch was gentle, and he seemed unfazed by the grizzly sight. "Uncle, I'm sorry. I should-"

"I was there. I know you weren't yourself." Silas looked to his side and saw Hayashi's still form on the floor. His severed arm lying nearby. *What a waste.*

Henry lowered his head in shame. "I never wanted to hurt anyone. I was trying to protect Lady Kaya."

Silas wanted to be mad at the boy. He wanted to blame him for what happened, but he knew that would be wrong. "I know."

Catherine looked much more upset and interrupted them. "We can talk about this another time. We need to get my father to the medical bay and secure the ship."

"Forget me. Find Captain Dvorak and secure the fleet. Contact Orzone and tell him what happened," Silas said.

"Orzone?" Jimmy asked, surprised.

Silas nodded. "His son commands the pirate fleet of Luna."

Jimmy laughed. "Ha, that bastard was Orzone this whole time. Don't worry, High Commander, we can set things right from here. Captain Dvorak is already securing the *Specter*, and we sent Bishop Vesivi and his crusade to help her. What should we do with these two," Jimmy said, motioning to the bodies.

Silas surveyed the two bodies. One had been perhaps his oldest teacher, and the other a lesson in trusting the honor of strangers.

"Ship Lancaster to my brother as a message. The other one we'll send to the Lunese," Silas said.

Jimmy walked over to Hayashi's body and picked up the hilt of Silas's blade. He walked back to place it in the crook of his arm. "Your blade, High Commander."

"I have to admit you're the last person I expected to walk through that door," Silas said, coughing.

"You and me both," Jimmy said with a grin. "Glad your timing was good for once."

Silas wiped his mouth and saw blood come away. He still smiled broadly. "Not good enough, but it's okay. Now I can die in peace, my daughter and friends by my side," he said, his muscles going limp as he let the joy of victory settle over him. He couldn't remember the last time he had been so happy.

"Oh no you don't," Catherine said. "Grab his other arm. We're taking him to the med bay. Why are you hesitating? Let's move!"

ARON

NOVEMBER, 4103 U.E.T. - *SPECTER*, GREAT CISLUNAR PLANE

SEVERAL DAYS HAD PASSED since they all almost died, but Aron thought he was getting used to that feeling. It was at least the third time in recent memory he had almost died. At least this time he had a nicer place to go to than a damp concrete room. He didn't think he would miss the underground living of Echus Canyon.

Jimmy and Captain Dvorak kept him busy over the last few days. He had saved them all from certain death, and all he got for it was more work, mostly filling the void until they could replace the bridge crew with qualified soldiers. Aron also thought Jimmy preferred dealing directly with him instead of other engineers.

With his shift finished, Aron went to find something to eat. He was amazed to find out the *Specter* had not only one mess hall but more than half a dozen spread throughout the massive vessel. He thought the food on the *Titan* was delicious, but this was a level of luxury he was completely unaccustomed to.

He made his way to one of the ward rooms that was typically reserved for the ship's officers. Captain Dvorak had given their crew access to it after it turned out they couldn't eat in peace with the regular crew. It was fine at first until the tales of Catherines miraculous recovery began to circulate.

Depending on who told the story, Aron and the rest of the crew were prophets or holy knights heralding the arrival of the Ashen Dawn. Aron felt like they were in the right place at the right time. Their denials only made the stories of their divine affiliation more fervent.

He went up to the food line and retrieved a tray of hot and delicious smelling food. It was some kind of bread stuffed with meat and sauce. They called it a pie, he'd never had one before, but it smelled wonderful. They even served fruit-flavored water, and you could have as much as you wanted. There were also slices of cake, and it wasn't even a holiday.

It was a busy time of day, and most of the tables were occupied. He preferred to eat alone, mostly to avoid any awkward conversations, but then he saw the professor sitting by herself and decided to join her.

"Hello, Professor Moreau. Mind if I join you?"

The older woman looked up from her digipad and waved to the empty seats. "Victoria isn't with me."

Aron felt his face turn red. "Oh, I... That's okay. I just wanted somewhere quiet to eat. Are you not having anything?"

"No more than I need to. The food is barely any better than sawdust," she said and went back to typing on her digipad. "I'm surprised you don't want to sit with the others and play the hero."

Aron shook his head. "That's only because you don't know me. I'm no hero. I'm an engineer."

"That's not what I heard," she said, looking up again.

"I did my job, that's all," he said modestly. "Anyway, the soldiers don't care about anything I did. They want to hear about Catherine or Lord Beckett."

"These people love their prophets," she said under her breath.

"You don't believe? That seems strange coming from a Sanctum professor. I guess it's okay for me to ask a question like that now." He second guessed himself, "Isn't it?"

The professor lowered her voice and said, "A word of advice. Don't assume anyone here is any less dogmatic simply because they don't want to take orders from the Vox and Manus any longer. You could get yourself into trouble that way."

Aron felt suddenly uncomfortable with how crowded the room was. He wanted to eat a delicious meal, not debate controversial topics.

He was glad when Henry arrived to join them. He liked the professor but found her very intimidating to speak to. She begrudgingly moved a stack of books off a seat to make room for the latest arrival.

Henry wore civilian clothes like Aron and the professor. Captain Dvorak had said it would keep things simpler while the dust settled. Aron hadn't liked the feel of a military uniform and was perfectly happy with the arrangement.

"Thank you, professor," Henry said, "I hope I'm not imposing."

Professor Moreau waved her hand absently. "Everyone always is, but it doesn't stop them."

Henry looked at Aron, and he shrugged. "Is there news of your uncle's condition?"

Henry placed his tray down and took his seat. "Catherine thinks he's through the worst of it.

The professor looked up. "Catherine is a trained physician, isn't she?"

Henry nodded. "Yes, she's a sworn Hospitaller."

"Interesting," Elyna said and typed something into her digipad. *Is she taking notes?* Aron wondered.

Aron said, "Dame Heather seemed relieved to not be the only medical expert anymore, and I think Clara is happy to have more teachers."

Henry grinned. "I heard your sister brow beat the knight commander into letting her work in the medical bay."

"She can be very persistent," Aron said. "But it's amazing how much she's learned. I still don't like her working there, but I like it better than her staying on the *Titan* with you know who." Aron knew they would understand he meant the berserkers. They had left them onboard their old ship for the time being, but it was uncertain what their future might look like now.

Henry nodded. "I understand that, but she's truly gifted and nearly an adult herself. In another year or so, she could have been joining the military."

Aron grimaced. "Don't remind me of that. I hope she never has to touch a gun."

Henry's expression became serious. "I hope one day that's true for all of us."

Professor Moreau said, "History has a horrible way of repeating itself, but maybe one day we can break that vicious cycle."

Aron contemplated that in the silence that followed. Then he looked at the stack of books beside the professor.

"That's the book I had from the Boundless Library, isn't it?" Aron asked, noticing the familiar spine on top. He could see several strips of colored paper marking different pages.

"Yes."

"Is it okay if I take a look at it?" he asked, curious what she found so interesting about the text. Aron really didn't know anything at all about the ancient American Empire, beyond its supposed existence.

"If you can read it, help yourself," she said casually.

Aron hesitated. "Is it not written in Standard? I've flicked through it to look at the pictures, but I didn't notice."

"No, but it's a similar language. You might be able to read some of it and discern context. It's an ancient form of the Martian language."

Aron thought that explained why there were many words he didn't understand. He had assumed his vocabulary was worse than he realized and decided not to mention the fact to anyone.

Henry looked curious too and leaned to look over Aron's shoulder as he grabbed the book and opened it. "I've only ever seen a few books on the topic of the ancient Americans in my family's library."

"That isn't surprising. Most of these histories are locked away in the archives of the Boundless Library or were burned during the Great Purge."

History books were a luxury Aron could never afford. As a result, all he ever read were the official accounts of the Republic's history.

Aron flipped through several pages. He could only understand several words, with many others having little to no meaning at all for him. What he was drawn to instead were the color photographs embedded in the book. There were beautiful pictures of Earth from orbit. The blue sphere gleaming. Pictures of its lush valleys and expansive oceans.

Something in him stirred at the images. Maybe it was some deep connection to Eden and the origins of man. "It was so beautiful."

Professor Moreau looked thoughtful. "Yes, it was. This was long before the Solar Empire existed and that blasted Iron Cage."

Aron continued to flip the pages, and the beautiful scenes of nature gave way to images of crowded cities, trash, and despair. It seemed almost inevitable that the latter portions of the book were dedicated to images of the machines of war during that period. Crude and hulking war ships fought over moons and asteroids that hadn't yet been colonized.

Aron flipped to one of the pages that the professor had marked and paused. There was an image of a man seated at a desk in an old-fashioned suit. He had a bald head, and his skin was very pale, like someone from the Far Coast.

"Professor, when was the Far Coast colonized?" he asked, trying to organize his thoughts.

She cocked her chin as she considered the best answer. "There were early missions but no permanent settlements like we have now until at least the 2600's."

He looked at the caption beneath the man's photo. He didn't understand most of what was written, but he sounded it out.

"2216 – Aelius Najm, 84th President of the USA&E." Aron looked up confused. "Is this a title?"

"Yes, he was a leader of their vast empire. He was critical in jump starting interplanetary expansion and the terraforming operations that followed in the subsequent centuries." The professor narrowed her eyes. "Why do you ask?"

"The name Aelius. And he looks like Aelius the Divine, you know, the prophet. I always thought Aelius was from the Far Coast somewhere, but now I think I may have gotten that wrong," Aron said. The similarities were incredible. Was Aelius really descended from some royal Gaian lineage? It would certainly explain a lot.

The professor relaxed. "Yes, Aelius the divine, everyone's favorite charlatan."

"I'm not so sure. He's strange, I'll give you that, but there's more to it," Aron said, still staring at the photo.

"You act like you know him personally," Henry joked.

"I do actually. He used to travel with Jimmy. Kaya and I talked to him plenty of times."

The professor perked up again. "Aelius was with you?"

"Sure, but I haven't seen him since before the Ashen Sunset. I couldn't say where he is now, but probably with Kaya if I had to guess. He always seemed to stay close to her." Aron said, unsure of why she was so interested. Then he studied the photo more closely, his mind wandering to tales of legend.

The professor slammed the book shut and took it back roughly. "Where is Jimmy now?" she demanded.

Henry answered quickly. "He was on the bridge."

Professor Moreau took her things and left without saying another word.

"What was all that about?" Aron asked, still a bit stunned.

Henry shrugged. "No idea. Something about that prophet, I guess. You said he might be with Kaya? Someone mentioned she was here, but no one will tell me where she is now. I assumed it was with the rest of the Mercurians back toward Venus."

"I heard the same thing," Aron said. "But I'd like to know for sure. I hope she's okay."

Henry agreed. "Maybe we can figure out where she went together, if you plan on sticking around."

Aron looked down at his meat pie and then at the fresh tattoo on his arm. "I don't want to leave, but it depends on Jimmy, I guess. Wherever he goes, I'll go."

Henry clasped his shoulder. "I hope you both stay. I don't want to imagine how things would have ended the other day without you two there."

Henry seemed like he was being genuine, and Aron took pride in knowing what he did had been important. "Same goes for you. It can't have been an easy decision, sacrificing so much." Aron felt like his own decisions up to this point had been driven by desperation more than any sense of duty or honor. He always had less to lose than someone like Henry.

Henry took a deep breath. "It was the hardest decision and also the easiest I have ever made."

"Then you don't regret it?"

Henry shook his head. "Do you?"

"Not for a moment." They clinked their glasses and returned to their meal.

CHAPTER

41

Silas sat up in the bed, going through the motions the physicians directed. Everything hurt, but he was feeling much more like himself. His mind was clearing, and he denied the additional painkillers they brought him. He didn't want to fall victim to the addiction he so criticized in others.

The surgeons completed a procedure on the stump of his right hand, sealing the skin, bone, and ligaments. He was lucky the cut was caused by a plasma blade, which cauterized the wound and saved him from bleeding to death. During the surgery, they also discovered his spleen had ruptured, along with other deep wounds on his body that required suturing.

At first, Silas wasn't sure if he was happy that he survived the ordeal. He knew Catherine was safe and was excited at the prospect of seeing Diana again, and the rest of his friends and family in the Celestial City. When Catherine walked into the room, he knew he was happy to still be alive.

"Hello, Cat," he said between slow breaths. The pain in his ribs made speaking difficult.

"Hi, Dad," she said, standing beside the bed. She wore the uniform of a hospitaller and looked so much like her mother. Her brown hair hung loosely above her shoulders. The pale pink color of her skin was the only sign of her recent injuries. "How are you feeling?"

"Sarding awful," he said with a smile.

"Glad to hear it," she said, putting a hand on his. "Not sure you're going to get too many more days off after this so you should enjoy it."

Silas tried to reach for a cup of water with his right hand and frowned when he realized what he had done. Catherine released his left hand and handed him the cup.

"You'll get used to it," she said, sounding hopeful. "We can start exploring options for prosthetics in a few weeks."

His chest twisted at the loss of his hand. He didn't think it would have meant this much to him. Then again, dueling had been nearly his entire personality as a youth and played no small part in his quick rise through the ranks of the military. He had lost his ability with a blade, and in that sense a part of what made him, him.

He took a sip from the cup to ease his throat. "How is Captain Dvorak doing?"

"Good so far. Jimmy has helped a lot with organizing all the different captains. Orzone is being difficult, but I have him pacified for now," Catherine said.

At least Orzone hadn't left. "What word is there from Taylor and Marcus?" He was anxious to find out that news most of all.

"Taylor was forced to fall back. The armies were scattered in the chaos, but the situation appears to be improving. Taylor was able to establish a defensive line on the Selenean Plain. The fleet has resumed air support, and the situation appears to be stabilizing. Based on Orzone's intel, the duchess should still be alive. So everything isn't lost."

Silas cursed. The blood of thousands wasted for nothing. They were back to where they were weeks ago. "What about Marcus? Was he able to reach the duchess?"

"His signal has gone dark, but we're working on finding him. I don't plan to abandon him, even if I need to go looking myself."

Silas hoped it would never come to that. "I'll go before I let anyone else. I'm the reason he's in this mess."

"Right now, you need to rest. That's the most important thing. Your people need you more than ever."

Silas cursed. He felt nothing but guilt for their predicament. "It's you they need. You're the one God chose, and I'm here to support you in that."

She looked at him sympathetically. "I know you believe that but..."

He could tell she wanted to tell him something.

"The situation is bigger than you or me."

He didn't think that was what she wanted to say. He didn't press her because he knew it wouldn't work. She would tell him when she wanted to, and for once he would have to be patient. "They tried to proclaim me king, even when I didn't want it. To my shame, there was a point I considered taking it. I realize now how much of a mistake that would have been."

She let out a sigh. "You won't like hearing that now they are calling you the King of Light or some such. They're even calling me Our Lady of Dawn. They think I'm the Ashen Dawn, made flesh. Imagine that, me, Catherine Beckett, the leader of a band of archangels." She shook her head. "Anyway, as my father, you get to claim your own piece of the divine."

Yes, I can believe it because I saw it with my own eyes, he thought and wanted to say. "You're deserving of all the praise you received for your bravery through the trial. You inspired billions with your actions." Silas thought she was blushing, or maybe getting angry. There would be time to sort through the politics. "How long have you been with the Coalition?" he asked.

"Since the time I enrolled in the Hospitaller University, more or less," she said, meeting his eyes, and he stiffened. That was more than seven years ago. "But I only borrowed the name Hex."

"It wasn't you I fought back on Ymir, was it?" Silas always knew there was a discrepancy in the fighting style he saw Hex display. It was similar but not the same, and an injury explained some of what he saw but not everything. He was worried he had lost his edge.

She shook her head. "No, I've never been to Ymir."

"You know who Hex really was then?" He couldn't resist the allure of knowing who his enemy had been all these years.

"I know who she is. She's still alive."

"Still alive? I nearly severed her leg..." He thought back to how Hex was carried away by someone else. How things were silent for a long time until the new Hex resurfaced with that same green armor. "She needed someone with a similar build and ability to sell the ruse."

"Yes, while she went to Triton to continue the next stage of her plan. You and Jimmy altered the schedule with your meddling. If you both weren't so competent, all of this may have happened a year ago," she explained, and he was trying to keep up.

"Jimmy was the one who led me to you on Deimos. Was he in on this the whole time?"

"No, Jimmy never knew who Hex was. In the beginning, he wanted to see Hex gone as much as you did. The two of you managed to stay one step ahead of us for years. Jimmy never thought the Hermes Conglomerate was on his side, but he was convinced to help eventually. You were always supposed to capture Hex, to capture me, on Deimos."

Silas lowered his eyes, feeling betrayed. He had been used as a pawn in some terrorist's game. Along with his daughter, Jimmy and who knew how many others. "Why did you never come to me before you got dragged into this? They used you as a decoy, meant to die for their cause. It's a miracle of God that you're still here."

"It's not-" She stopped herself from saying what she actually wanted to say. "I had a choice, and I made it. You had the same choice and said no."

"You never came to me. I never had any kind of choice. I would have never agreed to this lunacy," he said angrily. The agitation made him cough, and he struggled to catch his breath from the effort.

"Kaya al Vardan came to you. She offered you an opportunity, and you denied her. Then I came to you, and you denied me twice," she said, her own frustration evident. "You said you wouldn't deny me a third time, but now I'm having my doubts."

He tried to steady his breathing. "Tell me who the puppet master is?"

"Semiramis al Vardan."

"The Duchess of Mercury, but she's dead," he said in disbelief.

"There seems to be a lot of that going around lately."

Silas felt dizzy. The implications of what he heard racing through his head. The machines he was attached to began to beep more aggressively.

"I knew it was a bad idea to talk about this right now. Get some rest, and we can talk about this more. There's nothing that can't wait until you've recovered."

Catherine gave his hand a squeeze and left him to his thoughts.

All of this. Everything that happened during the last several years, maybe even longer, was an elaborate scheme. A plan meant to destroy the Republic he had dedicated his life to, and for what? That was the question. Was this an example of another noble trying to grab for power lost after the demise of the Solar Empire? Maybe it was something else entirely?

He knew Semiramis al Vardan, Kaya's mother. She was as honorable as anyone he had ever met and the one person who he feared to face in the dueling ring. On the one occasion he had met her, he lost. Then he considered the fight on Ymir against Hex, realizing it would have been her. He supposed that meant he had won that duel, and maybe now they were even. Except if there was ever a third fight, he would have to do it without his sword hand.

Perhaps that was a crazy thought. There was no evidence suggesting she was even his enemy at all. She *had* been his enemy, but was that still true? He didn't know, and that uncertainty haunted him. He was tired of being surprised, and there was no end in sight now. Then came the question of what that meant for the rest of the Mercurians. Were they in on this scheme too?

How would Catherine respond if he told her the truth of what he knew about Kaya's absence. *I guess she isn't the only one keeping secrets,* he thought. But maybe there was still hope she was alive. Marcus received that mysterious note after all. His heart twisted at the thought of Marcus. He wasn't ready to mourn another loss like that.

He considered now that he needed Kaya to be alive to preserve their unsteady alliance and create any lasting change. They wouldn't support him if he carried the blame for her death.

His mind continued to race until eventually exhaustion took over and he succumbed to sleep.

The next time he opened his eyes, he was greeted with the hulking form of Jimmy pacing in front of the bed. Silas had expected this visit.

Silas stared at him for a long moment before speaking. "Did you know you were sending me into a trap?"

Jimmy was startled out of his thoughts and approached the side of the bed. "Glad you're awake."

"Spare me Jimmy, just answer my question."

"Yeah…" he said slowly. "Hex came to me and gave me the data chip to give to you."

"You told me you stole it."

"…I lied."

Silas was glad he wasn't hiding from what he had done. Somehow it felt like less of a betrayal that way. "Why?"

"Hermes had a plan that was bigger than me or you. They had a path forward through the darkness. I could either stand in the way or grab a torch. I didn't want to be on the wrong side of history a second time. I told you I would do what it took to help the common people," Jimmy said passionately. "I swore a long time ago to face the darkness without fear and stay steadfast in my duty to safeguard the realms of man."

"Don't quote the fleet motto to me," Silas said, sitting up. "You led my only daughter to the pyre!"

"I swear I didn't know she was Hex, but it wouldn't matter if I had. She made her own choice, like the rest of us. We all want something better and are willing to sacrifice for it." Jimmy looked down at his stump. "I think we're all the same in that regard."

Silas took a deep breath. He wasn't happy that he had been so thoroughly played, but he knew he only had himself to blame. He had ignored the problem for far too long, and it festered into an angry, gangrenous wound. He had to accept the pain as the rotten flesh was carved from his body. "I will continue to give everything for the people who trust in me."

Jimmy nodded. "I'd never let anyone question your honor. It's why I came here. My operations on Mars are in shambles."

"I'm glad God saw fit to lead you here at the right time. A lot of people on this ship owe you and that engineer of yours a great debt." Their victory had been a close thing, and Silas was thankful for Jimmy's help. Except it didn't erase the lies. "After all our years together, Jimmy, I would have thought you'd tell me what was really going on."

Jimmy smiled sadly. "I had to pick the well-being of the majority over my own feelings. For what it's worth, I'm here with you now. What few resources I have left are at your disposal."

Silas didn't want to hold on to anymore pain. "You're right, we all had to make a choice. It took me longer to make mine. I'm glad you're here now."

Jimmy's expression lightened. He clasped Silas's uninjured arm with his large hand. "Too bad it feels less meaningful without Marcus here to berate me."

Silas laughed and then regretted it as he started coughing. "Any news on his location?"

"Not yet, but the Protean Company has teams on the ground searching. We'll find him."

Silas hoped it would be soon. Silas lowered his voice. "I have something else I need to ask you. In the top drawer," he said, motioning to a small dresser against the wall, "bring me the folder of papers on top."

Jimmy did as he asked, and Silas flicked through the documents clumsily with one hand until he found Reina's note. He handed it to Jimmy. "Does this handwriting look familiar?"

"This is Reina's... Is she still alive? I thought she went down with Kaya and the rest of the *Rubah's* crew."

"That's what I was told, but I don't know that it's the truth."

Jimmy handed the note back and ran his hand through his beard. "Then where are they now?"

"I don't know, but I want you to figure it out. Lancaster informed Lord Vardan that Kaya was dead and ordered him to return to Venus at haste. When we don't do that, we might find ourselves with a new enemy. I'm hoping we can avoid that."

Silas had been thinking about this problem and despite his misgivings knew Jimmy was the best person he had left to unravel the mystery.

"I'll find out what I can. I'm glad we're back on the same side, at least officially this time."

Silas clasped his arm. "Me too. Now let's make all this worth it."

CHAPTER
42

ARON

NOVEMBER, 4103 U.E.T. - *SPECTER*, GREAT CISLUNAR PLANE

ARON LEFT THE WARDROOM thoroughly bloated. He considered it might be easier to roll himself back to his room than to walk. Instead, he decided to take a long tour around the ship to digest. There would still be plenty of time left to sleep before his next shift.

The ship was large enough for him to easily cover several kilometers without taking the same corridor twice. He eventually cut his walk short due to fatigue, not because he ran out of corners of the ship to explore.

He made his way back to the small room he had been assigned, occasionally asking sailors for directions when he ended up in the wrong corridor.

His room was made up of a cluster of small berths surrounding a common living space. It was a space reserved for junior officers who needed quick access to the bridge. He didn't care if it was a broom closet, because it was a room he got all to himself. At least until they were able to reassign sailors and restore normal operations.

The common room was empty when he arrived. He opened the door to his berth, excited for the comfort of his mattress, only to find Jimmy sitting on his bed. Elyna was standing beside the small desk.

"Come in and shut the door," Jimmy said. "The professor wanted to speak with us."

Aron did as he asked, "What's this all about?"

"We needed somewhere to speak that others wouldn't be watching," Elyna said.

"Okay..."

Jimmy said, "We have some new information. Reina, Kaya, and the others might still be alive."

That surprised him. Aron didn't even know they might have been dead. "Are they with the Mercurian fleet? They sailed for Venus, didn't they?"

"We aren't sure, but we'll need your help to figure out what happened to their ship and where it might be. There is a lot of old data to comb through," Jimmy said.

Aron wasn't surprised to receive yet another request. "Alright, I can add it to my growing list."

Elyna spoke softly. "No, this needs to be your number one priority. We need to find that ship before anyone else does. Especially the Children."

Jimmy didn't offer any disagreement.

"The Children? Why does that matter? Why do you think they would even be looking?" Aron asked.

"The Children will want Kaya even more than they sought Victoria. That Aelius might be with them is an added benefit," Elyna said.

"Okay..." Aron said slowly, "but wasn't she here with the Mercurian fleet? Can't you reach out to her family? I don't understand why you're here in my bedroom asking me to help." He was genuinely confused.

Jimmy let out a long sigh. "Lord Beckett told me the Mercurians think she's dead and will be blaming him for it. We need to prove that isn't the case before things get much worse for us."

Aron thought that seemed like a good reason. "Alright, but why would the Children care about Aelius?"

Elyna's face was a rigid mask, and he was having trouble reading her. "The same reasons why Jimmy kept him around and never mentioned it. He knows a great many things that are useful. The kind of knowledge that's dangerous when placed in the wrong hands."

"I feel like there are things you aren't telling me," Aron said.

"It's not my place to divulge Hermes's business," she said, and Aron looked to Jimmy, wondering if he was the only one being left out.

Jimmy rubbed his beard. "All I know is finding Kaya and the missing Prometheus members is a priority. I also want to understand why the Children care so much about Victoria and the prophet."

"Do you not already understand that they want to build a new world?" Elyna said.

Jimmy laughed. "Sure, they always talk about it, but then they spend their time killing and destroying indiscriminately."

Aron agreed. "I don't think in my time with them I ever saw them rebuild anything at all."

Elyna shook her head. "You're both thinking too small. What they want to build is a new world on Earth, one in their own image to rival what came before it."

"Good thing that's impossible," Jimmy said flatly. "Those fools can get themselves blown up by the Iron Cage. Would be doing us all a favor really."

Aron wanted to laugh, but then he remembered the designs the Father had shown him. Maybe they did have a plan after all. "They want Aelius to build the tools they need to do it. I've seen his aptitude with machines. I always assumed he was an artificer at some point."

Elyna looked at him like only a proud professor could. "I can see why you've garnered the reputation you have, child. Yes, I think you're correct. The Children might think they can force him into service somehow."

From the look on Jimmy's face, it took him longer to put it together. When his face lit up in recognition, he looked at Aron as if he wanted to mention the designs. Instead, Jimmy kept his mouth shut.

"Alright, I'll get started right away," Aron said, and the others acknowledged him before leaving. He knew he would have to catch up with Jimmy separately.

When they were gone, his mind worked to try and piece together the mystery of the Children's plan. He would have to unlock the design files and figure out what they were trying to build. He assumed it must be something incredibly unique and powerful. Maybe weapons or terraforming tools. That they thought he might be able to build them filled him with a sense of pride. Even if he knew he'd never work for those monsters again.

That also made him wonder how Kaya or Victoria fit into everything. Then he remembered Jimmy asking him if they were related. He didn't think they were. They never said anything along those lines, and they looked very different. Except that thought made him wonder if instead their connection was through Aelius somehow. That might explain the interest the professor had in him.

In the end, he knew all it meant was that he would have a lot of work to do. His bed would have to wait for another time. With a heavy sigh, he shut the light and made his way back to the bridge.

EPILOGUE

Marcus

November, 4103 U.E.T. – Selenean Summit, Luna

Marcus fell roughly into the pit, landing in something wet and fetid. "Sarding hell. Worthless sacks," he muttered grimly, trying to brush himself off.

Thin beams of light trickled in from a metal grate high above his head. He tried to get his bearings, but his left eye was swollen shut, and his head throbbed awfully.

"God's bones, where am I?"

"In the oubliette under the archbishop's castle, I think," a female voice said from the darkness.

Marcus turned sharply toward the sound. His hand instinctively went for his pistol but came up empty. He raised his fist instead. "Who's there?"

Marcus thought he recognized the voice.

"The evil mistress of the deep. Daughter of the darkness, keeper of the endless night," the voice said dramatically.

The sarcastic tone was instantly recognizable. "Lady Engstrom? Is that you?"

"You recognize me, darling? How lovely. I didn't expect a Martian to be so cultured," she replied, stepping into the faint light.

He hadn't seen Duchess Olivia Engstrom in years, but her appearance was striking. She had a strong angular face with light-beige skin and light brown, almost blond features. She was around his age in her late forties or early fifties.

"Talk about luck. They took me right to you," he said with a bitter laugh.

She narrowed her eyes, appraising him. "What are you talking about? Who are you, and why are you in my pit."

Marcus shook his head. "Looks like it's my pit now. Nice of you to remember an old friend though."

Lady Engstrom stepped closer. "Marcus...Marcus Higgins?"

"The one and only," he said, spreading his arms like a performer.

"Is Silas with you?" she asked quickly.

"Yes, good to see you too, My Lady."

She punched him in the chest, and he winced. The archbishop's agents spent a good amount of time questioning him before throwing him into the pit to rot. "Sarding hell, woman, knock it off. He was in orbit with our fleet last time I saw him. I don't know how much you know about what's going on."

"Not nearly enough. They threw me in here when the siege started."

"Have they come back for you since?" he asked.

"No, although I have some benefactor who periodically throws bundles of food into the pit. I don't expect it to last for long though. The entire point of an oubliette is to make people disappear."

Marcus rubbed his face and immediately realized his mistake when he felt the slimy liquid of the pit on his cheek. "Silas sent me here to find you, and here I am. Now we need to find a way out."

"You aren't listening. There isn't a way out. That's the entire point. Just that one little hole up there," she said, pointing to the heavy steel gate above them.

Marcus considered the situation, his mind compartmentalizing the discomfort he felt and his own anxieties. He had a task, and that task gave him purpose. "Then why not kill you and get it over with? They must want to keep you around for something, even down here and out of sight. Same with me, I guess."

Lady Engstrom shrugged. "I have my suspicions. I think it's partially a test to see how long we last."

Marcus scrunched his brow. "Not that I think they're beyond petty torture, but it seems pointless."

"Not if you believe in fairy tales."

Marcus shook his head. "Listen, my head is killing me, and I have no sarding patience for riddles. There must be a way out of here, and we're going to find it."

Lady Engstrom spread her arms to encompass the small room. "Knock yourself out, soldier."

Marcus pushed past her with a huff and began studying the walls. He was particularly looking for anywhere the water dripping down the walls was draining. A task that wasn't very easy in the dark.

"Can you stop blocking all the light? Also, feel free to give me a hand."

"I have been here for days. Do you think I haven't already looked?" she snapped back.

"Yes," he said, not hiding his annoyance.

"I remember now why we never kept in touch."

Marcus let out a short laugh. "It was because you broke my friend's heart."

"Then he married your sister, so what do you care?"

"That's exactly why I care. Now, if you aren't going to help me, do you at least have any snacks?"